Tree-House Comix Proudly Presents

DOG MAN
UNLEASHED

WRITTEN AND ILLUSTRATED BY **DAV PILKEY**

AS GEORGE BEARD AND HAROLD HUTCHINS

WITH INTERIOR COLOR BY JOSE GARIBALDI

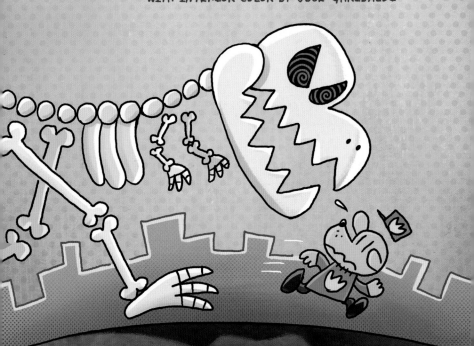

graphix

AN IMPRINT OF

■SCHOLASTIC

FOR PHIL FALCO

Library of Congress Control Number 2016936340

978-1-338-74104-9 (POB)
978-1-338-61198-4 (Library)

10 9 8 7 6 5 4 3 2 1   21 22 23 24 25

Printed in China   62
This edition first printing, August 2021

Edited by Anamika Bhatnagar
Book design by Dav Pilkey and Phil Falco
Color by Jose Garibaldi
Creative Director: Phil Falco
Publisher: David Saylor

Chapters

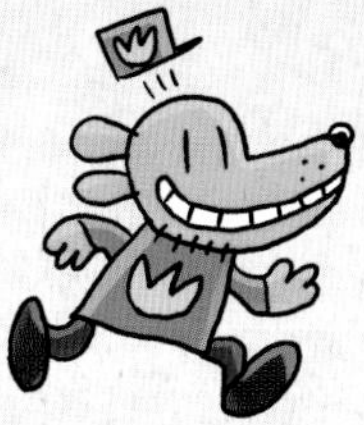

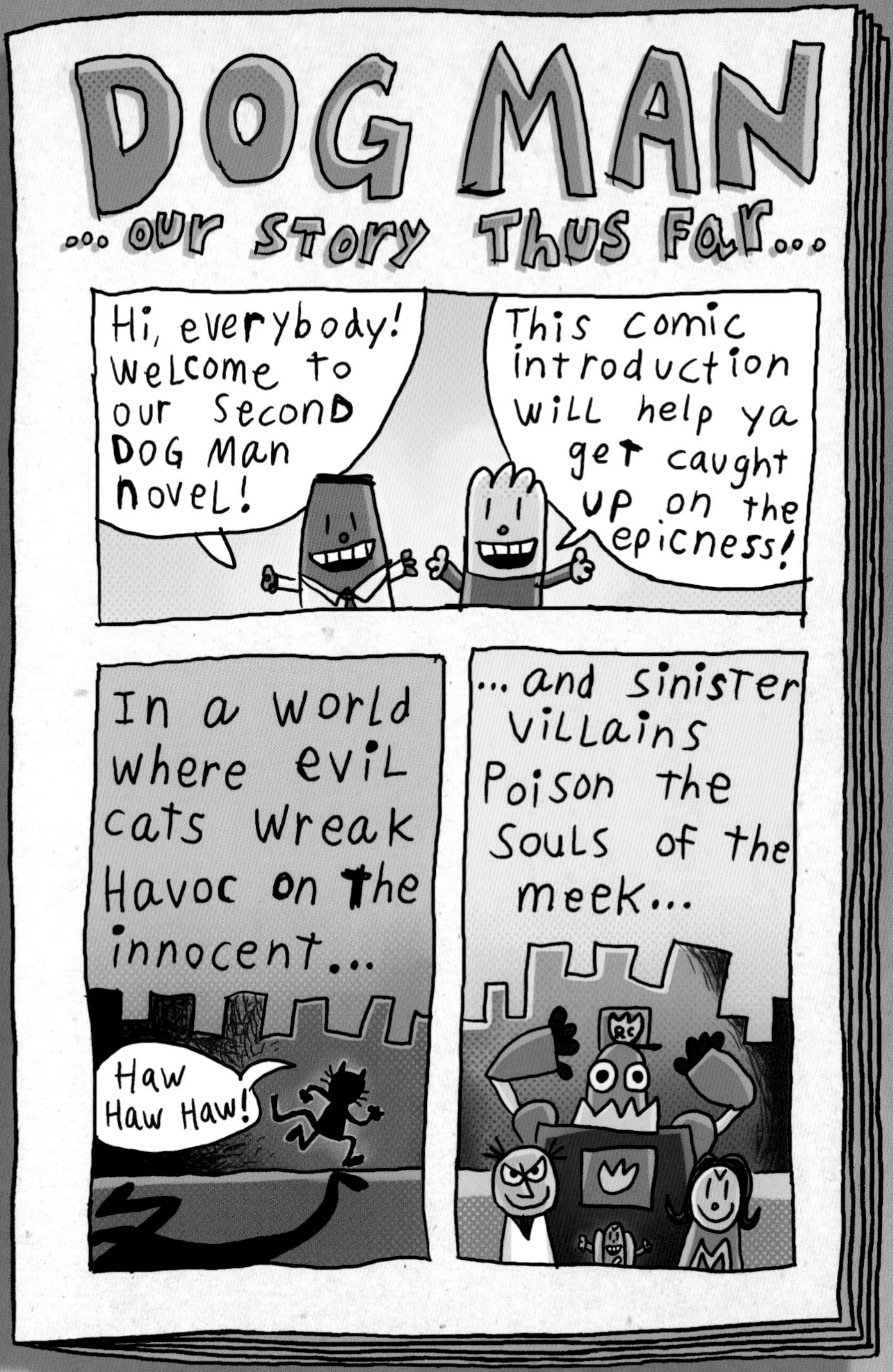
DOG MAN
... our story thus far...
Hi, everybody! Welcome to our second DOG MAN novel!
This comic introduction will help ya get caught up on the epicness!
In a world where evil cats wreak havoc on the innocent...
Haw Haw Haw!
...and sinister villains poison the souls of the meek...
RC

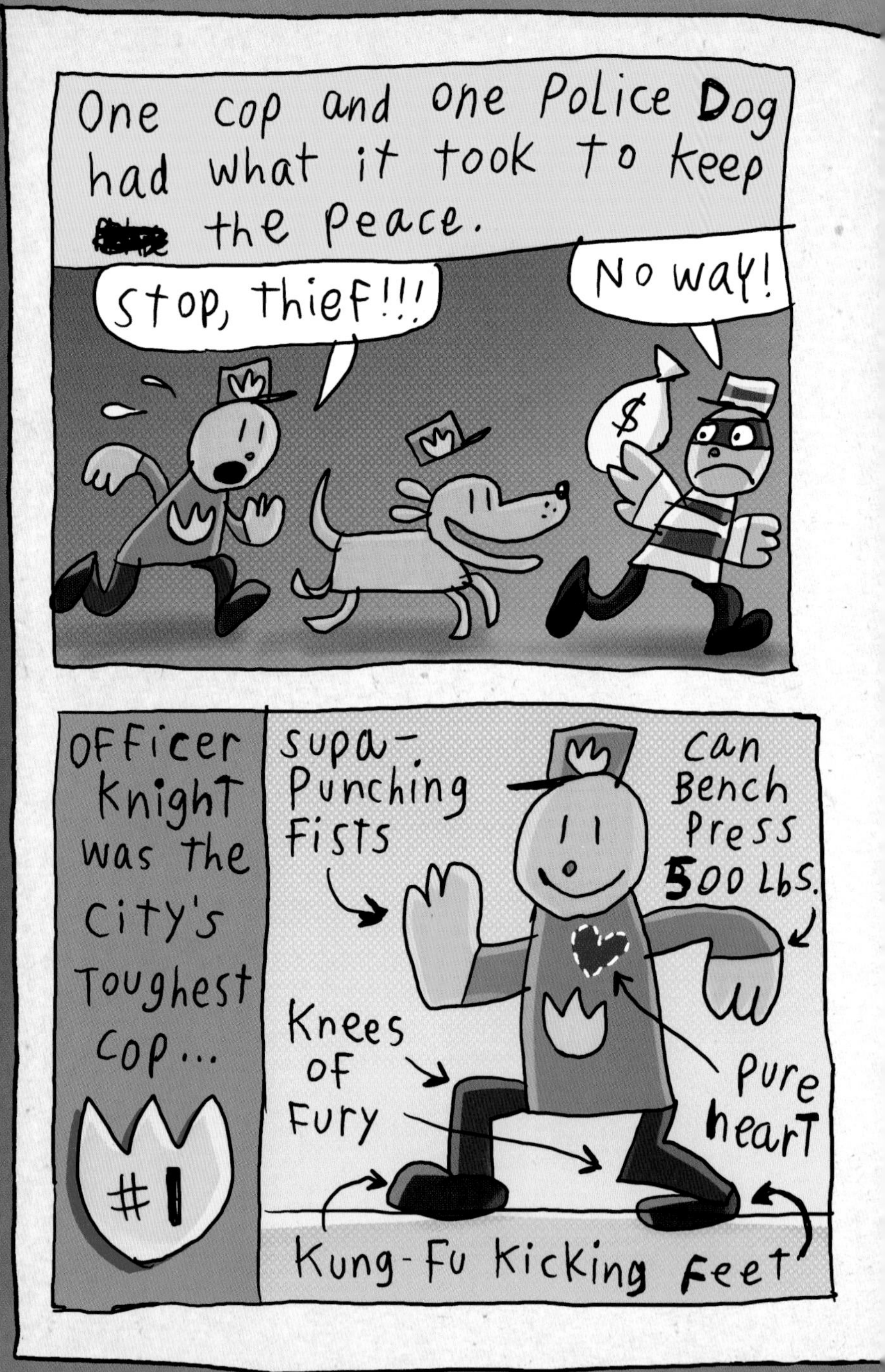

One cop and one Police Dog had what it took to keep [redacted] the peace.
Stop, thief!!!
No way!
$
Officer Knight was the city's Toughest cop...
#1
supa-Punching Fists
can Bench Press 500 Lbs.
Knees of Fury
Pure heart
Kung-Fu Kicking Feet

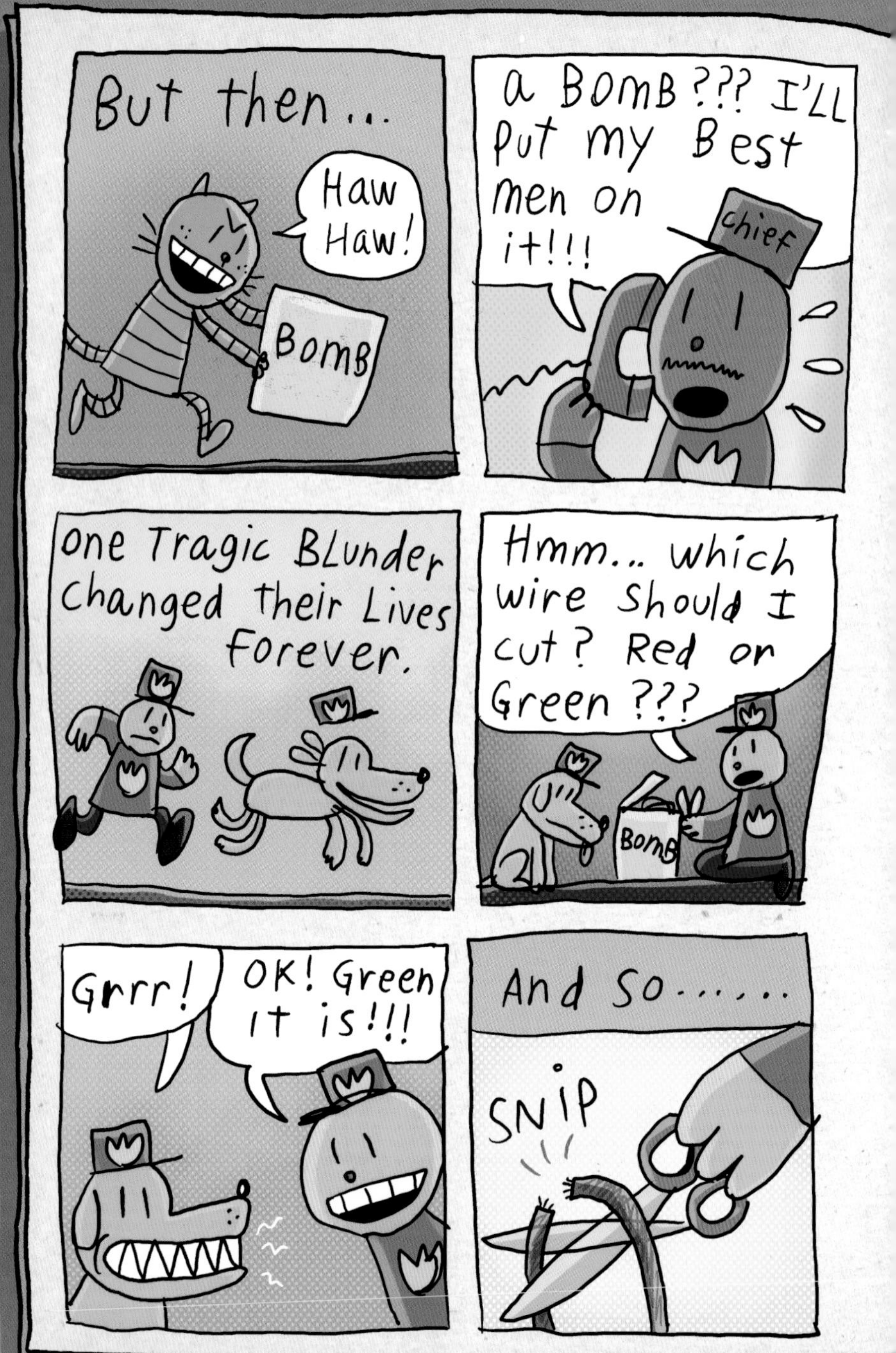

But then...
Haw Haw!
BOMB
a BOMB??? I'LL put my Best men on it!!!
Chief
One Tragic BLunder changed their Lives Forever.
Hmm... which wire Should I cut? Red or Green???
BOMB
Grrr!
OK! Green it is!!!
And So......
SNIP

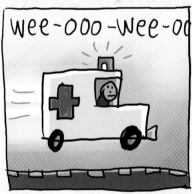

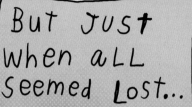

But just when all seemed Lost...

Hey!

← Nurse Lady

Why don't we sew Greg's head onto Cop's Body?

Good idea, nurse Lady! You're a genius!!!

I know.

and soon, a brand new crime fighter was born.

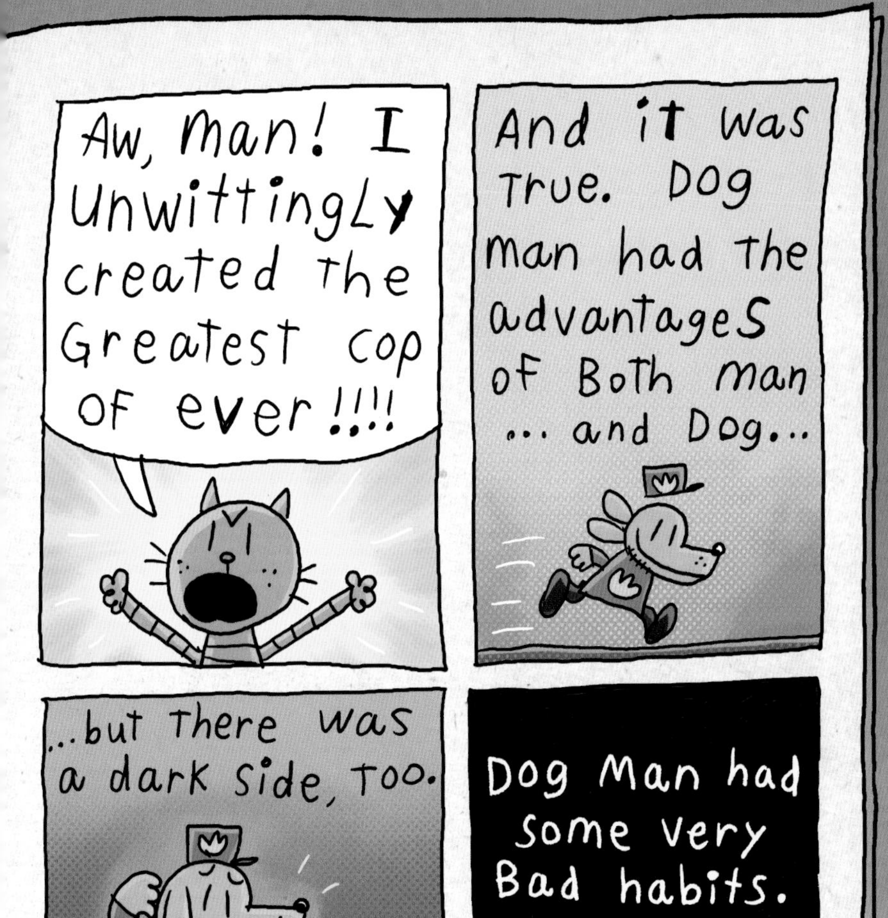
Aw, man! I unwittingly created the greatest cop of ever!!!!
And it was true. Dog man had the advantages of both man ... and dog...
...but there was a dark side, too.
Dog Man had some very bad habits.
He slobbered all over everybody...
chief
aw, gross!
...he was obsessed with balls...
squeak
squeak
squeak

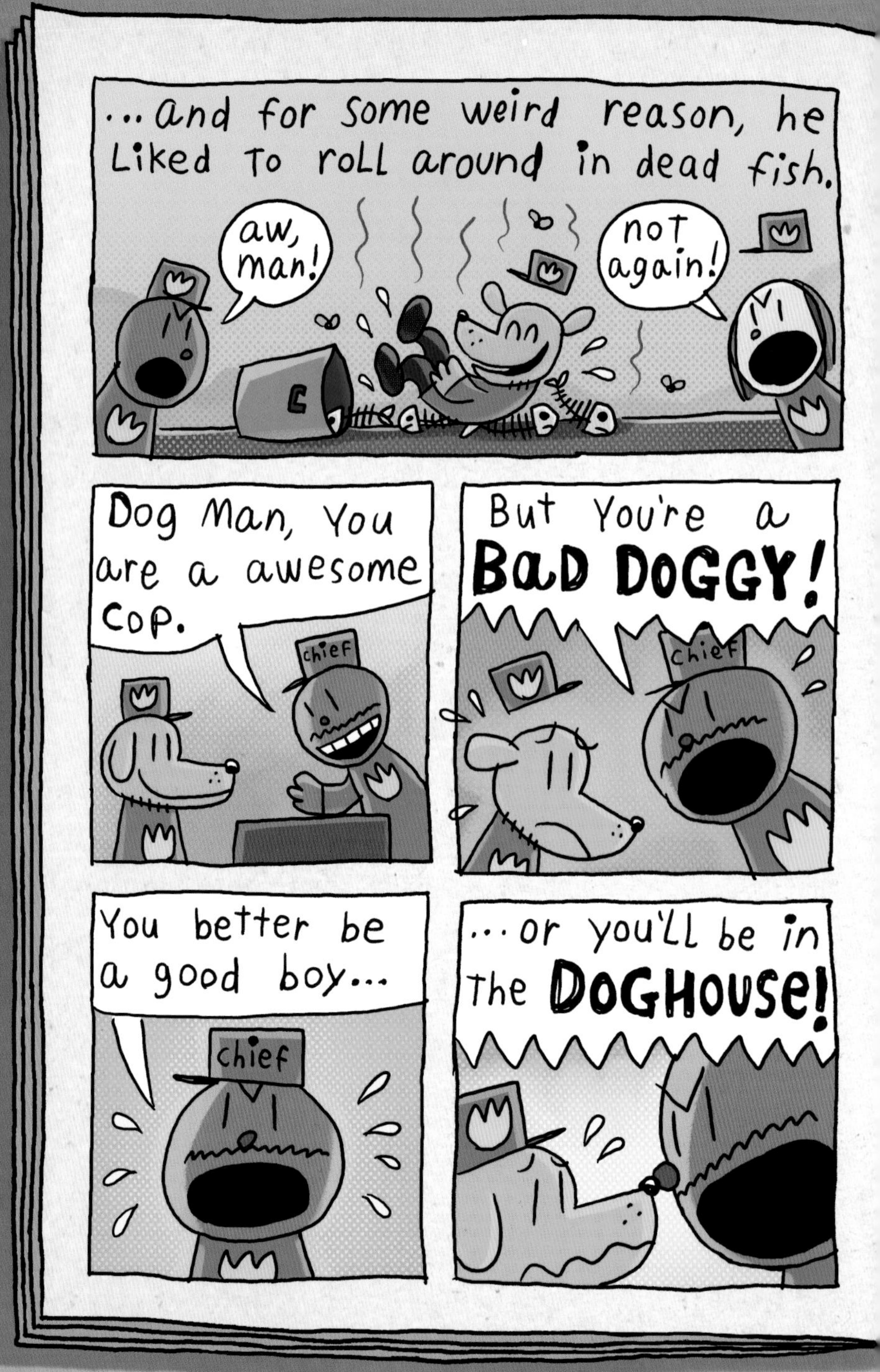
...and for some weird reason, he Liked To roLL around in dead fish.
aw, man!
not again!
C
Dog Man, You are a awesome cop.
chief
But You're a BAD DOGGY!
chief
You better be a good boy...
chief
...or you'LL be in The DOGHOUSE!

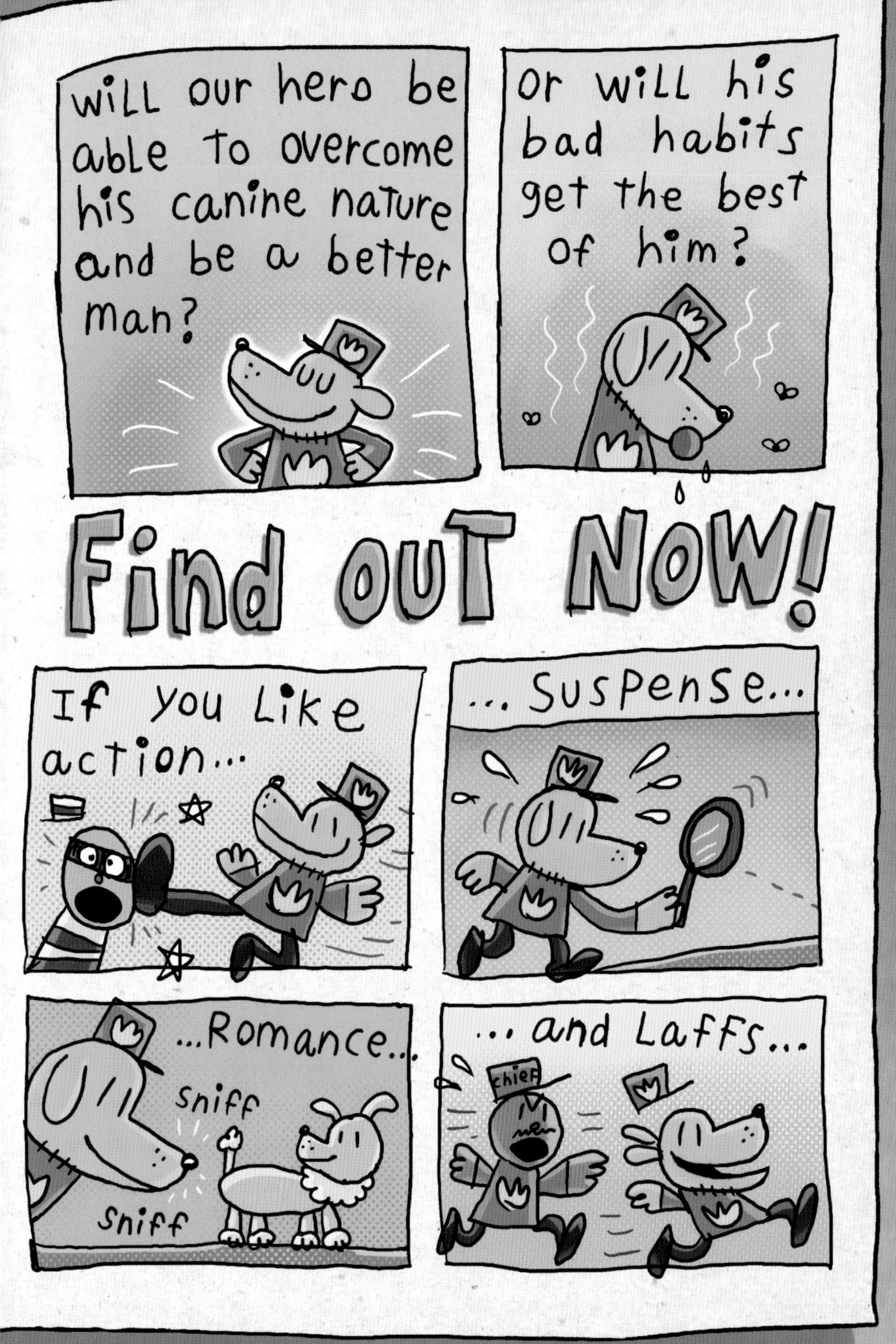

Will our hero be able to overcome his canine nature and be a better man?
Or will his bad habits get the best of him?
Find out NOW!
If you Like action...
...SusPense...
...Romance...
sniff
sniff
...and Laffs...
Chief

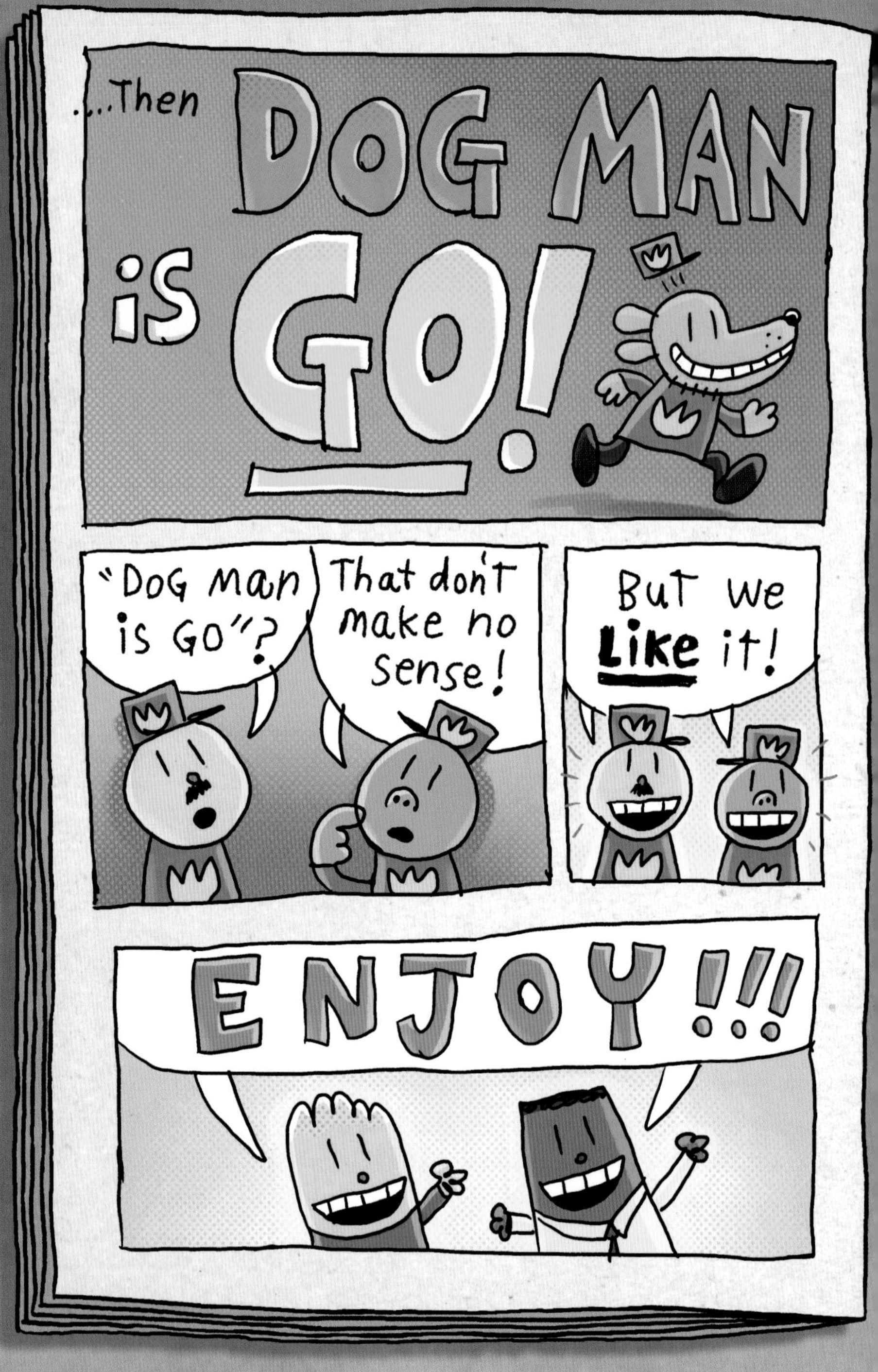
...Then
DOG MAN
is GO!
"DOG Man is GO"?
That don't make no sense!
But we **Like** it!
ENJOY!!!

Tree House comix Proudly Presents

Chapter 1
The Secret Meeting

by George and Harold

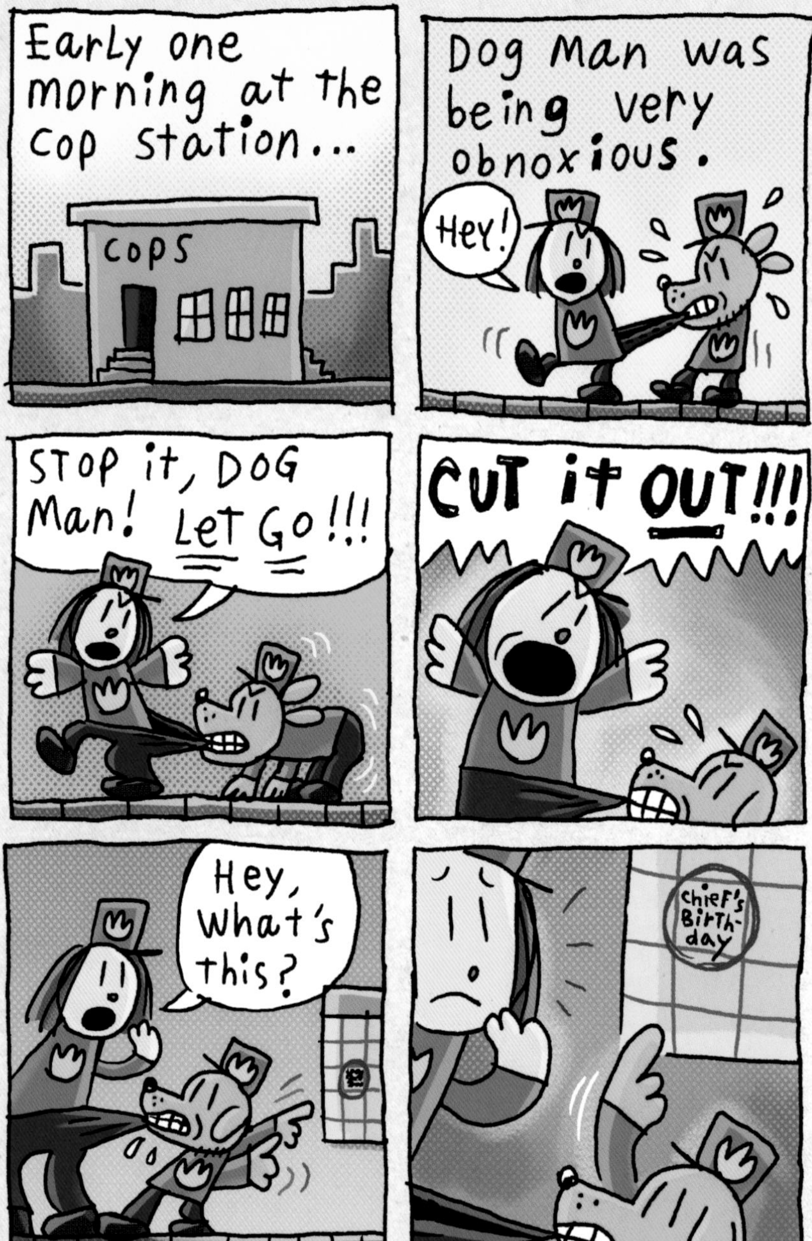
Early one morning at the cop station...
COPS
Dog Man was being very obnoxious.
Hey!
STOP it, DOG Man! LeT GO!!!
CUT it OUT!!!
Hey, What's this?
chief's BirTh-day

CHIEF'S birthday is TODAY!!!

CHIEF'S BIRTHDAY

Let's have a Party!

we can all help plan it!!!

CALLING ALL COPS!

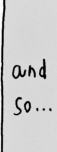

and so...

I'll make a card!

I'll bake a cake!

We'll do the decorations!!!

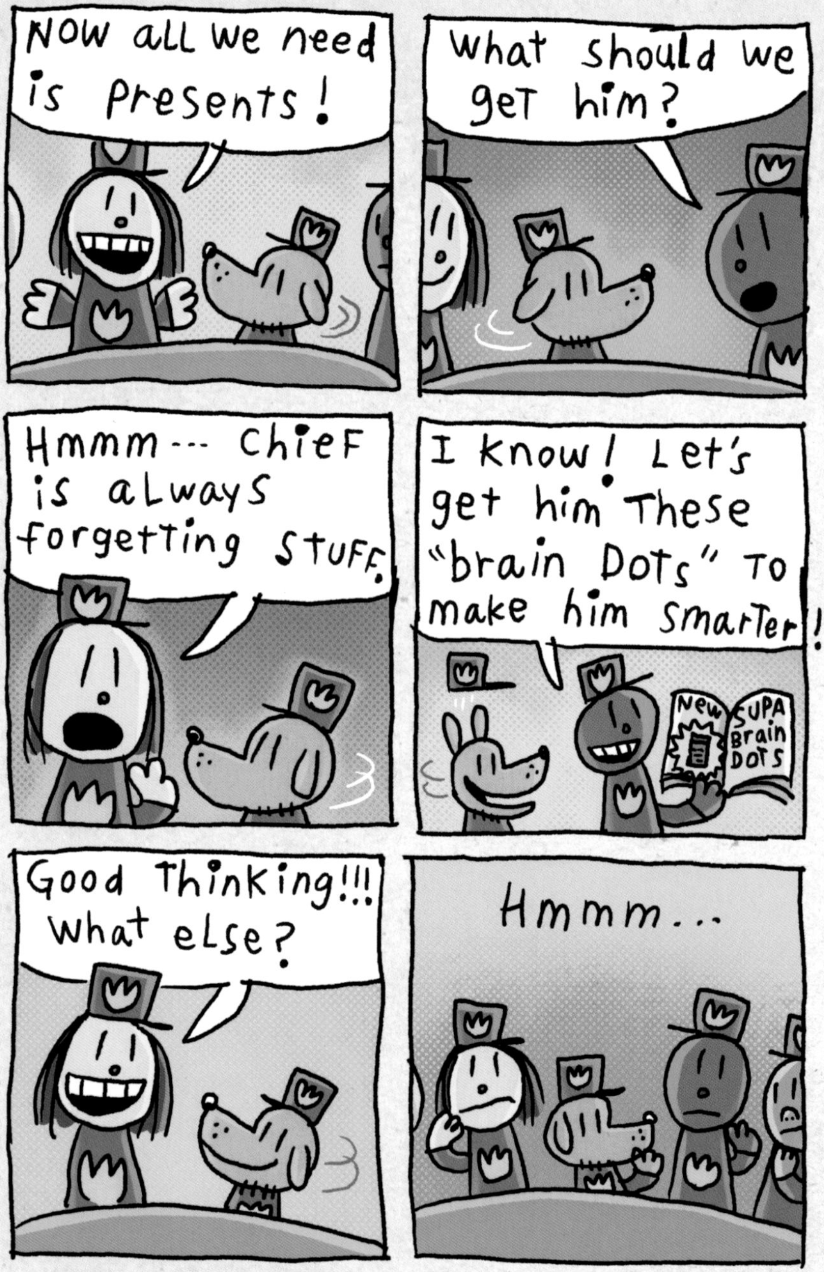
NOW all we need is presents!
What should we get him?
Hmmm... Chief is always forgetting stuff.
I know! Let's get him these "brain dots" to make him smarter!
New SUPA Brain Dots
Good thinking!!! What else?
Hmmm...

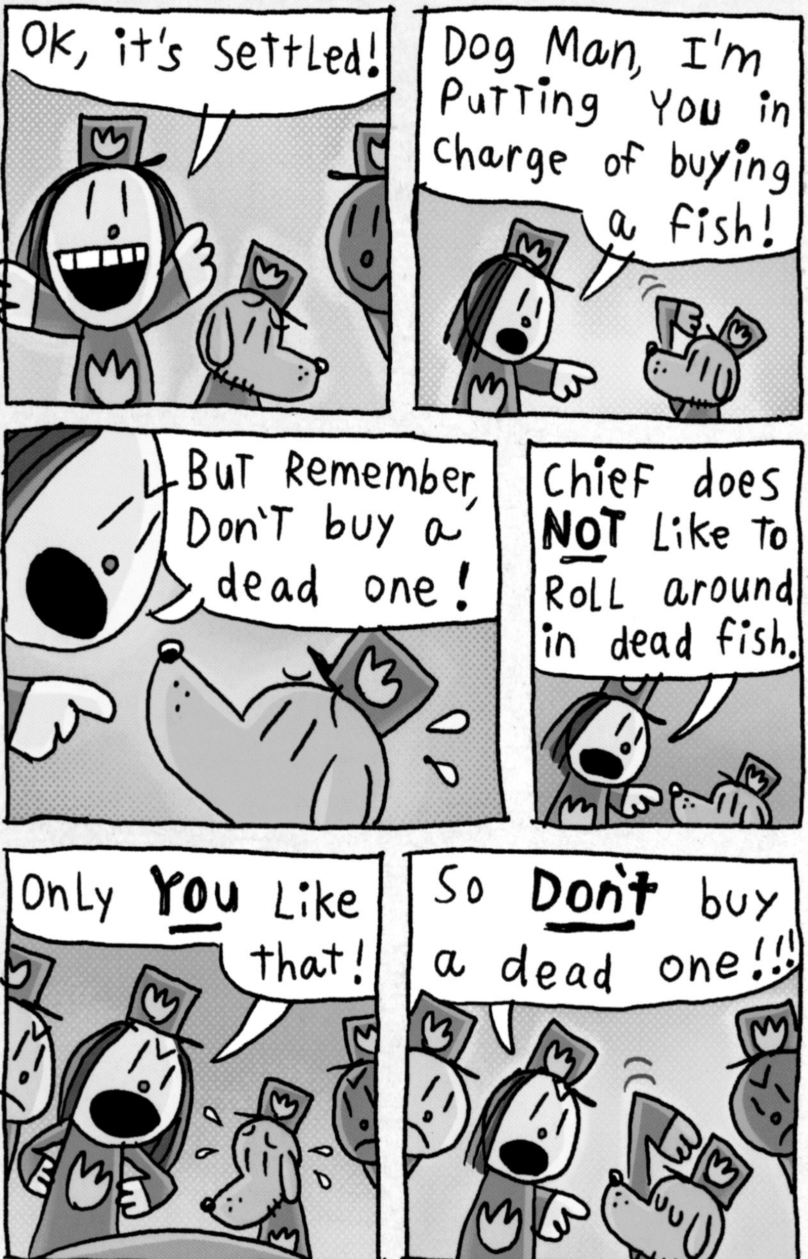
OK, it's settled!
Dog Man, I'm putting you in charge of buying a fish!
But remember, don't buy a dead one!
Chief does NOT like to roll around in dead fish.
Only YOU like that!
So DON'T buy a dead one!!!

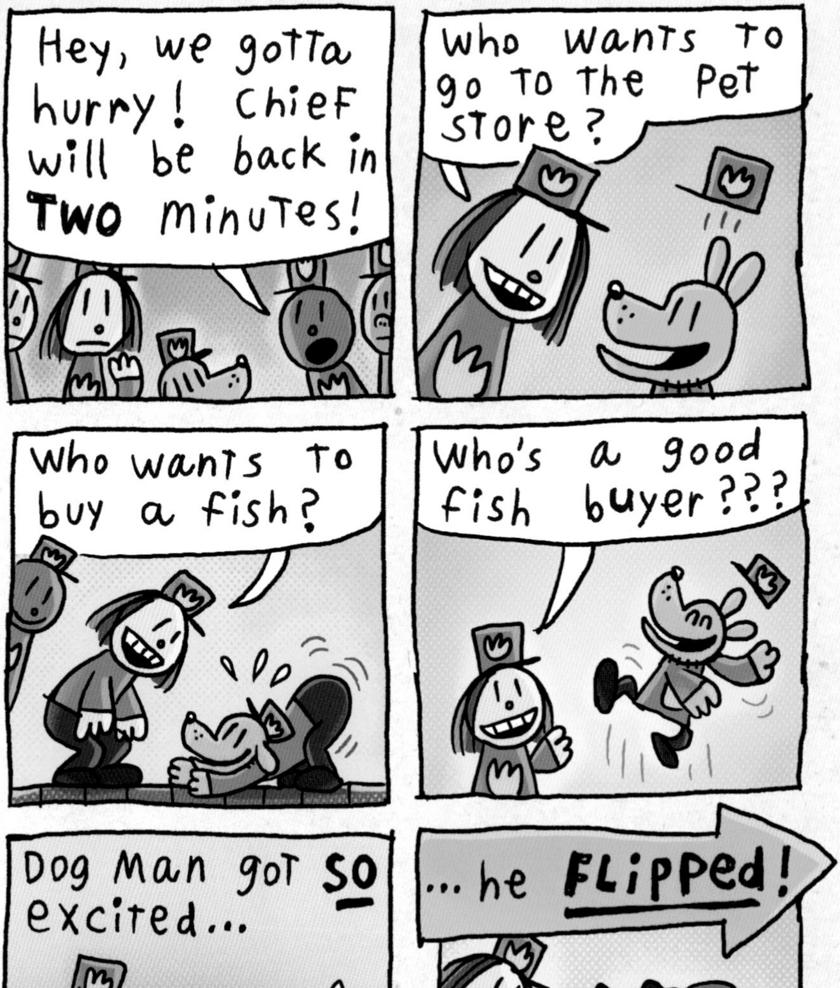

Hey, we gotta hurry! Chief will be back in TWO minutes!
Who wants to go to the pet store?
Who wants to buy a fish?
Who's a good fish buyer???
Dog Man got SO excited...
... he FLIPPED!

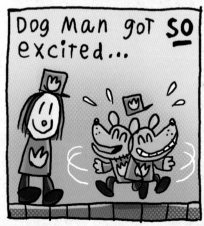

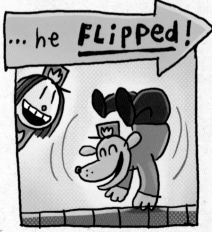

Introducing FLIP-O

Be a Flip Master!

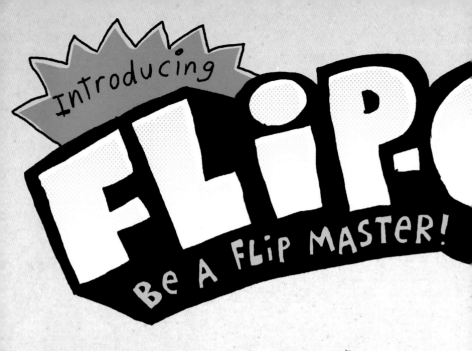

Flip-o-rama is
Easy if you know the rules:
Flip it, don't rip it!

a haiku
by
Dog Man.

犬男

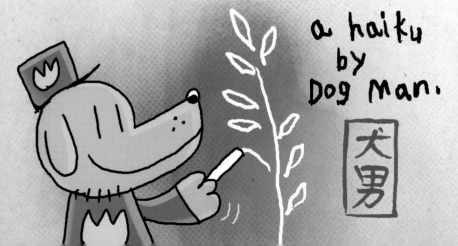

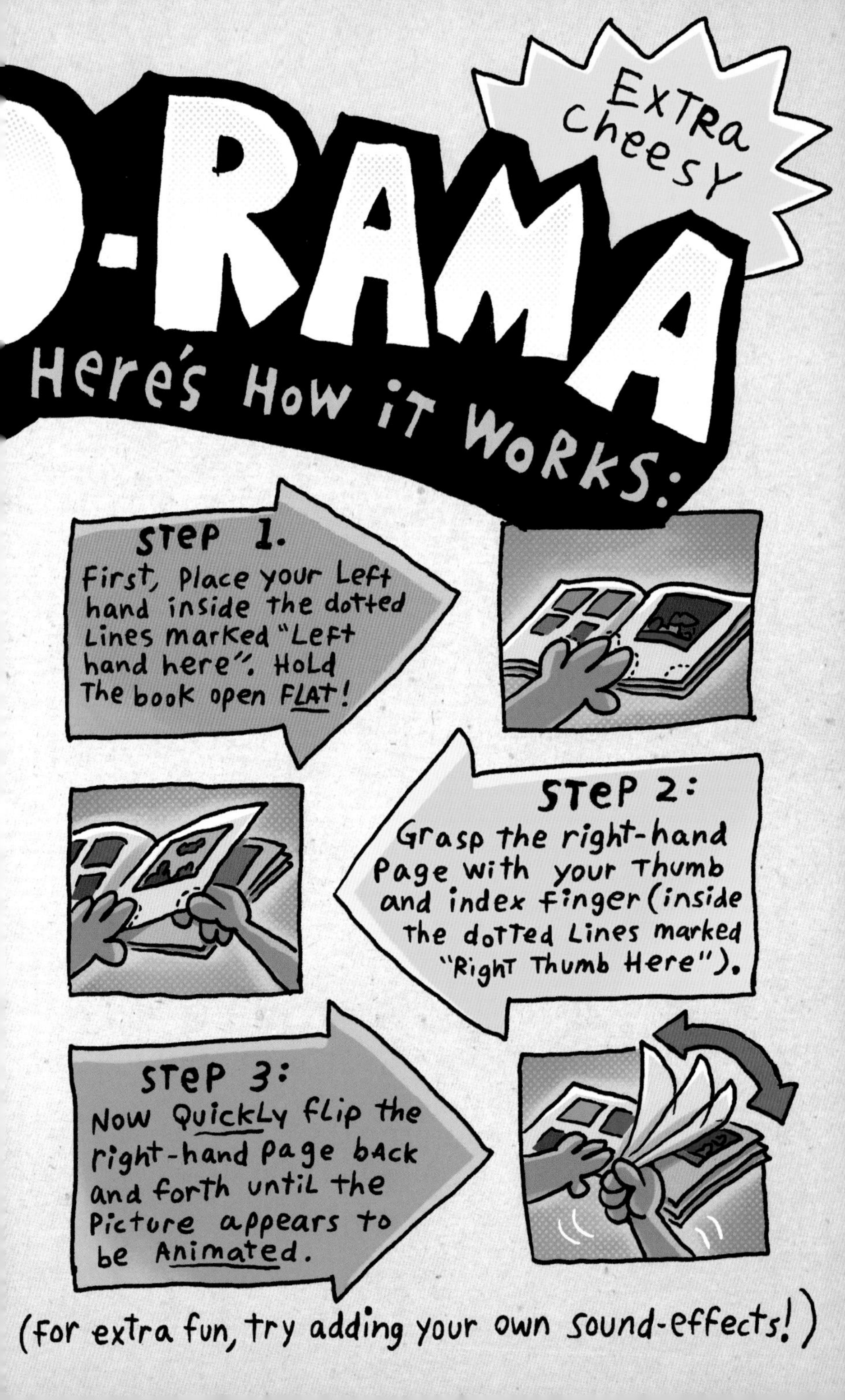

O-RAMA
EXTRA cheesy
Here's How it WORKS:
STEP 1.
First, Place your Left hand inside the dotted Lines marked "Left hand here". Hold The book open FLAT!
STEP 2:
Grasp the right-hand Page with your Thumb and index finger (inside the dotted Lines marked "Right Thumb Here").
STEP 3:
Now QUICKLY flip the right-hand page back and forth until the Picture appears to be Animated.
(For extra fun, try adding your own sound-effects!)

Remember,

while you are flipping,
be sure you can see
the images on page 25
AND the images on page 27.

If you flip quickly,
the pictures will
start to look like
one **Animated** cartoon!

Don't forget to
add your own
sound-effects!

Left
hand here.

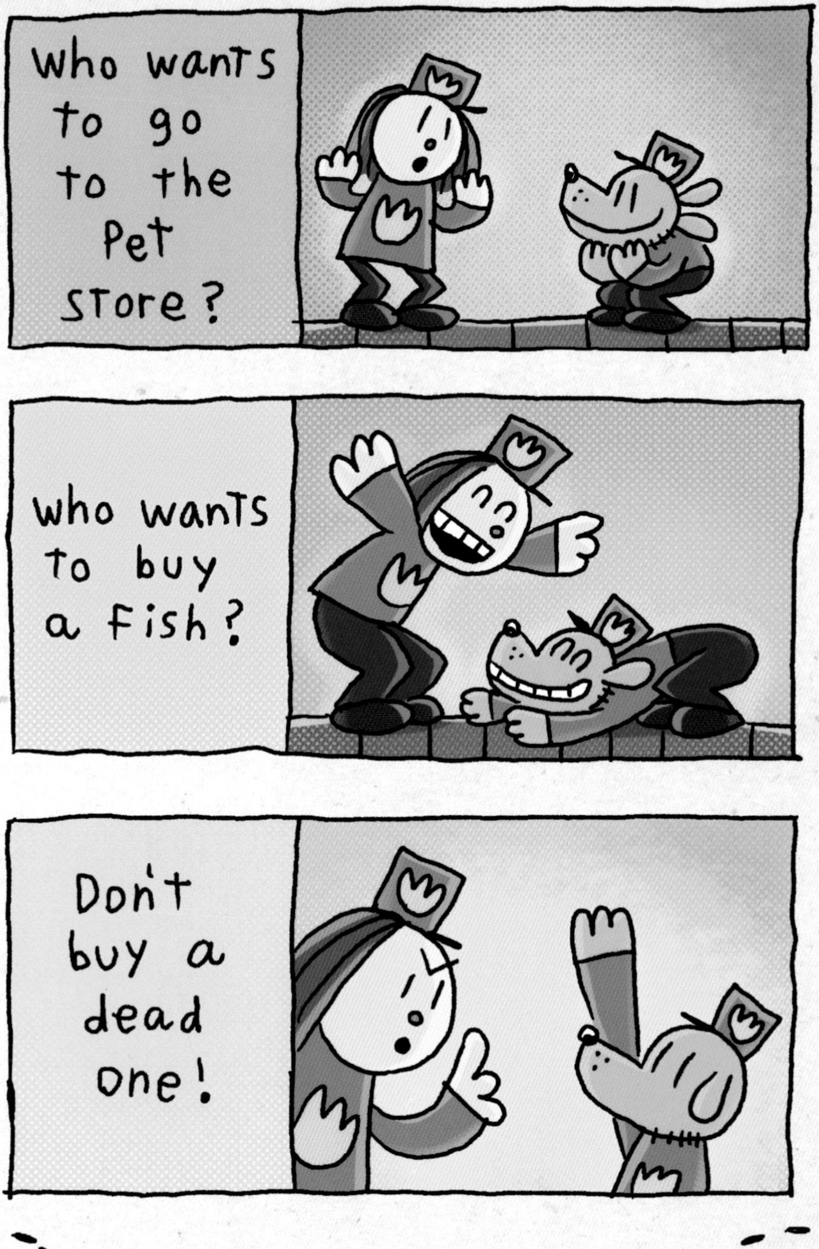
Who wants to go to the pet store?
Who wants to buy a fish?
Don't buy a dead one!

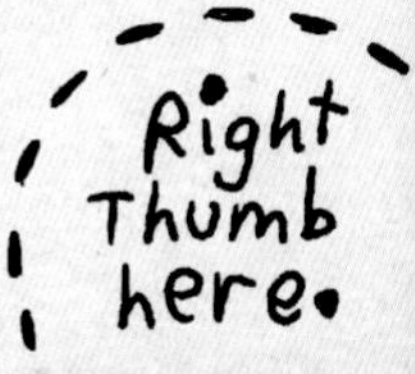
Right Thumb here.

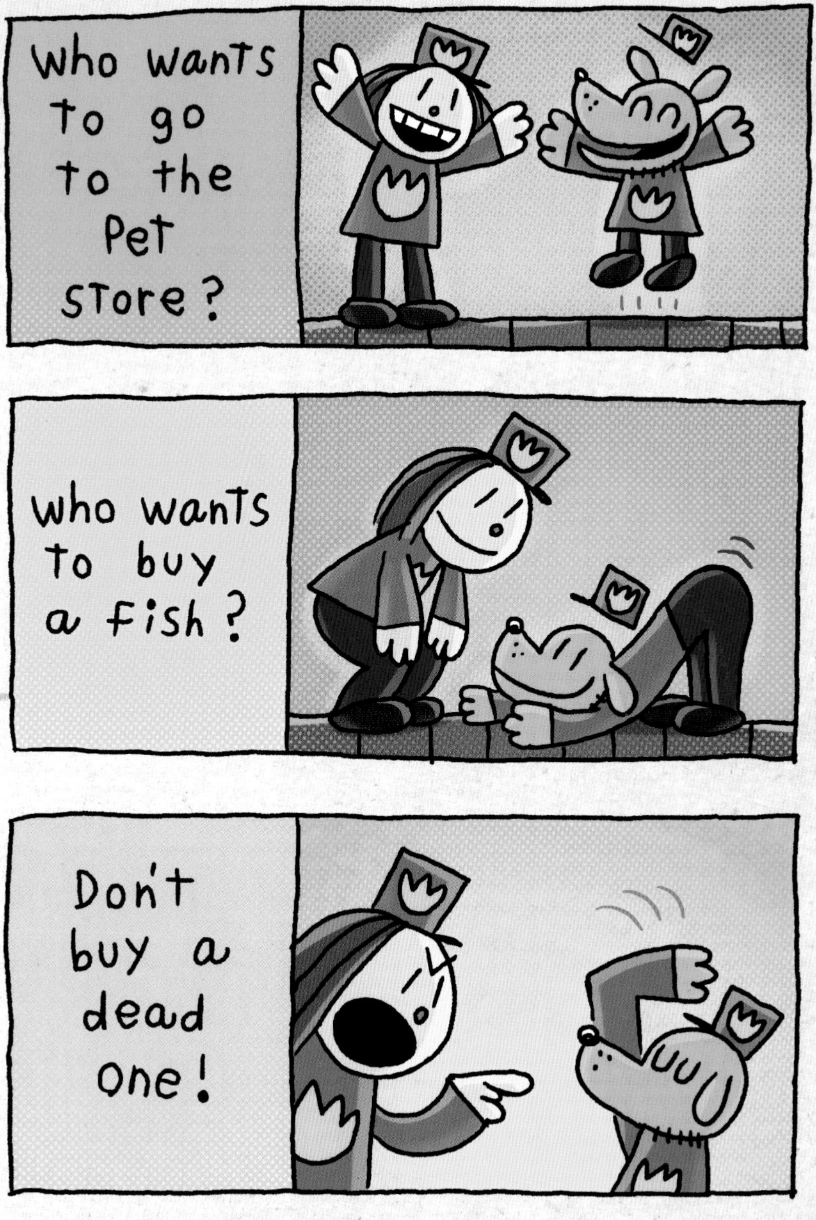
Who wants to go to the Pet store?
Who wants to buy a fish?
Don't buy a dead one!

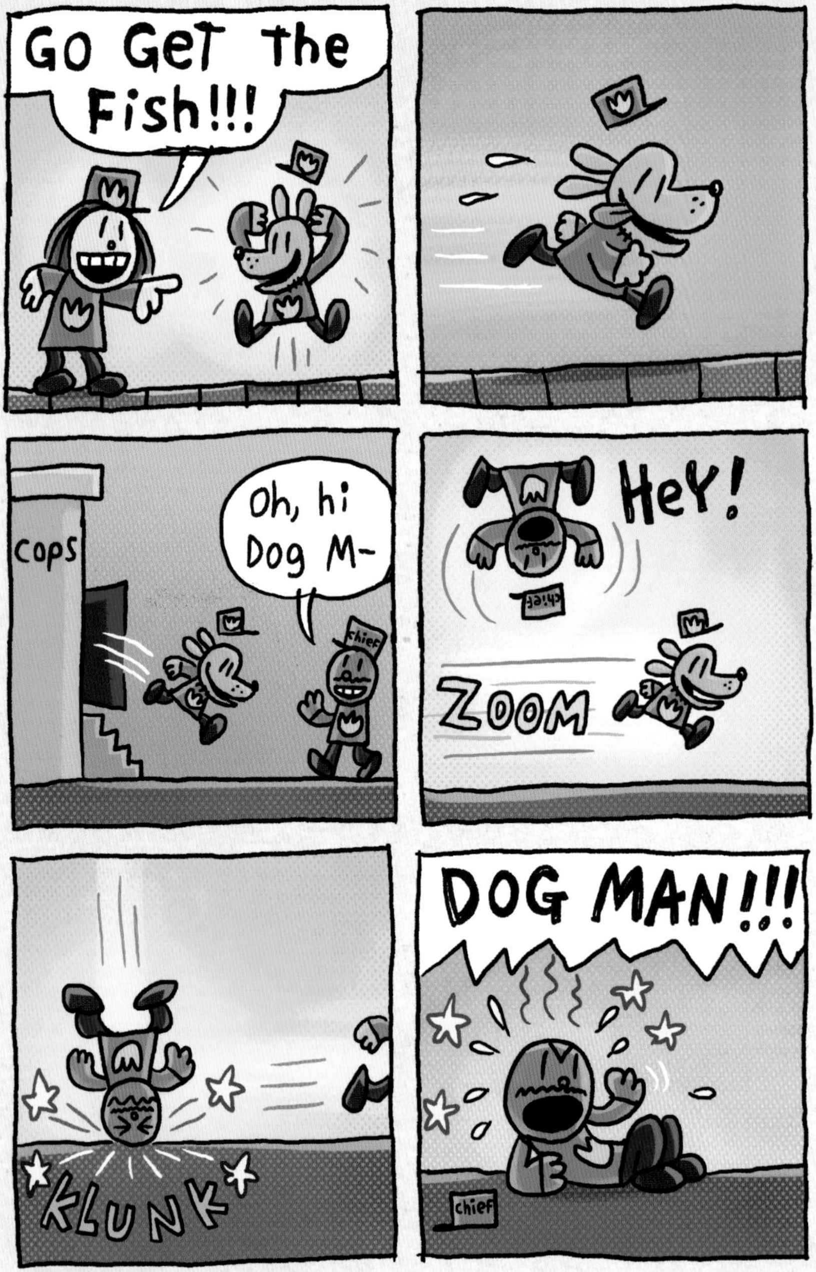

Go Get the Fish!!!
COPS
Oh, hi Dog M-
chief
HEY!
ZOOM
KLUNK
DOG MAN!!!
chief

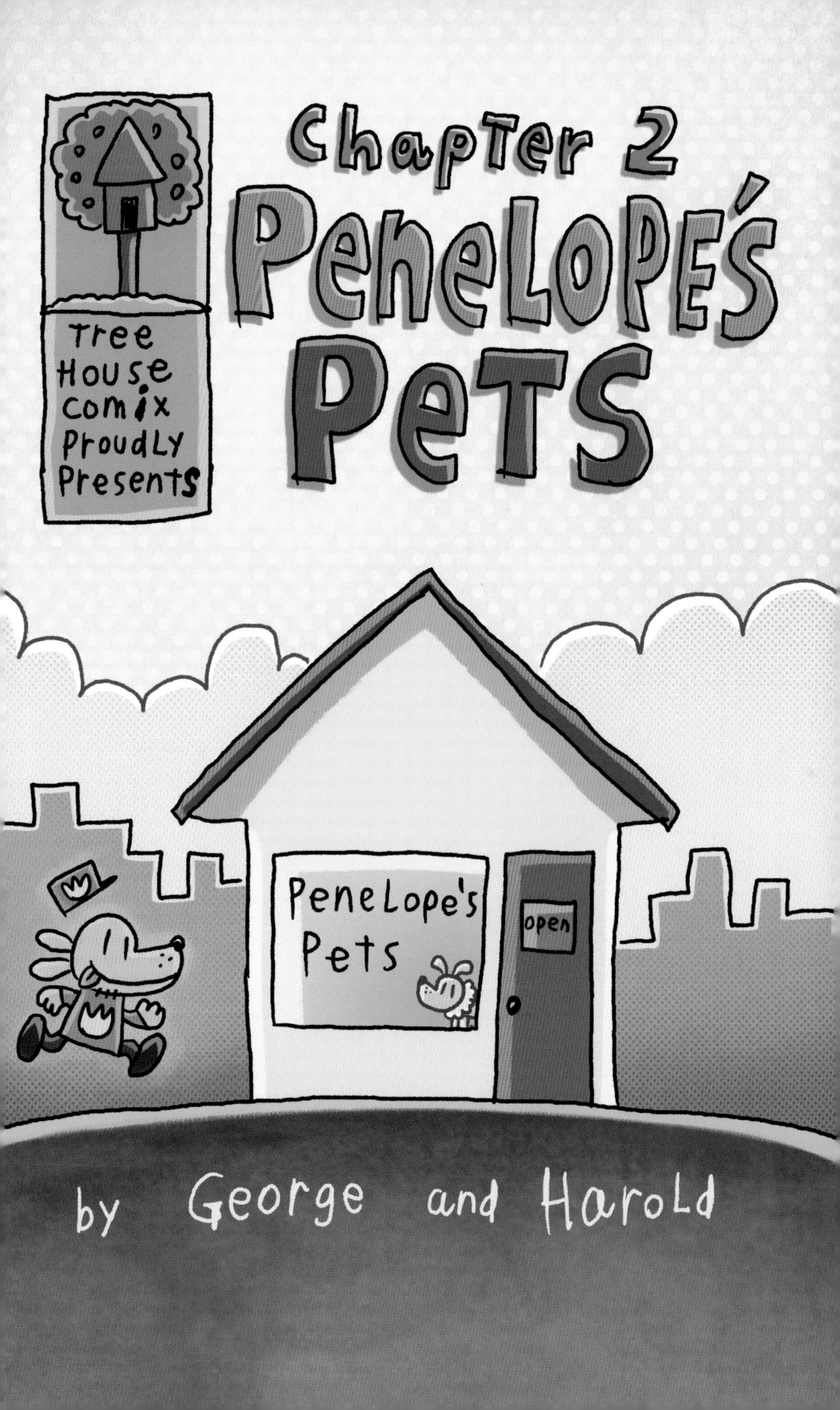
Tree House Comix Proudly Presents
Chapter 2
Penelope's Pets
Penelope's Pets
open
by George and Harold

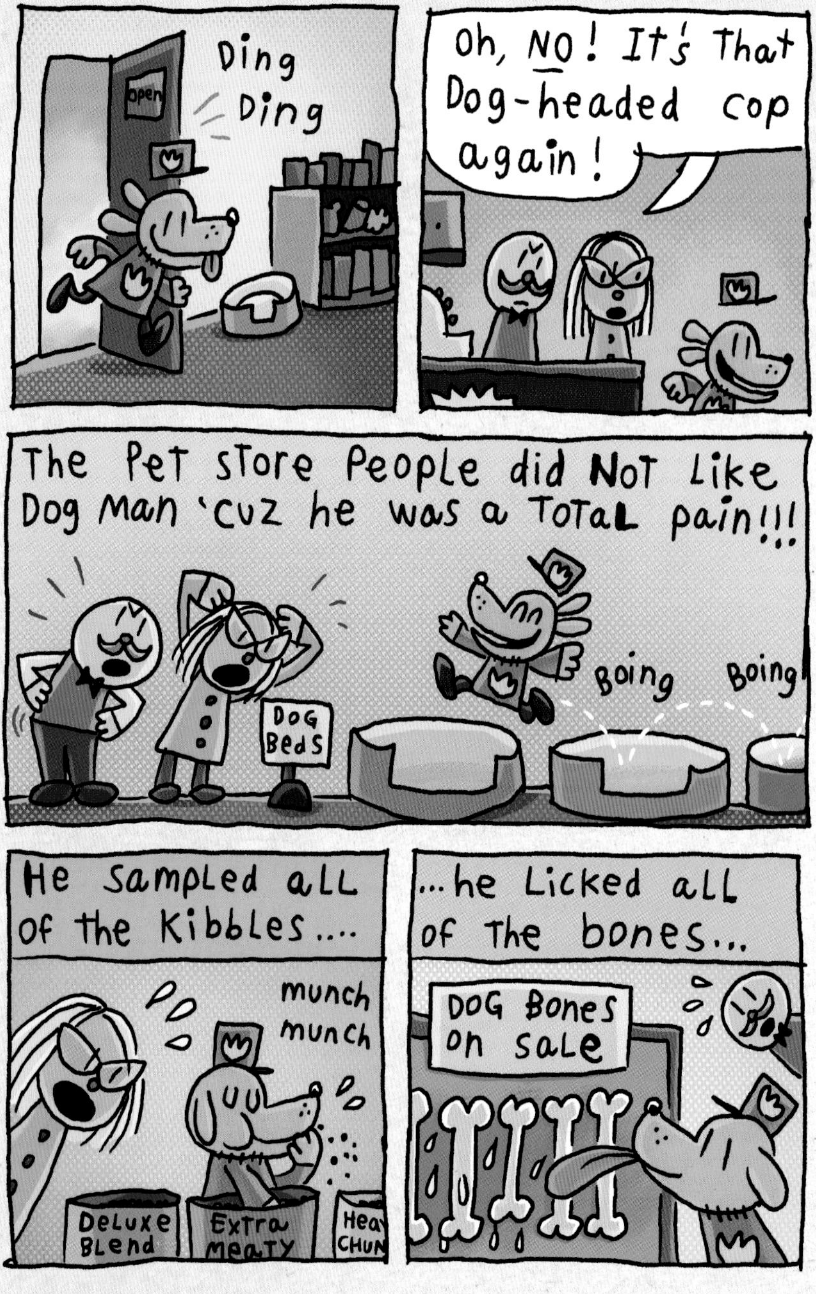

Ding Ding
Open
Oh, NO! It's That Dog-headed cop again!
The Pet store People did NOT Like Dog Man 'cuz he was a TOTAL pain!!!
DOG Beds
Boing Boing
He sampled all of the Kibbles....
munch munch
Deluxe Blend
Extra Meaty
...he Licked all of the bones...
DOG Bones on sale

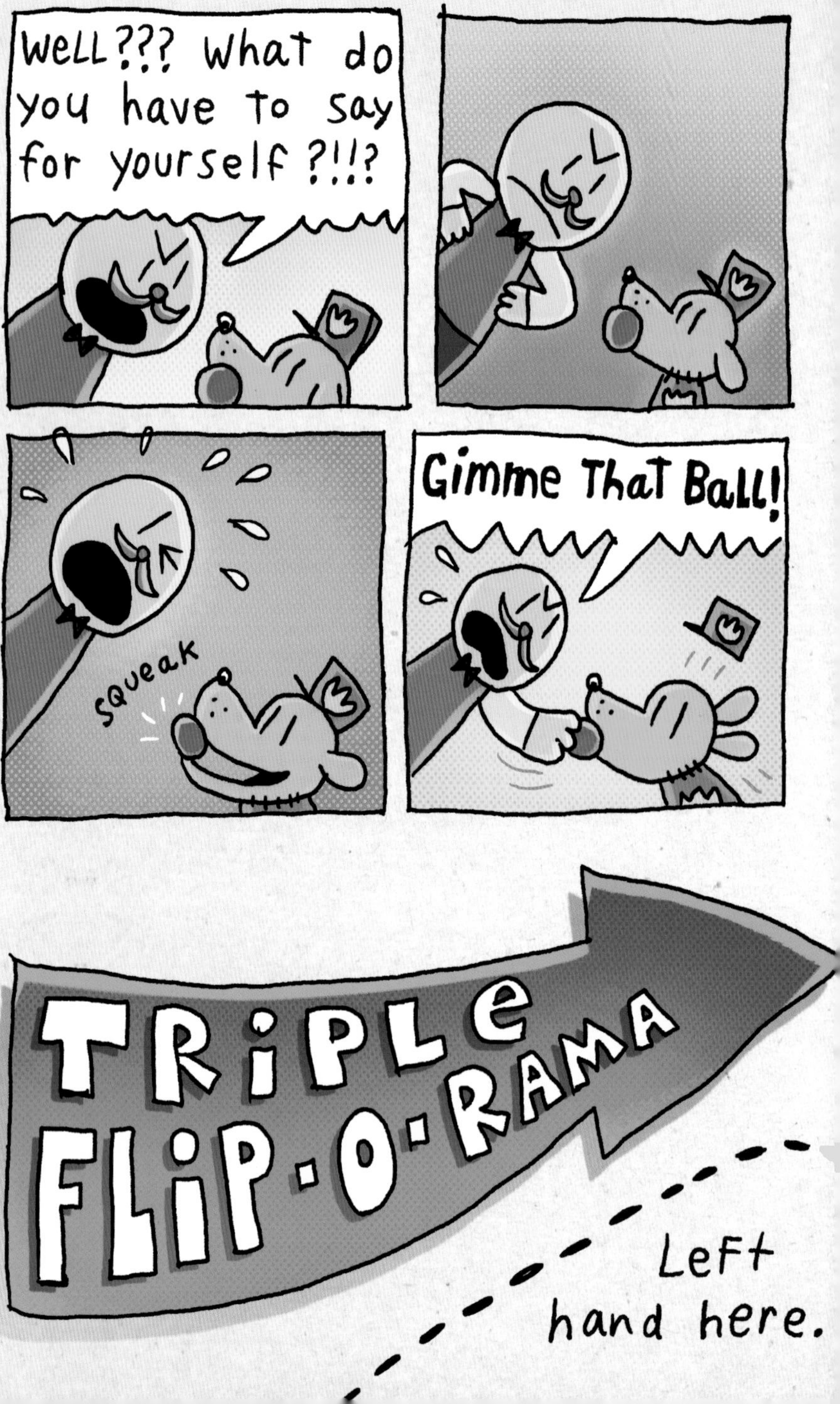
WELL??? What do you have to say for yourself?!!?
SQUEAK
Gimme That Ball!
TRIPLE FLIP-O-RAMA
Left hand here.

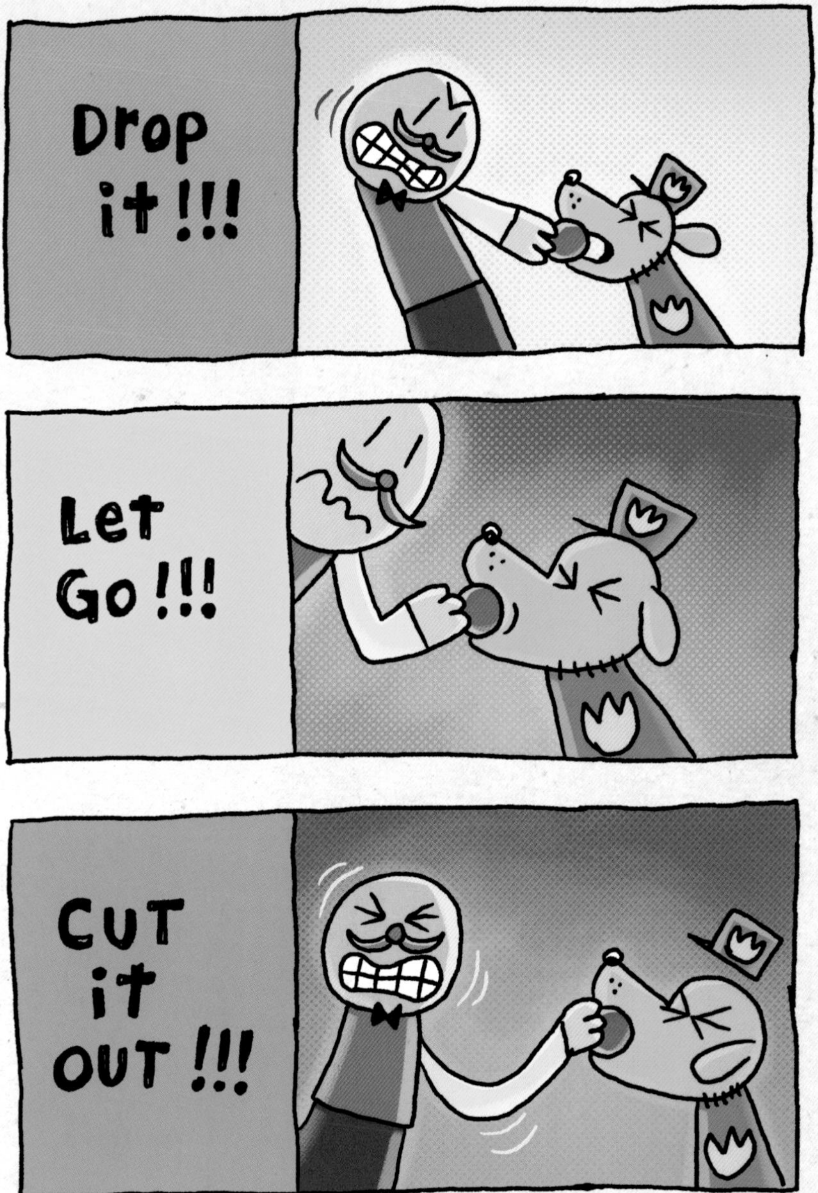

Drop it!!!
Let Go!!!
CUT it OUT!!!

Right Thumb here.

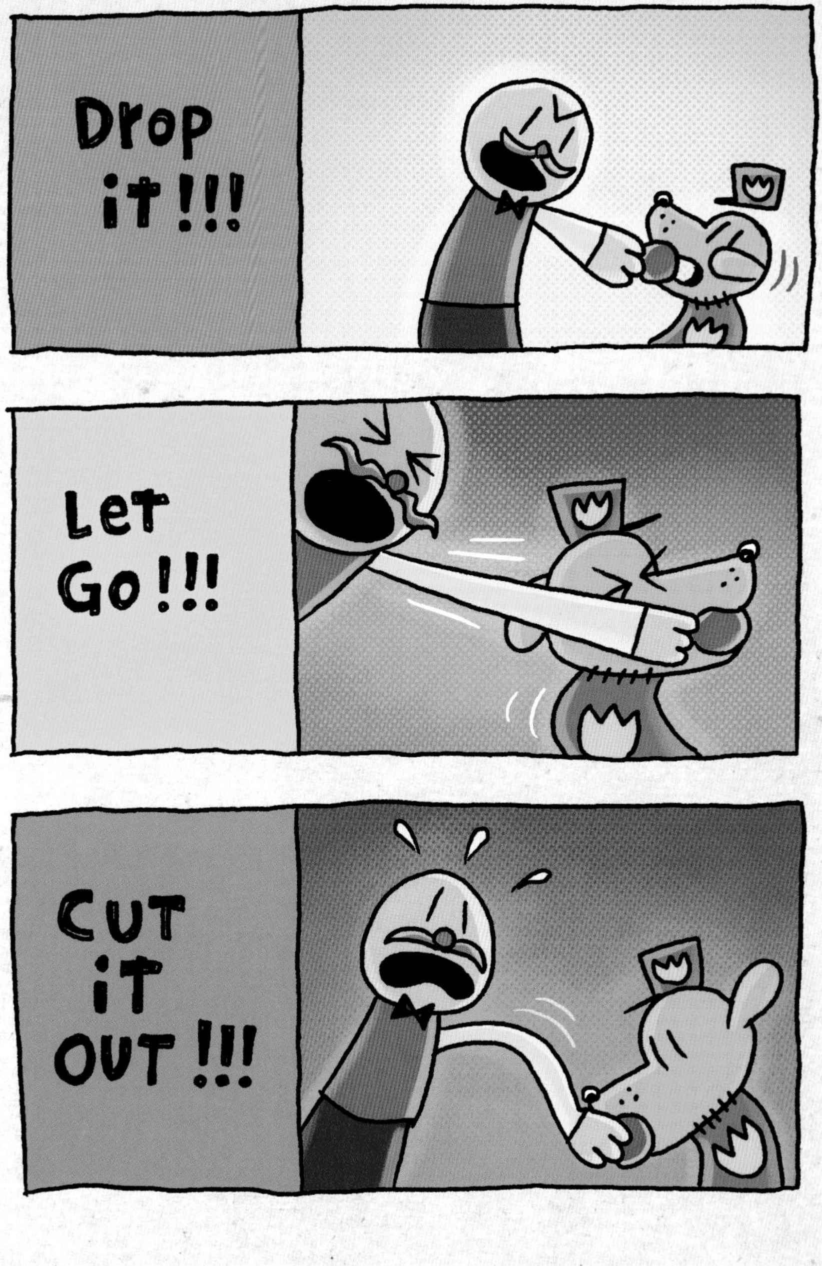
Drop it!!!
Let Go!!!
CUT iT OUT!!!

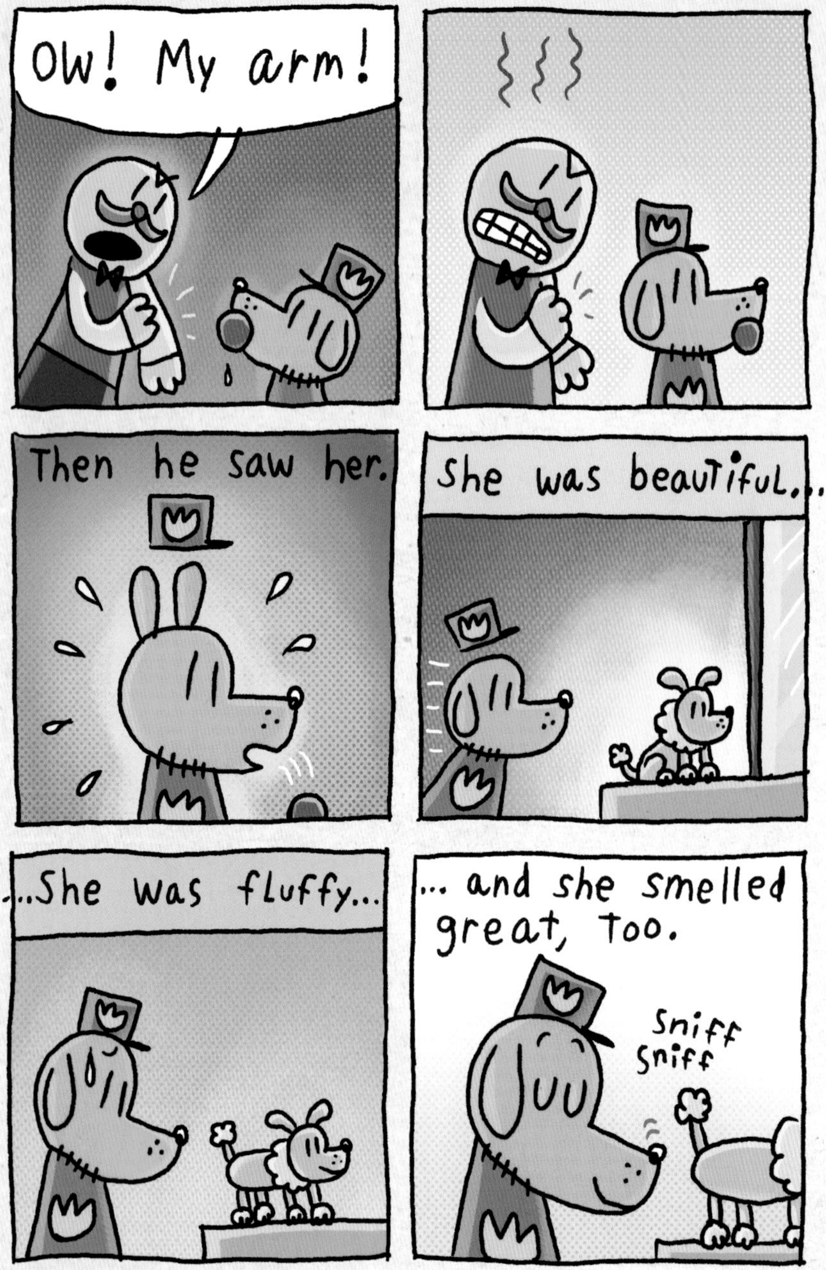
OW! My arm!
Then he saw her.
She was beautiful...
...She was fluffy...
... and she smelled great, too.
Sniff
Sniff

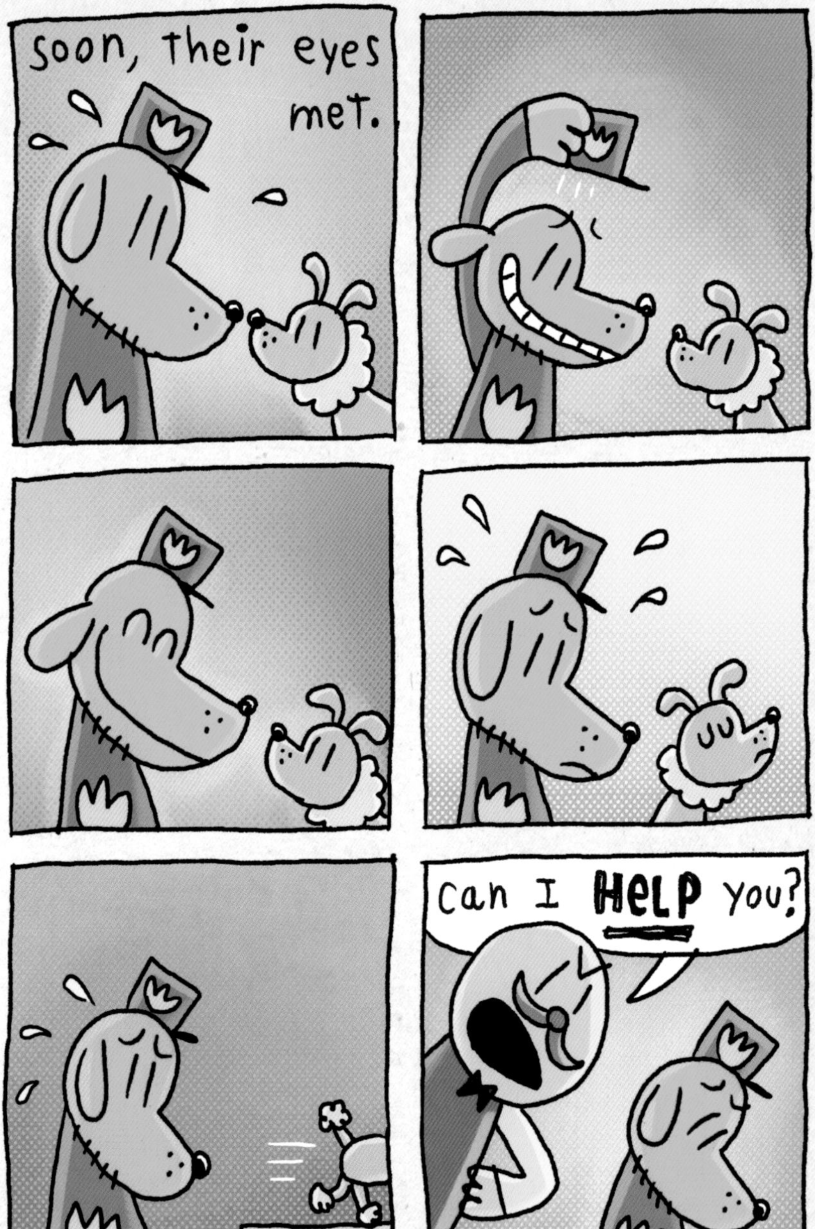
Soon, their eyes met.
Can I HELP you?

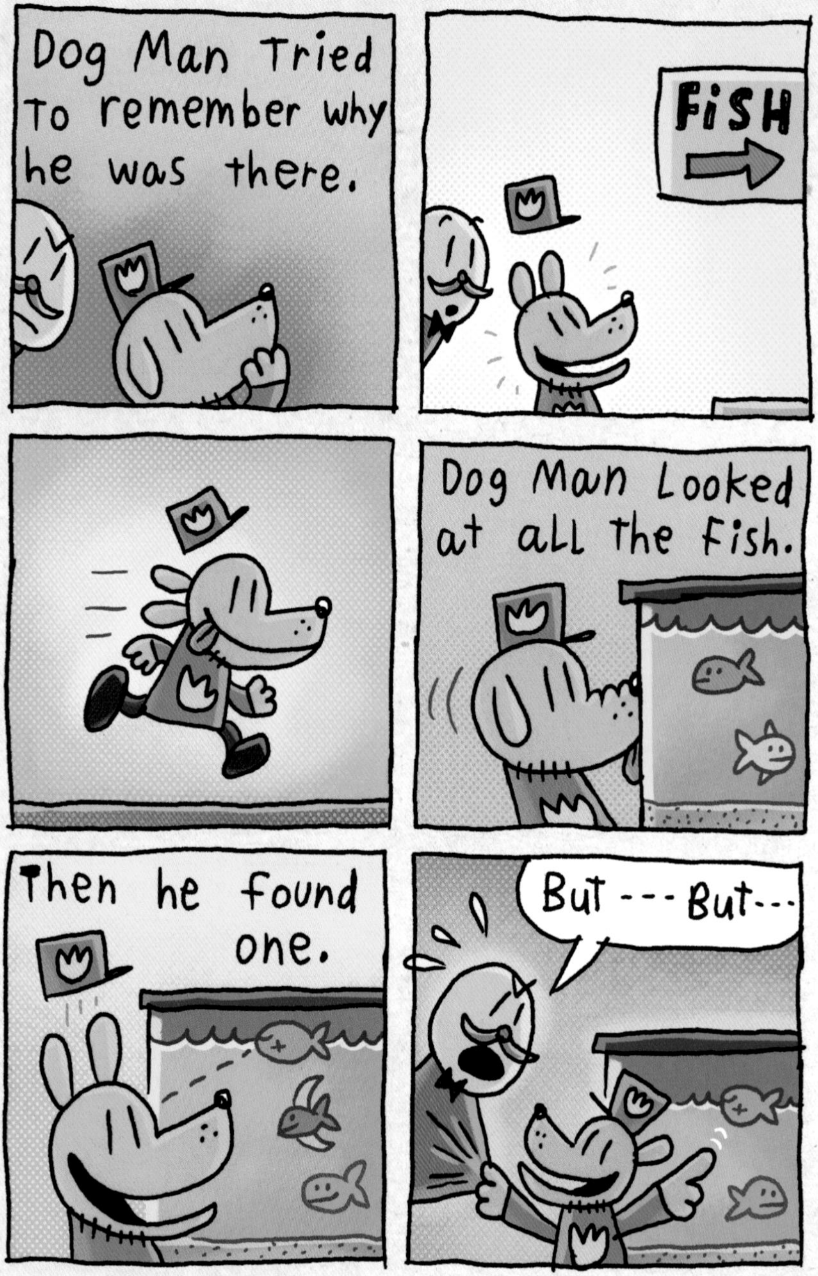

Dog Man Tried To remember why he was there.
FiSH
Dog Man Looked at aLL The Fish.
Then he found one.
But --- But---

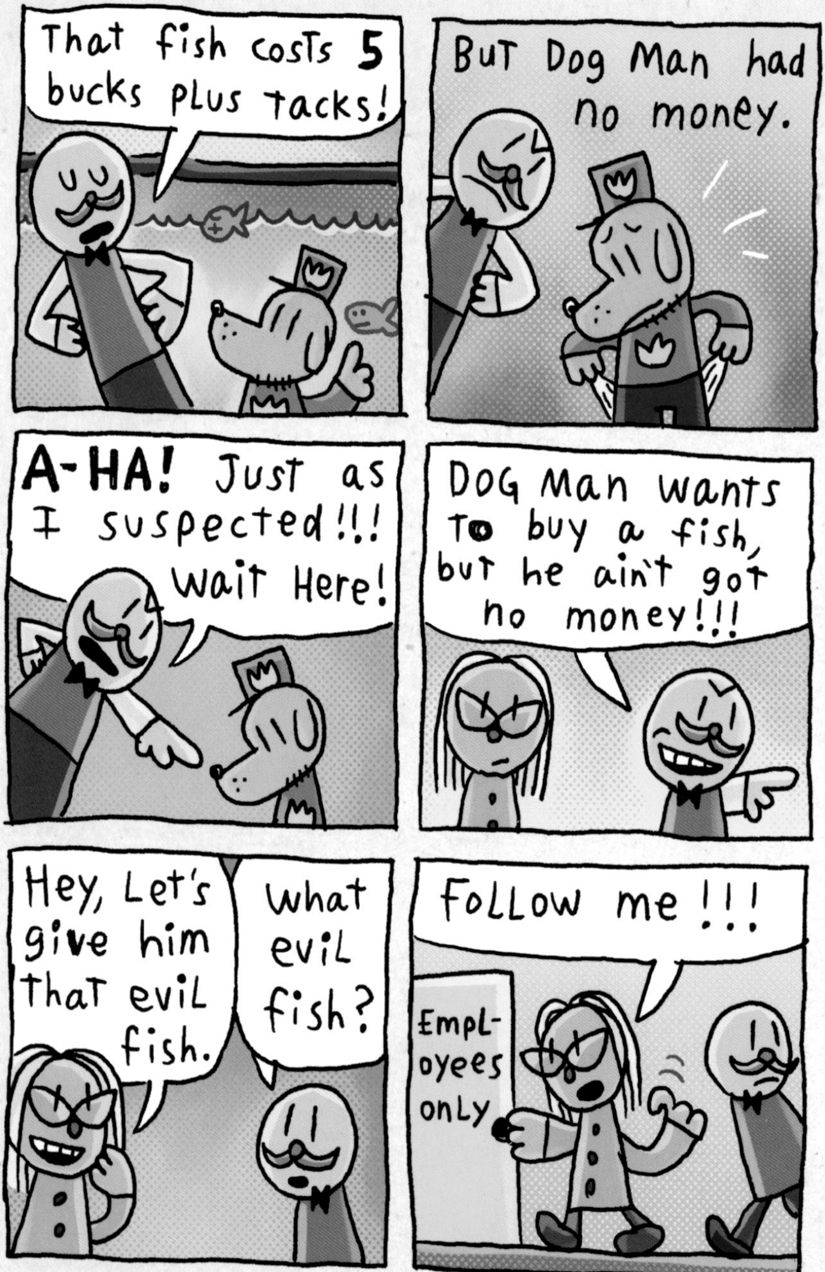

That fish costs 5 bucks plus tacks!
But Dog Man had no money.
A-HA! Just as I suspected!!! Wait Here!
DOG Man wants to buy a fish, but he ain't got no money!!!
Hey, Let's give him that evil fish.
What evil fish?
Follow me!!!
Employees only

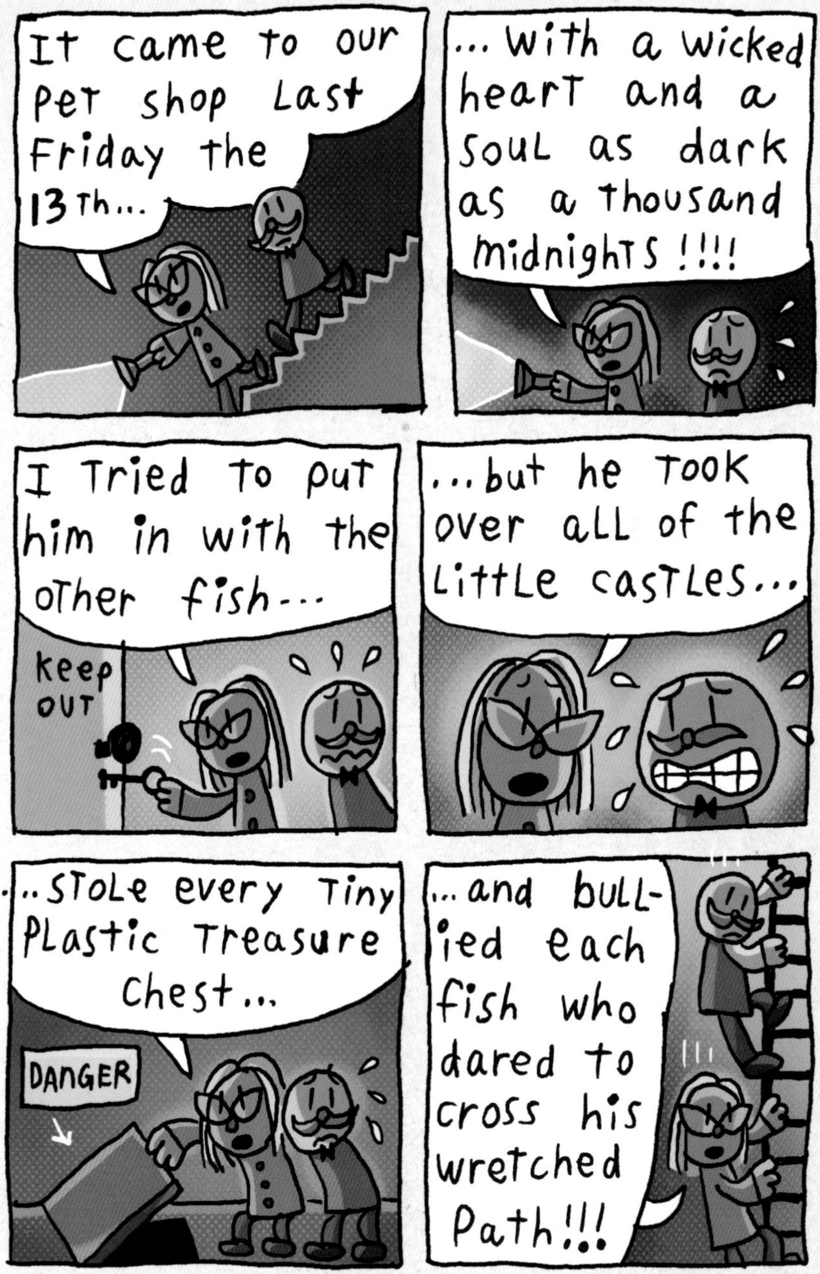
It came to our pet shop Last Friday the 13th...
...with a wicked heart and a soul as dark as a thousand midnights!!!!
I Tried to put him in with the other fish...
keep out
...but he took over all of the little castles...
..stole every tiny plastic treasure chest...
DANGER
...and bull-ied each fish who dared to cross his wretched path!!!

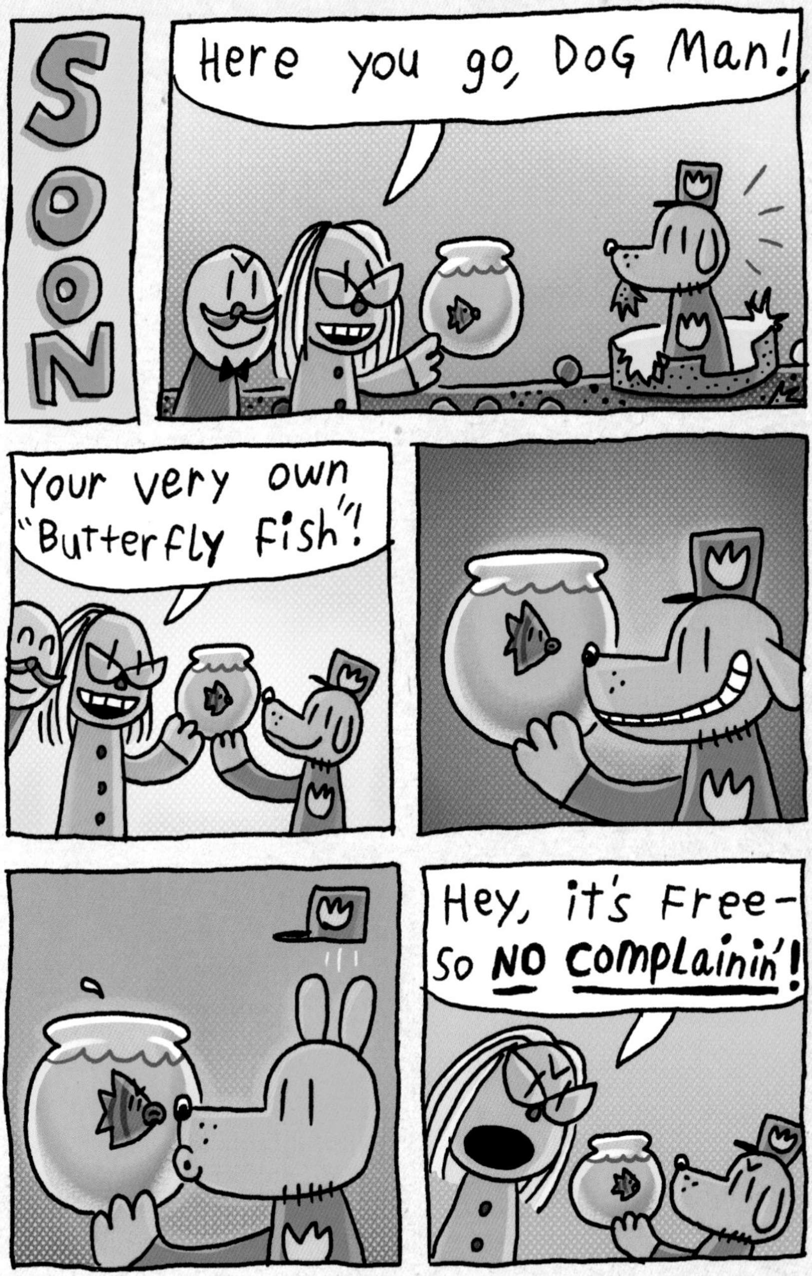
SOON
Here you go, DOG Man!
Your very own "Butterfly Fish"!
Hey, it's Free-
So NO Complainin'!

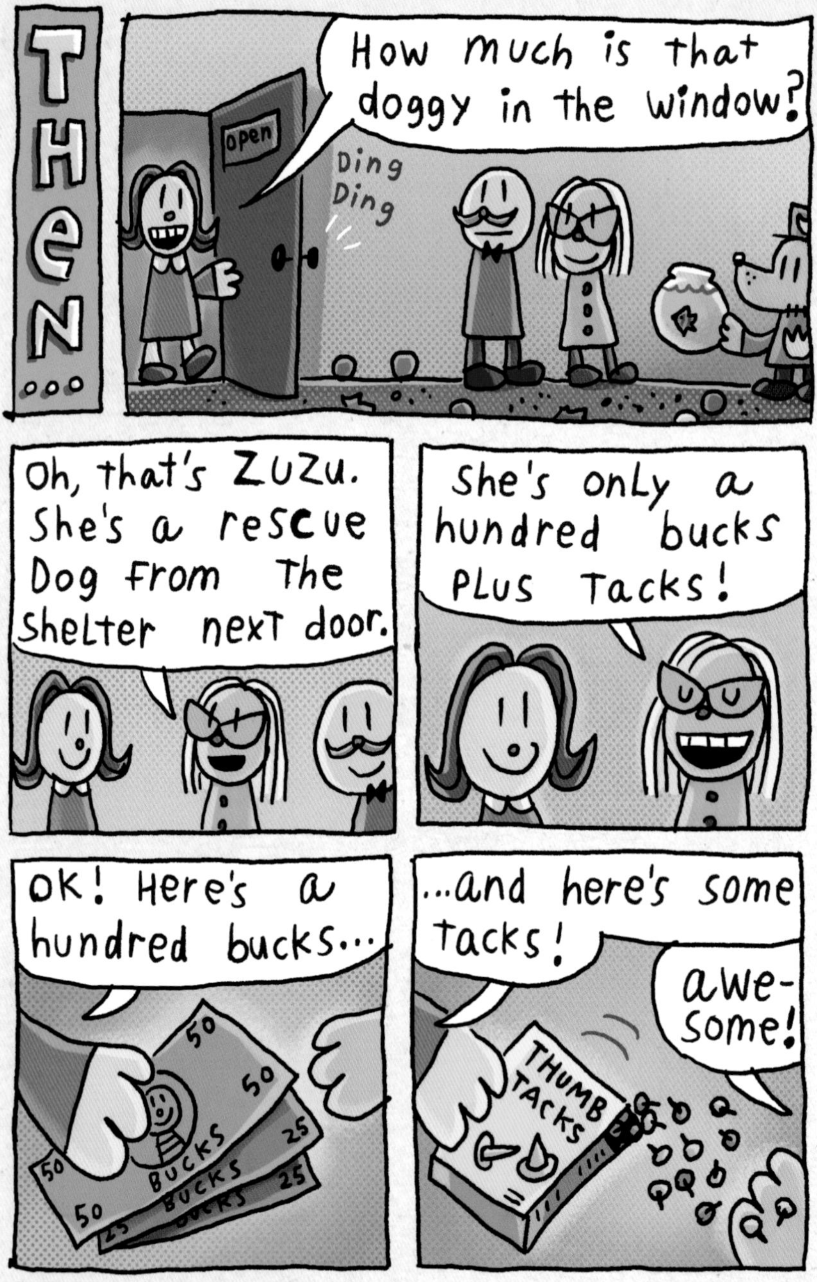
THEN...
How much is that doggy in the window?
Ding Ding
open
Oh, that's ZUZU. She's a rescue Dog from The Shelter next door.
She's only a hundred bucks plus Tacks!
OK! Here's a hundred bucks...
50
50
50
50
25
25
BUCKS
BUCKS
...and here's some tacks!
awe-some!
THUMB TACKS

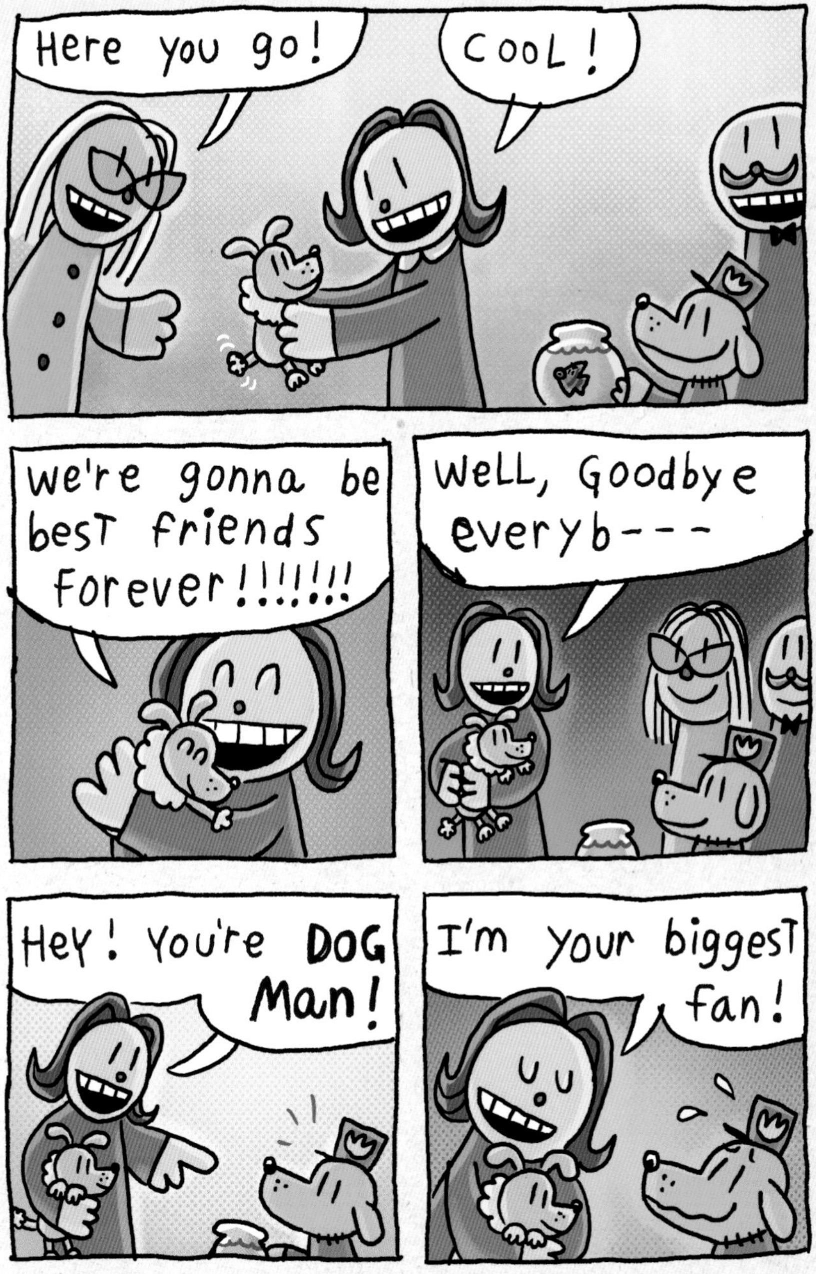
Here you go!
COOL!
We're gonna be best friends Forever!!!!!!!
WeLL, Goodbye everyb---
Hey! You're DOG Man!
I'm your biggest fan!

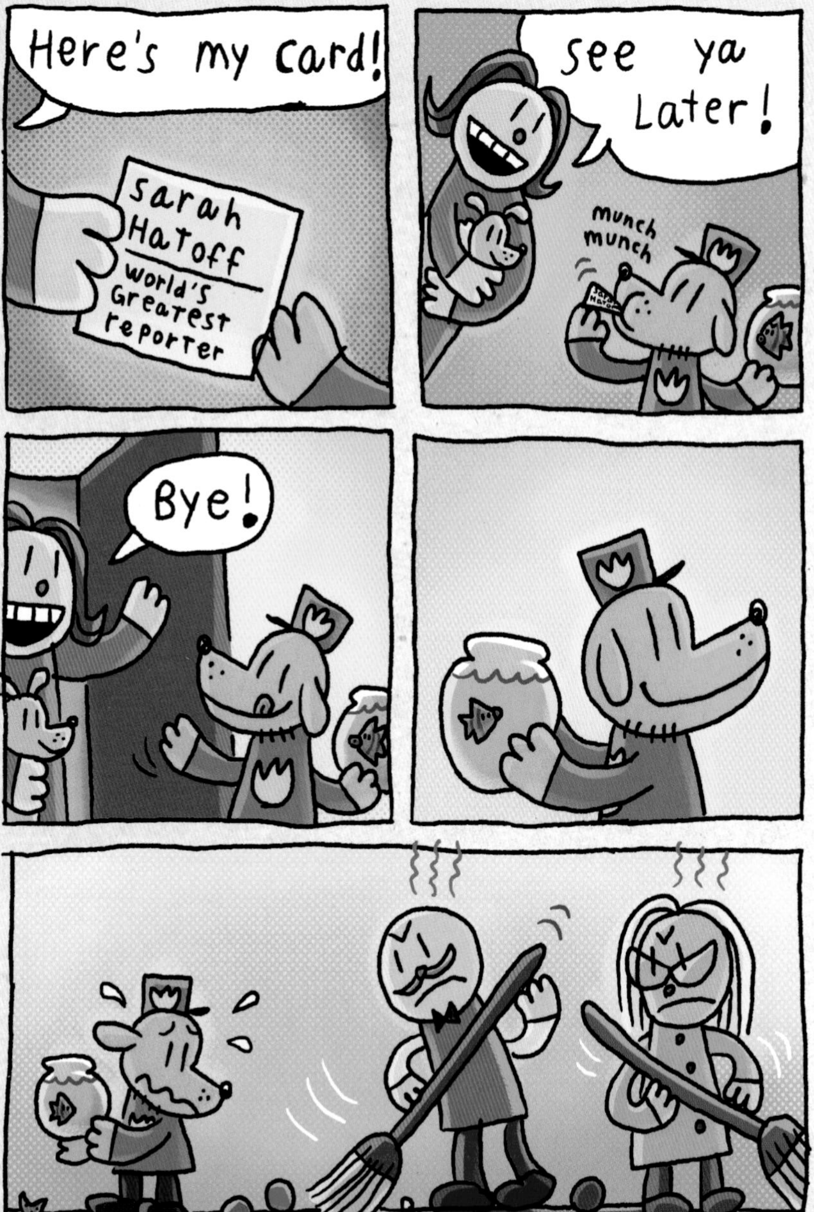
Here's my card!
Sarah Hatoff
World's Greatest reporter
See ya Later!
munch munch
Bye!

CHAPTER 3

HAPPY BIRTHDAY, CHIEF

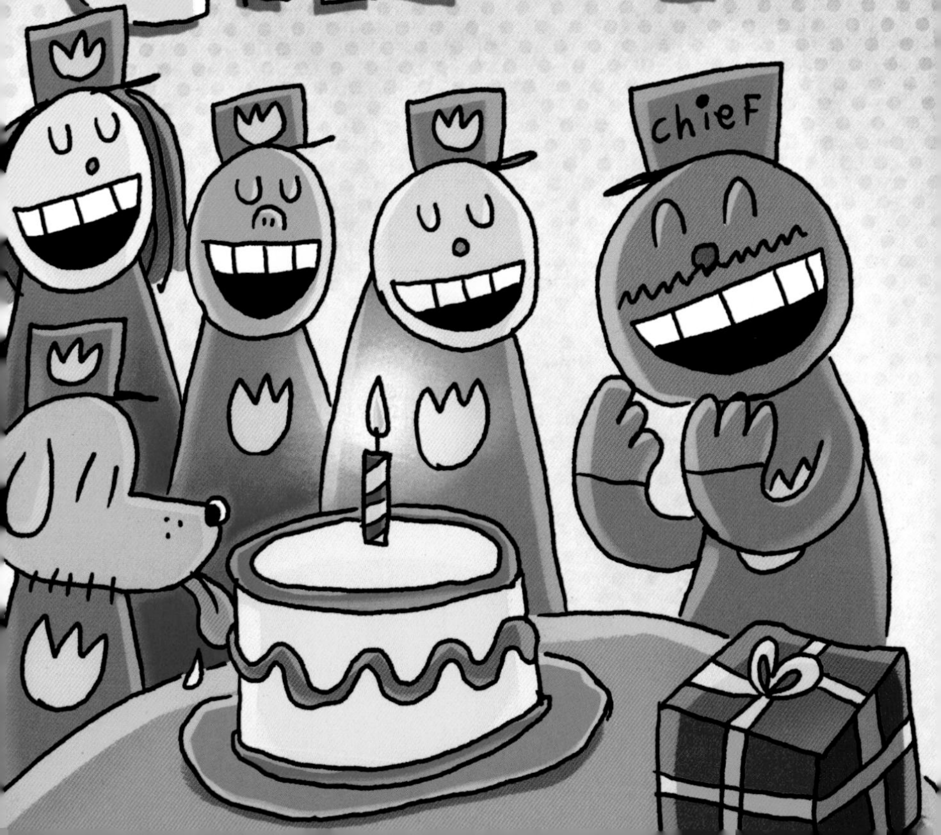

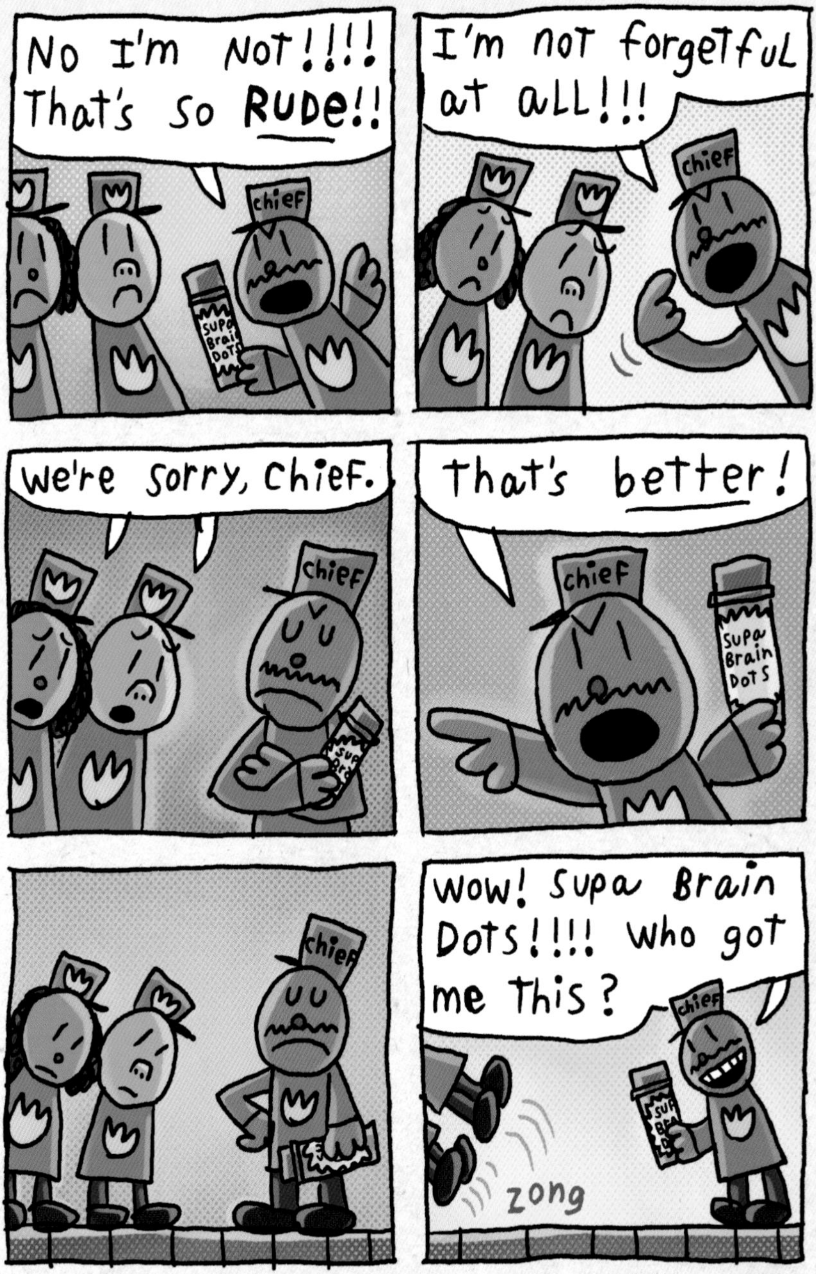
No I'm NOT!!!! That's so RUDE!!
chief
SUPA Brain DOTS
I'm not forgetful at all!!!
chief
We're sorry, Chief.
chief
That's better!
chief
SUPA Brain DOTS
chief
Wow! Supa Brain Dots!!!! Who got me this?
chief
ZONG

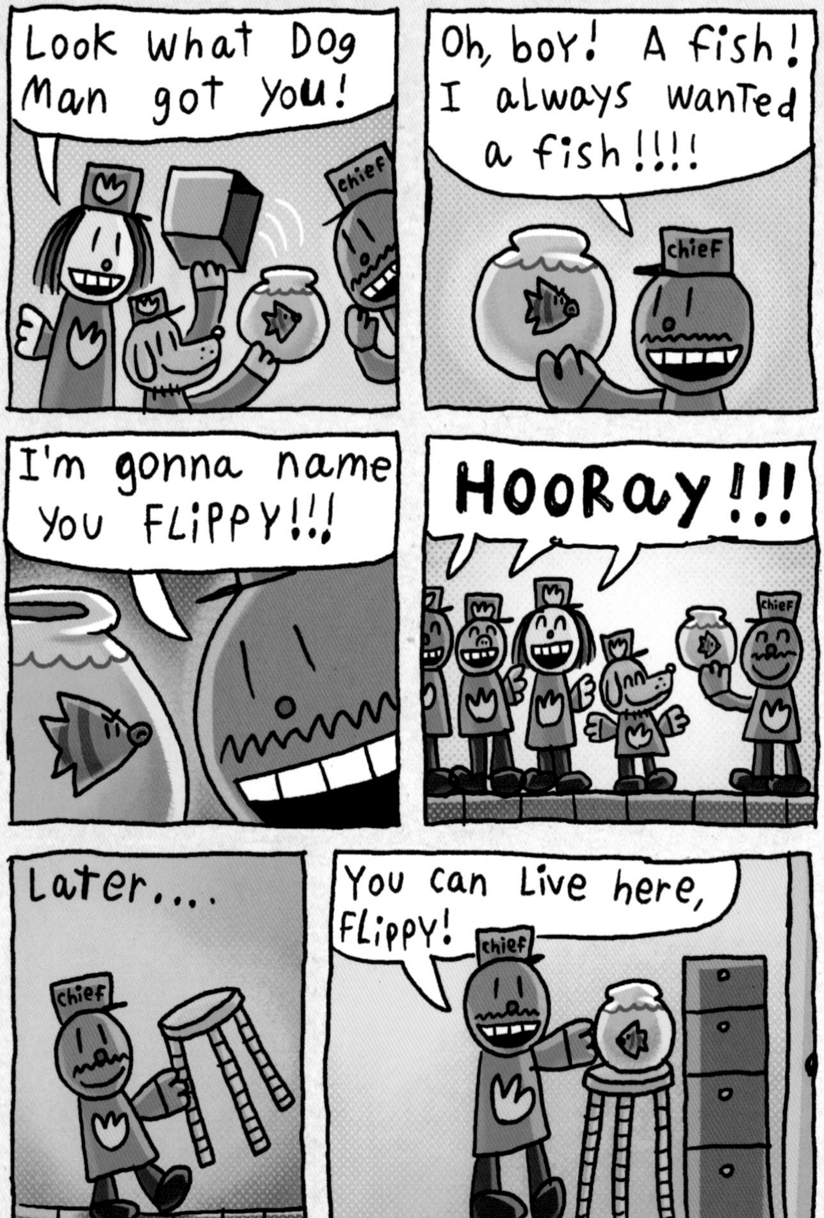
Look what Dog Man got you!
chief
Oh, boy! A fish! I always wanted a fish!!!!
chief
I'm gonna name you FLIPPY!!!
HOORAY!!!
chief
Later....
chief
You can live here, FLiPPY!
chief

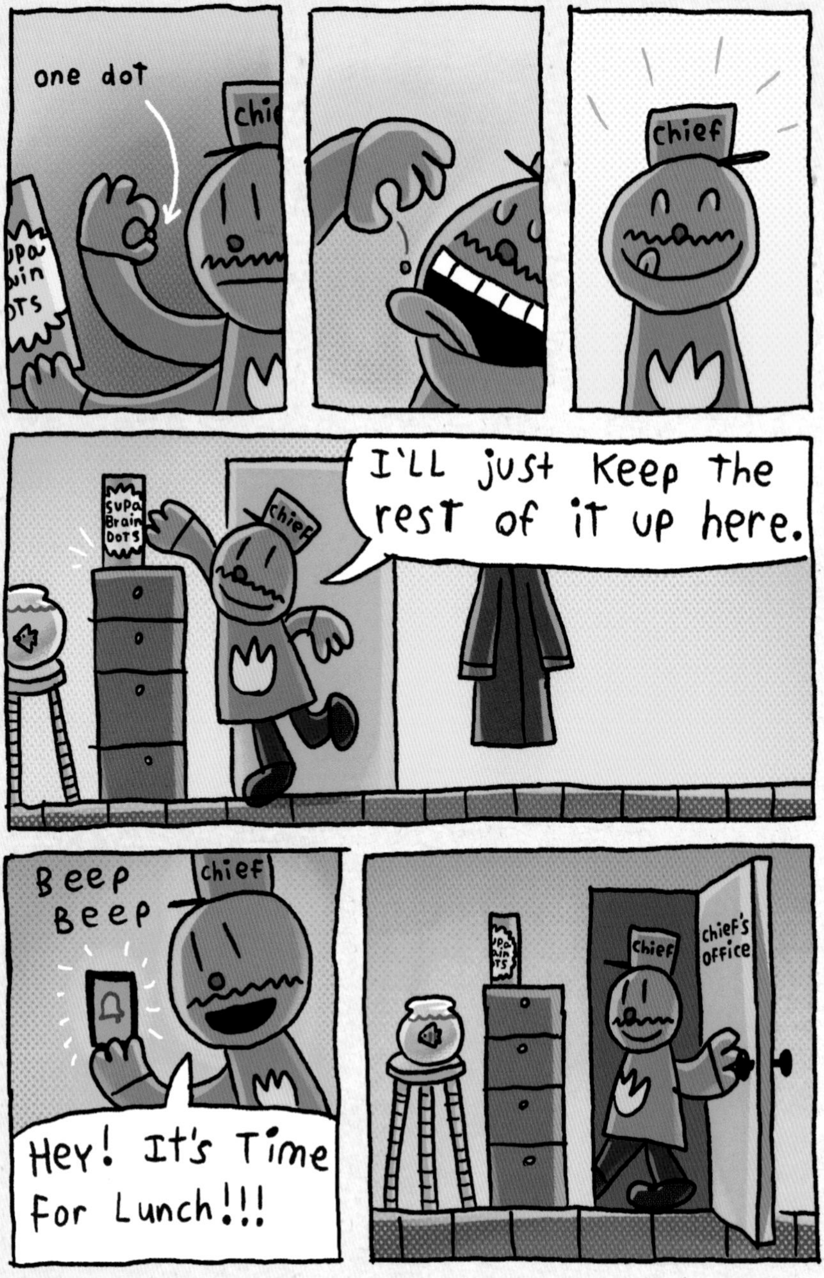
one dot
chie
UPA
AIN
OTS
chief
SUPA
Brain
DOTS
chief
I'LL just Keep the rest of it up here.
Beep
Beep
chief
Hey! It's Time For Lunch!!!
chief
chief's office

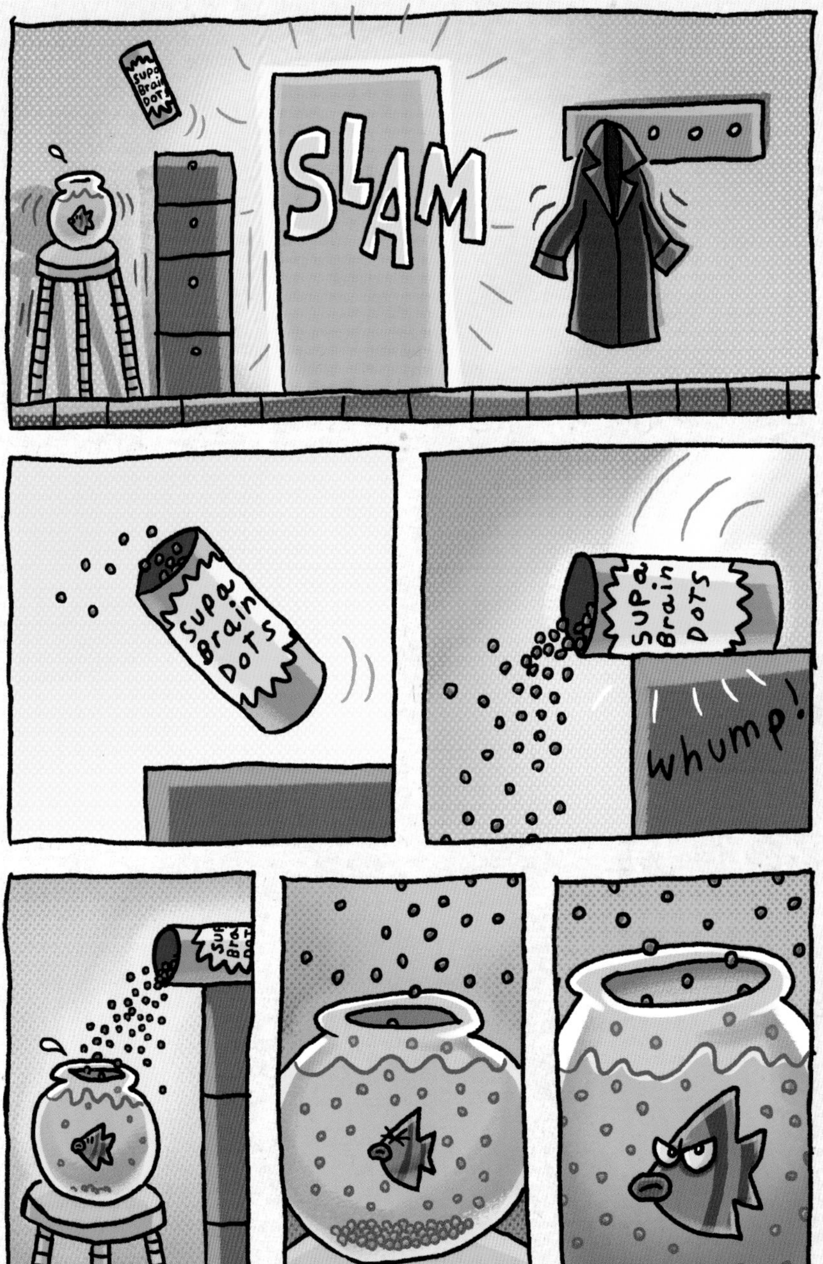
Supa Brain Dots
SLAM
Supa Brain Dots
Supa Brain Dots
whump!

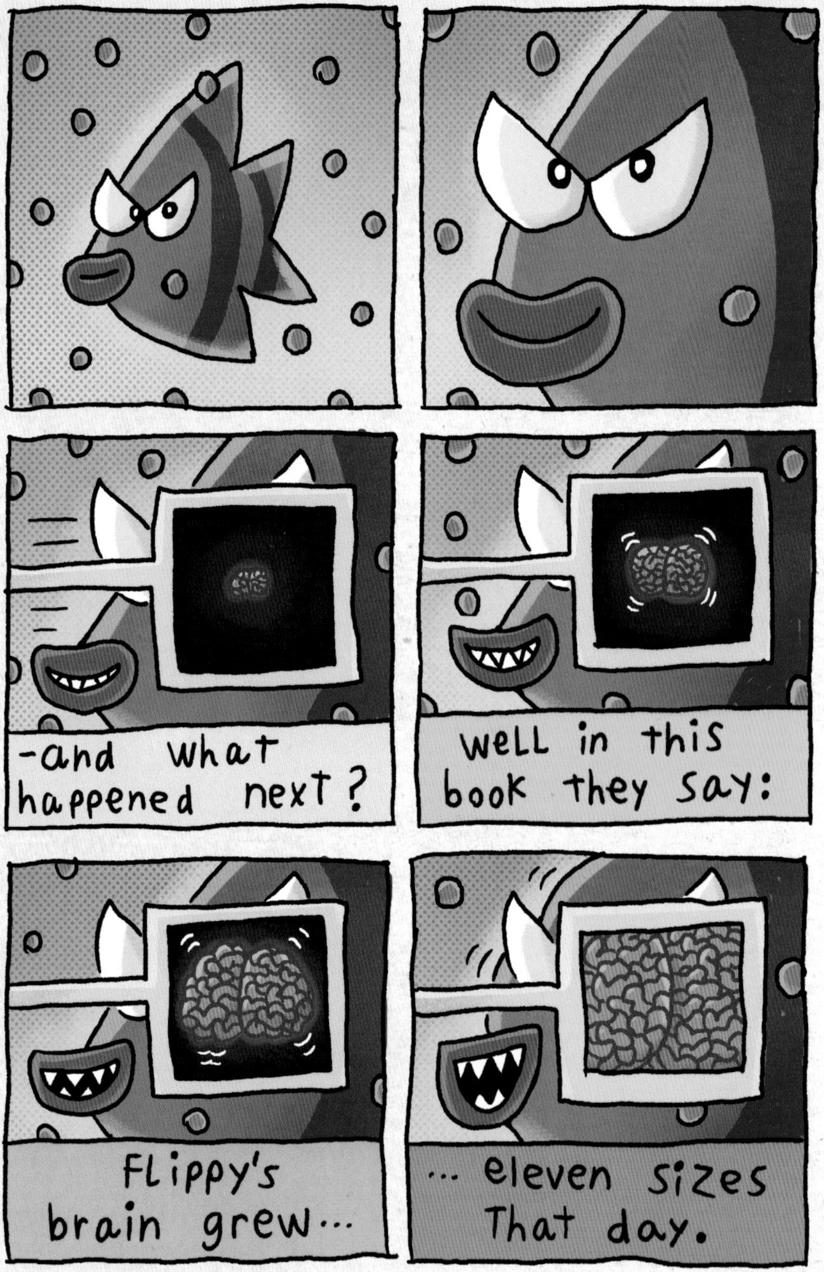
-and what happened next?
well in this book they say:
Flippy's brain grew...
... eleven sizes That day.

Chapter 4
The Big
ROBBERY

By George and Harold

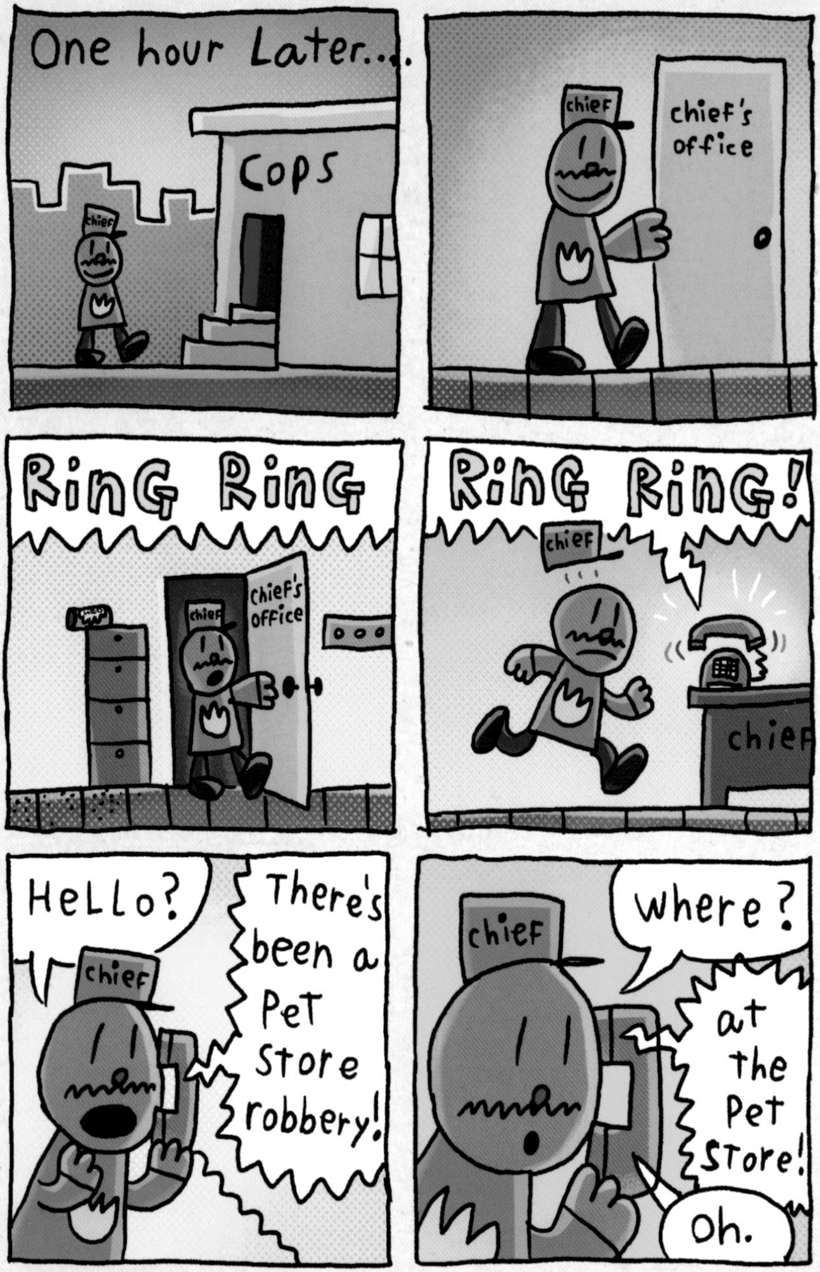

One hour Later....
Cops
chief
chief
chief's office
RinG RinG
chief
chief's office
RinG RinG!
chief
chief
Hello?
chief
There's been a Pet Store robbery!
chief
Where?
at the Pet Store!
Oh.

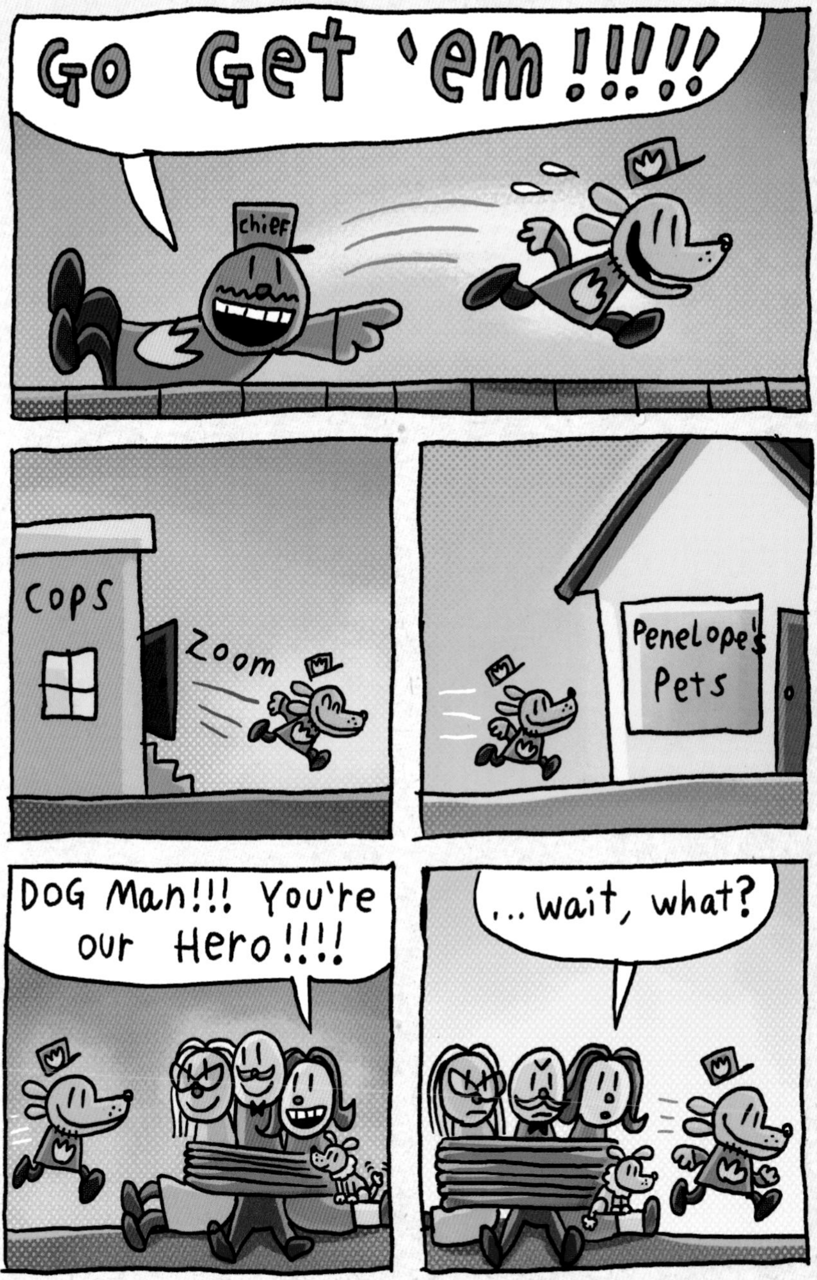
GO GET 'EM!!!!!
chief
COPS
Zoom
Penelope's
Pets
DOG Man!!! You're our Hero!!!!
...wait, what?

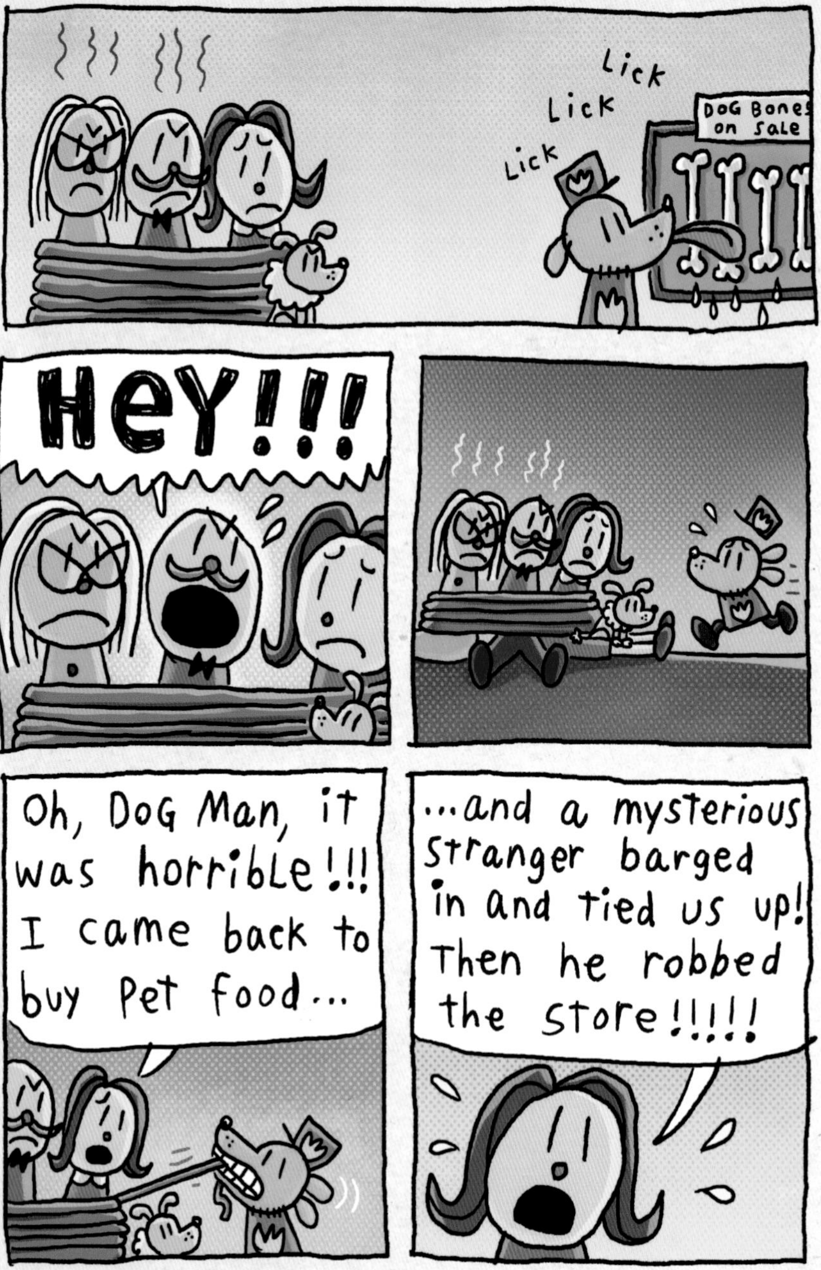
Lick
Lick
Lick
DOG Bones on Sale
HEY!!!
Oh, Dog Man, it was horrible!!! I came back to buy pet food...
...and a mysterious stranger barged in and tied us up! Then he robbed the store!!!!!

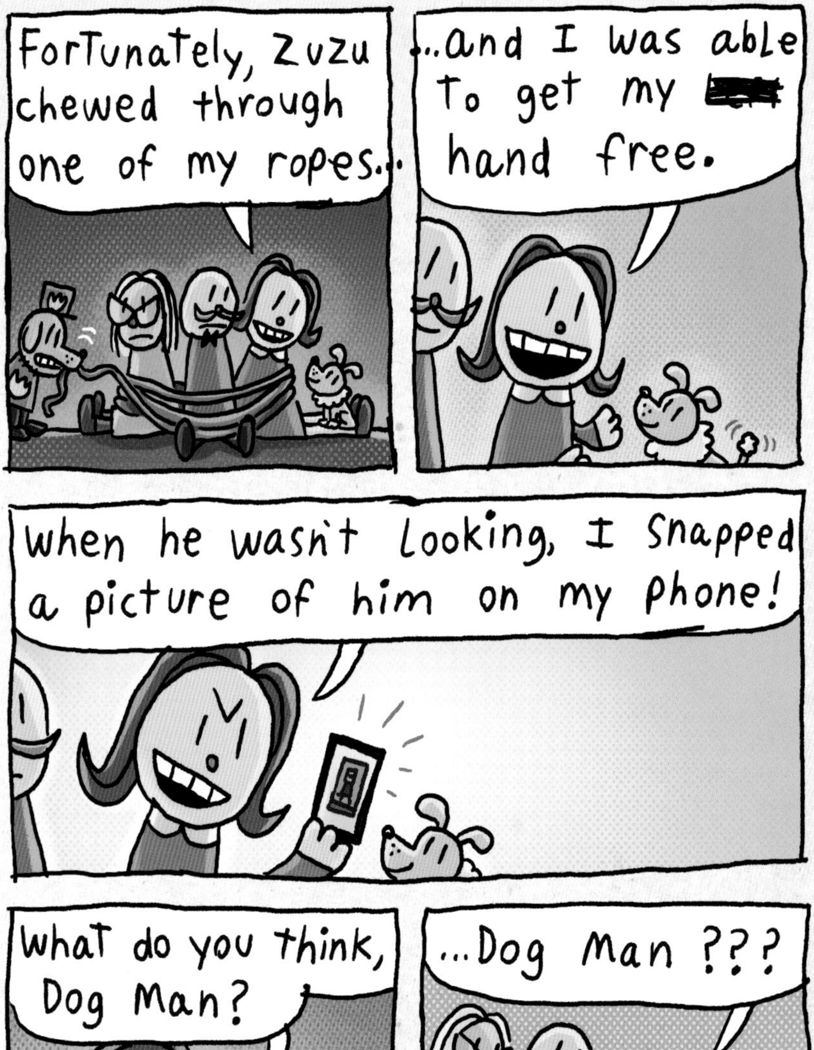

Fortunately, Zuzu chewed through one of my ropes...
...and I was able to get my [redacted] hand free.
When he wasn't looking, I snapped a picture of him on my phone!
What do you think, Dog Man?
...Dog Man???

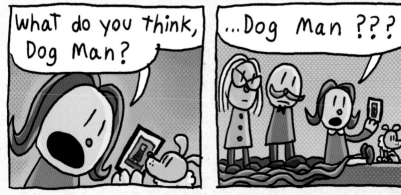

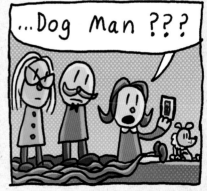

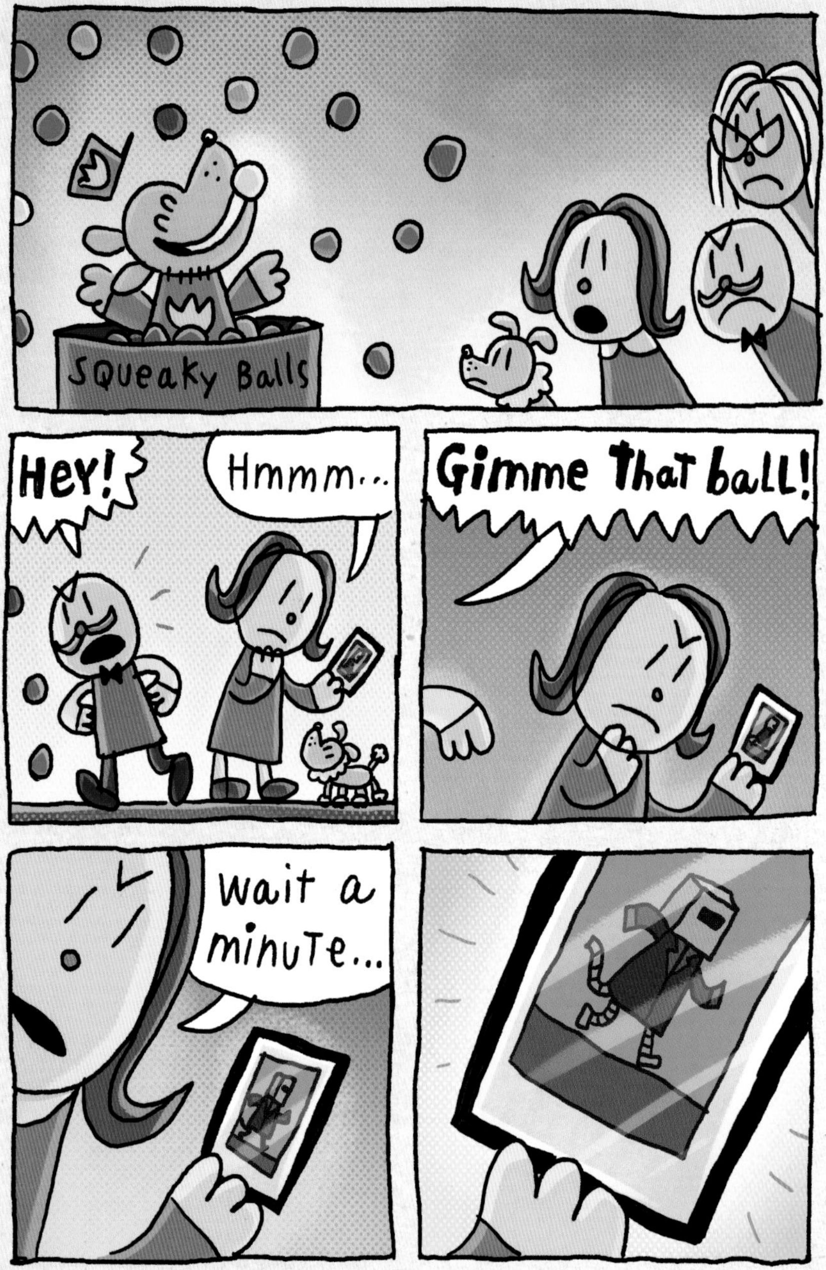
SQUEAKY BALLS
HEY!
Hmmm...
Gimme That ball!
wait a minute...

ChapTer 5
PeTey'S BiG EScapE

CaT JaiL

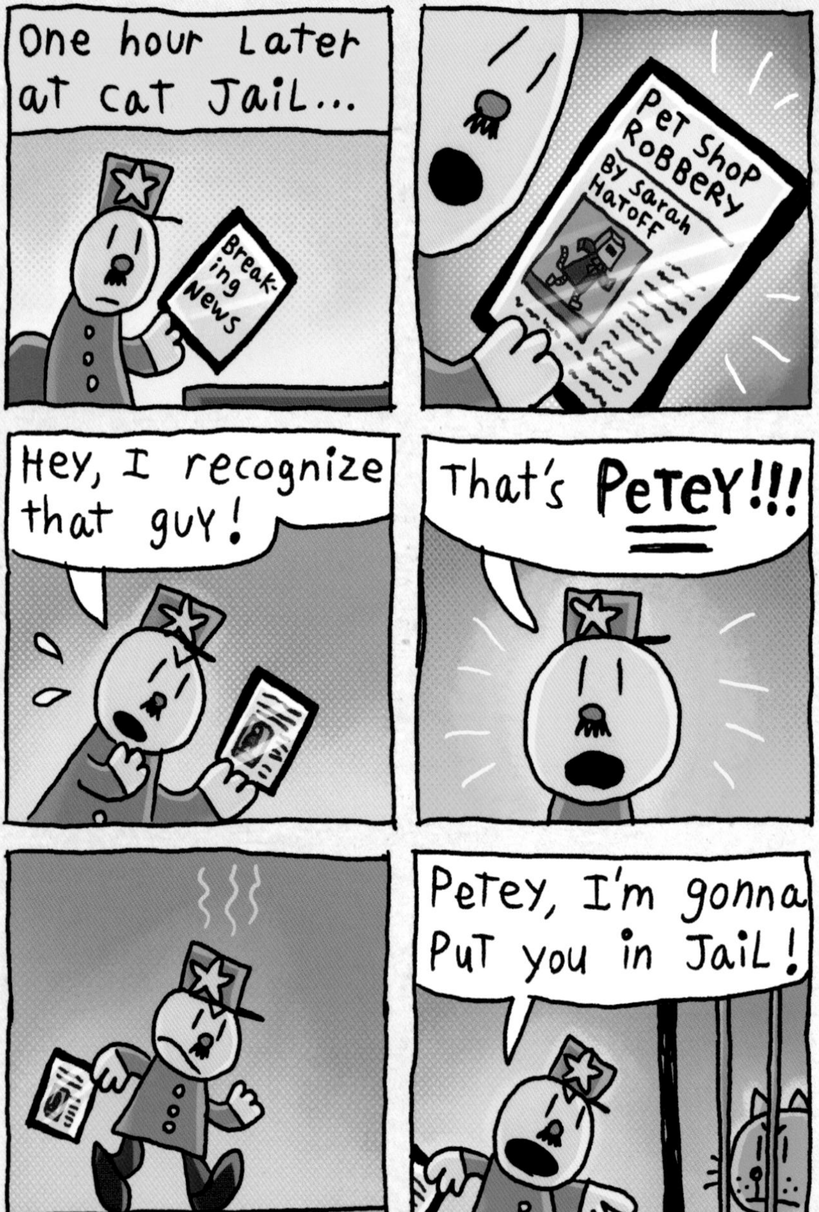
One hour Later at cat JaiL...
Break-ing News
PeT ShoP RoBBeRY
By Sarah HaToFF
Hey, I recognize that guy!
That's PeTeY!!!
PeTey, I'm gonna PuT you in JaiL!

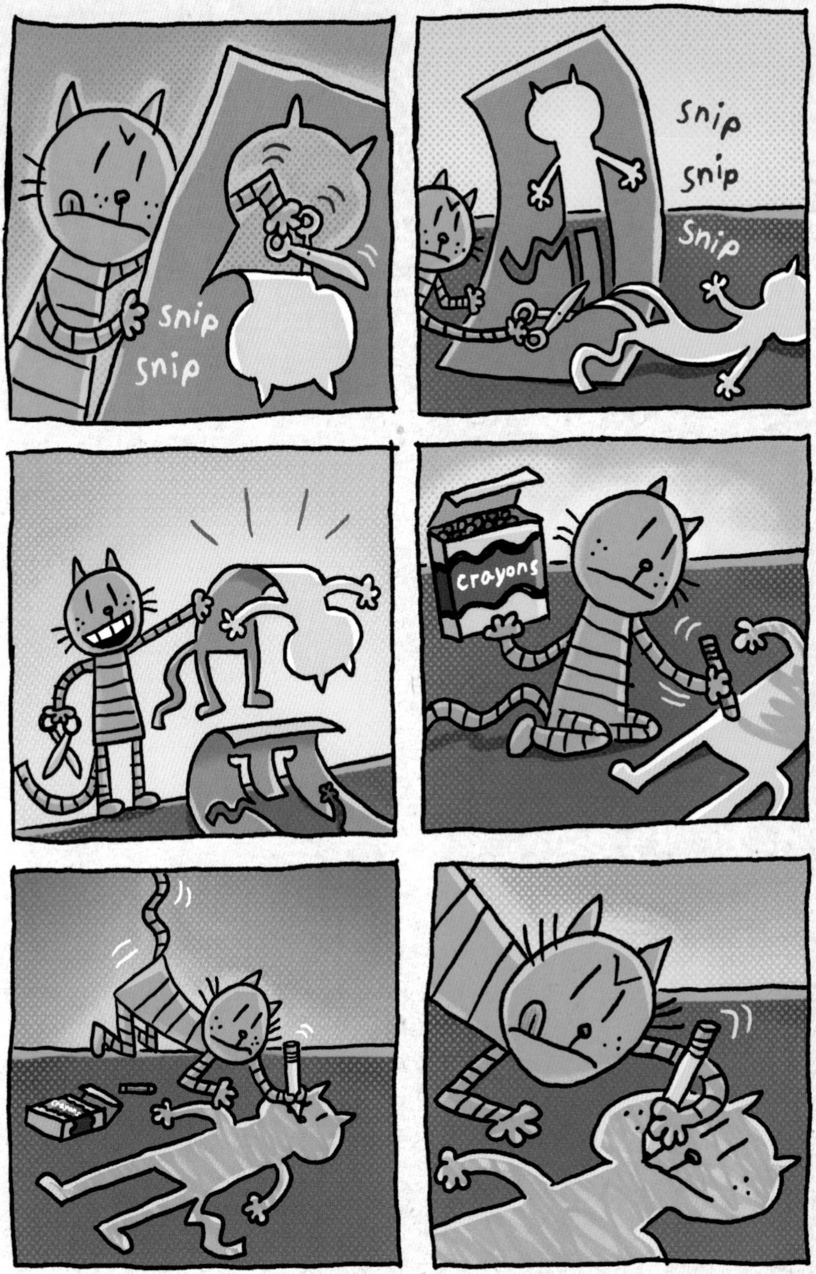
snip
snip
snip
snip
snip
crayons
crayons

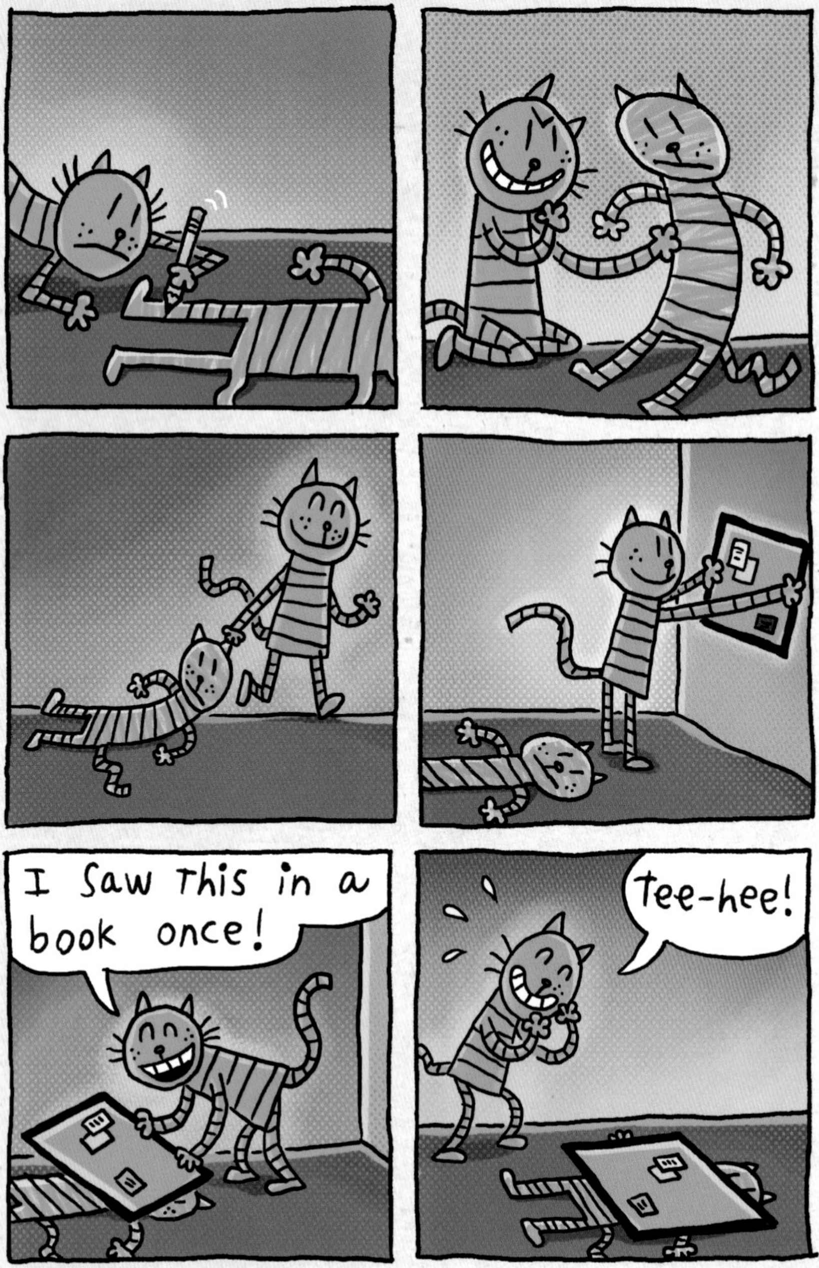
I saw this in a book once!
tee-hee!

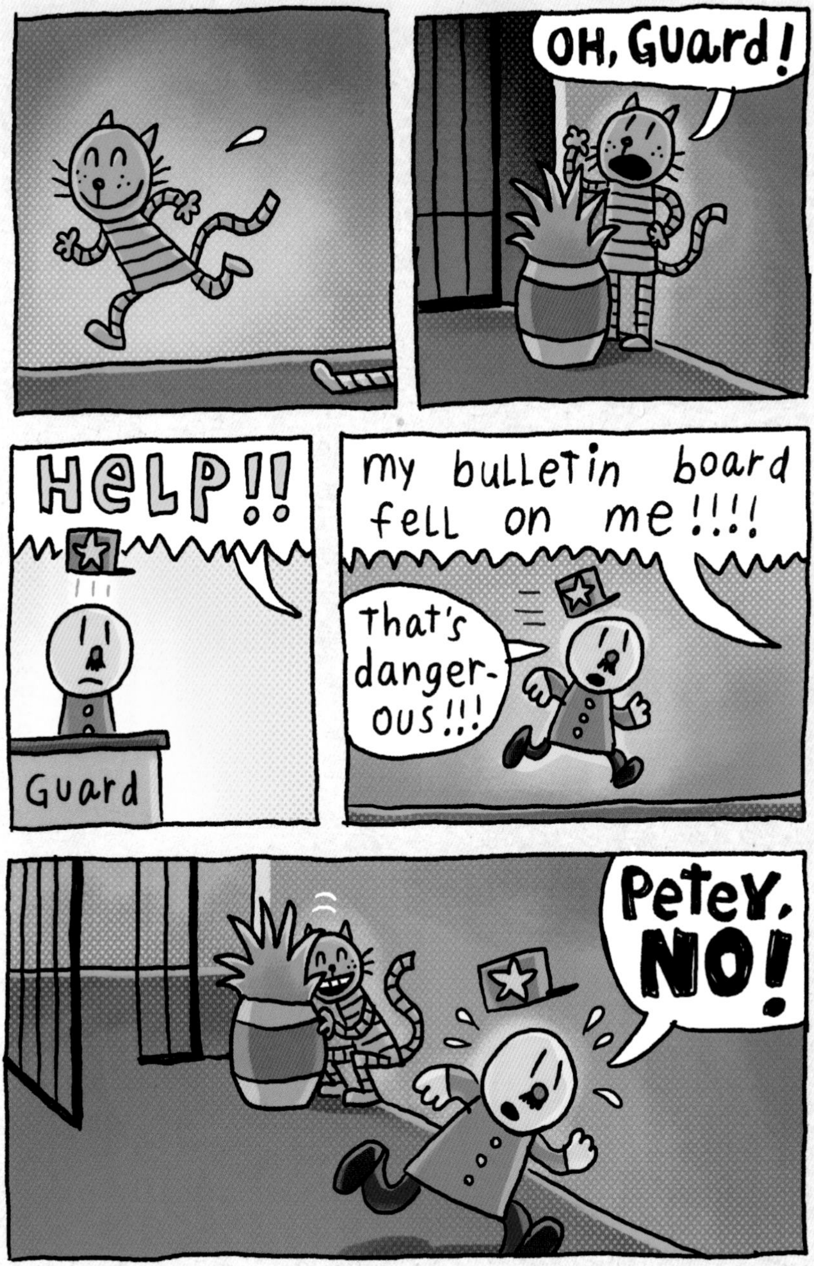
OH, GUARD!
HELP!!
GUARD
My bulletin board fell on me!!!!
That's danger-ous!!!
PETEY, NO!

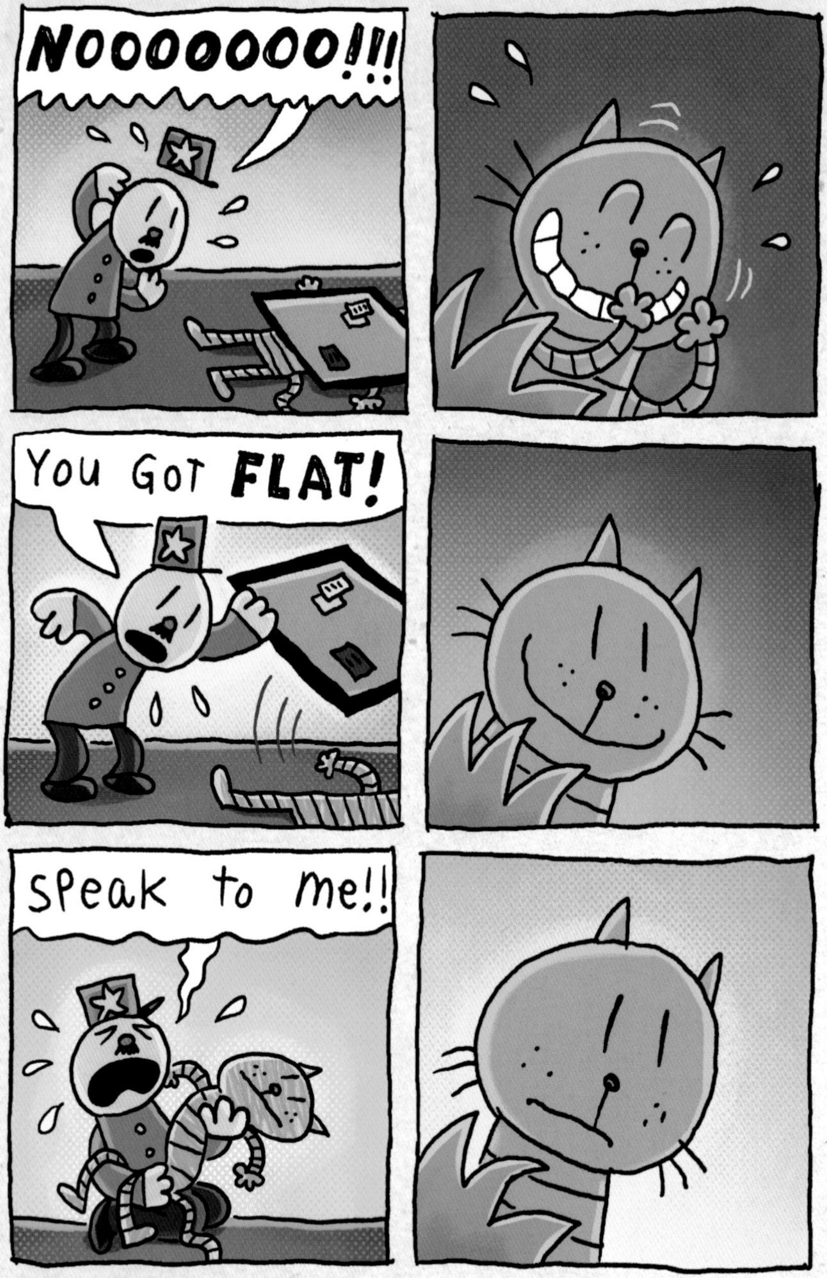
NOOOOOOO!!!
You Got FLAT!
Speak to me!!

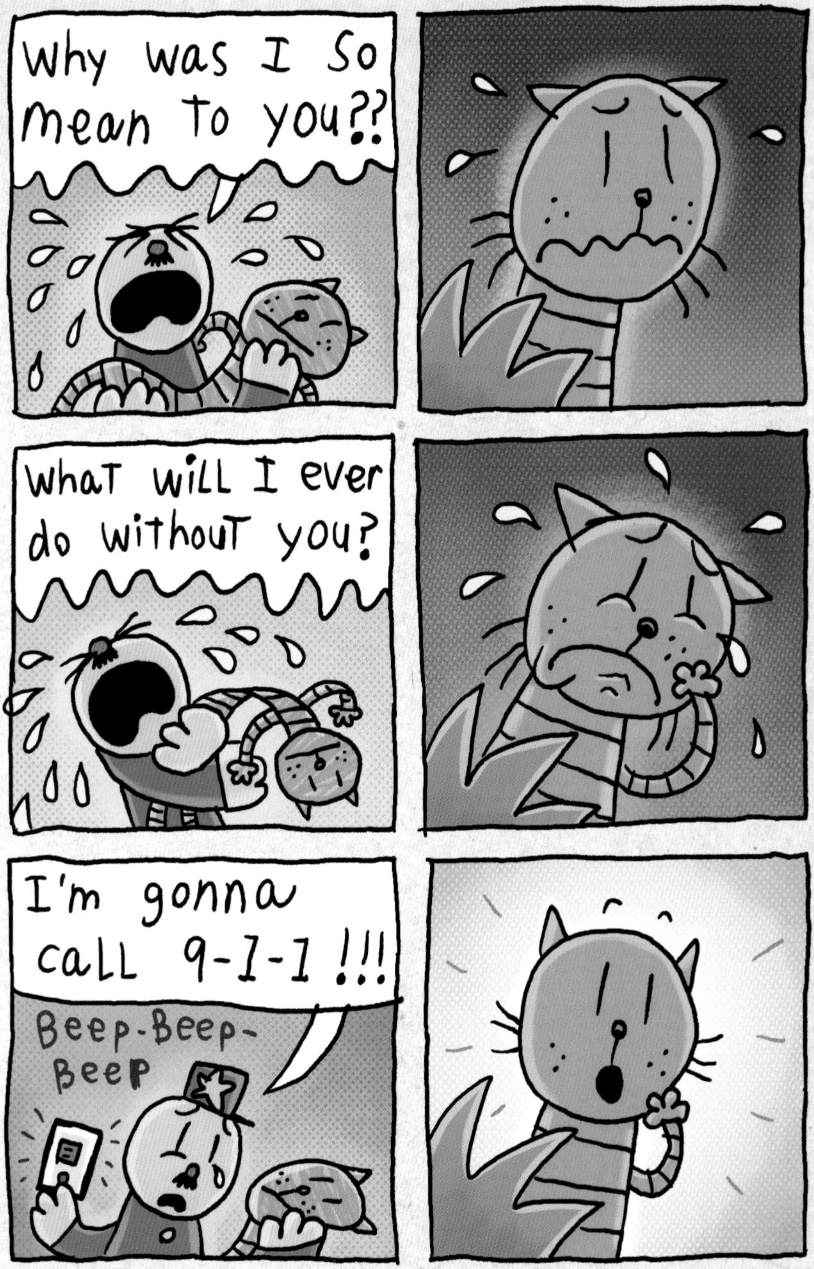
Why was I so mean to you??
What will I ever do without you?
I'm gonna call 9-1-1!!!
Beep-Beep-Beep

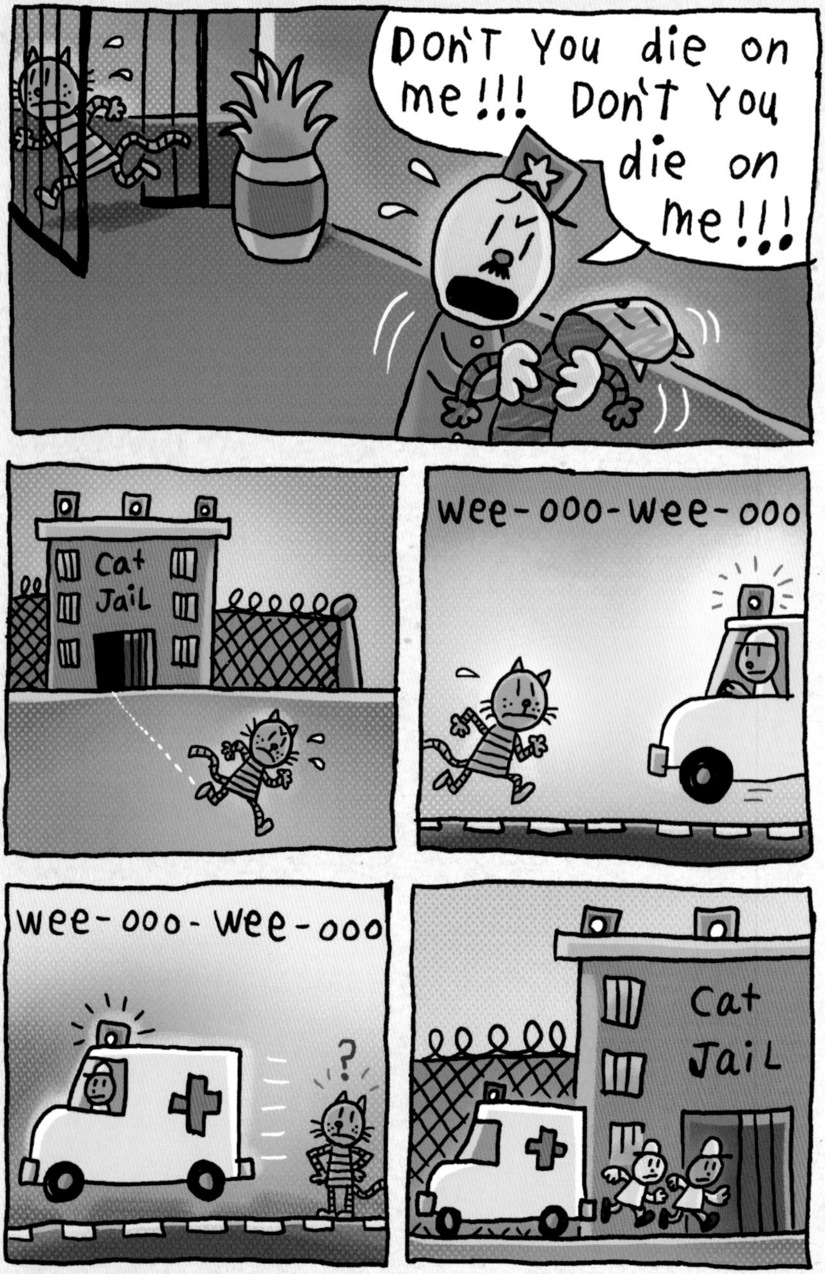
DON'T YOU die on me!!! DON'T YOU die on me!!!
Cat Jail
wee-ooo-wee-ooo
wee-ooo-wee-ooo
?
Cat Jail

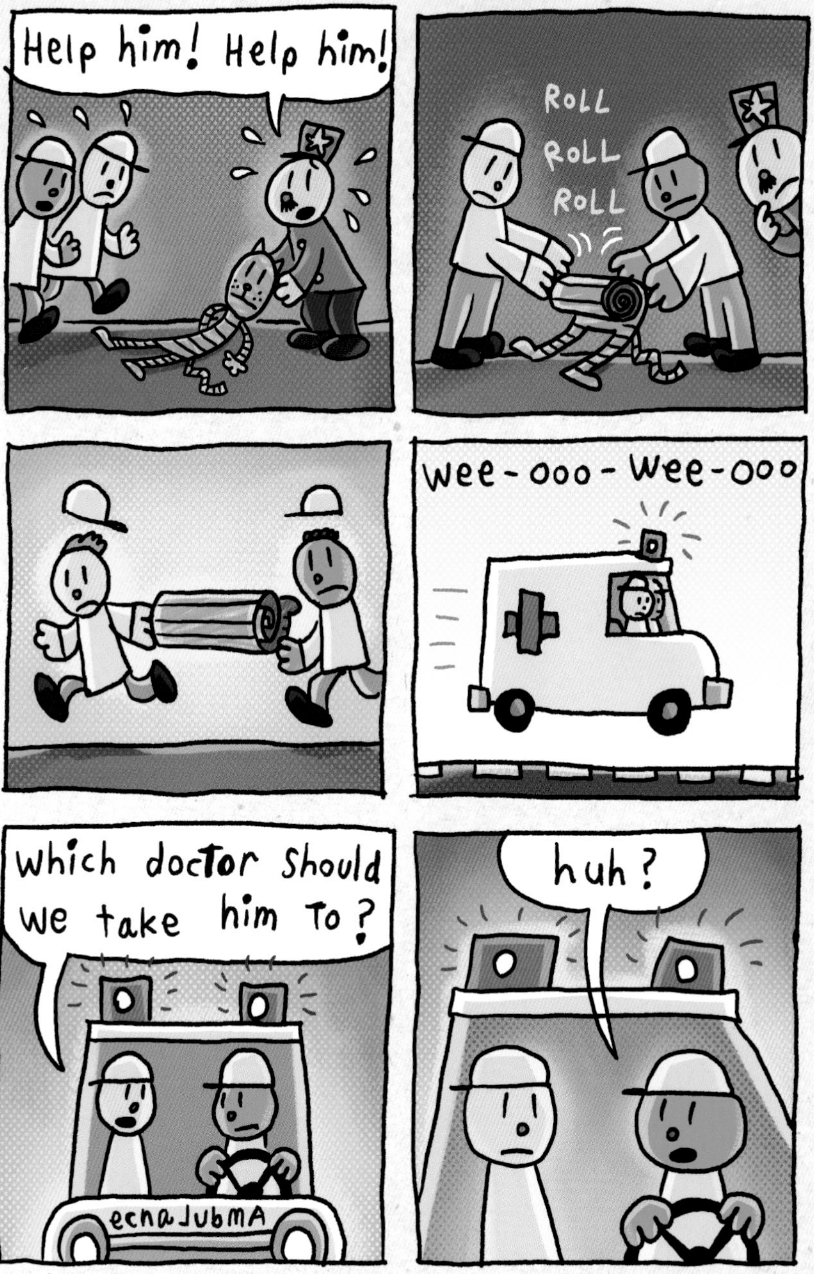

Help him! Help him!
ROLL
ROLL
ROLL
wee-ooo-wee-ooo
Which doctor should we take him to?
ecnaLubmA
huh?

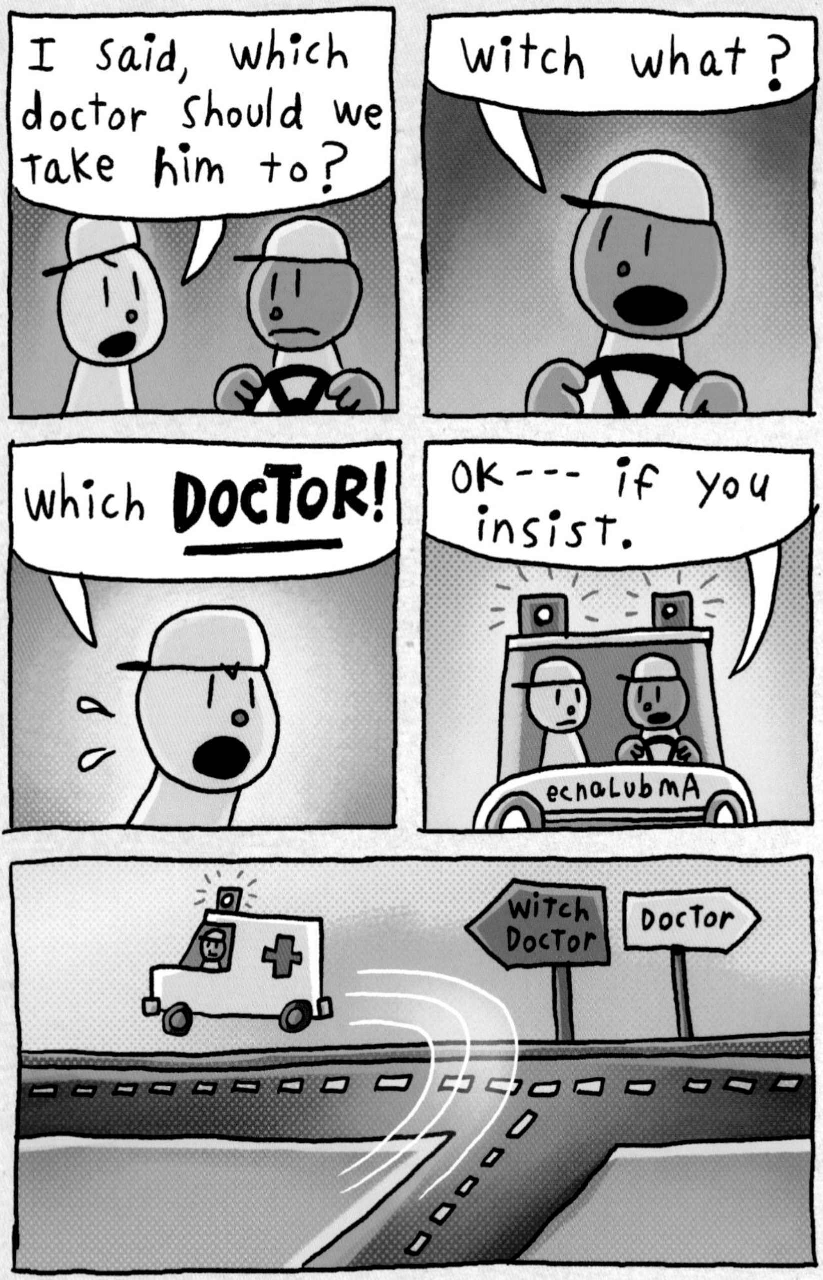

I said, which doctor should we take him to?
Witch what?
Which DOCTOR!
OK --- if you insist.
echaLubmA
Witch Doctor
Doctor

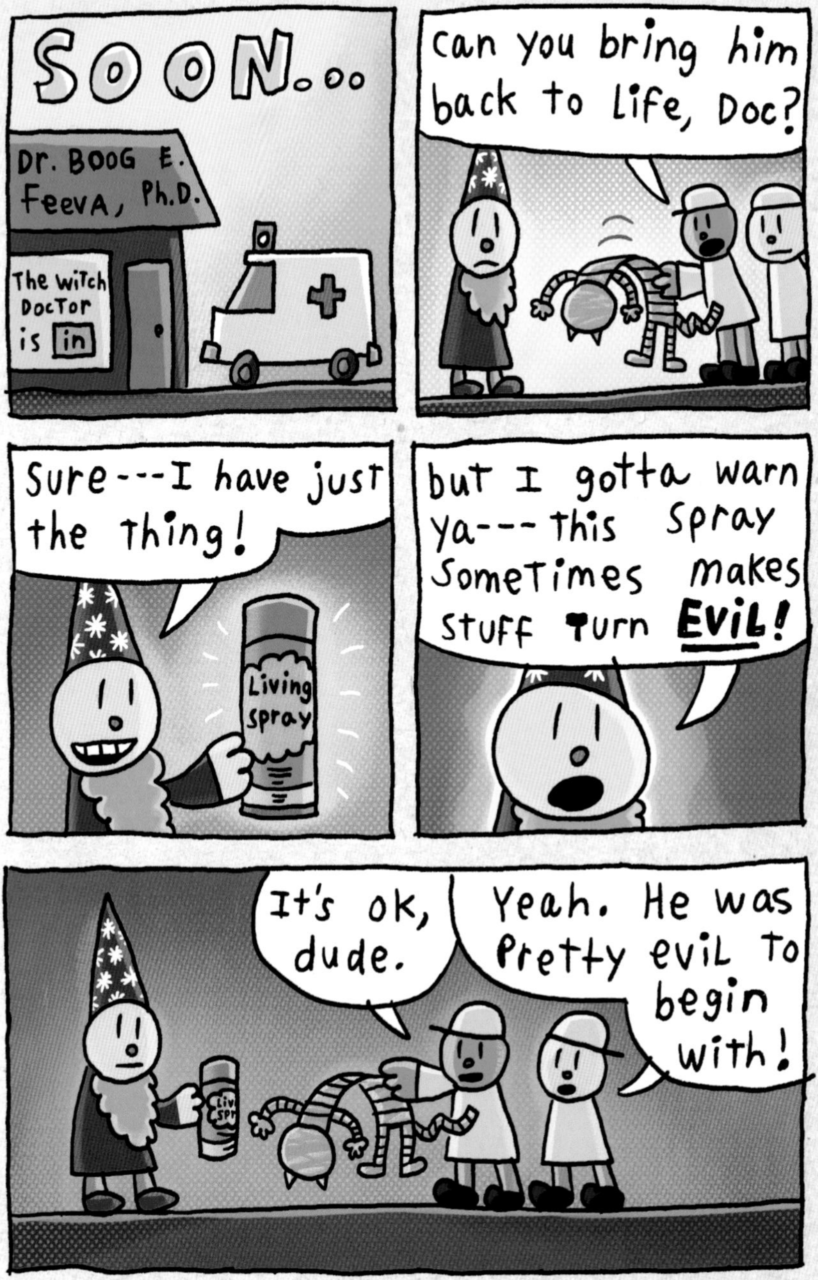
SOON...
DR. BOOG E. FeevA, Ph.D.
The WiTch DocTor is in
can you bring him back to Life, Doc?
Sure---I have just the Thing!
Living Spray
but I gotta warn ya--- this Spray SomeTimes makes STUFF Turn EVIL!
It's ok, dude.
Yeah. He was Pretty eviL To begin with!

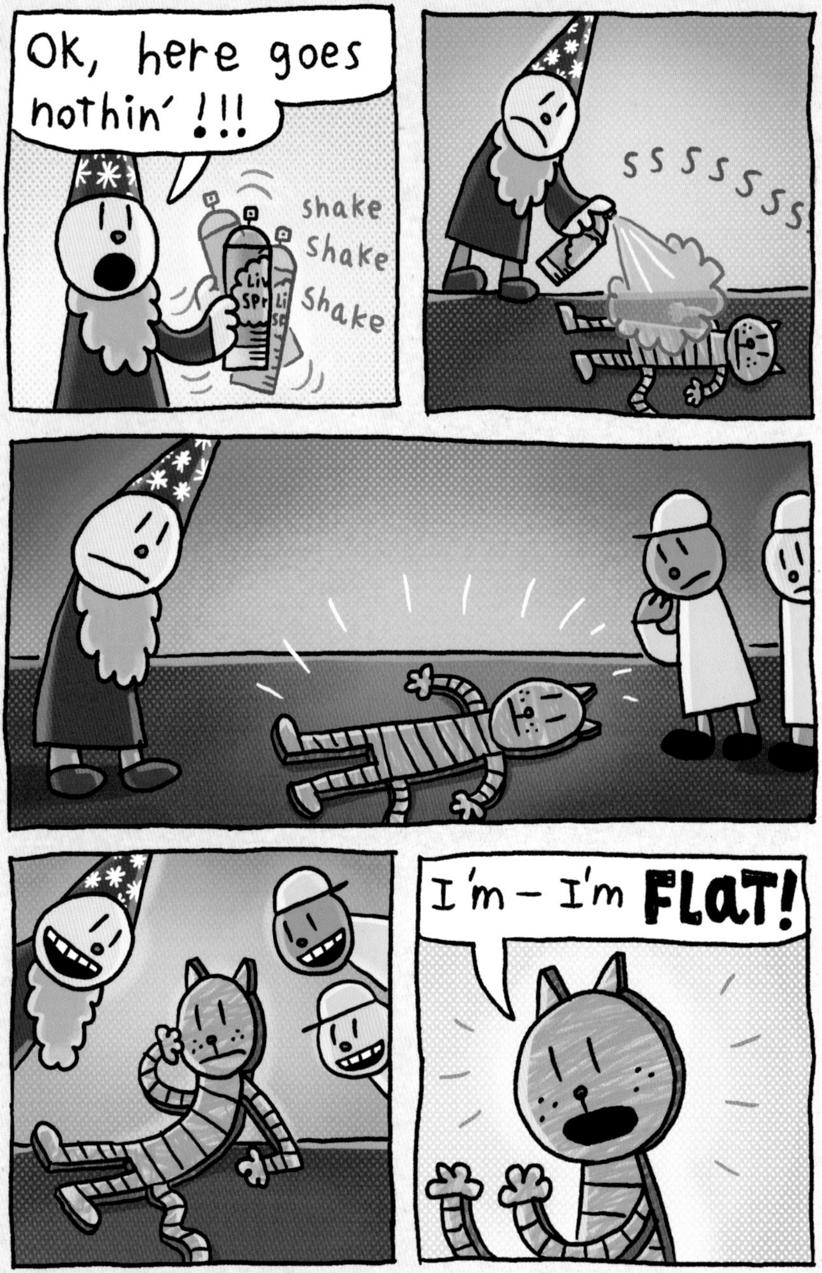
Ok, here goes nothin' !!!
shake
Shake
Shake
SSSSSSSS
I'm – I'm FLAT!

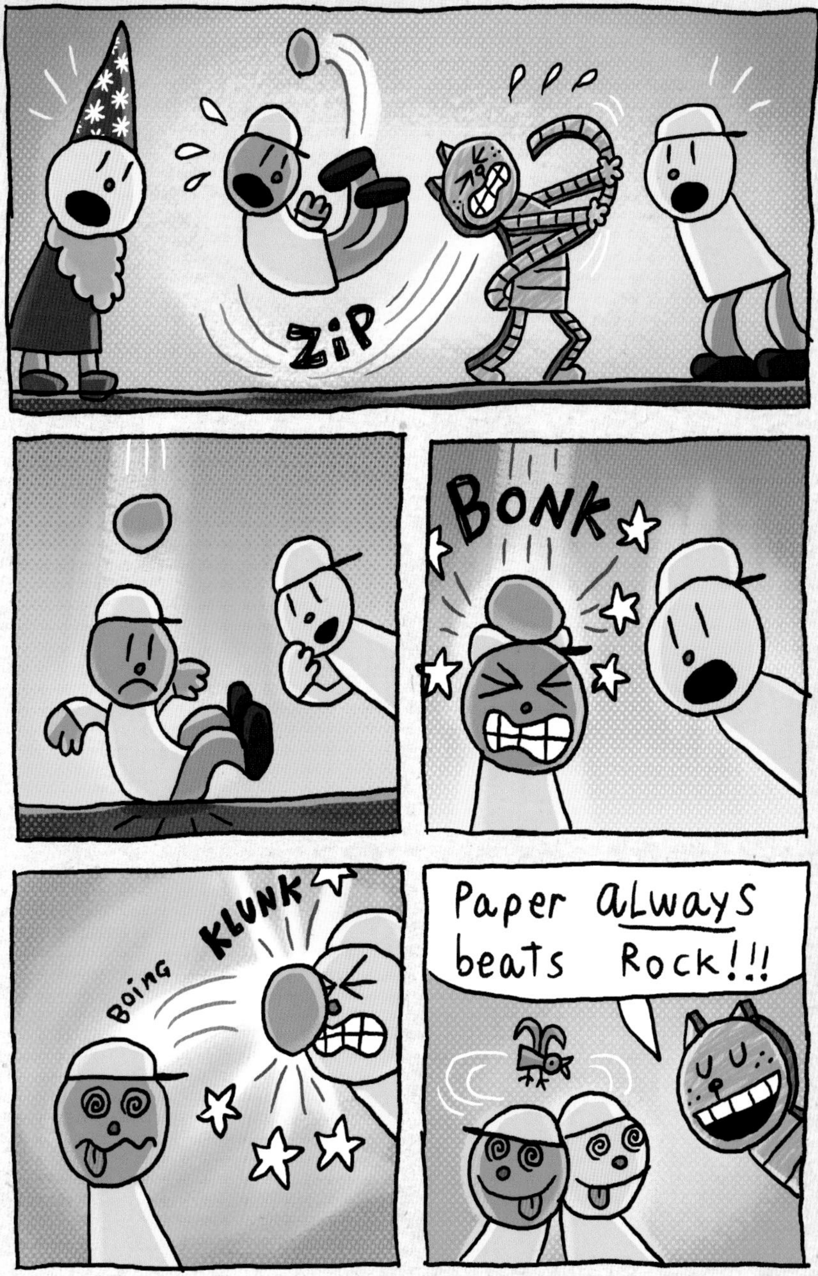
ZiP
BONK
BOING
KLUNK
Paper aLways beats Rock!!!

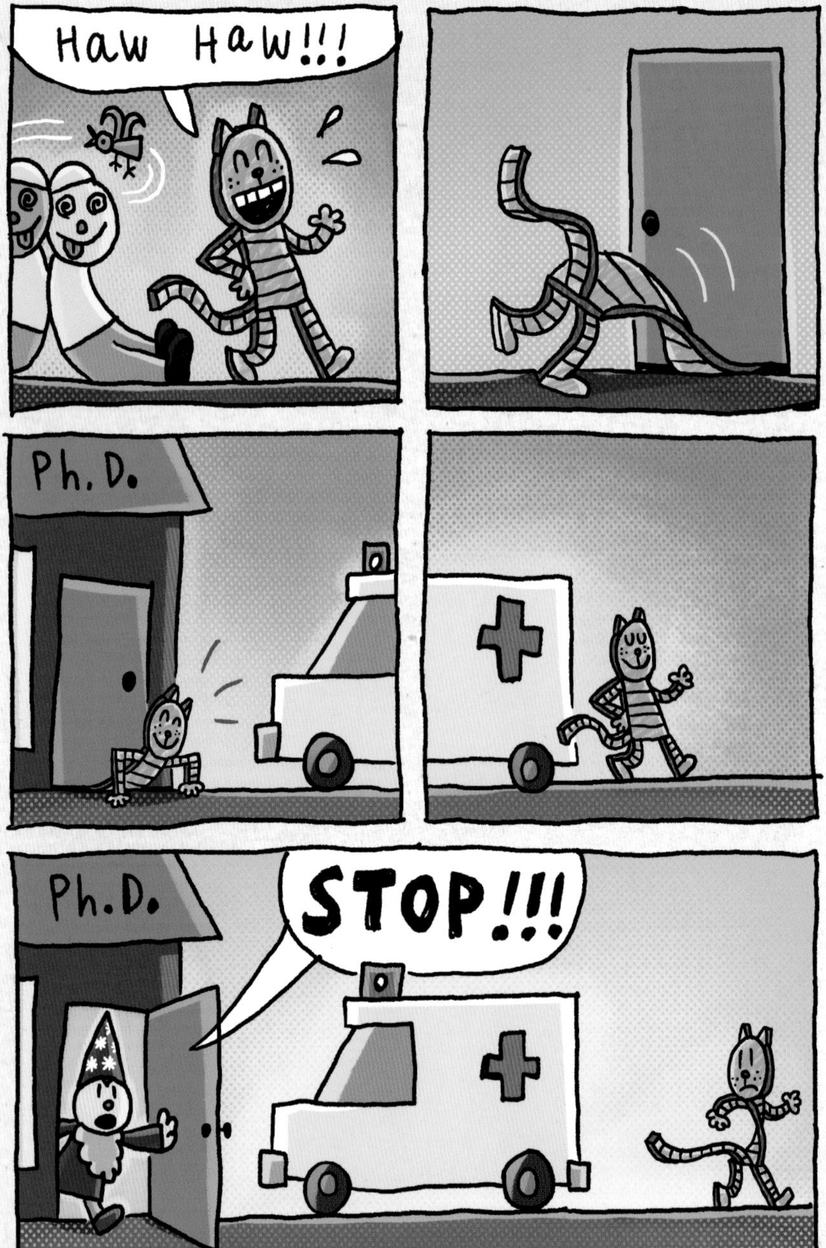
HAW HAW!!!
Ph.D.
Ph.D.
STOP!!!

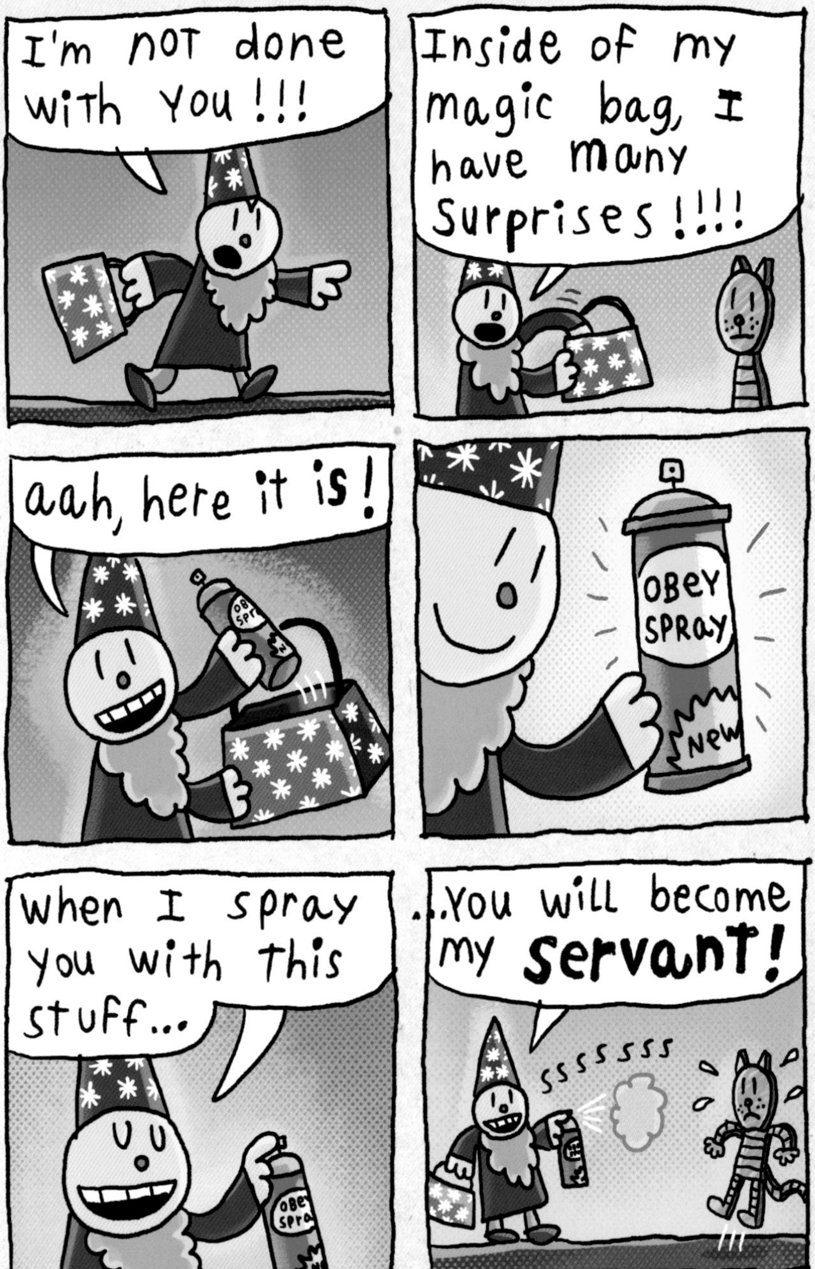
I'm NOT done with YOU!!!
Inside of my magic bag, I have many Surprises!!!!
aah, here it is!
OBEY SPRAY
NEW
when I spray you with this stuff...
...YOU will become my servant!
SSSSSSS

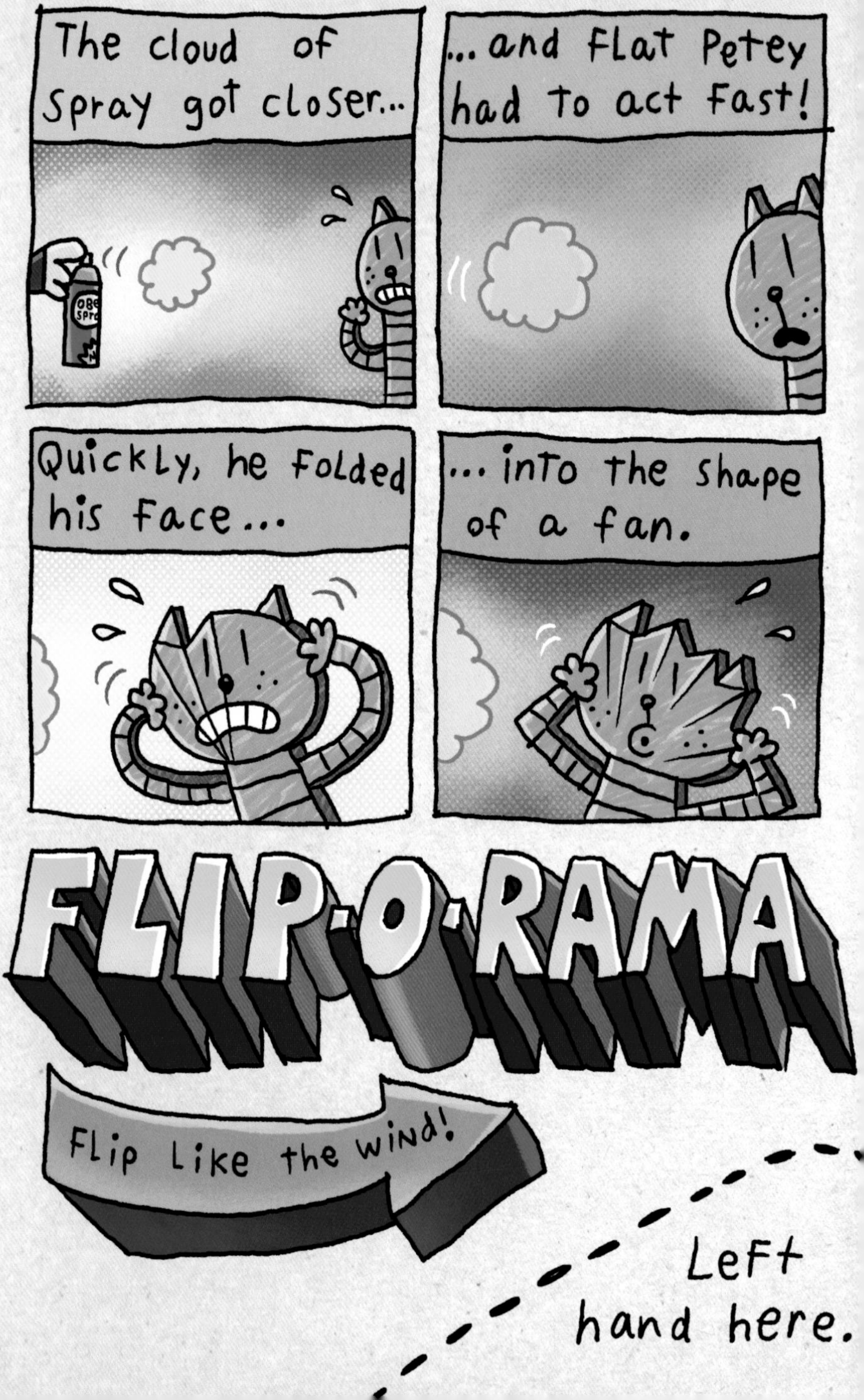
The cloud of spray got closer...
OBE SPRA
...and Flat Petey had to act fast!
Quickly, he folded his face...
...into the shape of a fan.
FLIP-O-RAMA
Flip like the wind!
Left hand here.

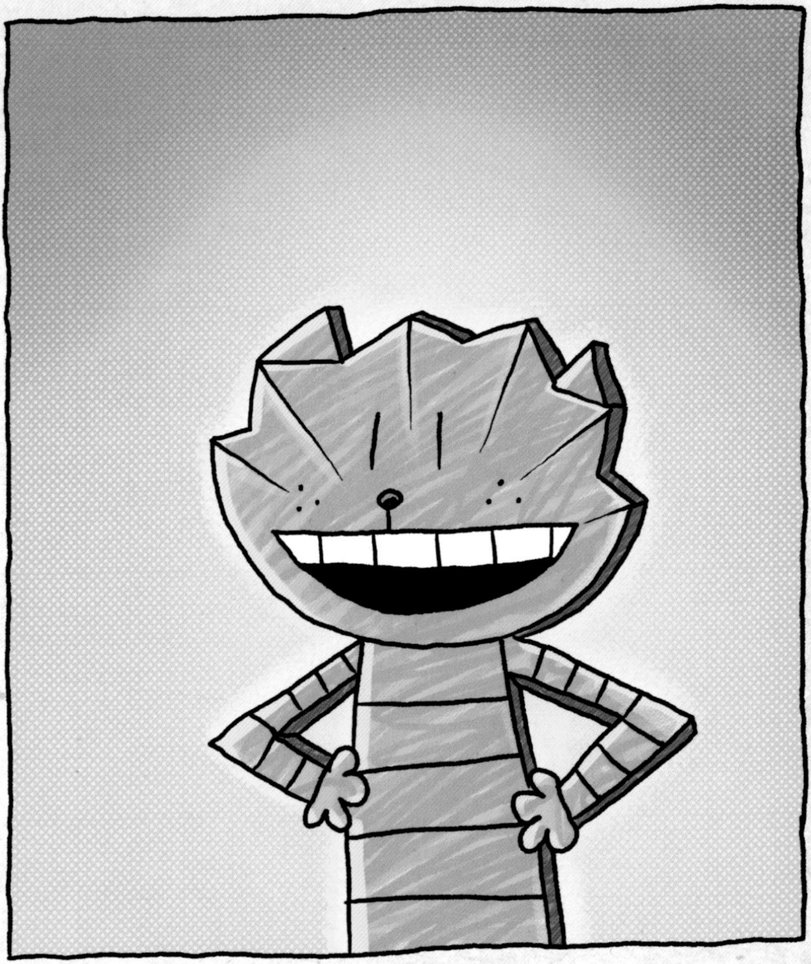

A Fan
with a Plan!

Right
Thumb
here.

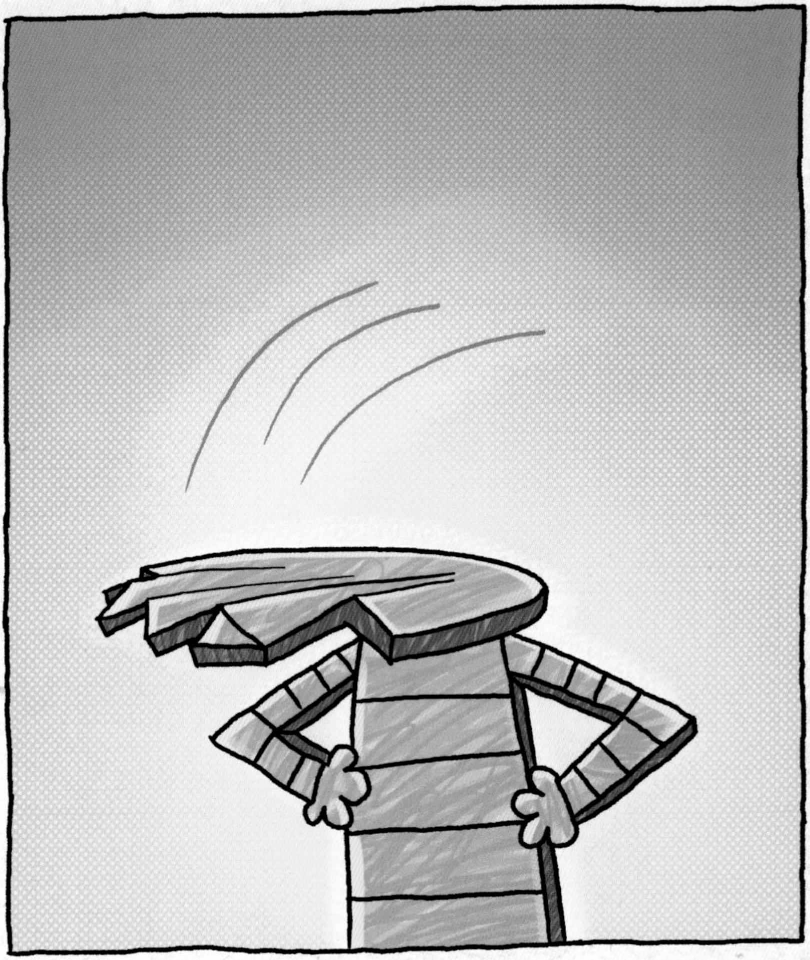

A Fan
With a Plan!

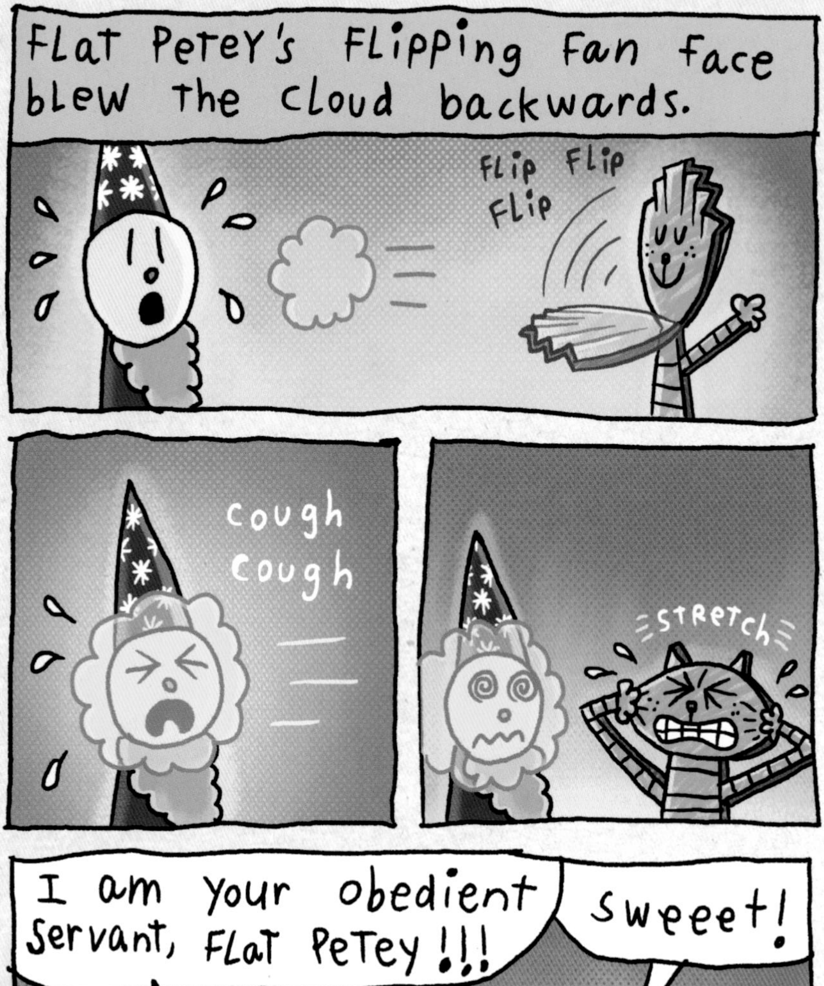
Flat Petey's Flipping Fan face blew the cloud backwards.
Flip Flip Flip
cough cough
STRETCH
I am your obedient servant, Flat Petey!!!
Sweeet!

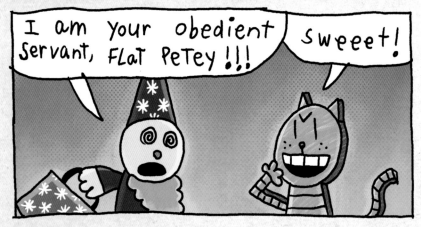

Chapter 6

A Buncha STUFF That Happened Next

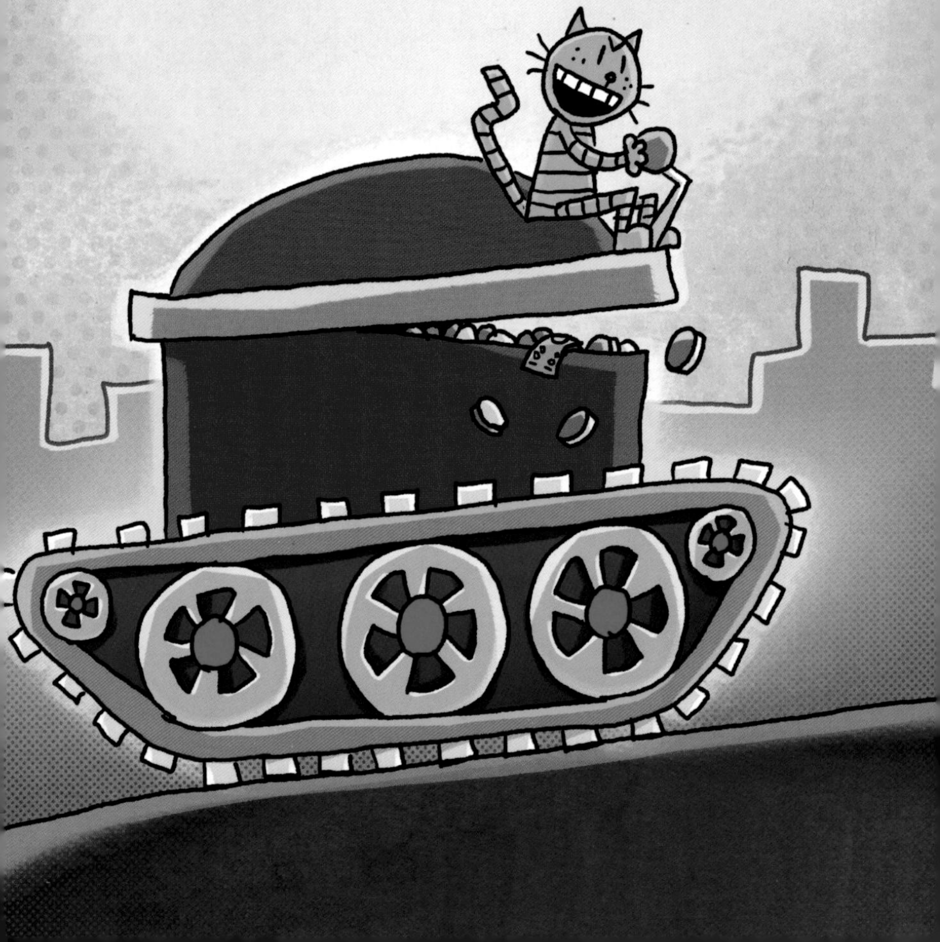

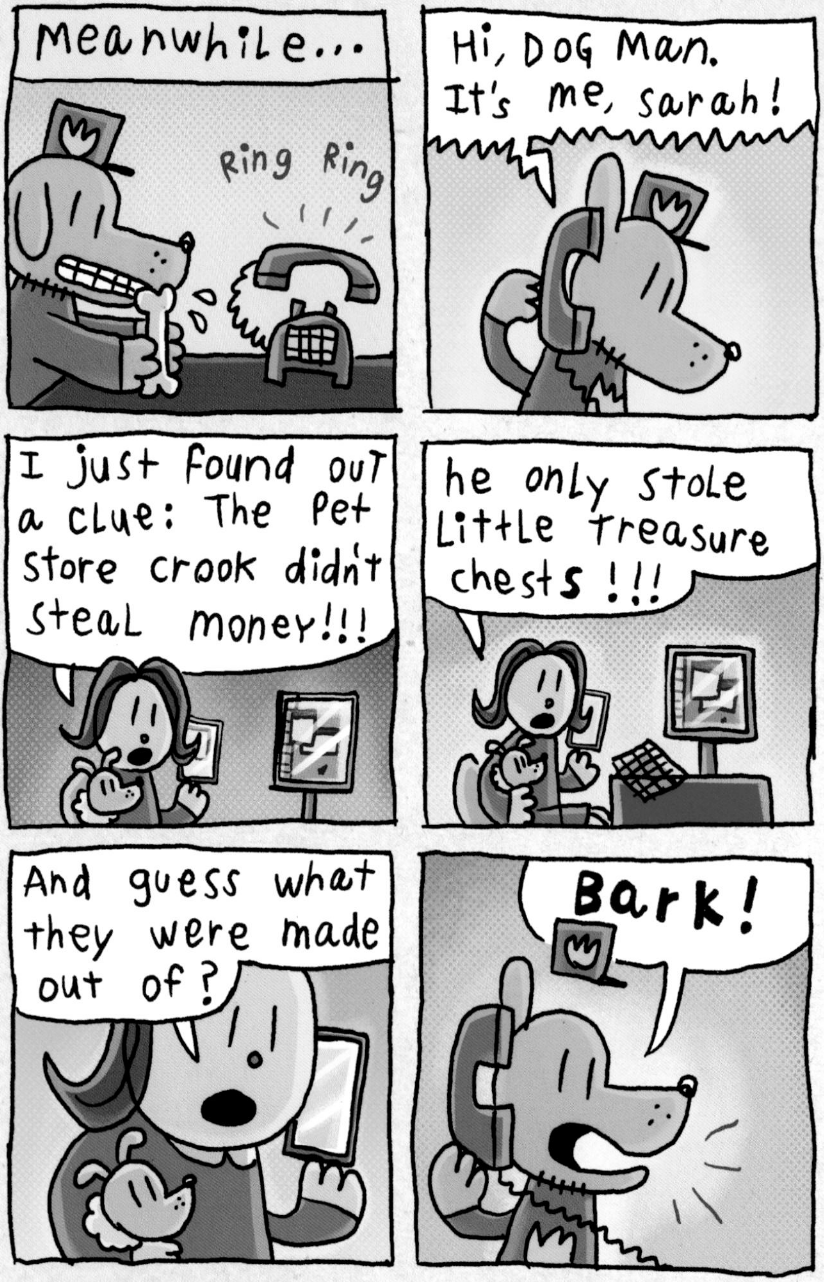
Meanwhile...
Ring Ring
Hi, DOG Man. It's me, sarah!
I just found out a clue: The pet store crook didn't steal money!!!
he only stole little treasure chests!!!
And guess what they were made out of?
Bark!

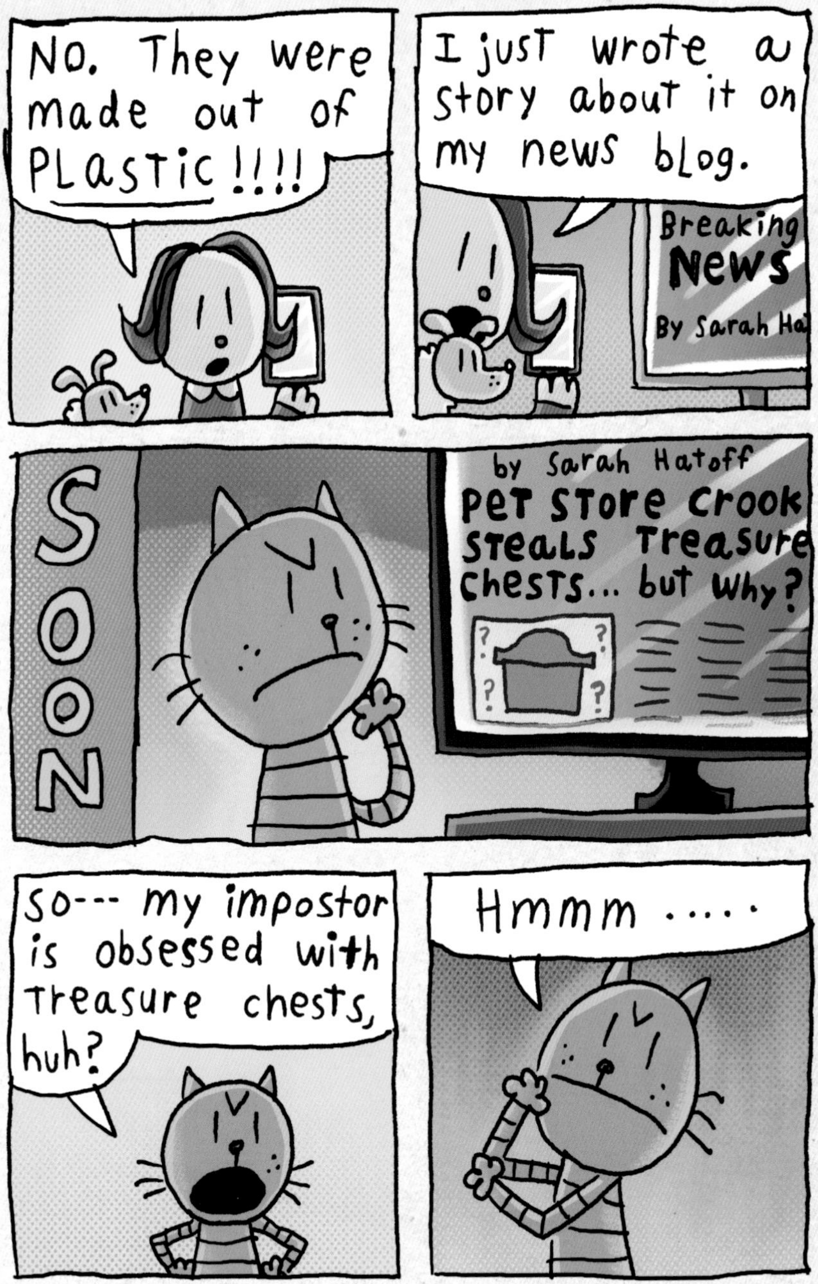

No. They were made out of PLASTIC!!!!
I just wrote a story about it on my news blog.
Breaking News
By Sarah Ha
SOON
by Sarah Hatoff
PET STORE CROOK STEALS TREASURE CHESTS... but Why?
So--- my impostor is obsessed with treasure chests, huh?
Hmmm.....

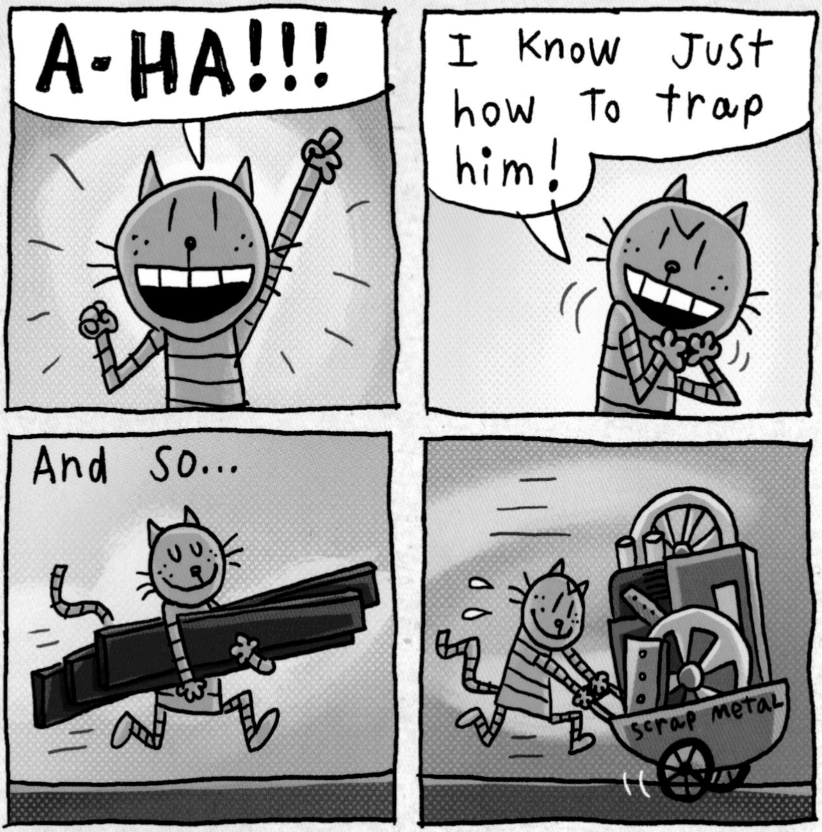
A-HA!!!
I Know Just how To trap him!
And so...
scrap metal

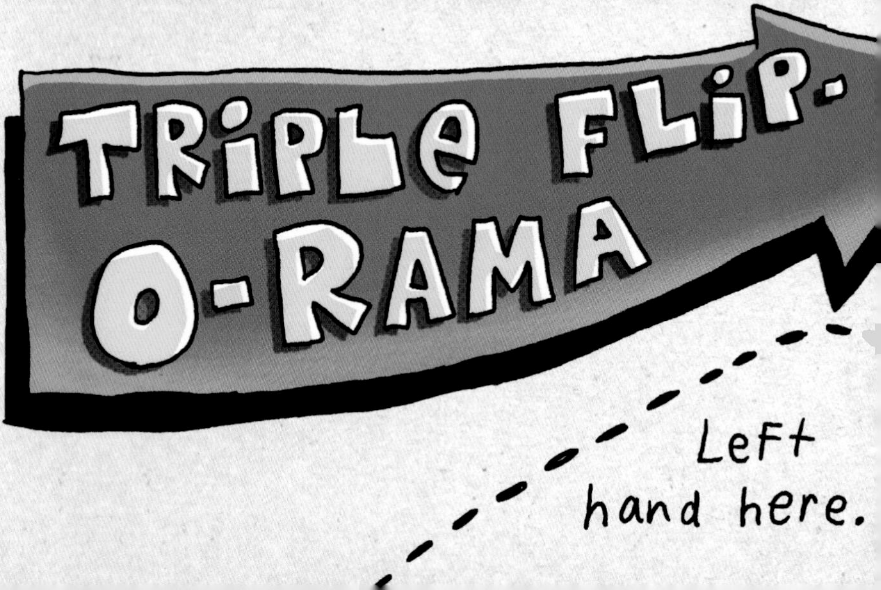
TRIPLE FLIP-O-RAMA
Left hand here.

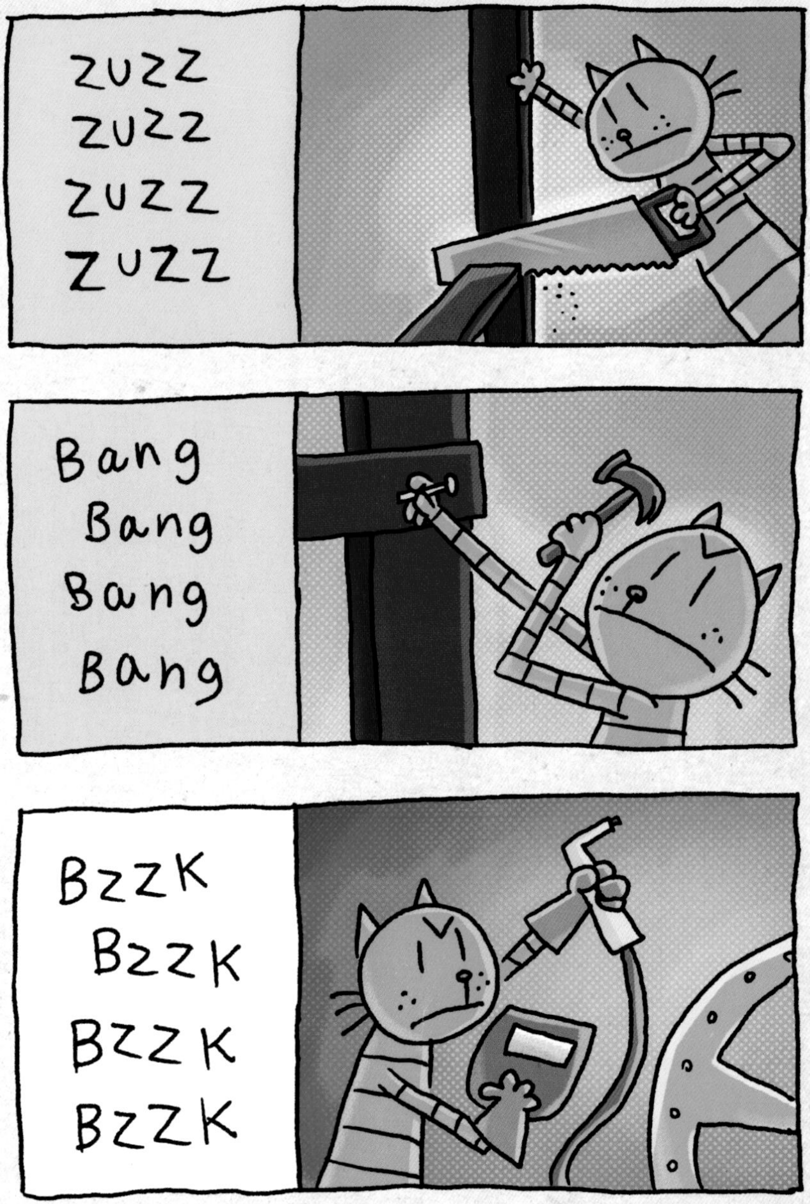
ZUZZ
ZUZZ
ZUZZ
ZUZZ
Bang
Bang
Bang
Bang
BZZK
BZZK
BZZK
BZZK

Right Thumb here.

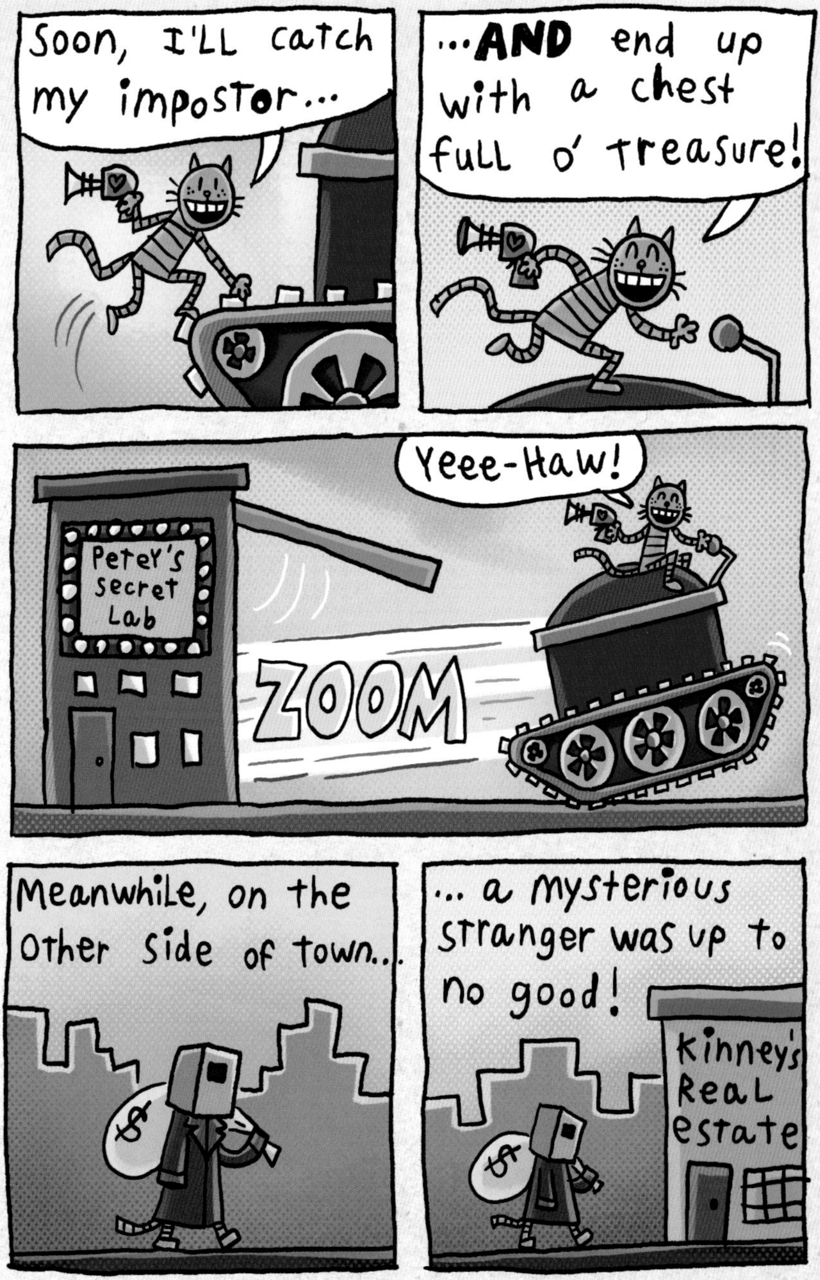
Soon, I'LL catch my impostor...
...AND end up with a chest full o' treasure!
Yeee-Haw!
Peter's Secret Lab
ZOOM
Meanwhile, on the other side of town...
... a mysterious stranger was up to no good!
Kinney's Real estate

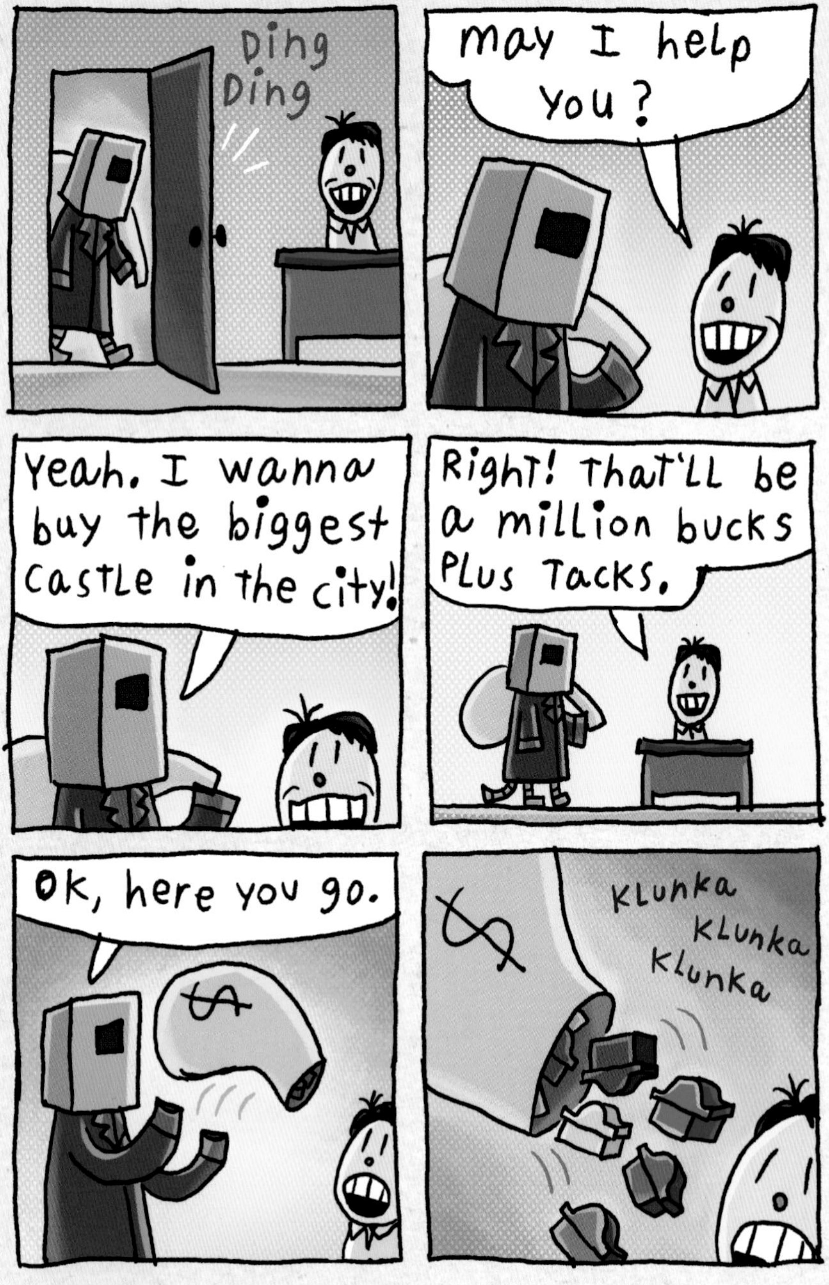

Ding
Ding
may I help you?
Yeah. I wanna buy the biggest castle in the city!
Right! That'll be a million bucks plus tacks.
Ok, here you go.
Klunka
Klunka
Klunka

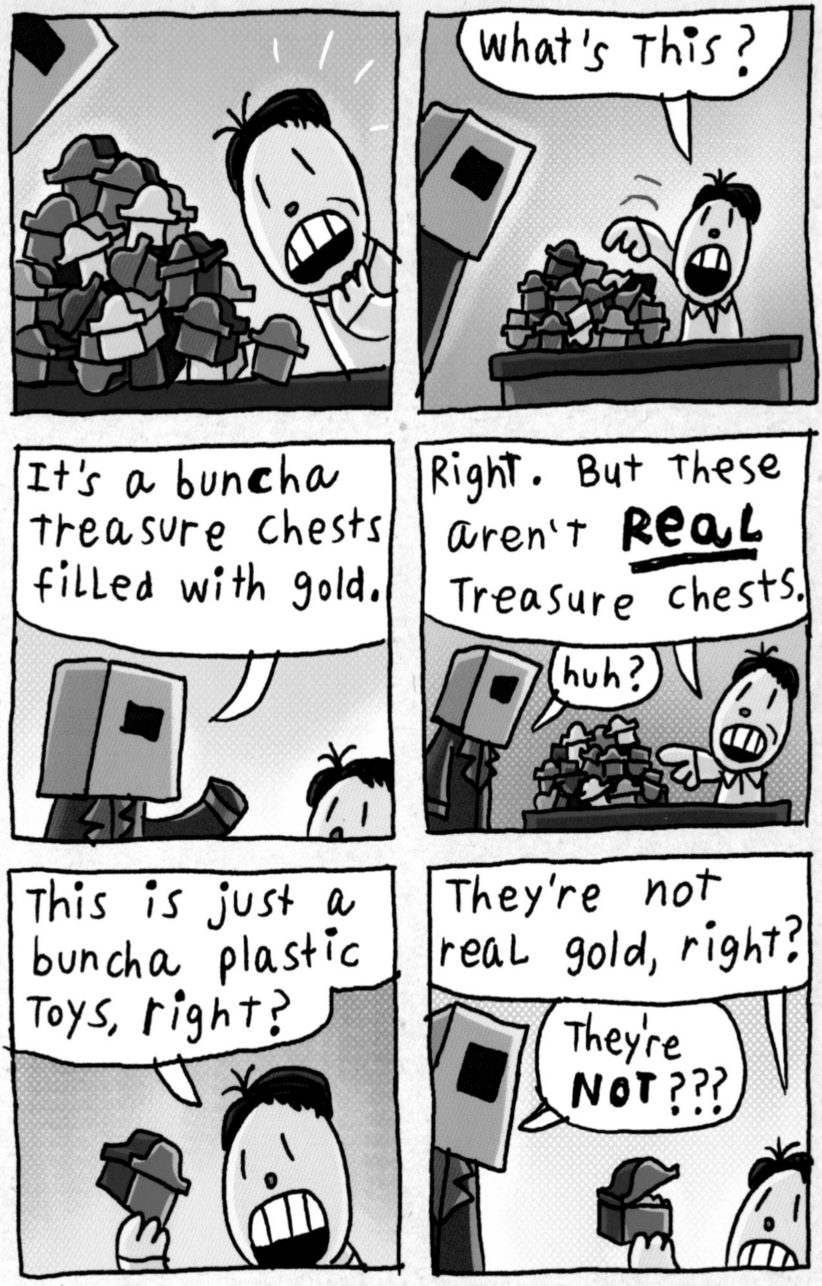
What's This?
It's a buncha treasure chests filled with gold.
Right. But these aren't REAL Treasure chests.
huh?
This is just a buncha plastic Toys, right?
They're not real gold, right?
They're NOT???

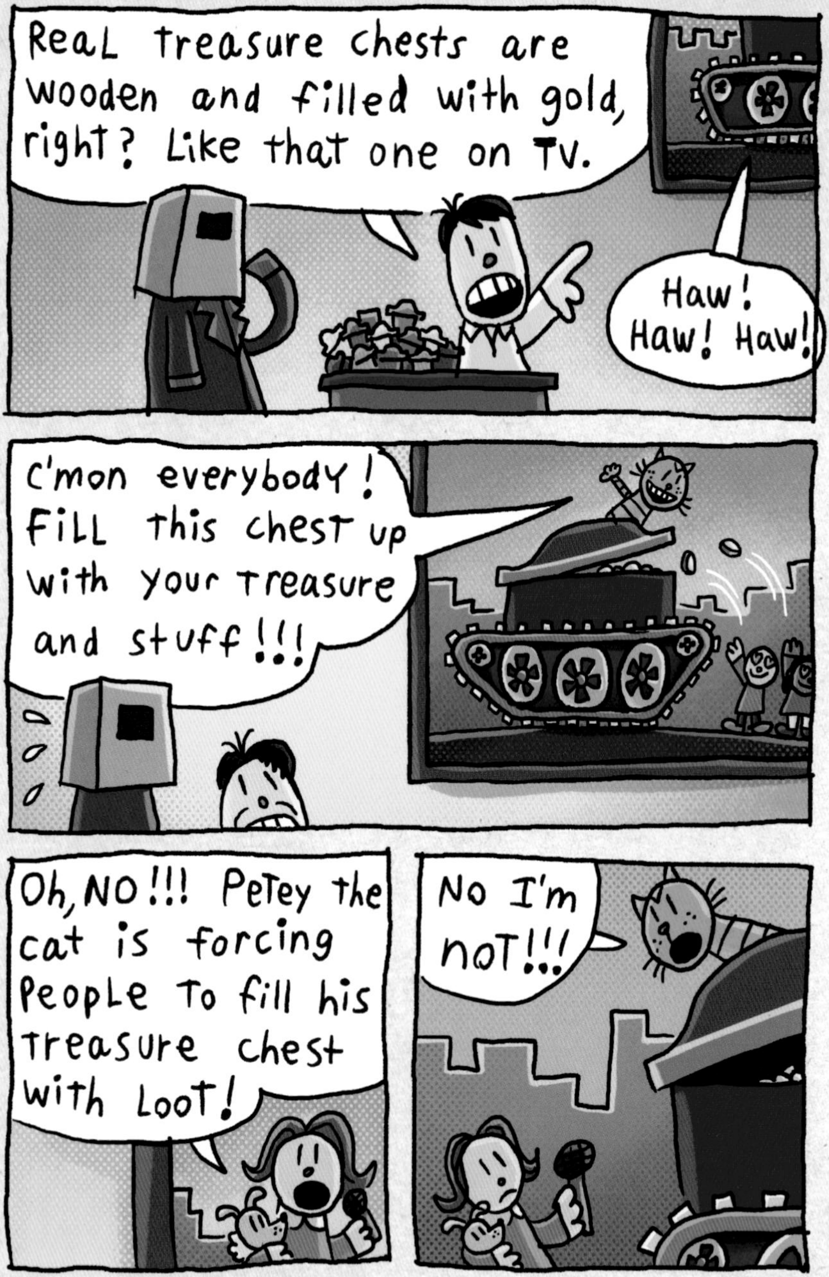
Real treasure chests are wooden and filled with gold, right? Like that one on TV.
Haw! Haw! Haw!
C'mon everybody! Fill this chest up with your treasure and stuff!!!
Oh, NO!!! Petey the cat is forcing people to fill his treasure chest with loot!
No I'm not!!!

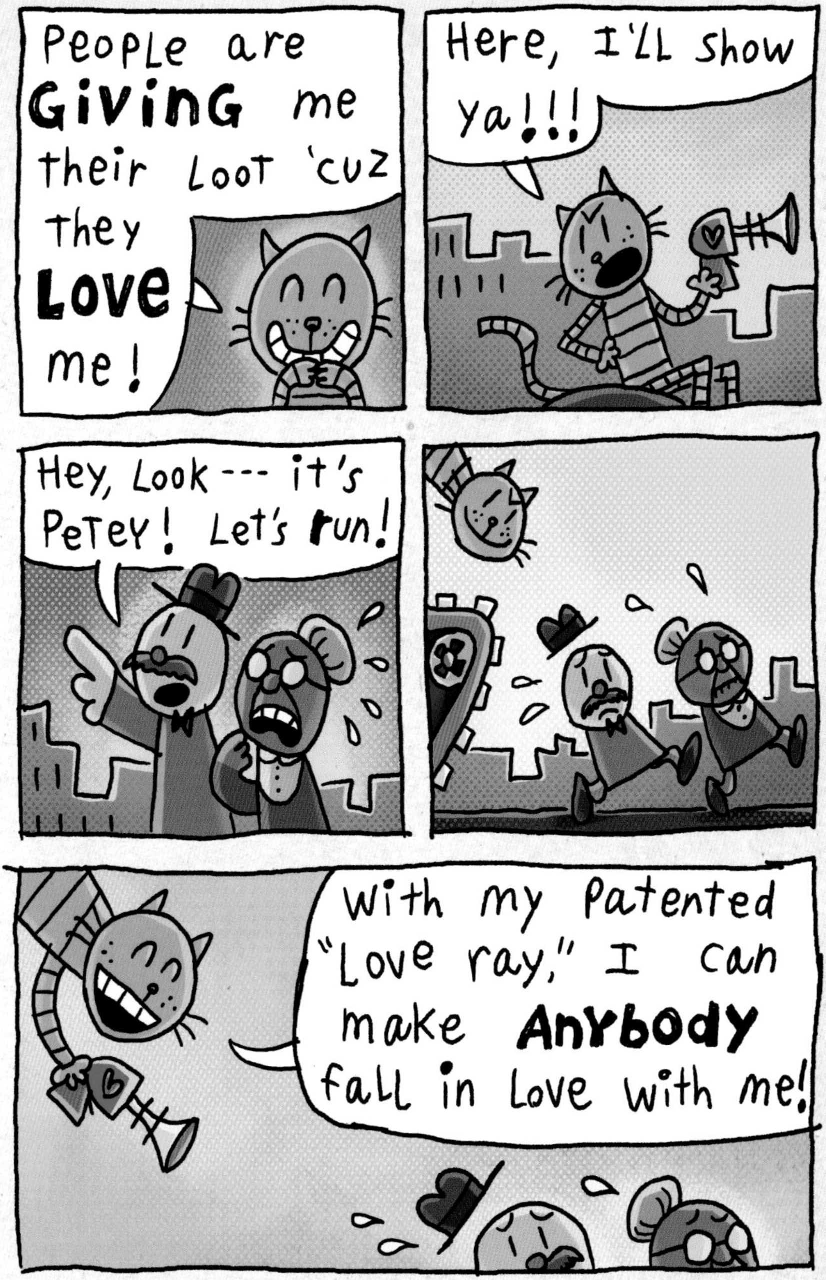
People are GIVING me their Loot 'cuz they LOVE me!
Here, I'LL show ya!!!
Hey, Look --- it's Petey! Let's run!
With my Patented "Love ray," I can make ANYBODY fall in Love with me!

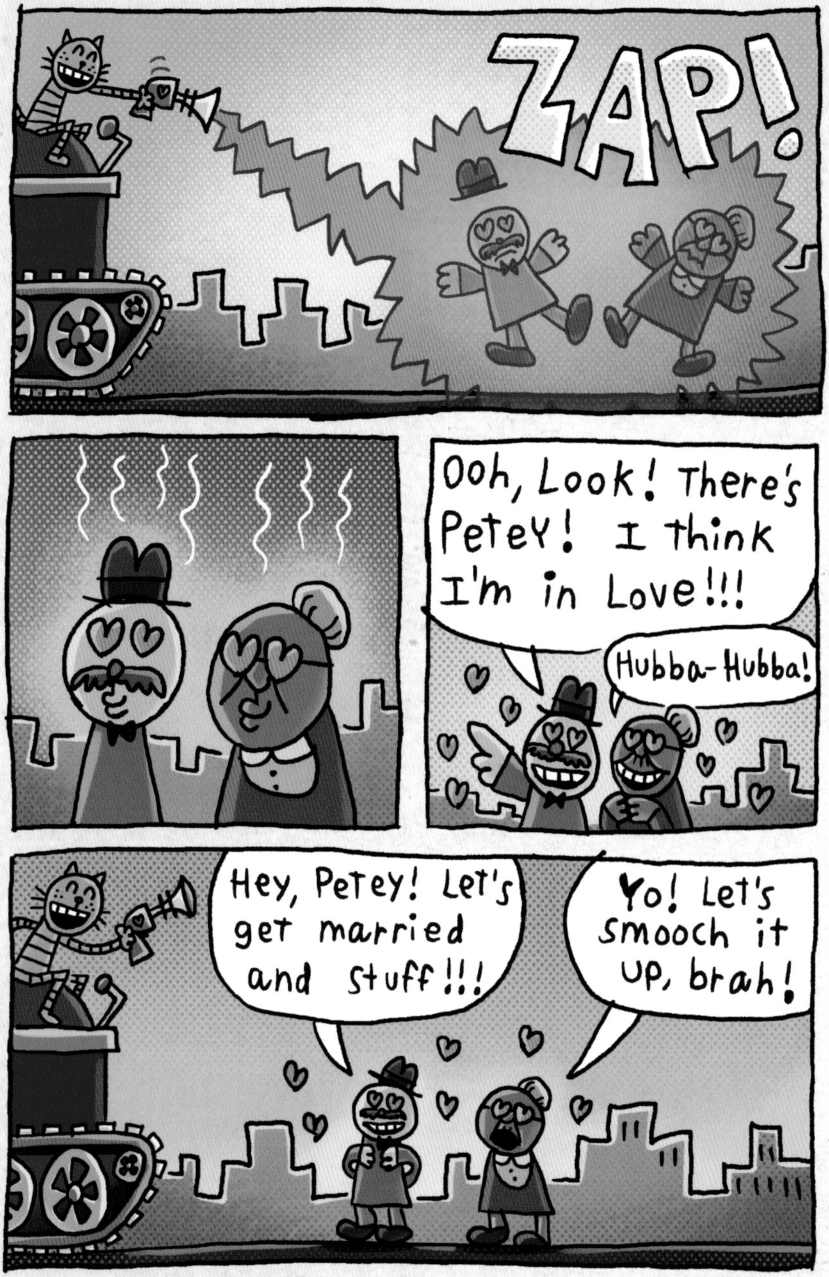
ZAP!
Ooh, Look! There's Petey! I think I'm in Love!!!
Hubba-Hubba!
Hey, Petey! Let's get married and stuff!!!
Yo! Let's smooch it up, brah!

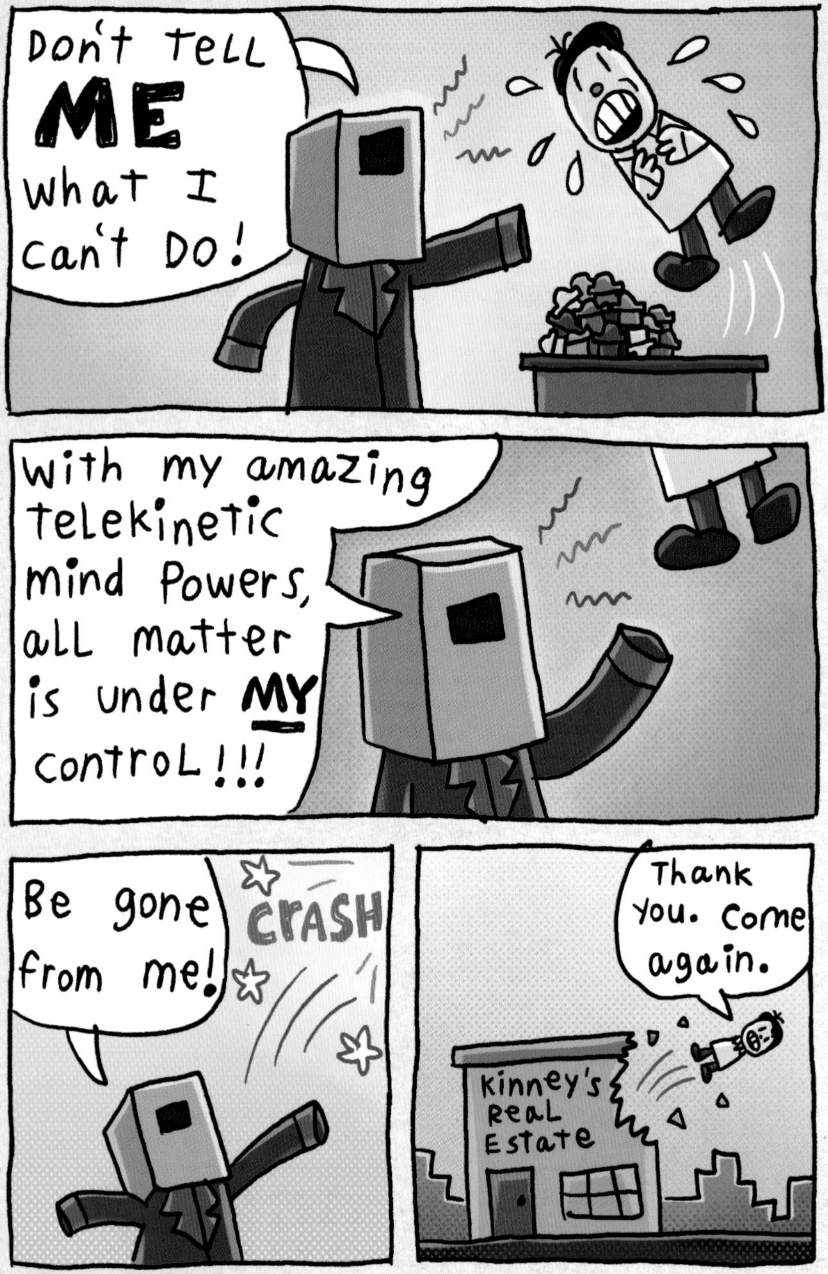
Don't TeLL ME what I can't Do!
With my amazing telekinetic mind Powers, aLL matter is under MY controL!!!
Be gone from me!
CRASH
Thank You. Come again.
Kinney's ReaL Estate

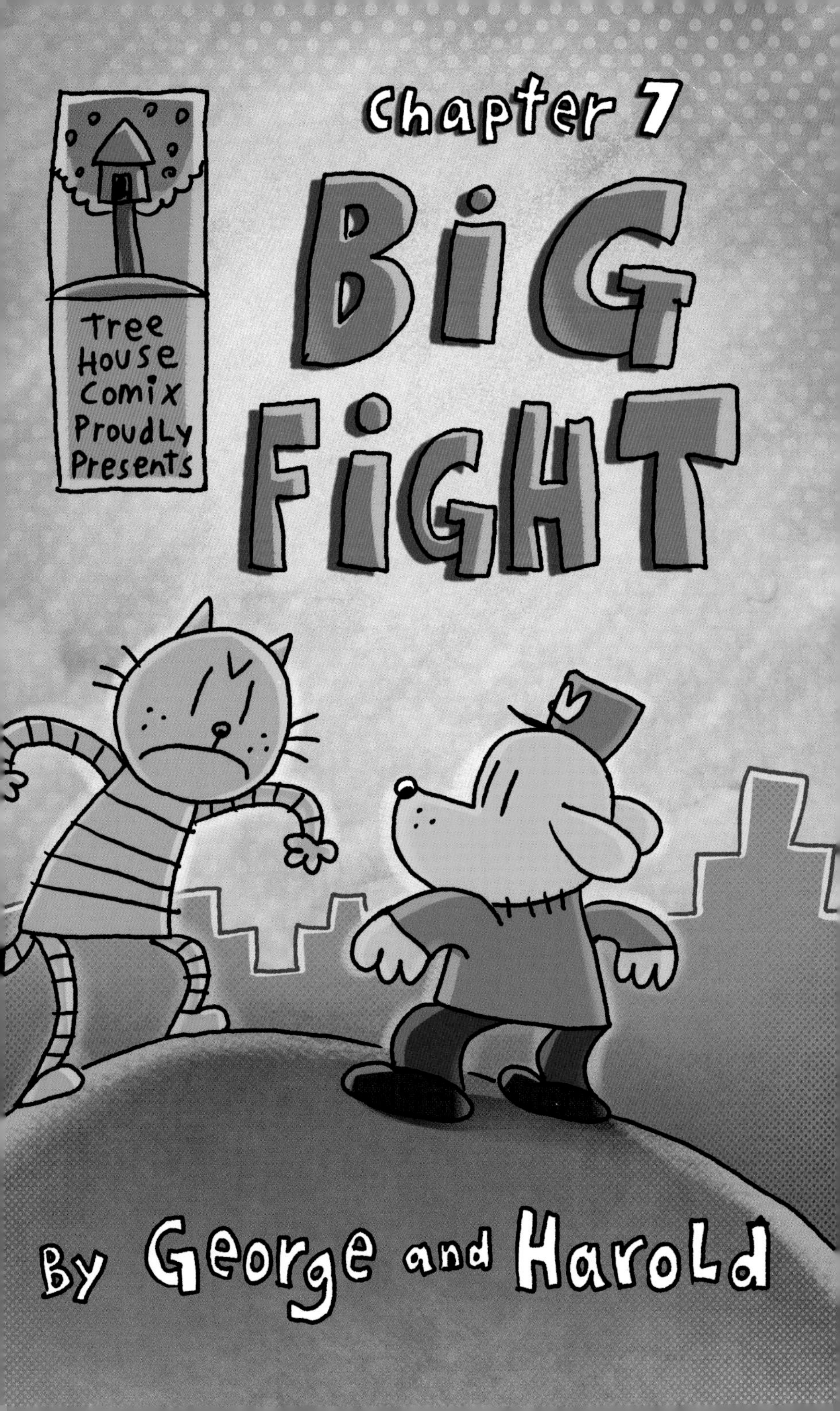
Tree House Comix Proudly Presents
Chapter 7
Big Fight
By George and Harold

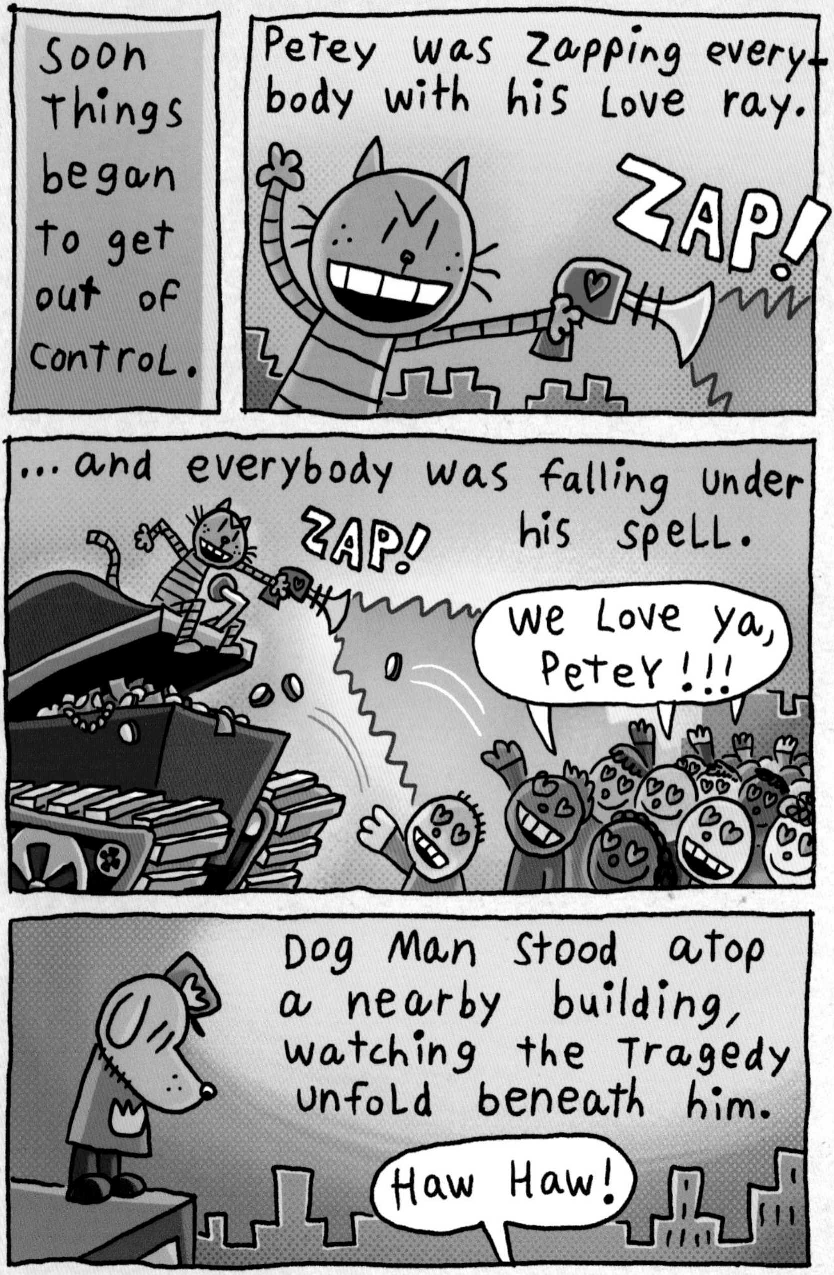
Soon things began to get out of control.
Petey was Zapping everybody with his Love ray.
ZAP!
...and everybody was falling under his spell.
ZAP!
We Love ya, Petey!!!
Dog Man Stood atop a nearby building, watching the Tragedy unfold beneath him.
Haw Haw!

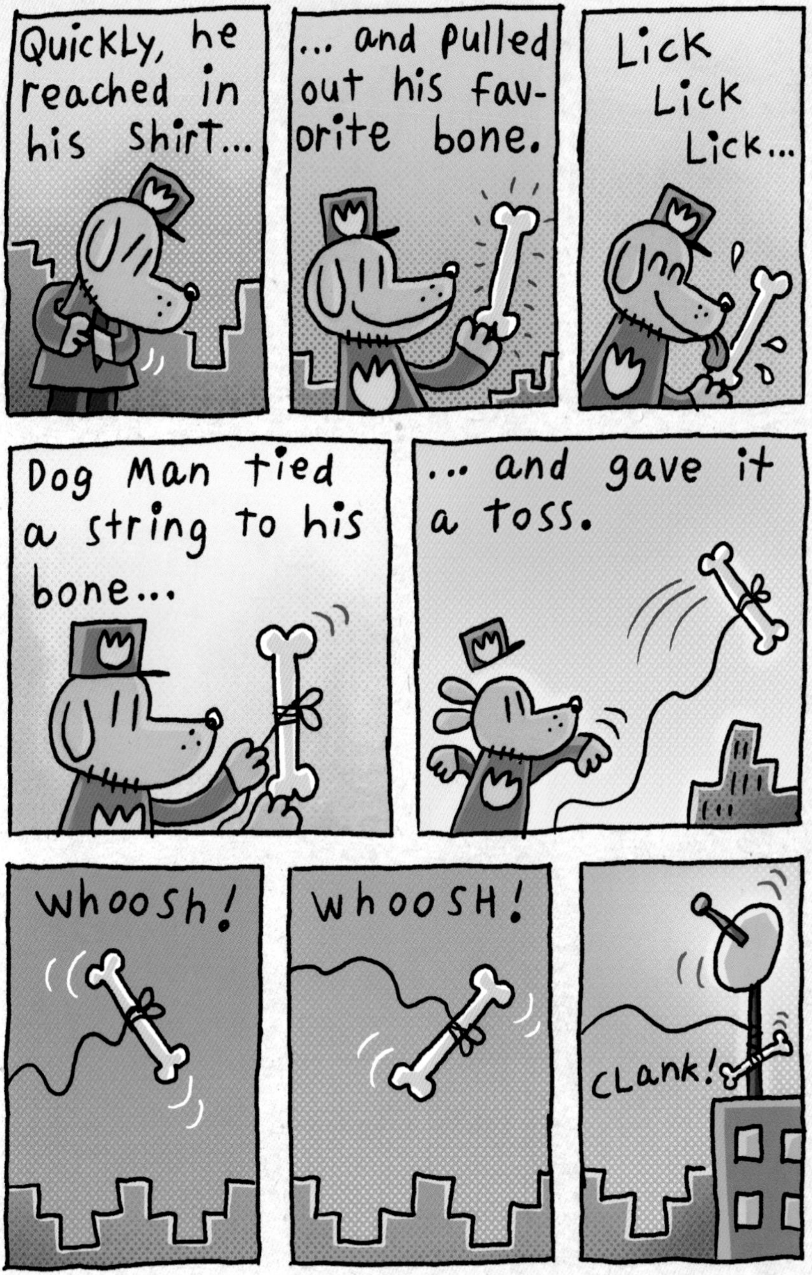

Quickly, he reached in his shirt...
... and pulled out his fav-orite bone.
Lick Lick Lick...
Dog Man tied a string to his bone...
... and gave it a toss.
whoosh!
whooSH!
CLank!

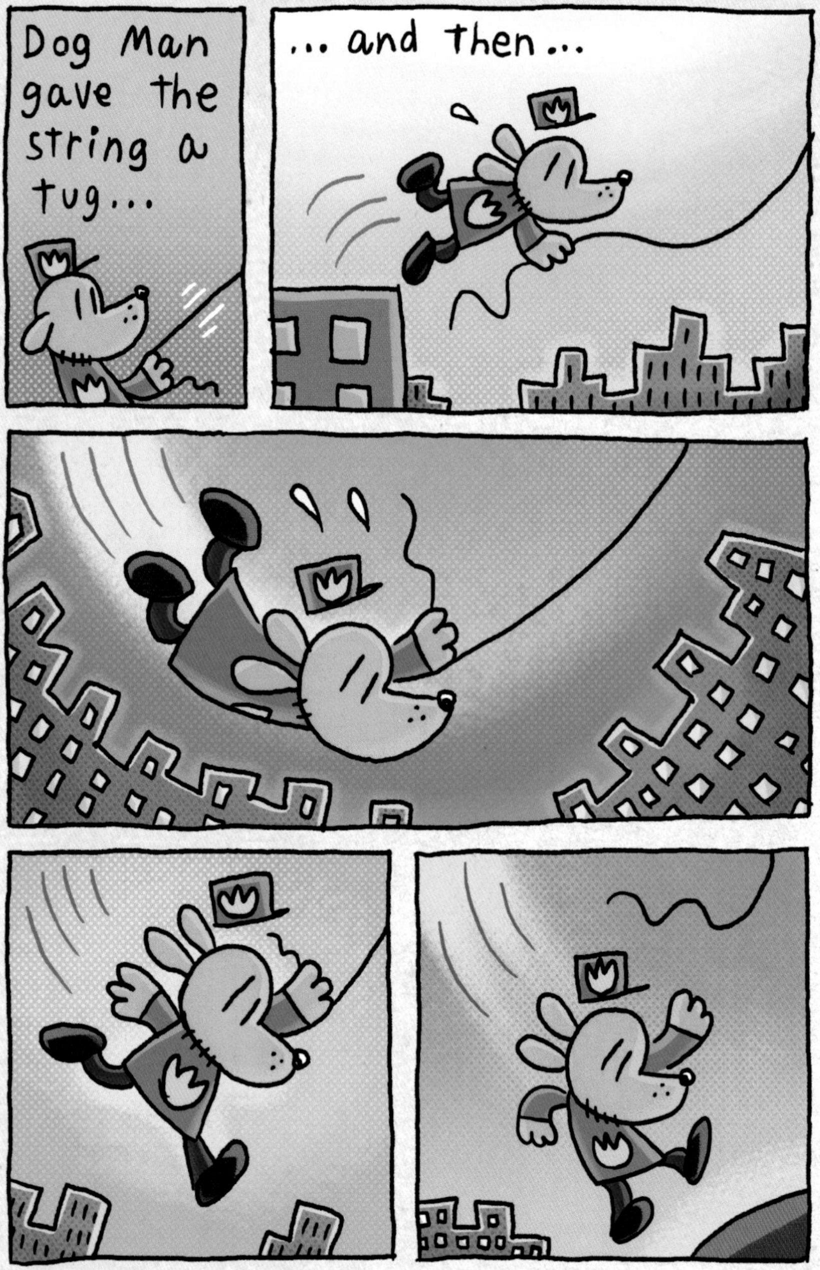
Dog Man gave the string a tug...
... and then...

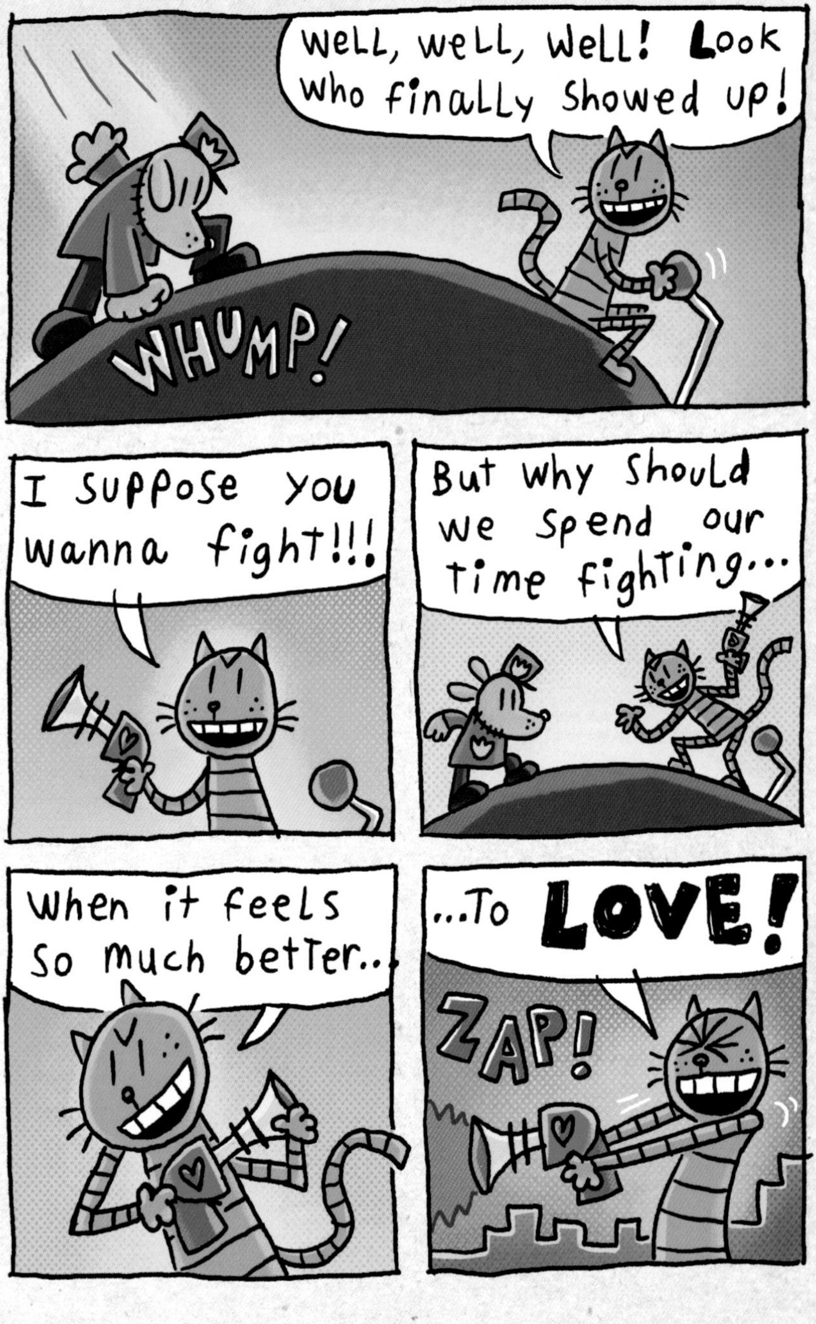

WELL, WELL, WELL! LOOK WHO FINALLY SHOWED UP!
WHUMP!
I SUPPOSE YOU WANNA FIGHT!!!
BUT WHY SHOULD WE SPEND OUR TIME FIGHTING...
WHEN IT FEELS SO MUCH BETTER...
...TO LOVE!
ZAP!

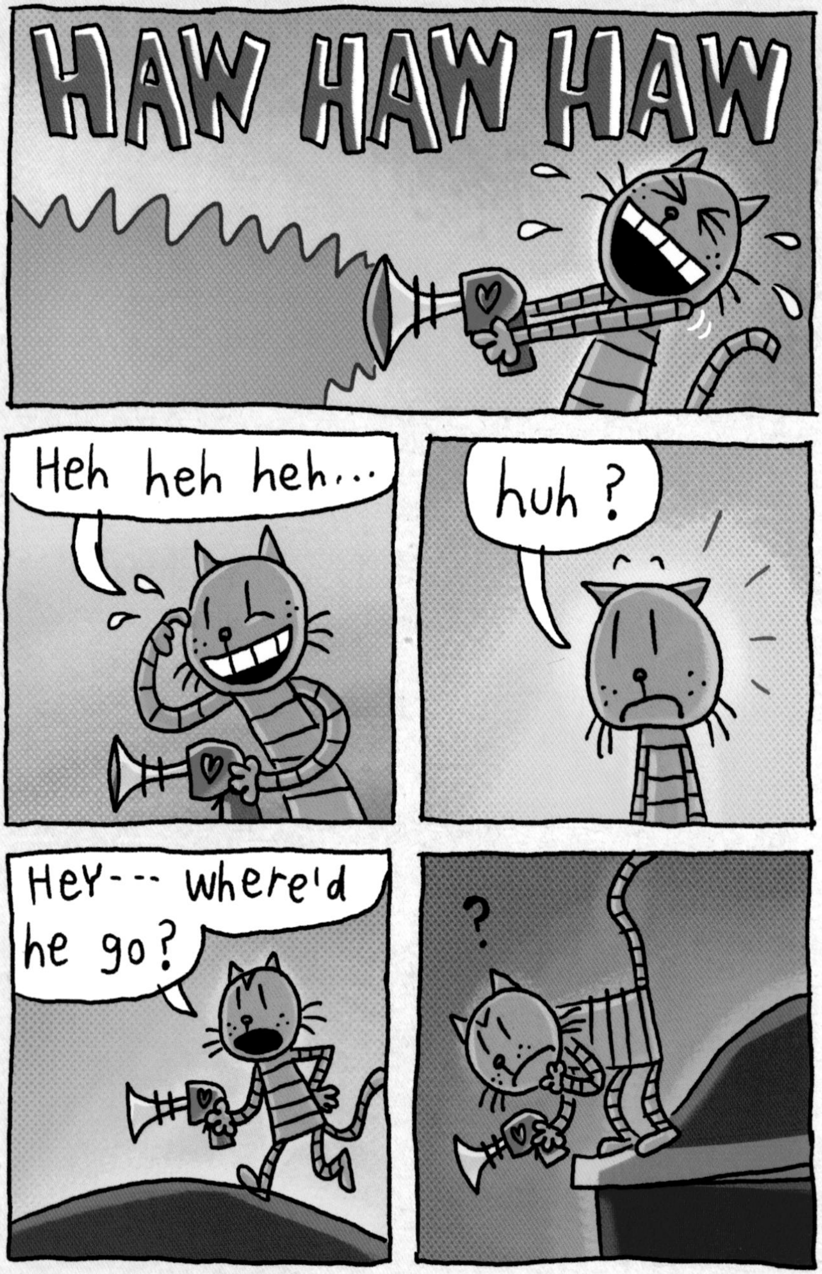
HAW HAW HAW
Heh heh heh...
huh ?
Hey--- where'd he go?
?

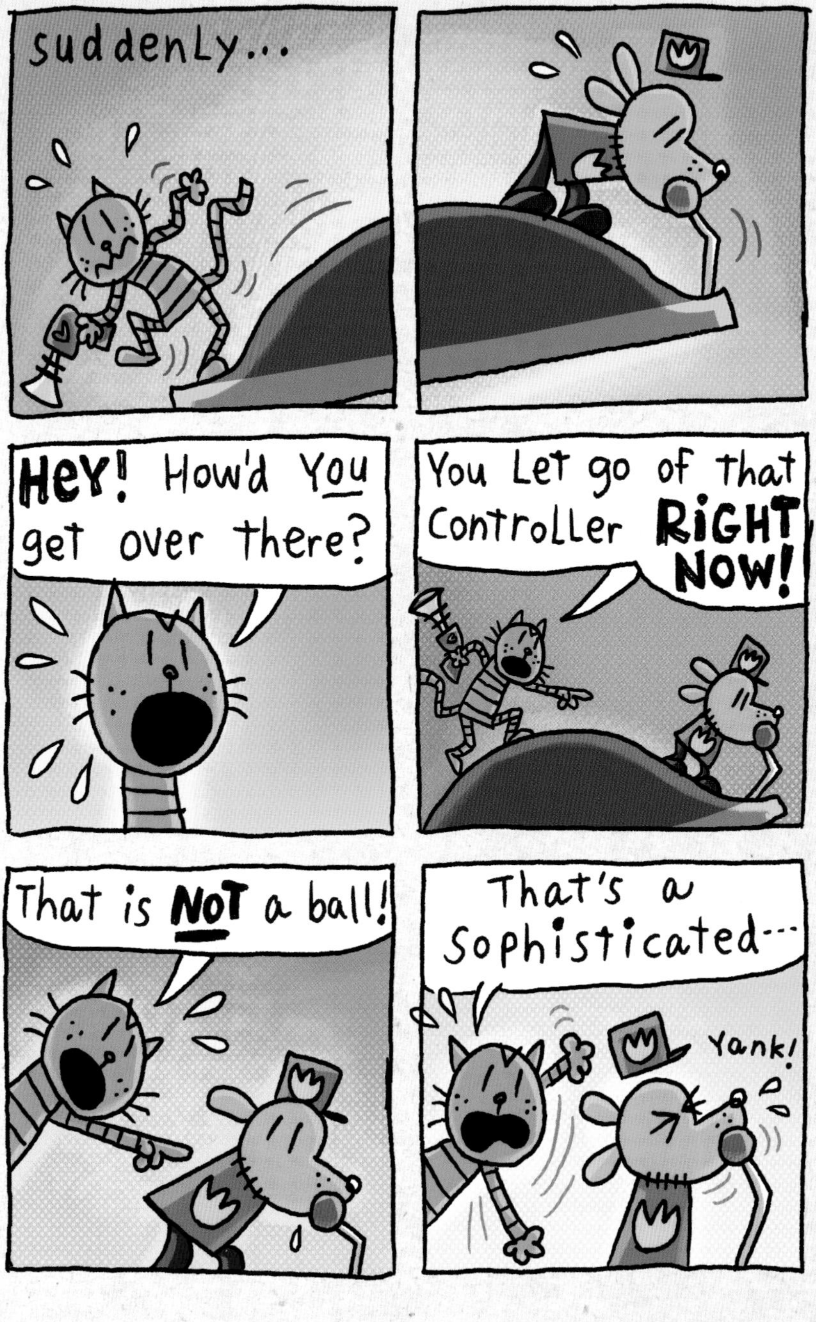
Suddenly...
HEY! How'd You get over there?
You Let go of that Controller RIGHT NOW!
That is NOT a ball!
That's a Sophisticated...
Yank!

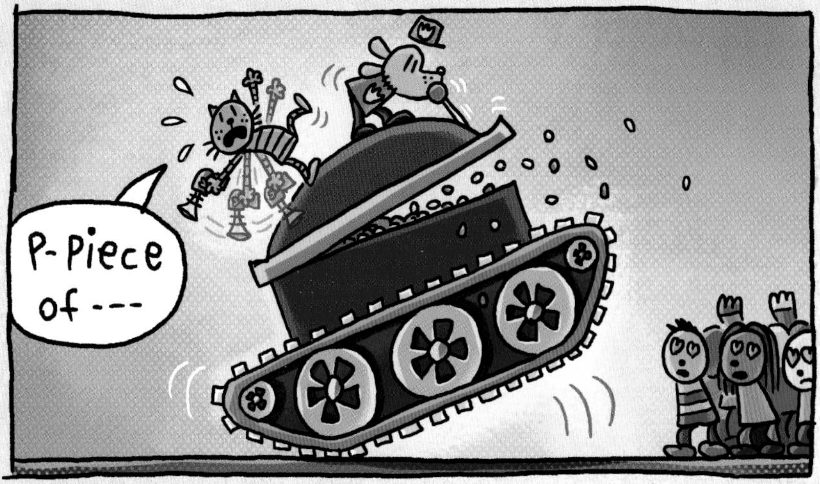
P-Piece of ---

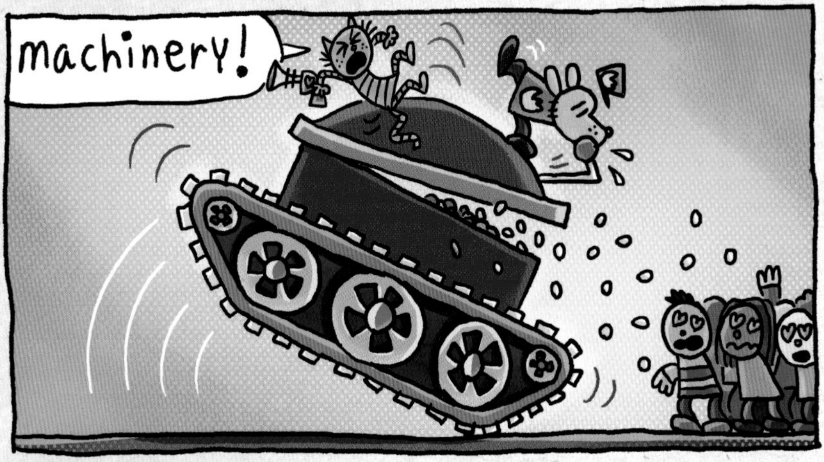
machinery!

TRIPLE FLIP-O-RAMA

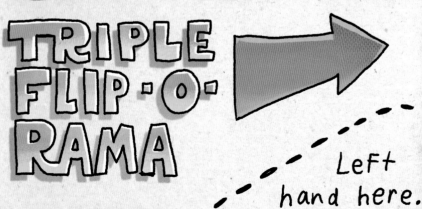

Left hand here.

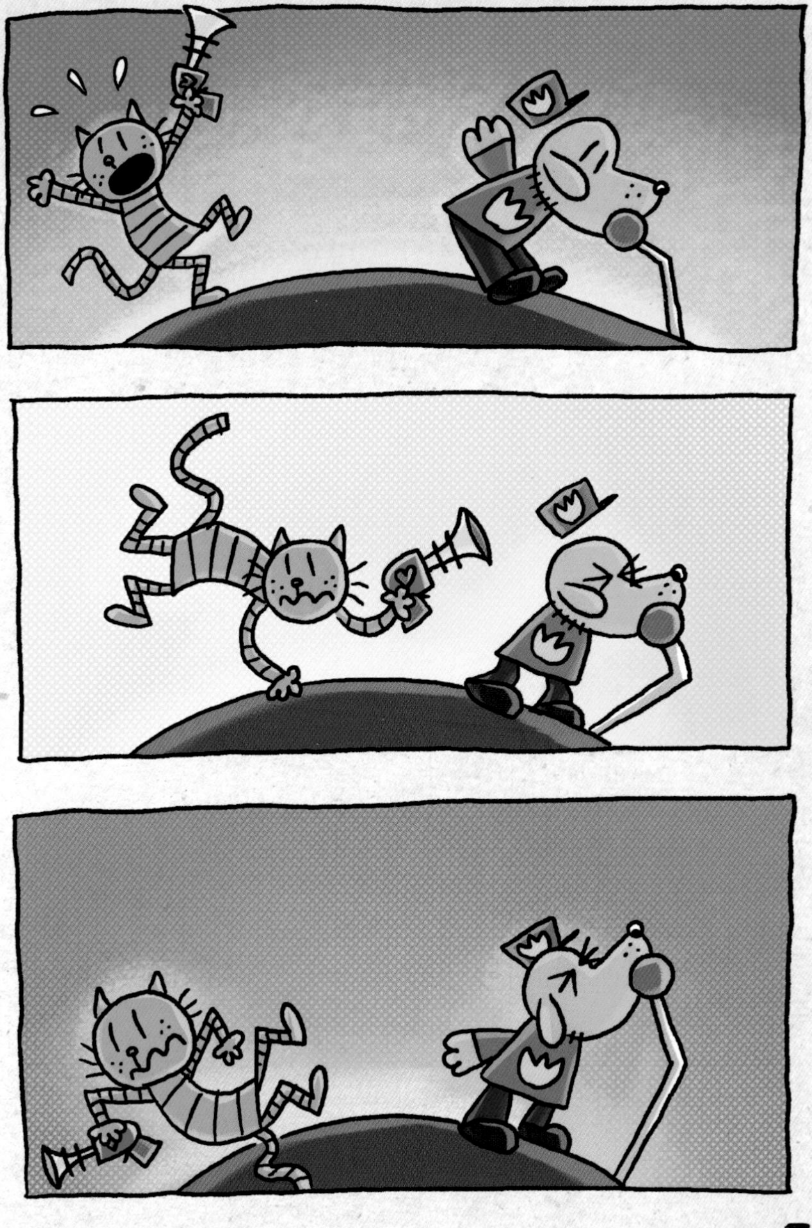

Right Thumb here.

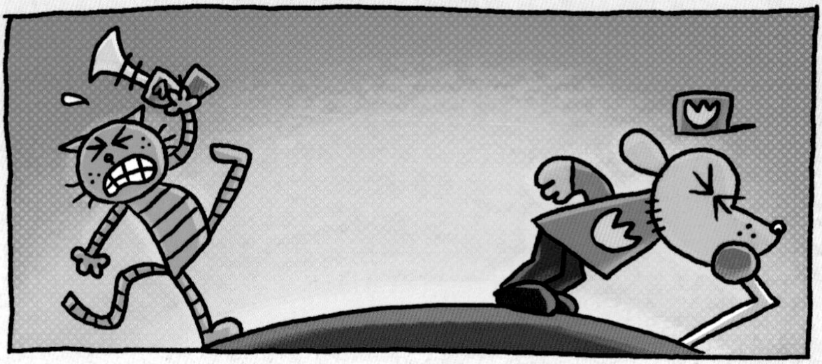

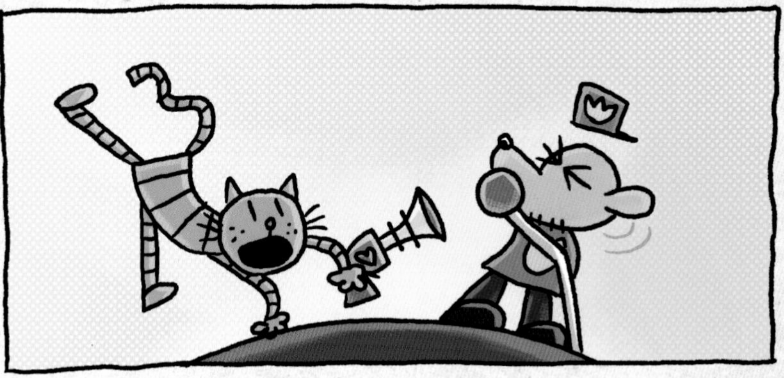

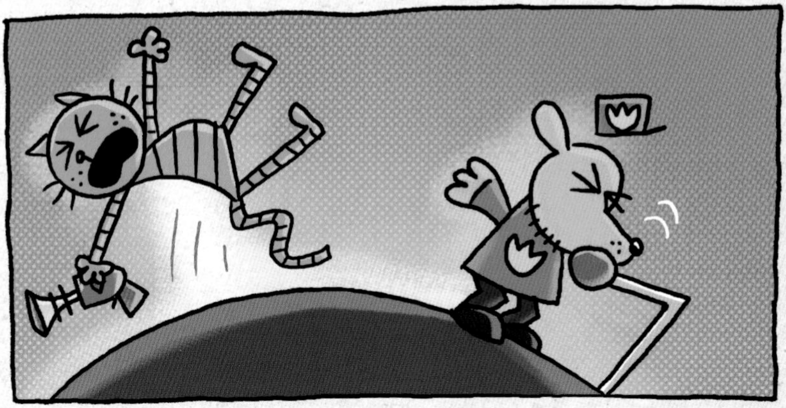

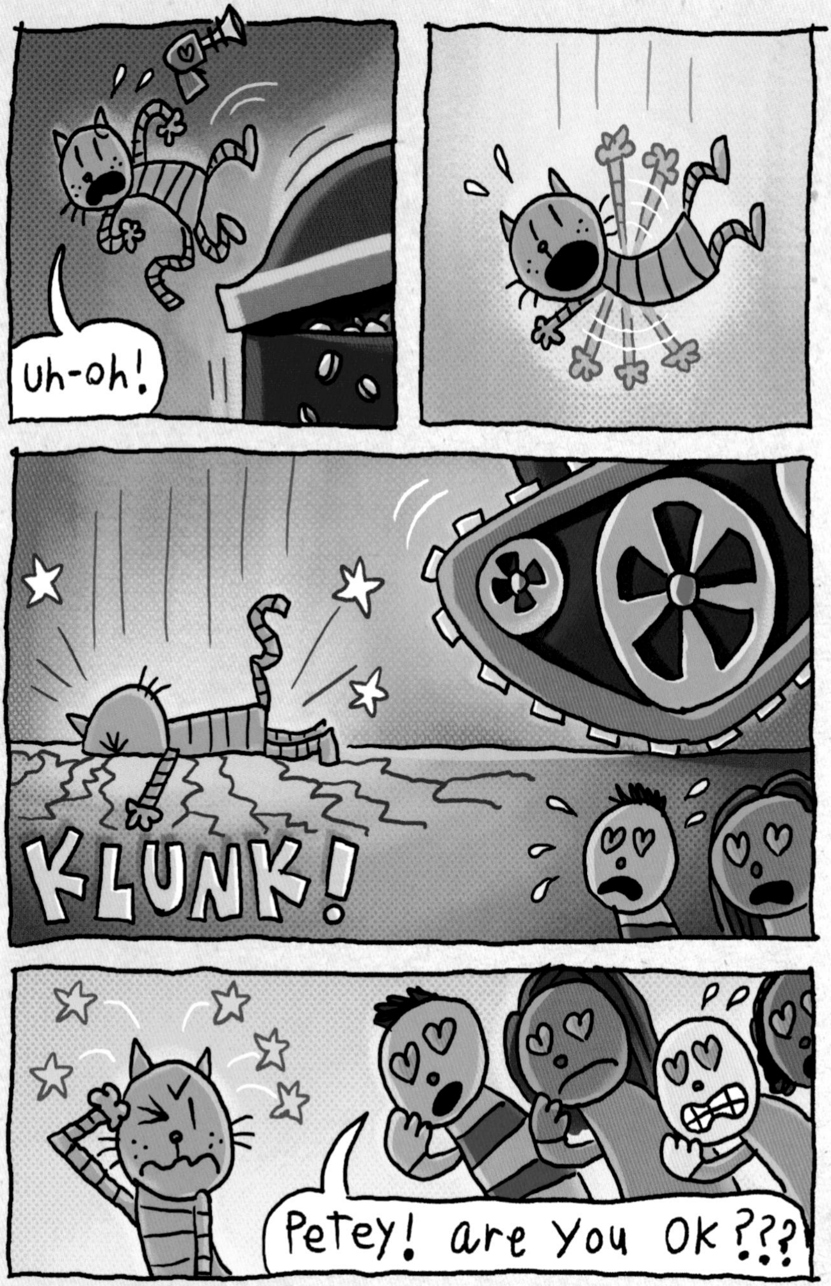

Uh-oh!
KLUNK!
Petey! are you OK???

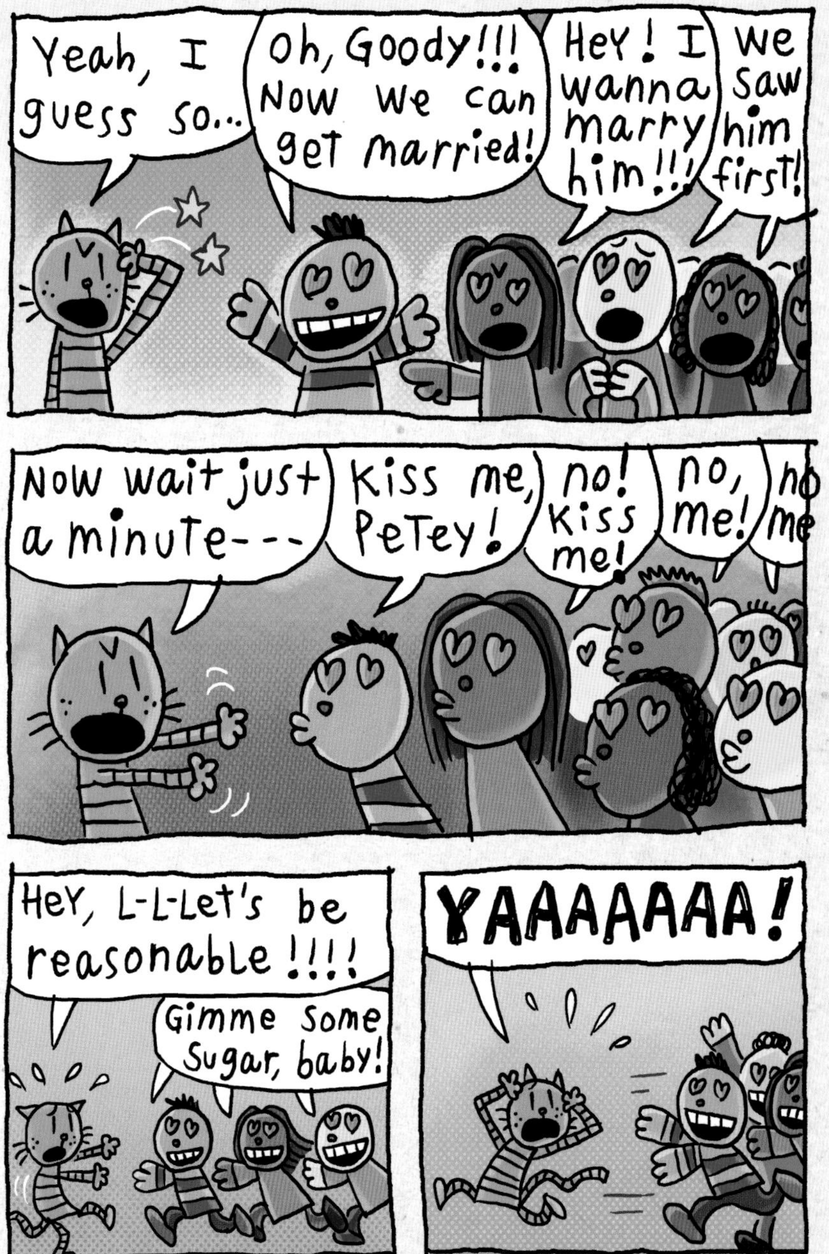
Yeah, I guess so...
Oh, Goody!!! Now we can get married!
Hey! I wanna marry him!!!
We saw him first!
Now wait just a minute---
Kiss me, PeTey!
no! Kiss me!
no, me!
Gimme some Sugar, baby!
Hey, L-L-Let's be reasonable!!!!
YAAAAAAA!

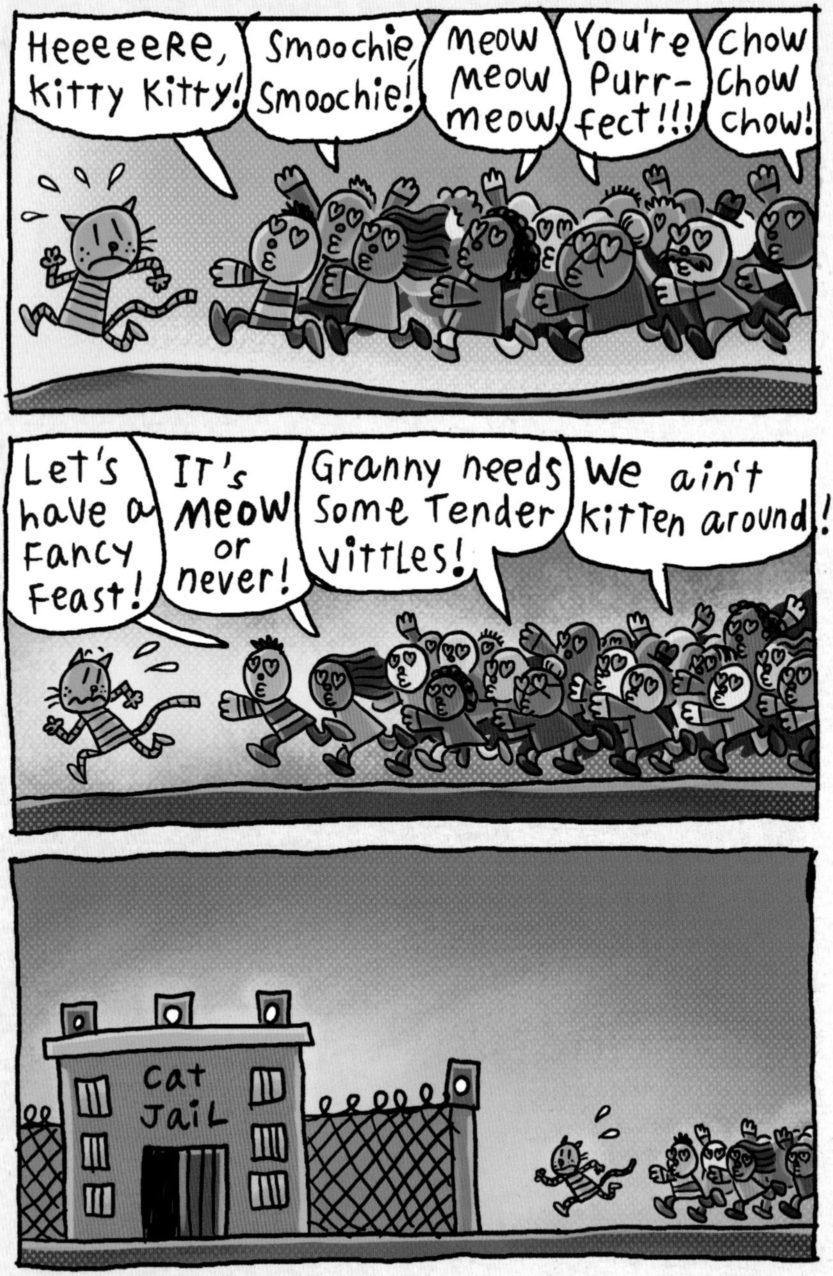
Heeeeere, kitty kitty!
Smoochie, Smoochie!
Meow meow meow
You're Purr-fect!!!
Chow chow chow!
Let's have a Fancy Feast!
IT's MEOW or never!
Granny needs some Tender vittles!
We ain't kitten around!
Cat Jail

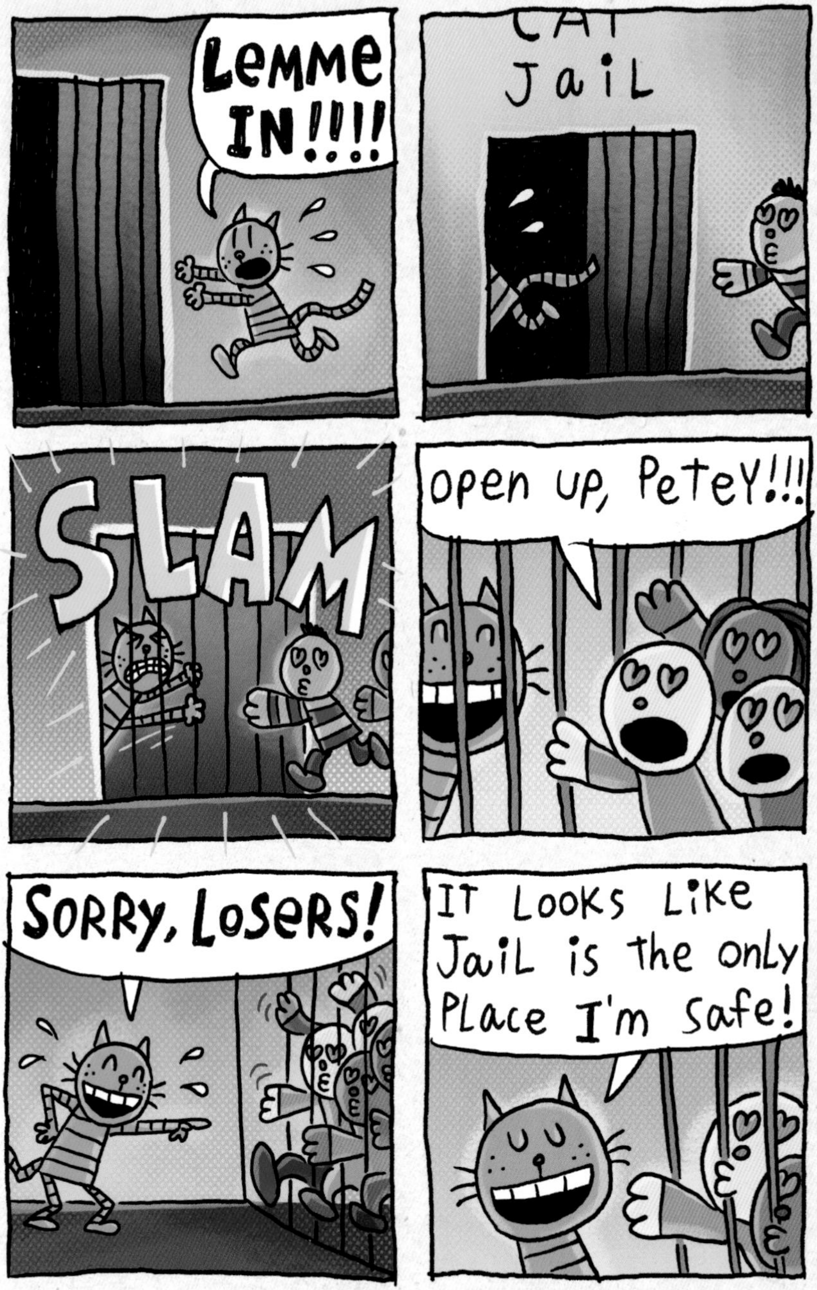
LEMME IN!!!!
CAT JAIL
SLAM
OPEN UP, PETEY!!!
SORRY, LOSERS!
IT LOOKS LIKE JAIL IS THE ONLY PLACE I'M SAFE!

Chapter 8

FLAT CAT FEVER

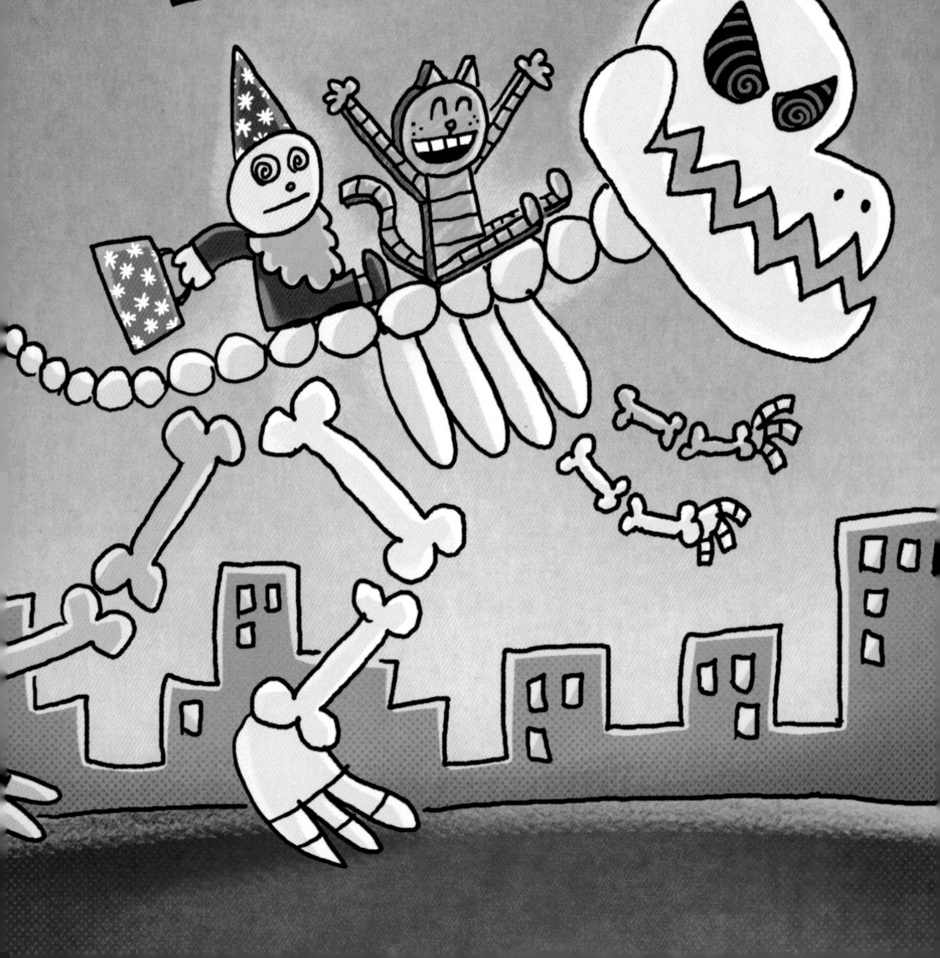

Meanwhile, back in Town, Tensions were still high...

Dog Man would not let go of the ball.

Sarah Tried to Convince him...

Drop the Ball, DOG Man!!!!

Zuzu Tried, too!

RuFF! RuFF! RuFF!

Even Chief couldn't make Dog Man Listen to reason.

BAD DOGGY

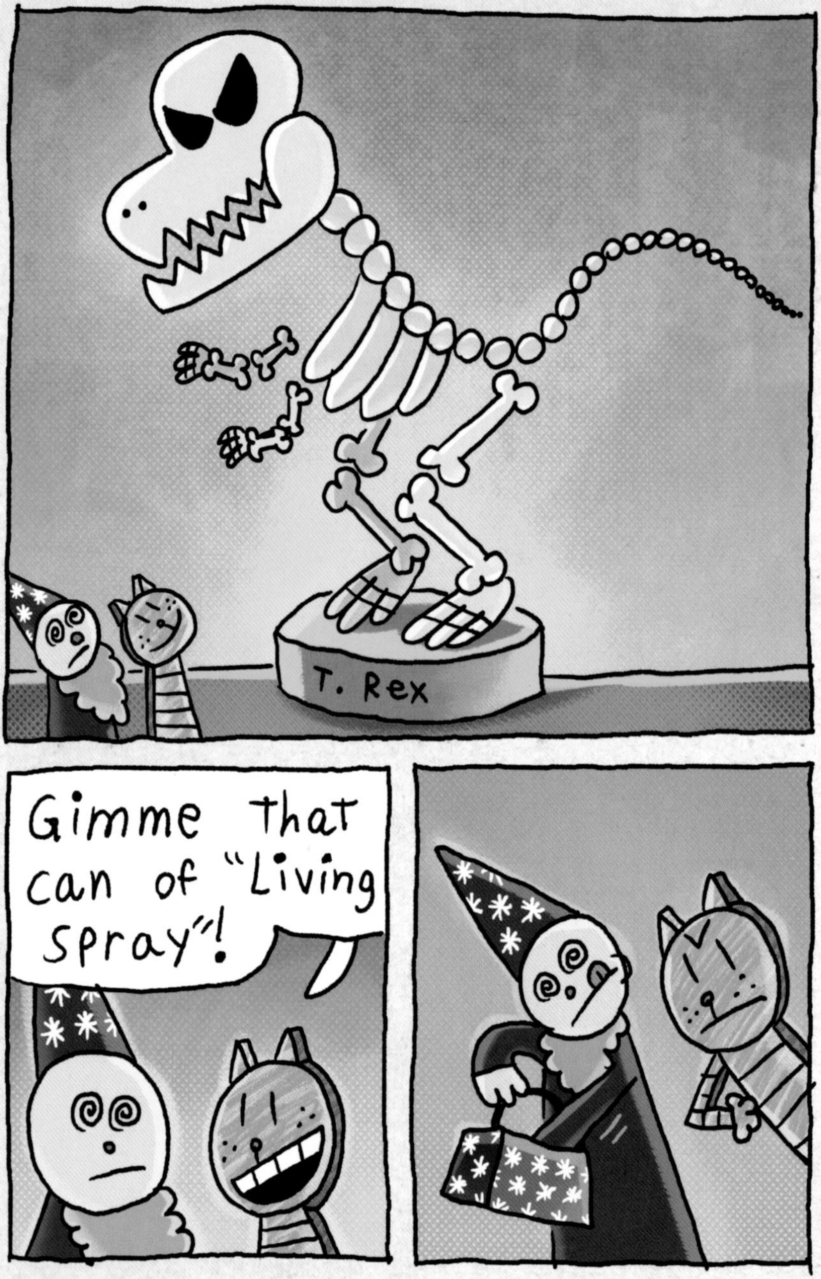
T. Rex
Gimme that can of "Living spray"!

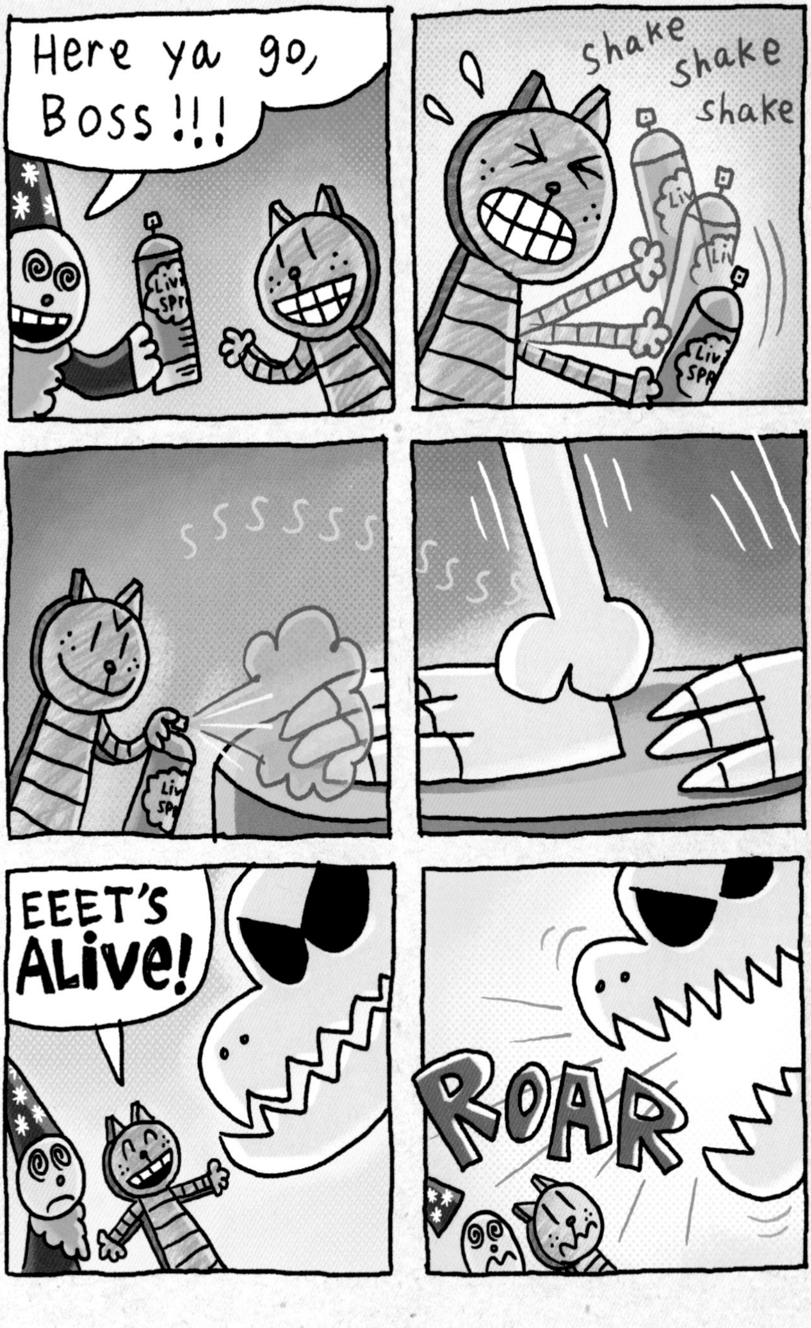
Here ya go, Boss!!!
shake shake shake
SSSSSS
SSSS
EEET'S ALIVE!
ROAR

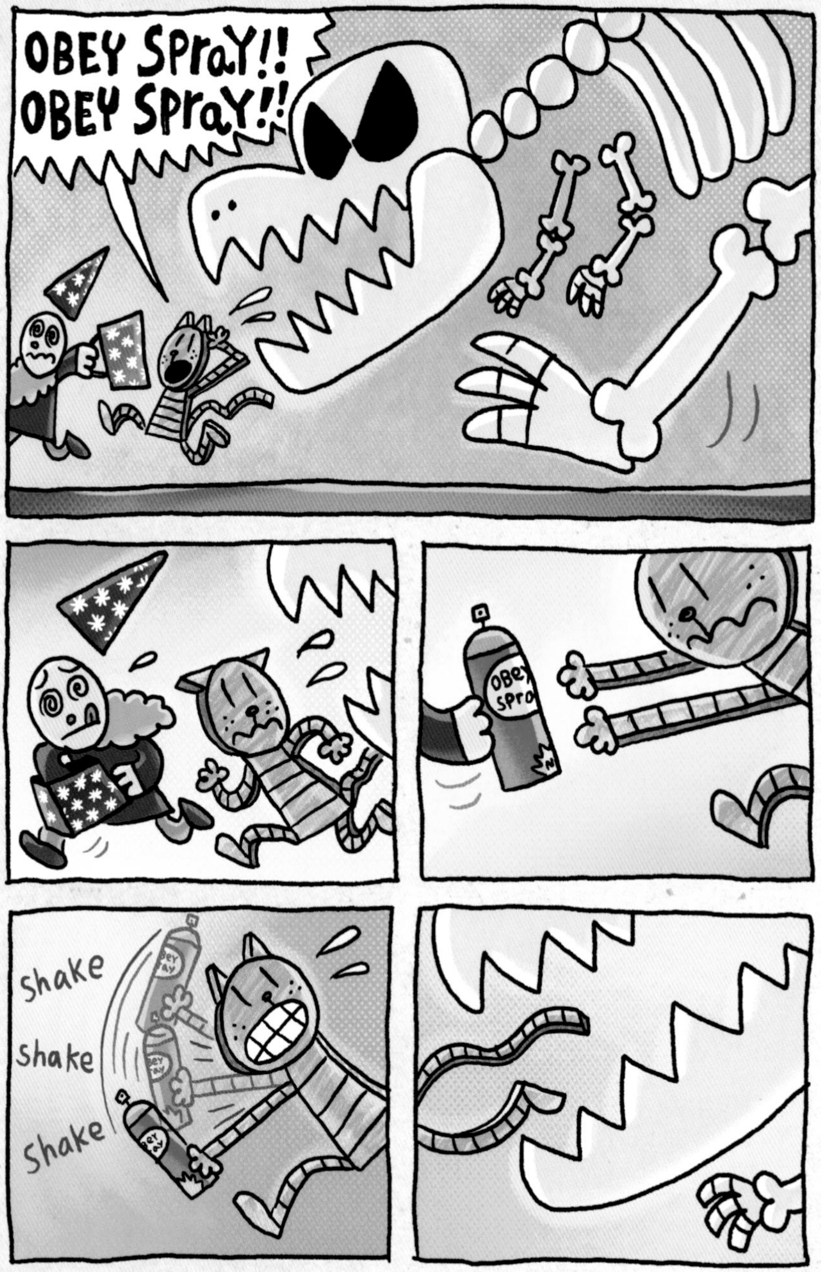
OBEY SPRAY!!
OBEY SPRAY!!
OBEY
SPRA
SHAKE
SHAKE
SHAKE

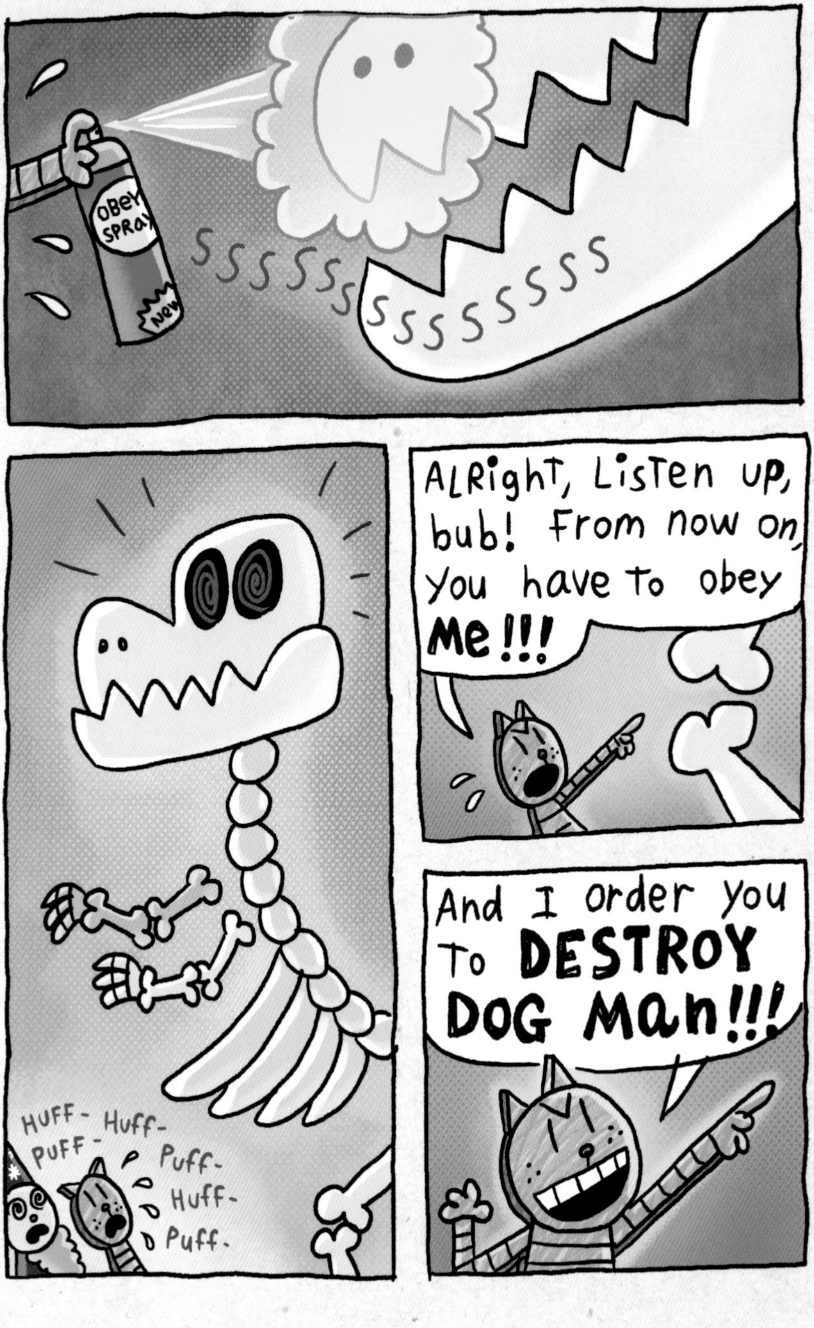
OBEY SPRAY
NEW
SSSSSSSSSSSSSSSSS
ALRight, LiSTen UP, bub! From now on, You have to obey Me!!!
HUFF- Huff- PUFF- Puff- Huff- Puff-
And I order you To DESTROY DOG Man!!!

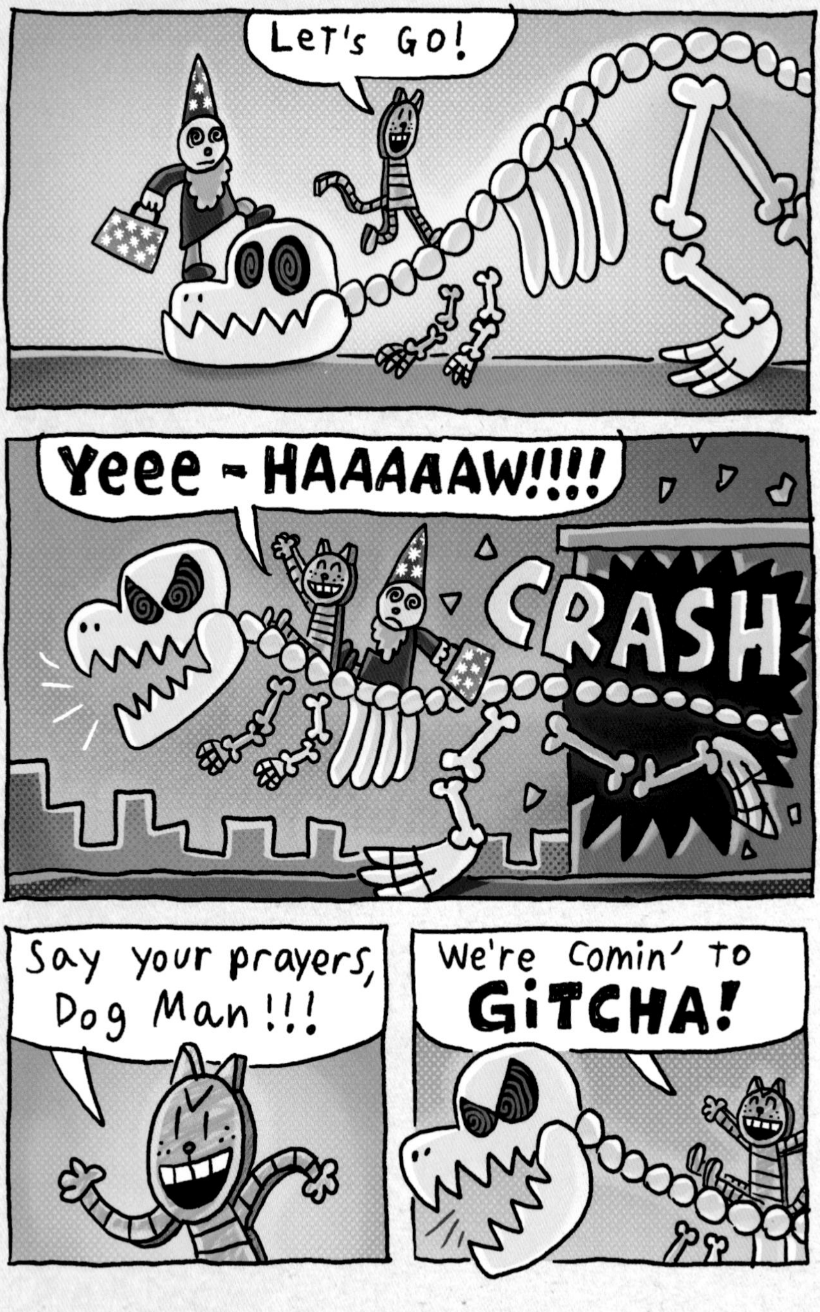
Let's GO!
Yeee-HAAAAAW!!!!
CRASH
Say your prayers, Dog Man!!!
We're Comin' to GiTCHA!

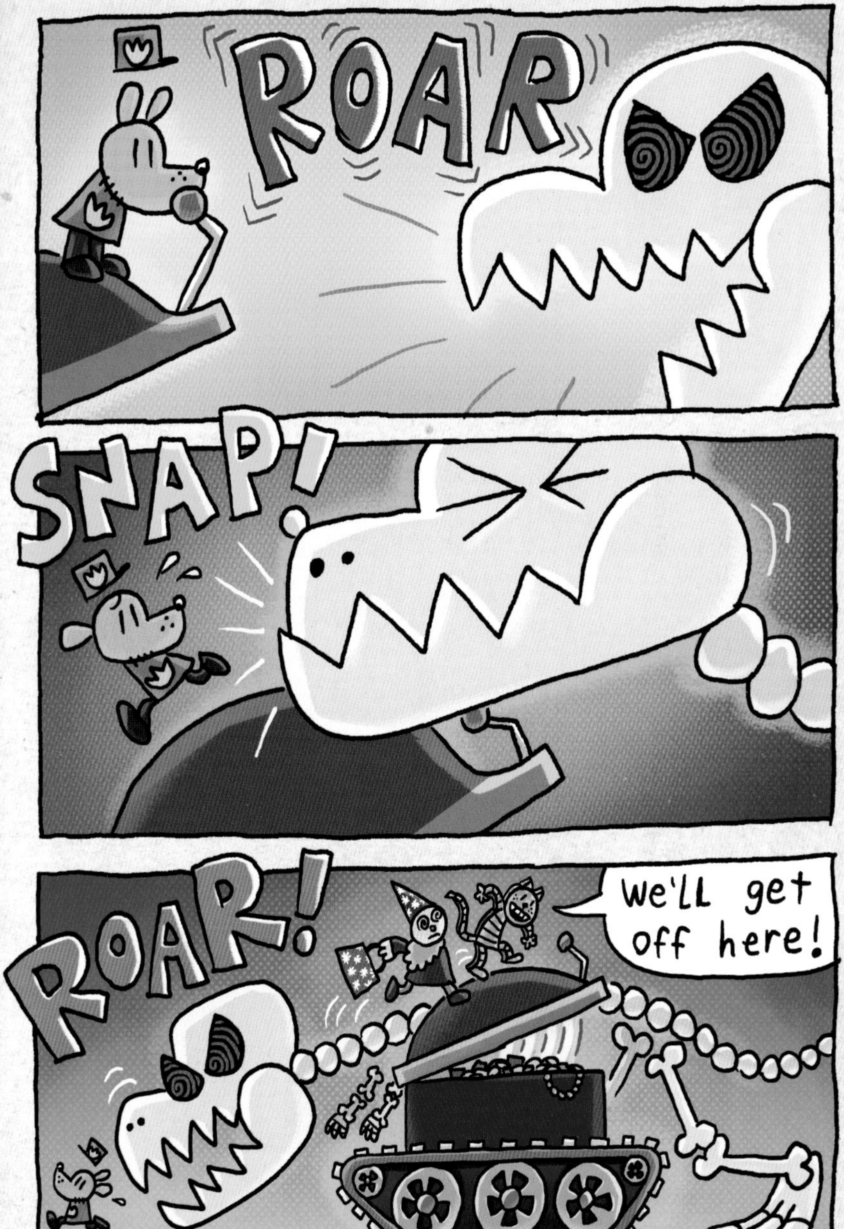
ROAR
SNAP!
ROAR!
We'll get off here!

FLIP·O·RAMA

cheesy Animation Technology...

Left
hand here.

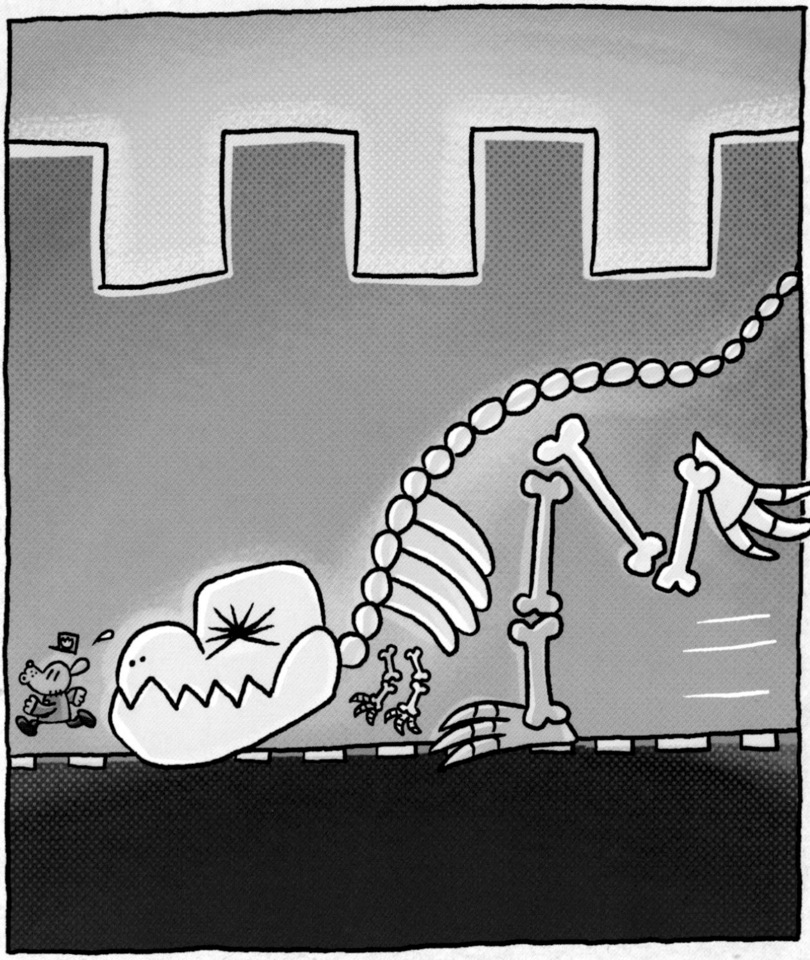

Jurassic Bark

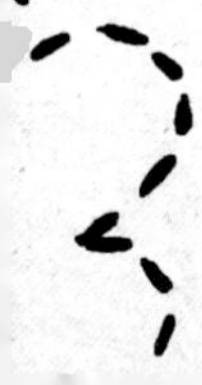

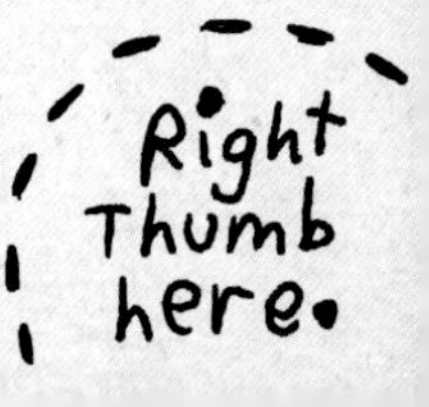
Right
Thumb
here.

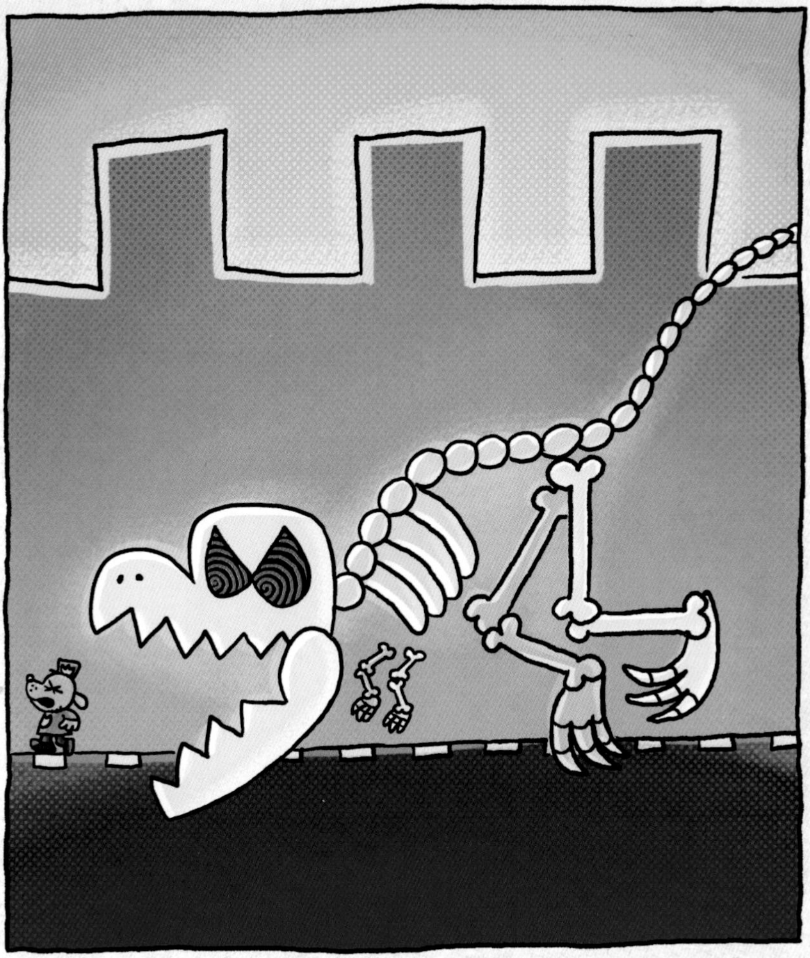

Jurassic Bark

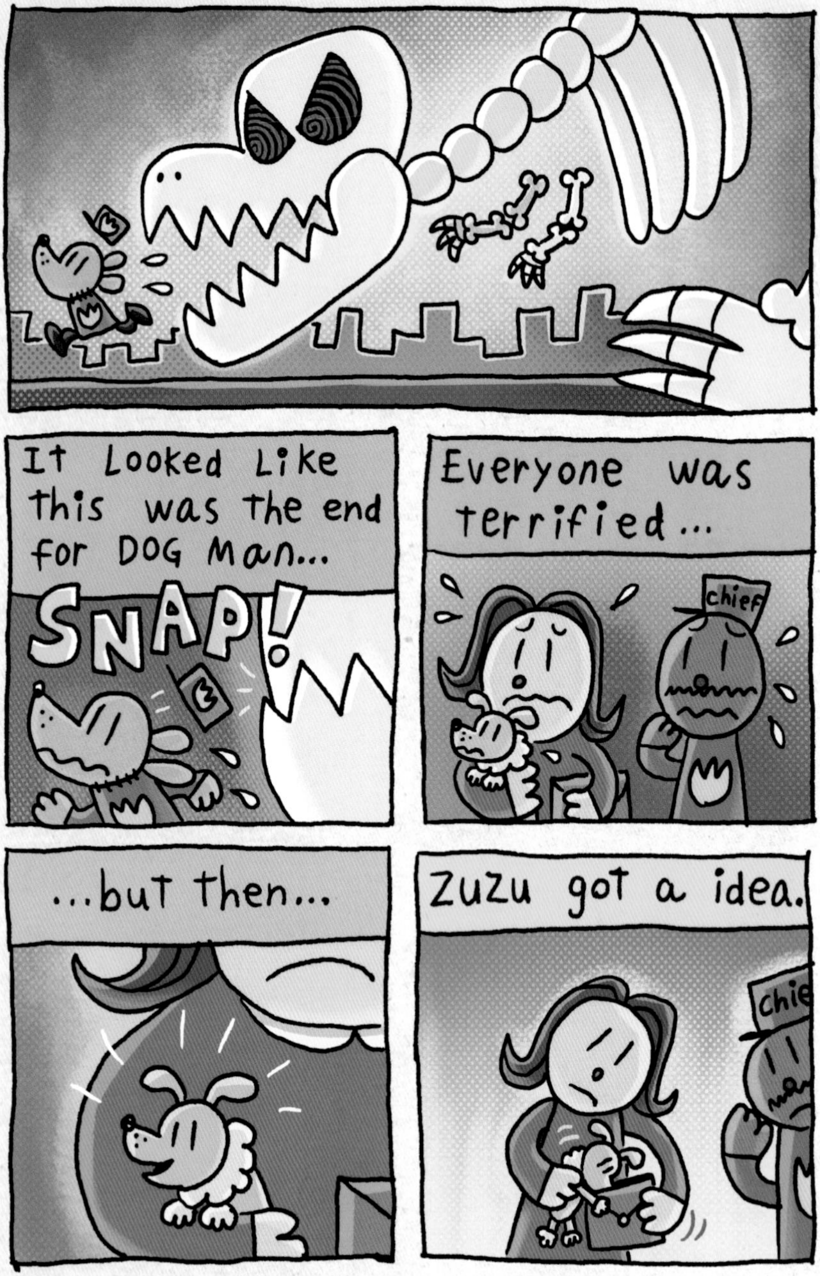
It Looked Like this was the end for DOG Man...
SNAP!
Everyone was terrified...
chief
...but then...
Zuzu got a idea.

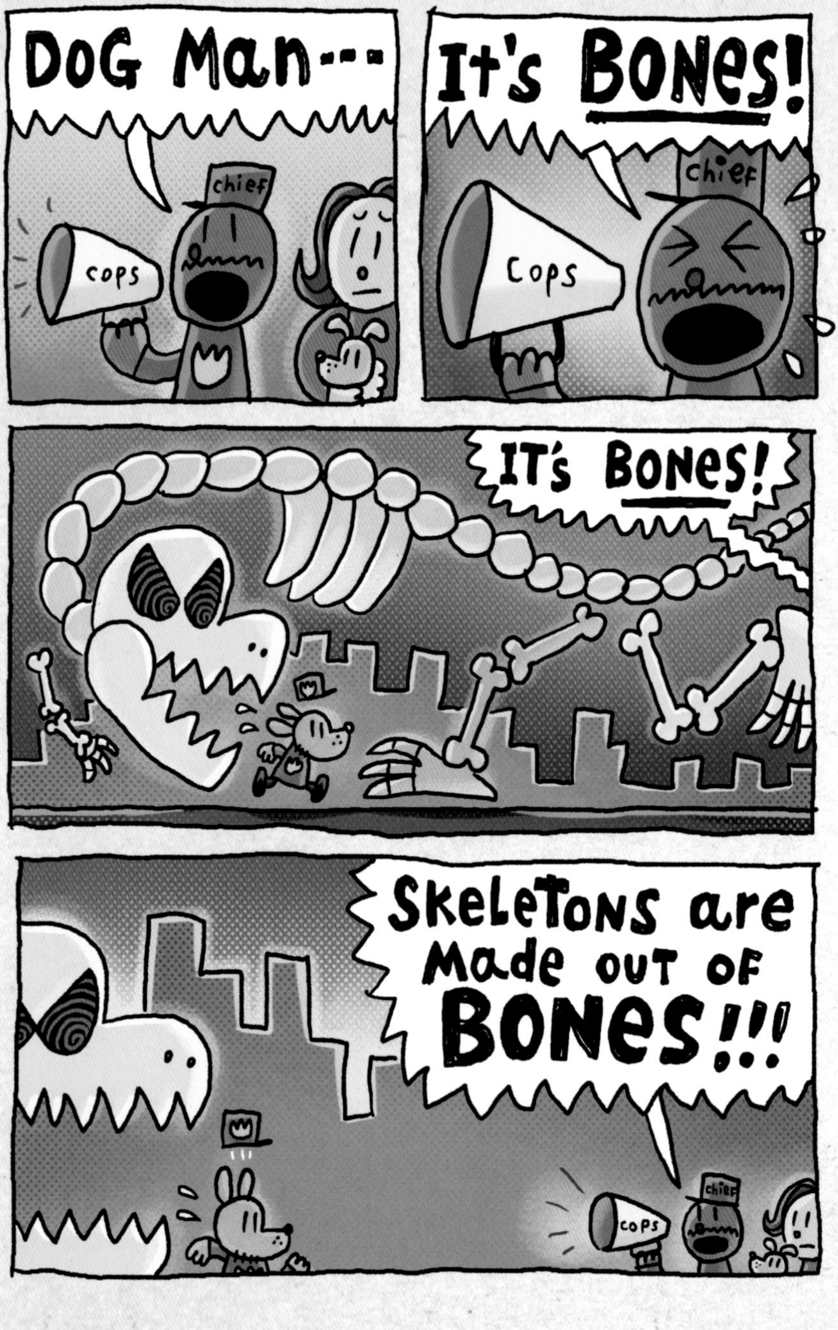

DOG Man...
It's BONES!
cops
chief
IT's BONES!
SkeLeTONS are Made OUT OF BONES!!!

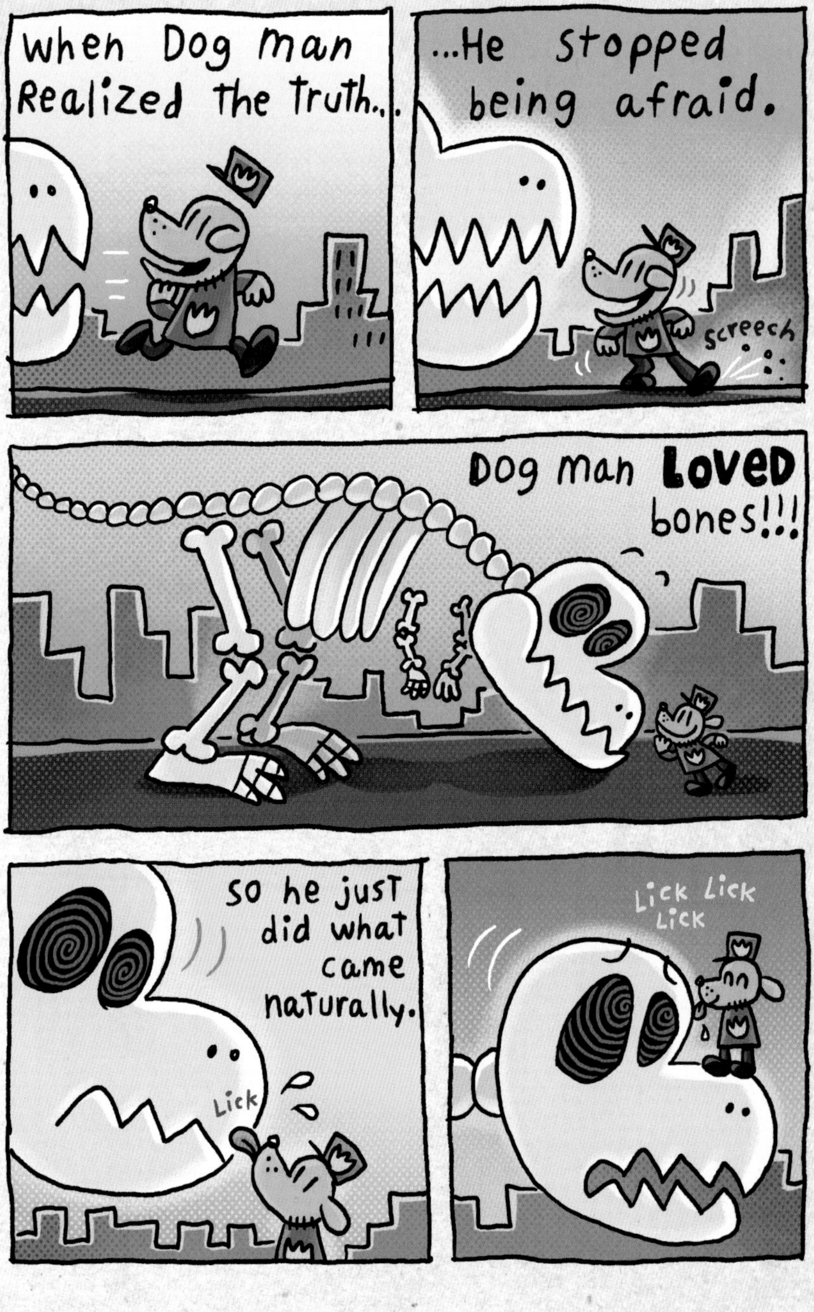

When Dog Man Realized the Truth...
...He stopped being afraid.
Screech
Dog Man LOVED bones!!!
So he just did what came naturally.
Lick
Lick Lick Lick

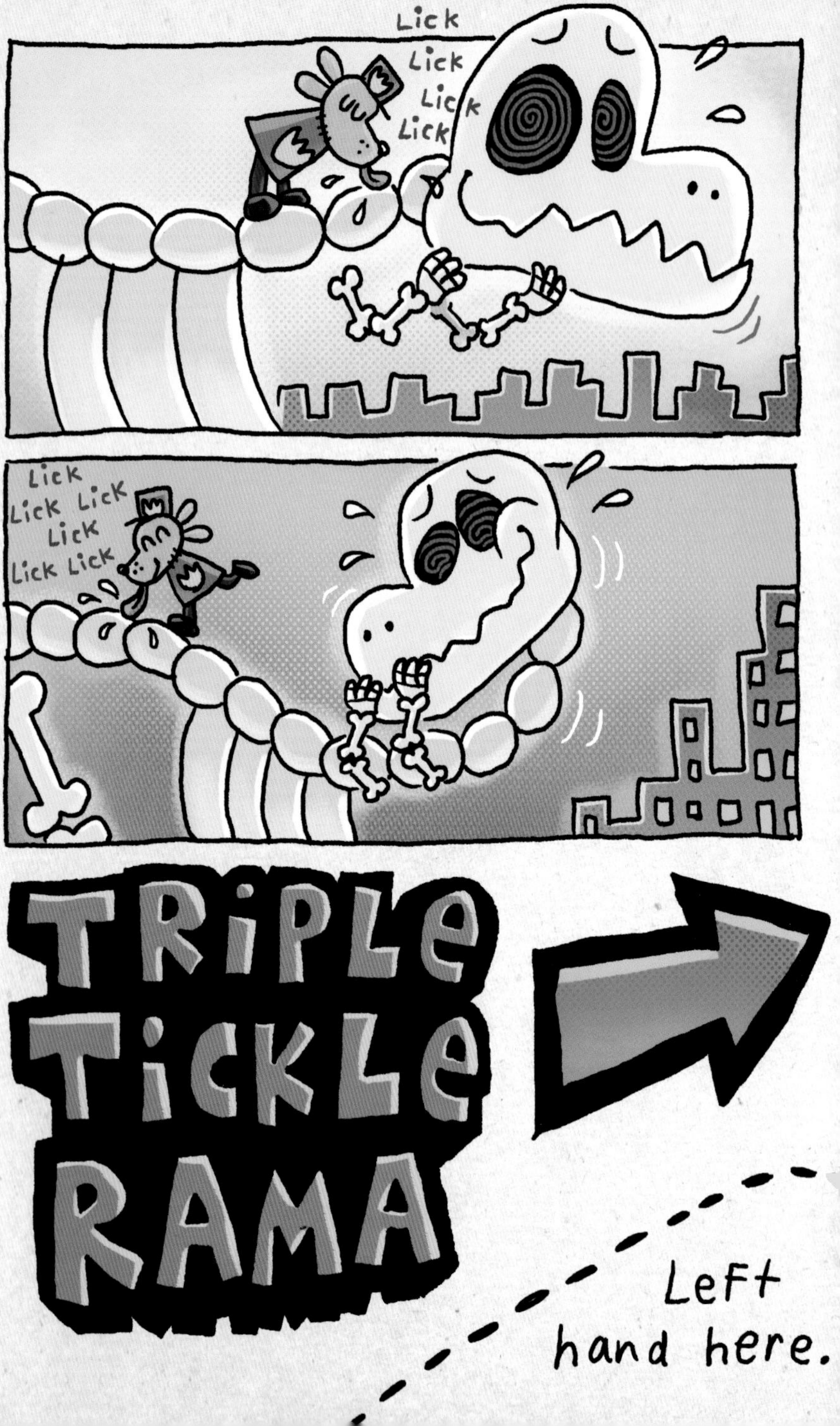

Lick
Lick
Lick
Lick
Lick
Lick Lick
Lick
Lick Lick
TRIPLE TICKLE RAMA
Left hand here.

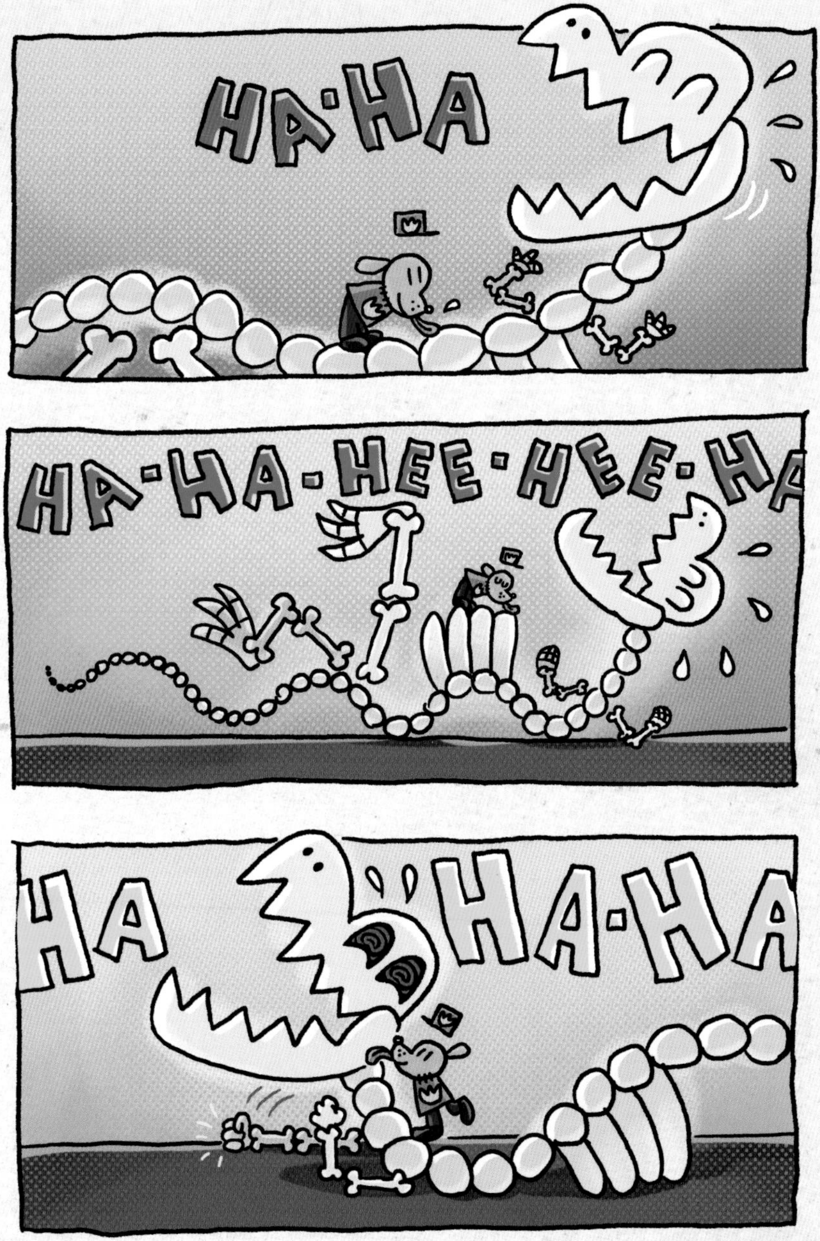
HA-HA
HA-HA-HEE-HEE-HA
HA-HA-HA-HA

Right Thumb here.

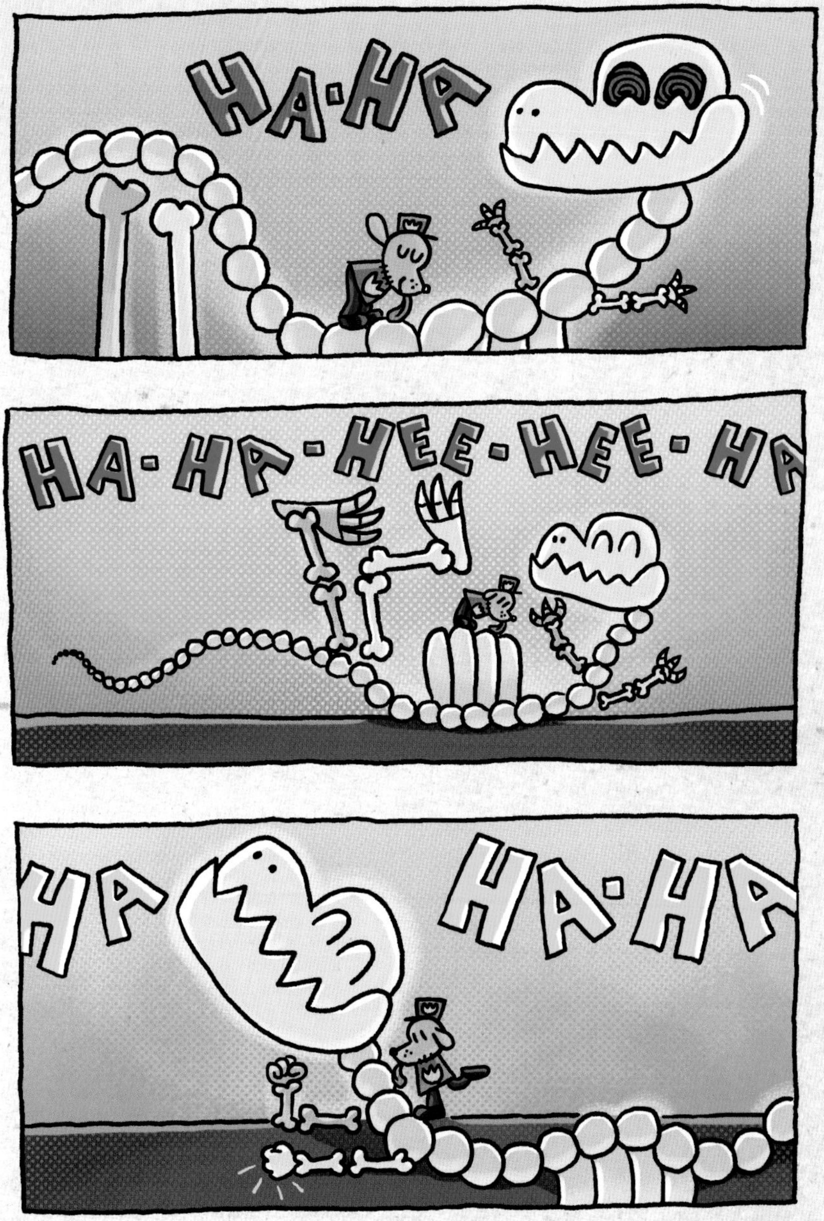
HA-HA
HA-HA-HEE-HEE-HA
HA
HA-HA

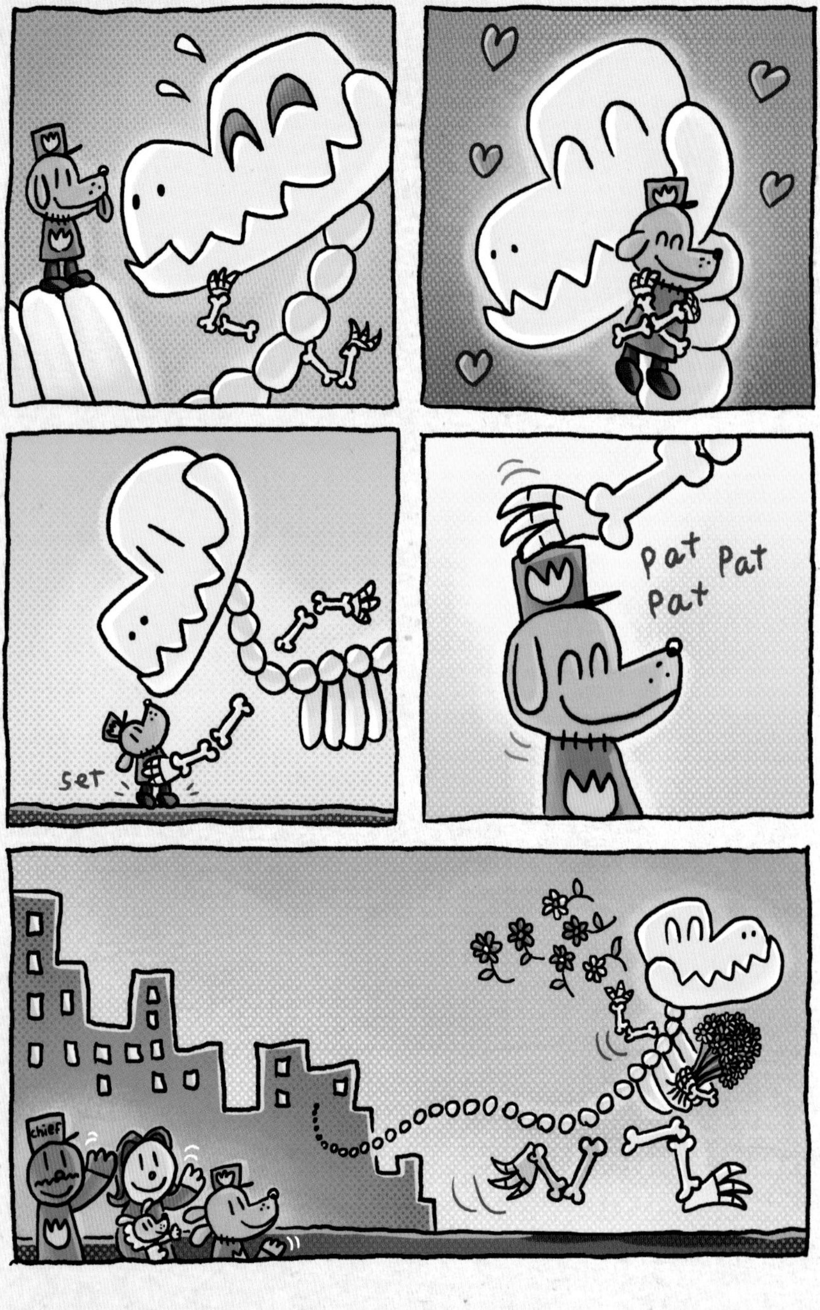
set
Pat
Pat
Pat
chief

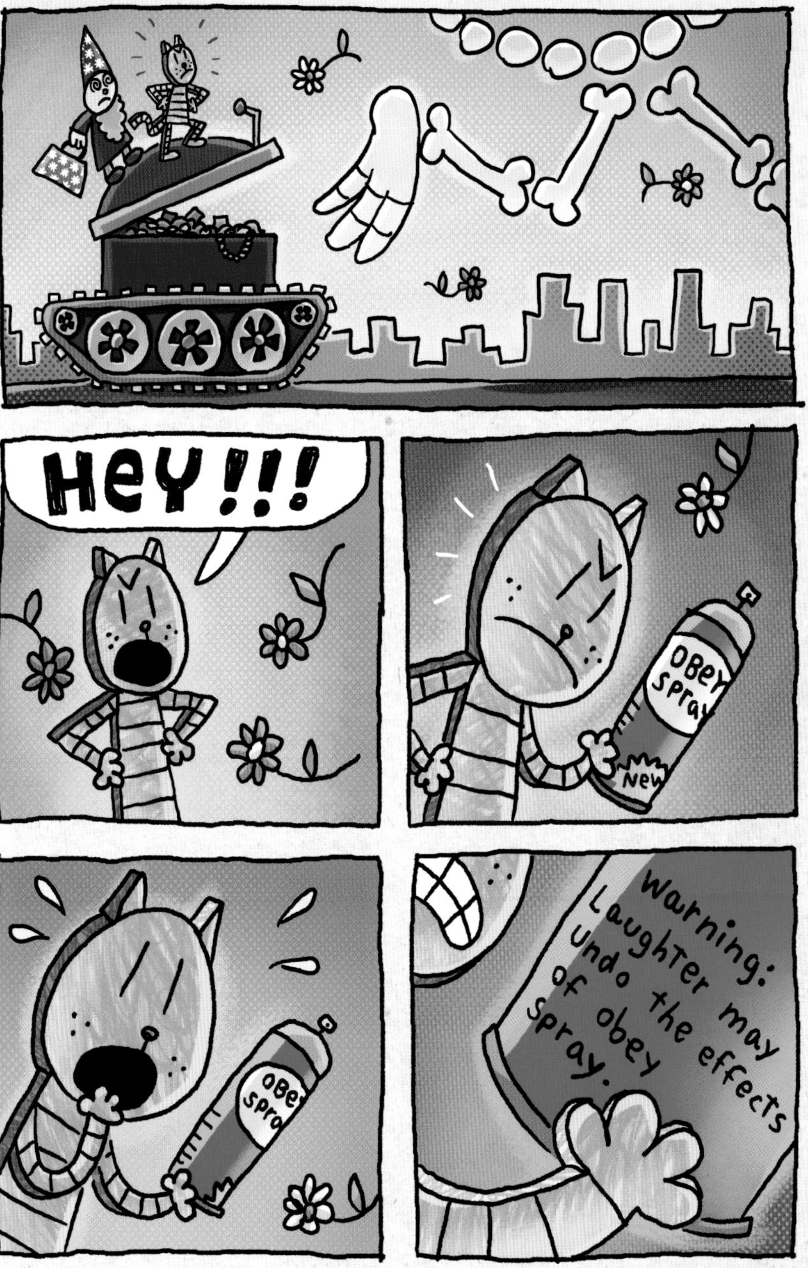
HEY!!!
OBEY SPRAY
NEW
OBEY SPRA
Warning: Laughter may undo the effects of obey spray.

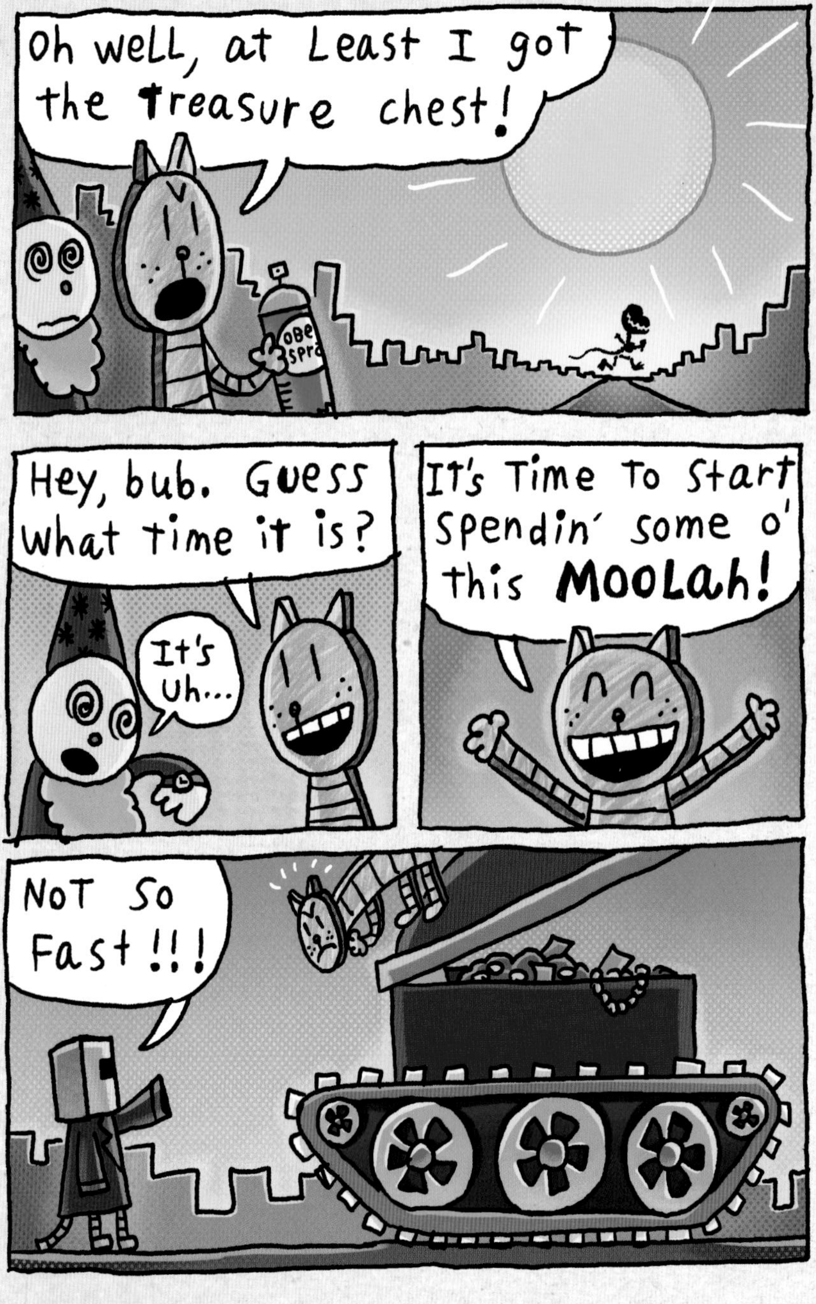

Oh well, at Least I got the treasure chest!
OBE SPR
Hey, bub. Guess what time it is?
It's uh...
It's Time To Start spendin' some o' this MOOLah!
NoT So Fast!!!

Chapter 9
The Mysterious Stranger Returns

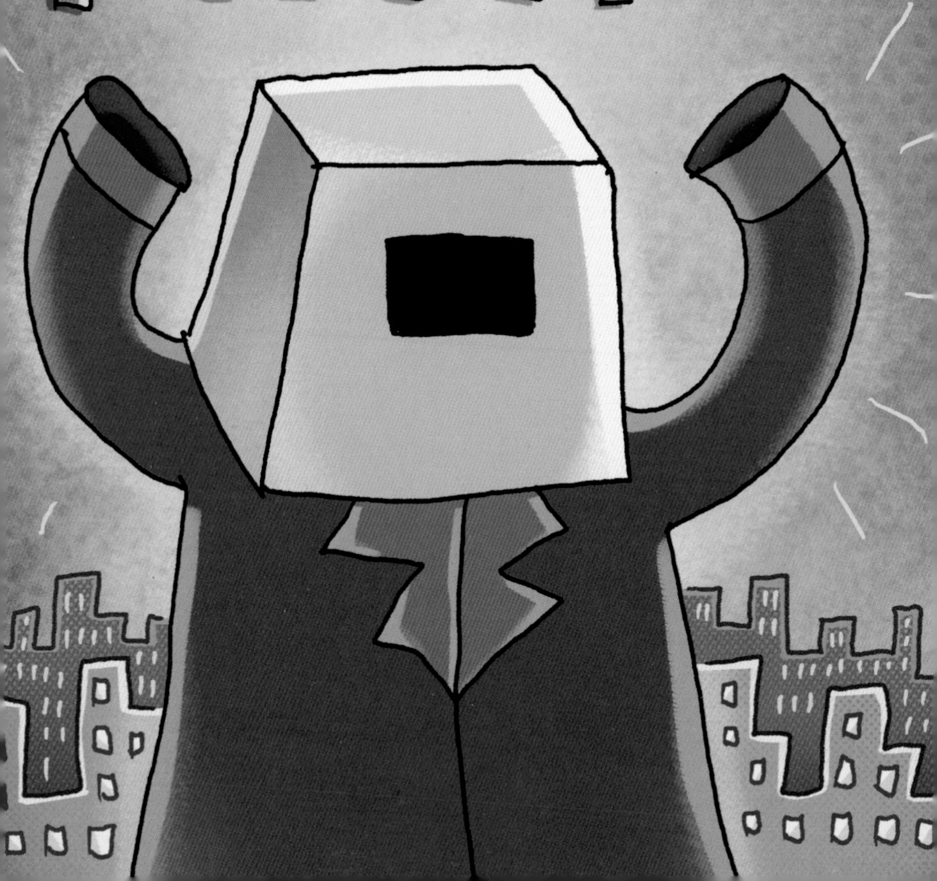

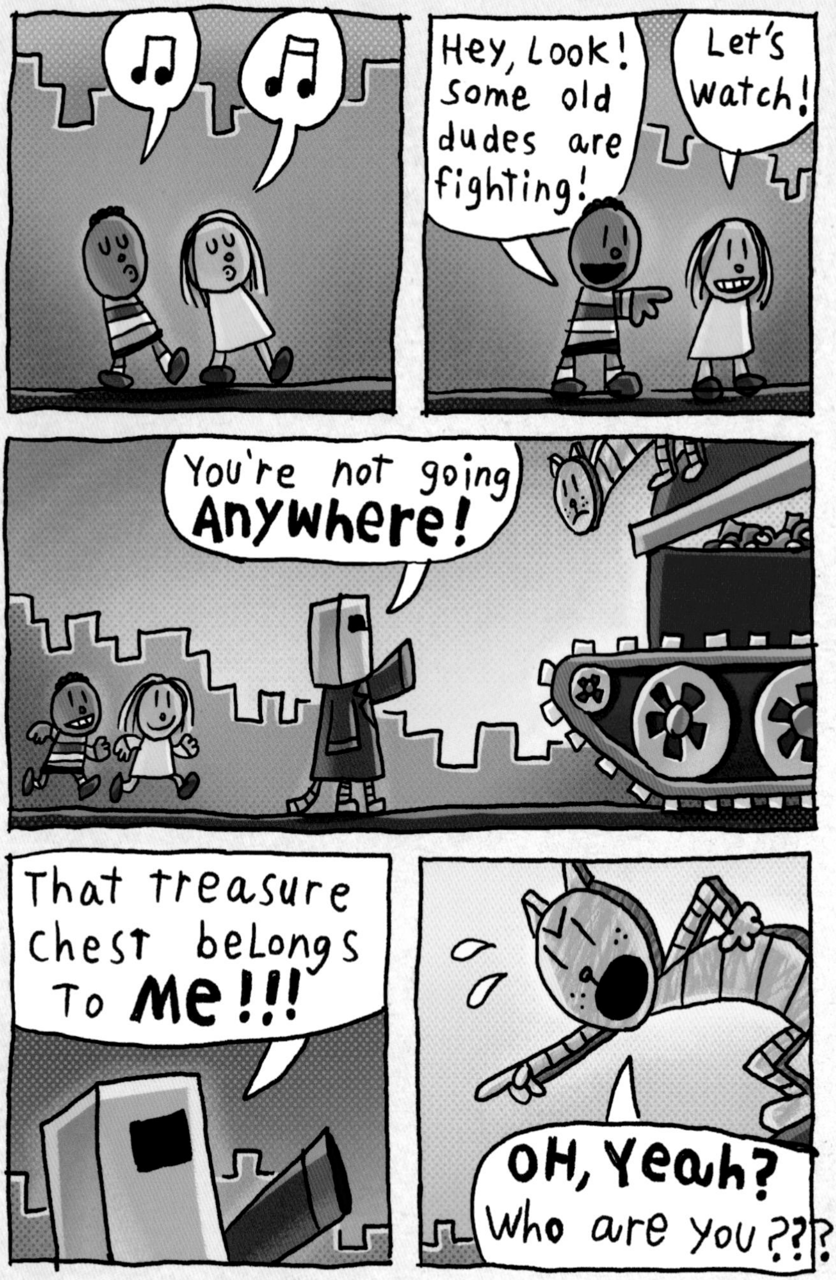

Hey, Look! Some old dudes are fighting!
Let's watch!
You're not going Anywhere!
That treasure chest belongs To Me!!!
OH, Yeah? Who are you???

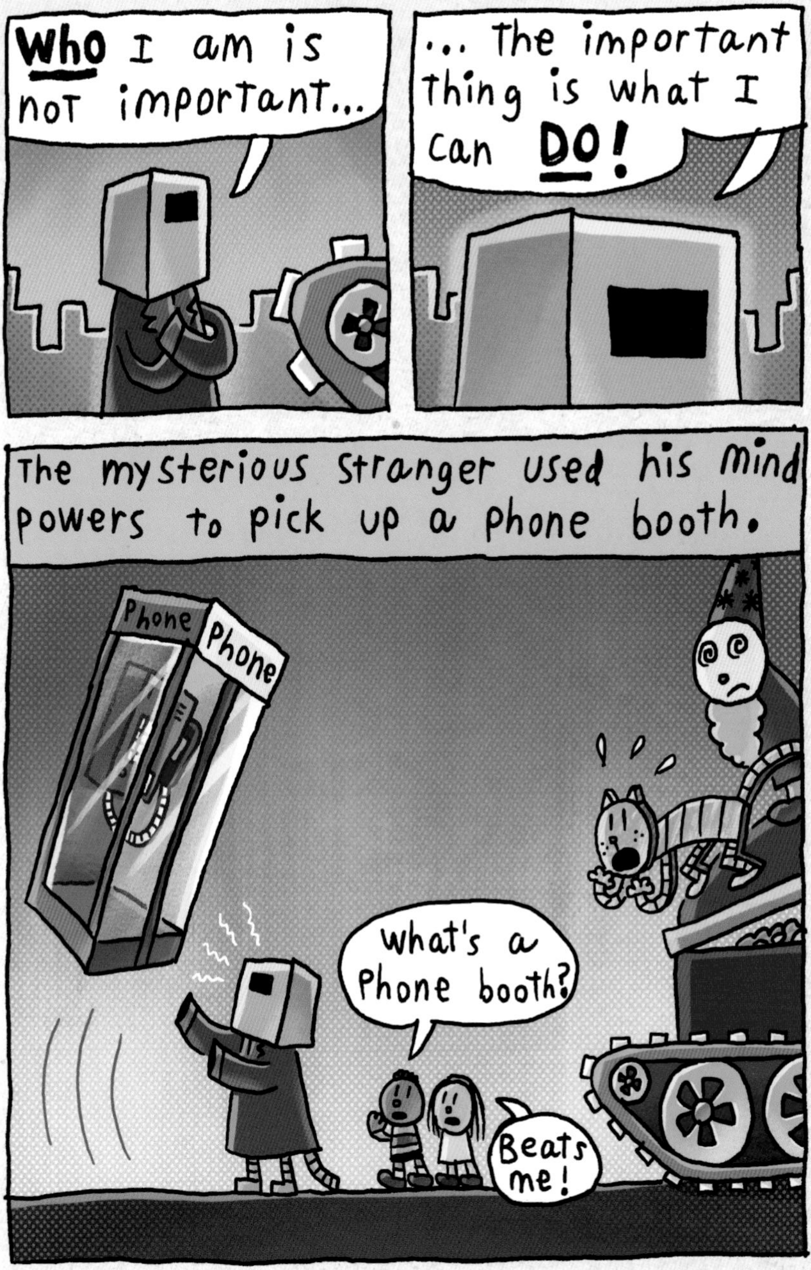
WHO I am is not important...
... The important thing is what I can DO!
The mysterious stranger used his mind powers to pick up a phone booth.
Phone
Phone
What's a phone booth?
Beats me!

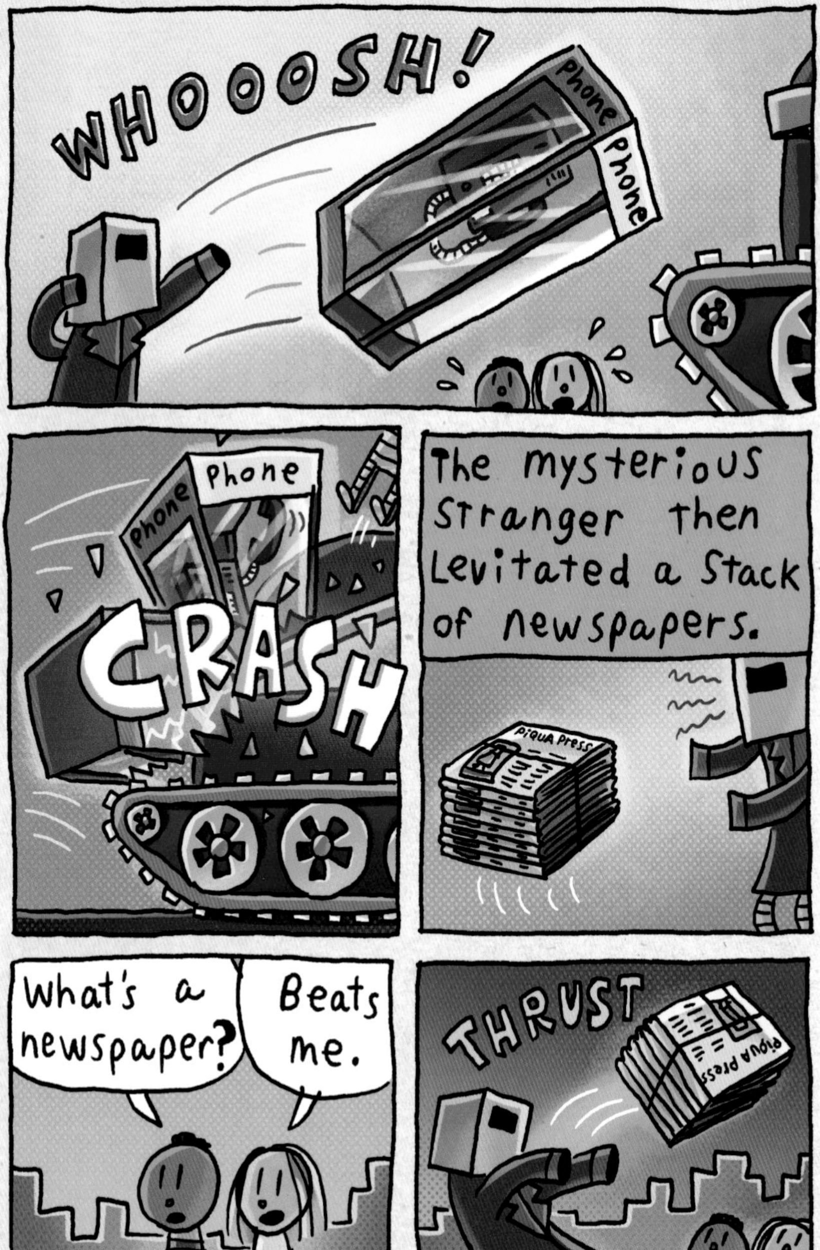
WHOOOSH!
Phone
Phone
Phone
Phone
CRASH
The mysterious Stranger then Levitated a Stack of newspapers.
PiQUA Press
What's a newspaper?
Beats me.
THRUST
PiQUA Press

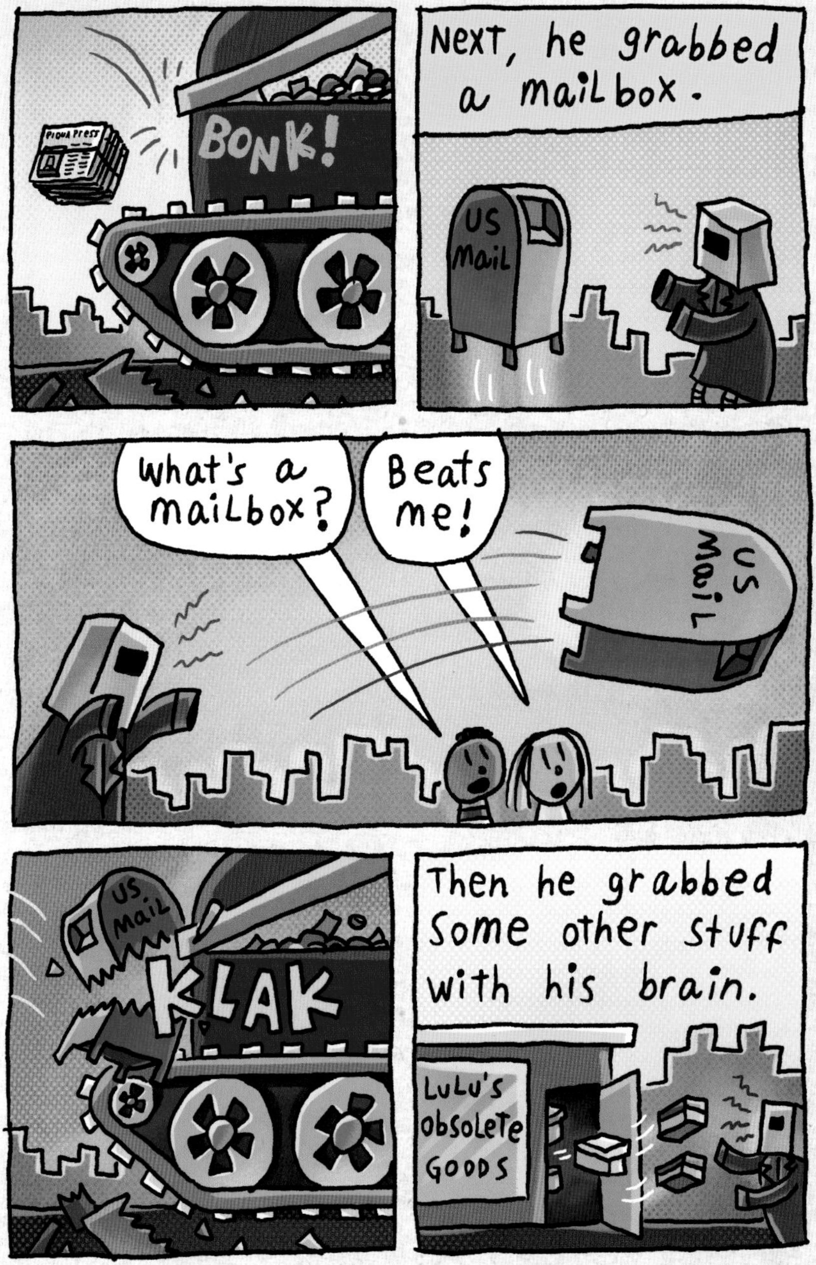

BONK!
PIQUA PRESS
NEXT, he grabbed a mailbox.
US Mail
What's a mailbox?
Beats me!
US Mail
US Mail
KLAK
Then he grabbed some other stuff with his brain.
LuLu's Obsolete Goods

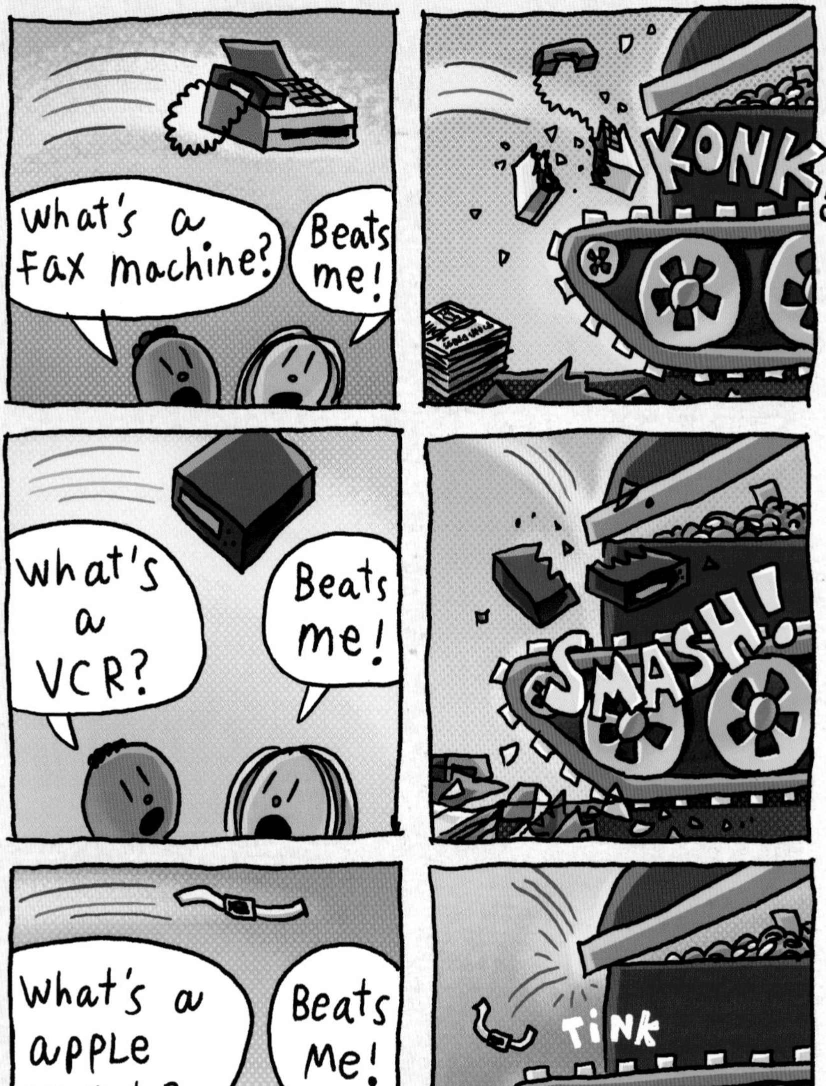
What's a fax machine?
Beats me!
KONK!
What's a VCR?
Beats me!
SMASH!
What's a apple watch?
Beats me!
TINK

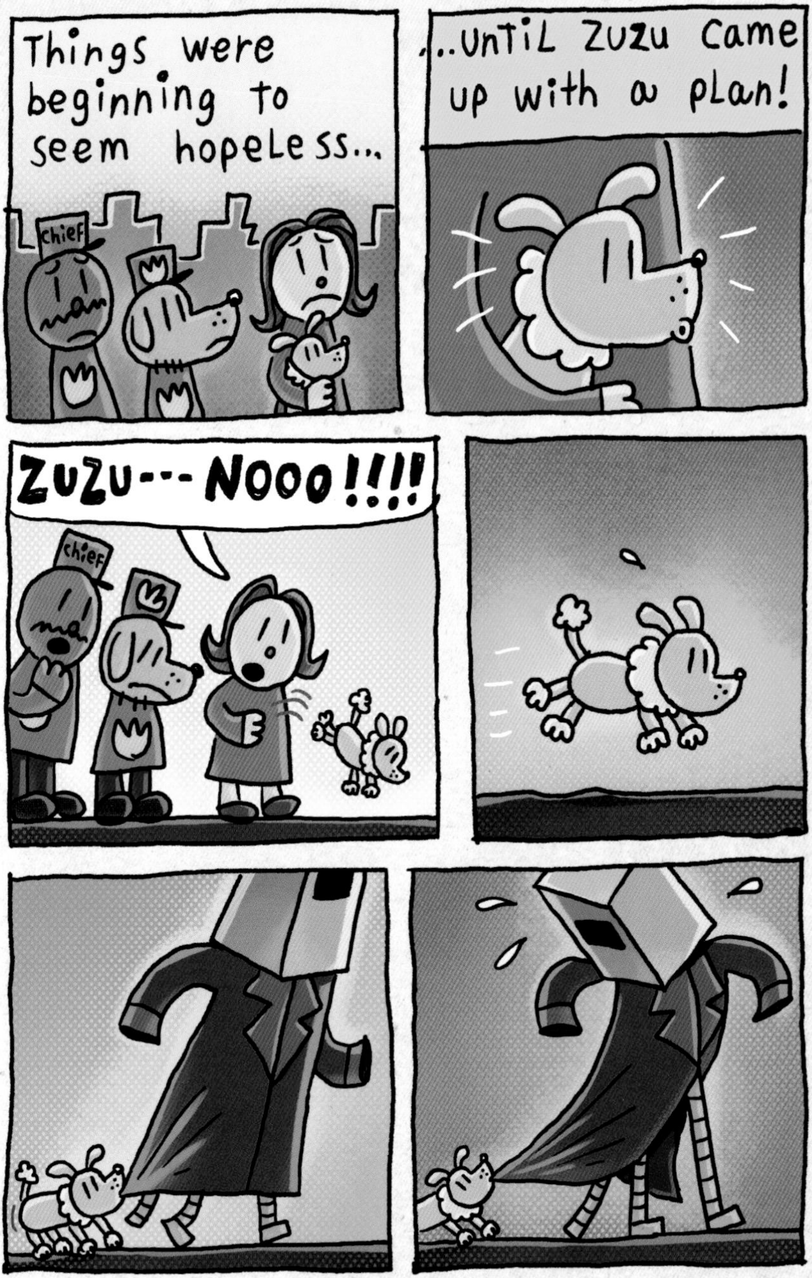
Things were beginning to seem hopeless...
chief
...UNTIL ZUZU came up with a plan!
ZUZU---NOOO!!!!
chief

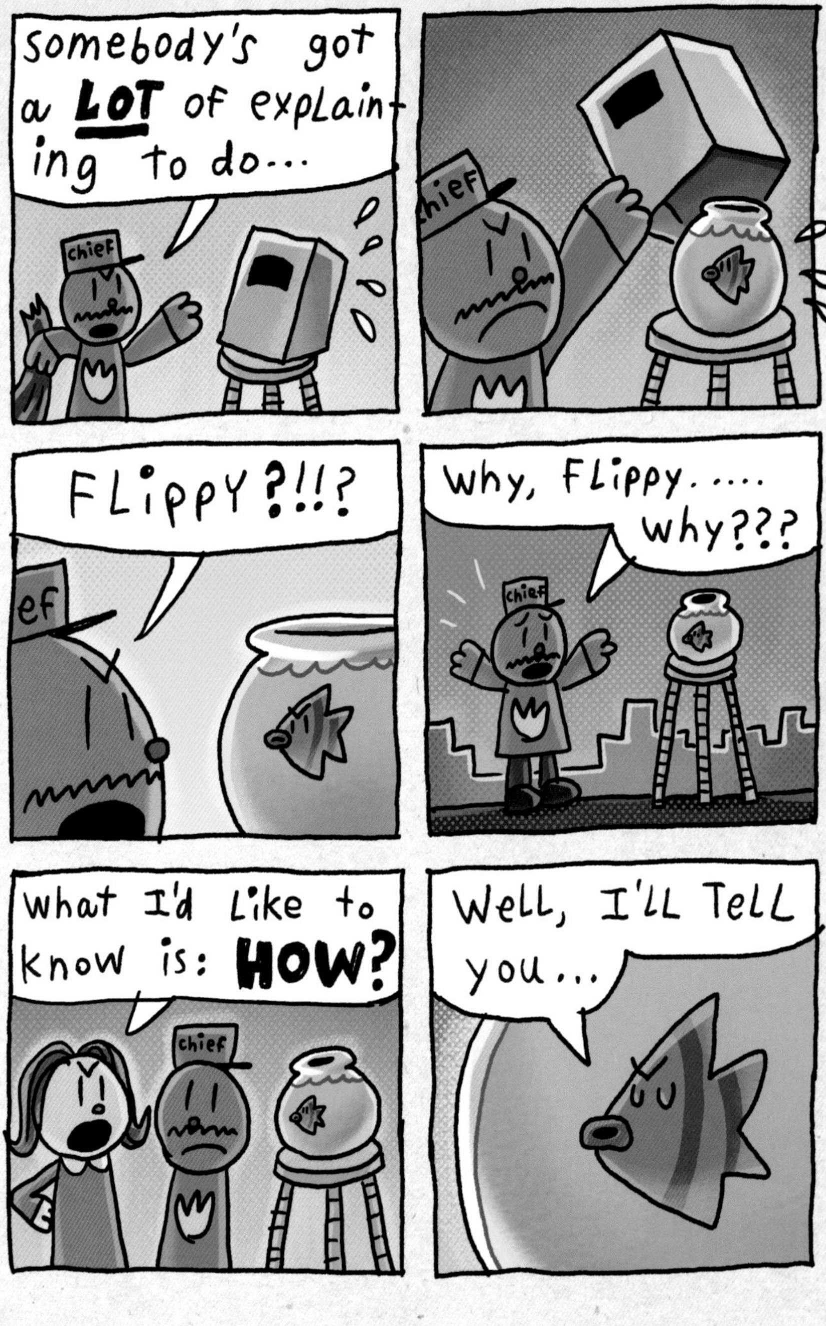
somebody's got a LOT of explaining to do...
Chief
hief
FLIPPY?!!?
ef
Why, FLIPPY.... why???
Chief
What I'd Like to know is: HOW?
Chief
WeLL, I'LL TeLL you...

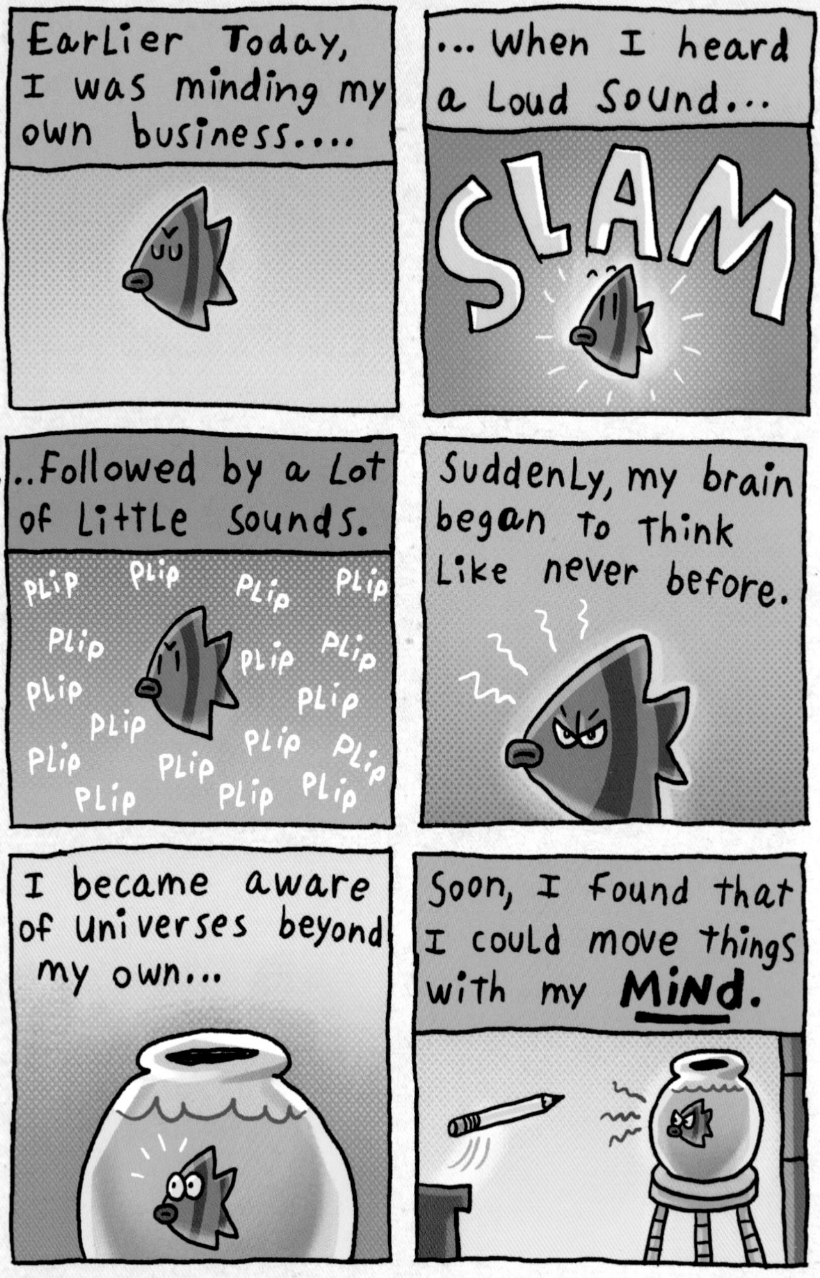
Earlier Today, I was minding my own business....
... When I heard a Loud Sound...
SLAM
...Followed by a Lot of Little sounds.
PLiP PLiP PLiP PLiP PLiP PLiP PLiP PLiP PLiP PLiP PLiP PLiP PLiP PLiP PLiP PLiP PLiP
Suddenly, my brain began to Think Like never before.
I became aware of Universes beyond my own...
Soon, I found that I could move things with my MIND.

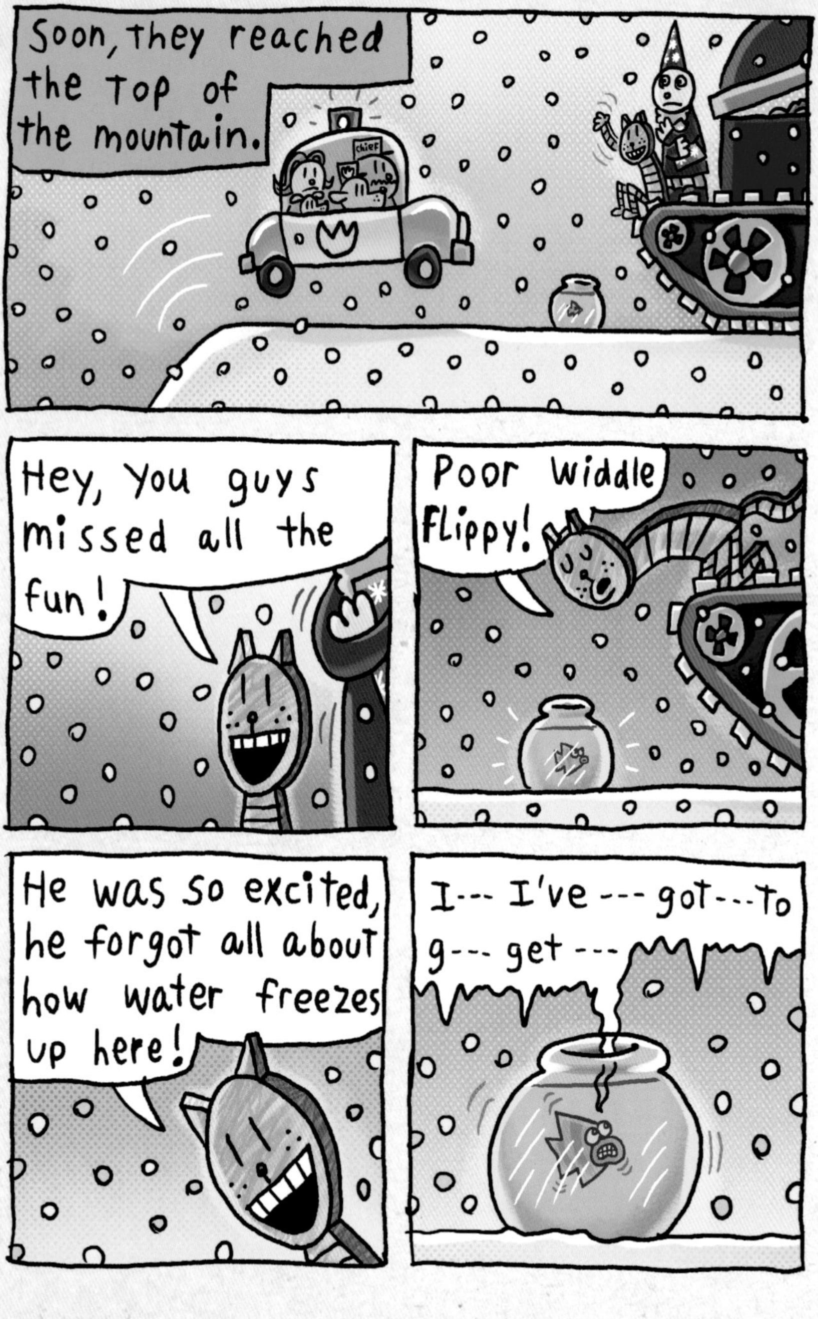
Soon, they reached the top of the mountain.
chief
Hey, You guys missed all the fun!
Poor widdle Flippy!
He was so excited, he forgot all about how water freezes up here!
I--- I've --- got---to g--- get ---

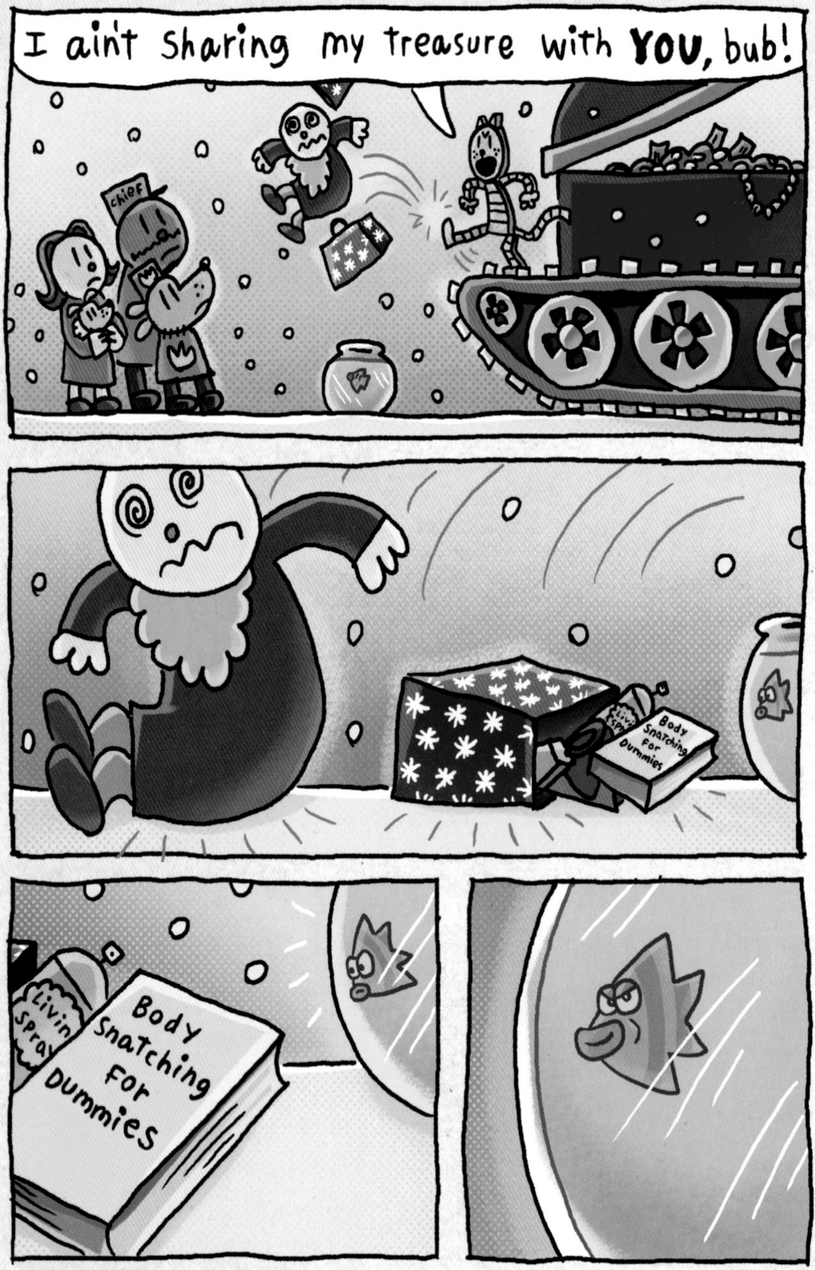
I ain't sharing my treasure with YOU, bub!
CHIEF
Body Snatching For Dummies
Body Snatching For Dummies
Livin
Spray

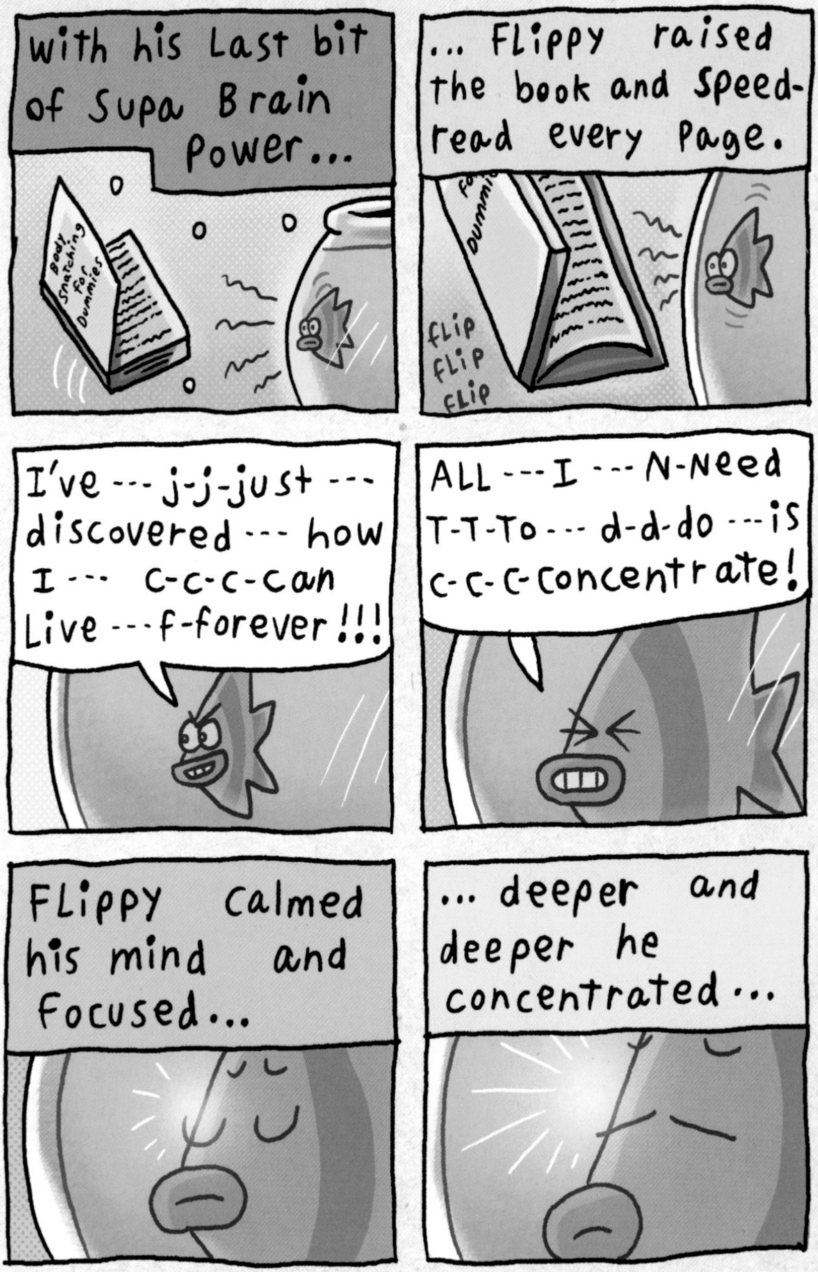
With his Last bit of Supa Brain Power...
Body Snatching for Dummies
... Flippy raised the book and Speed-read every Page.
FLIP FLIP FLIP
I've --- j-j-just --- discovered --- how I --- c-c-c-can Live --- f-forever!!!
ALL --- I --- N-Need T-T-To --- d-d-do --- is c-c-c-concentrate!
Flippy calmed his mind and Focused...
... deeper and deeper he concentrated...

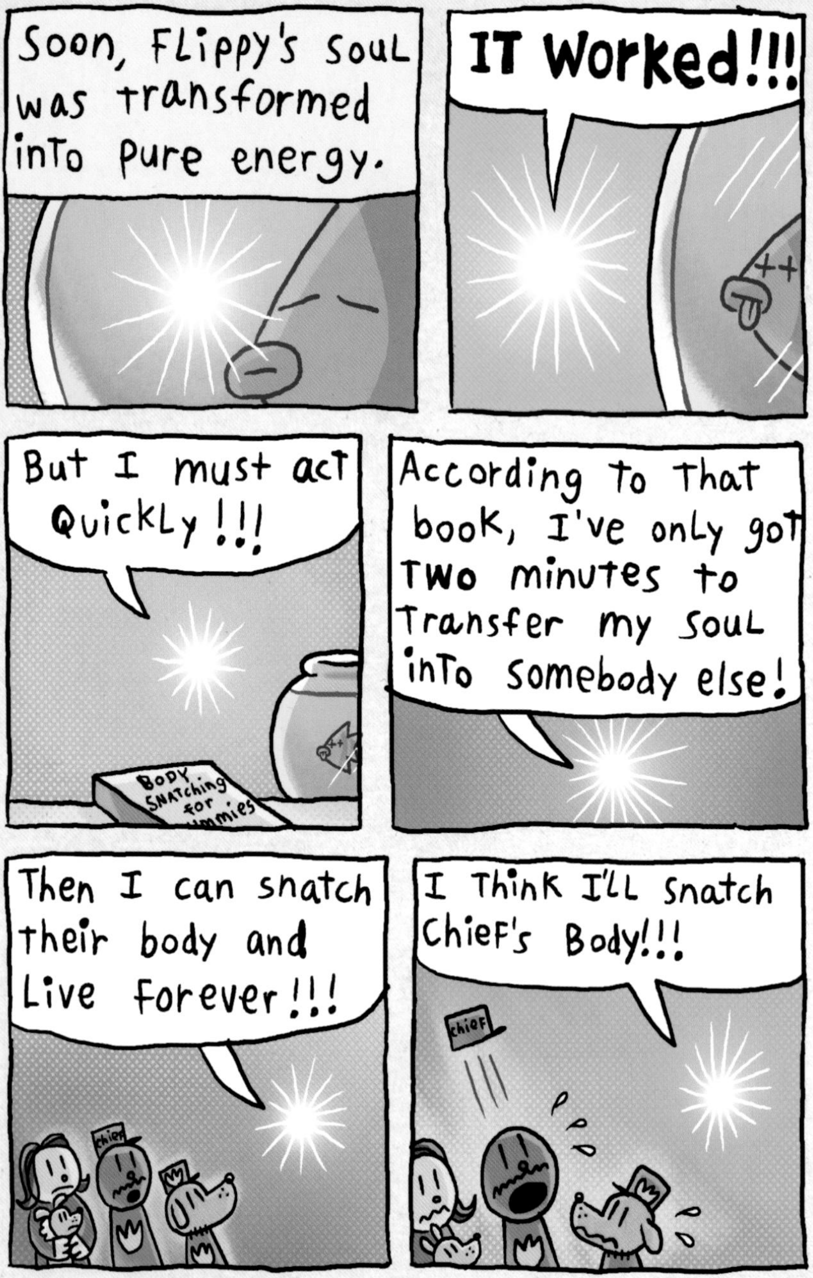

Soon, FLippy's souL was transformed into pure energy.
IT Worked!!!
But I must act QuickLy!!!
BODY SNATCHING FOR DUMMIES
According to That book, I've onLy got TWO minutes to Transfer my souL into somebody else!
Then I can snatch their body and Live forever!!!
I Think I'LL snatch Chief's Body!!!

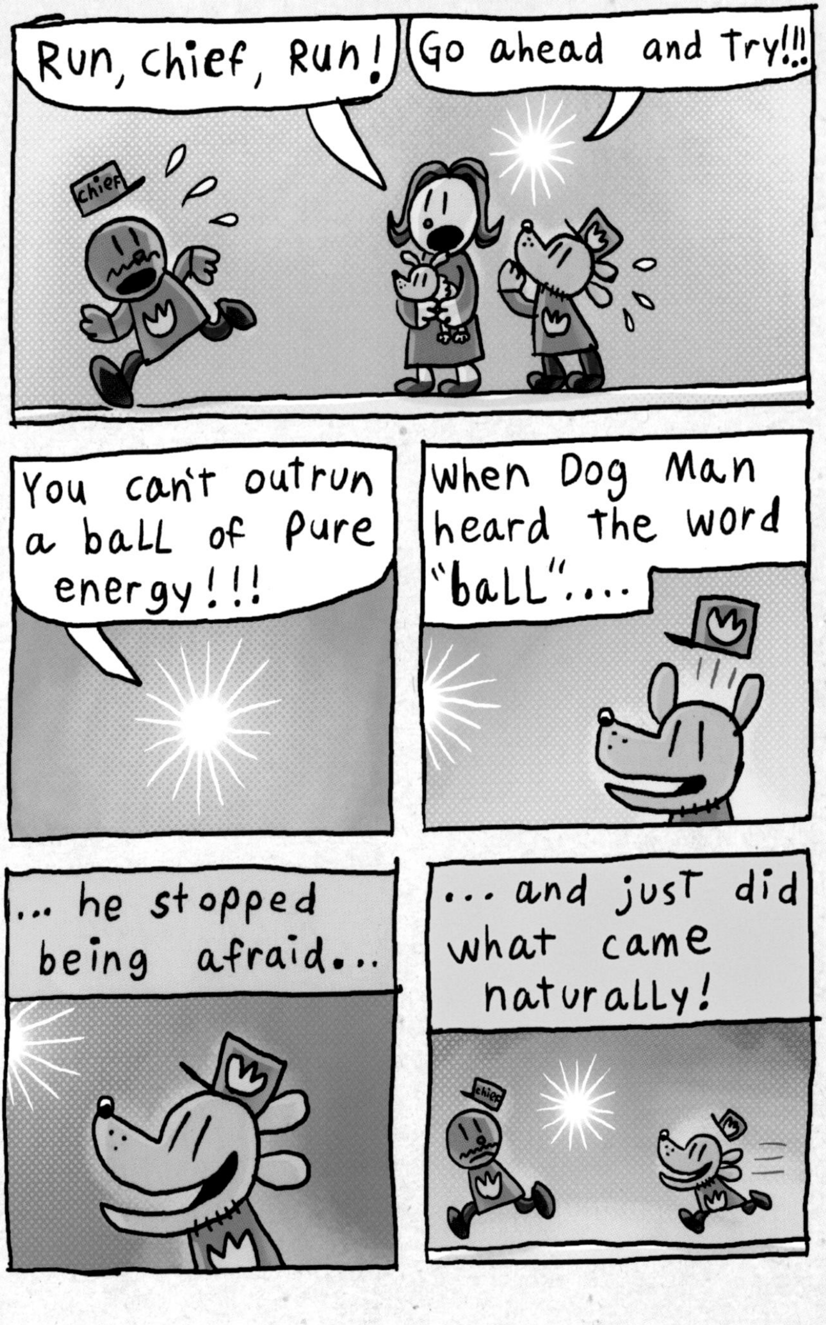

Run, chief, Run!
Go ahead and Try!!!
chief
You can't outrun a ball of Pure energy!!!
When Dog Man heard the word "ball"....
... he stopped being afraid...
... and just did what came naturally!
chief

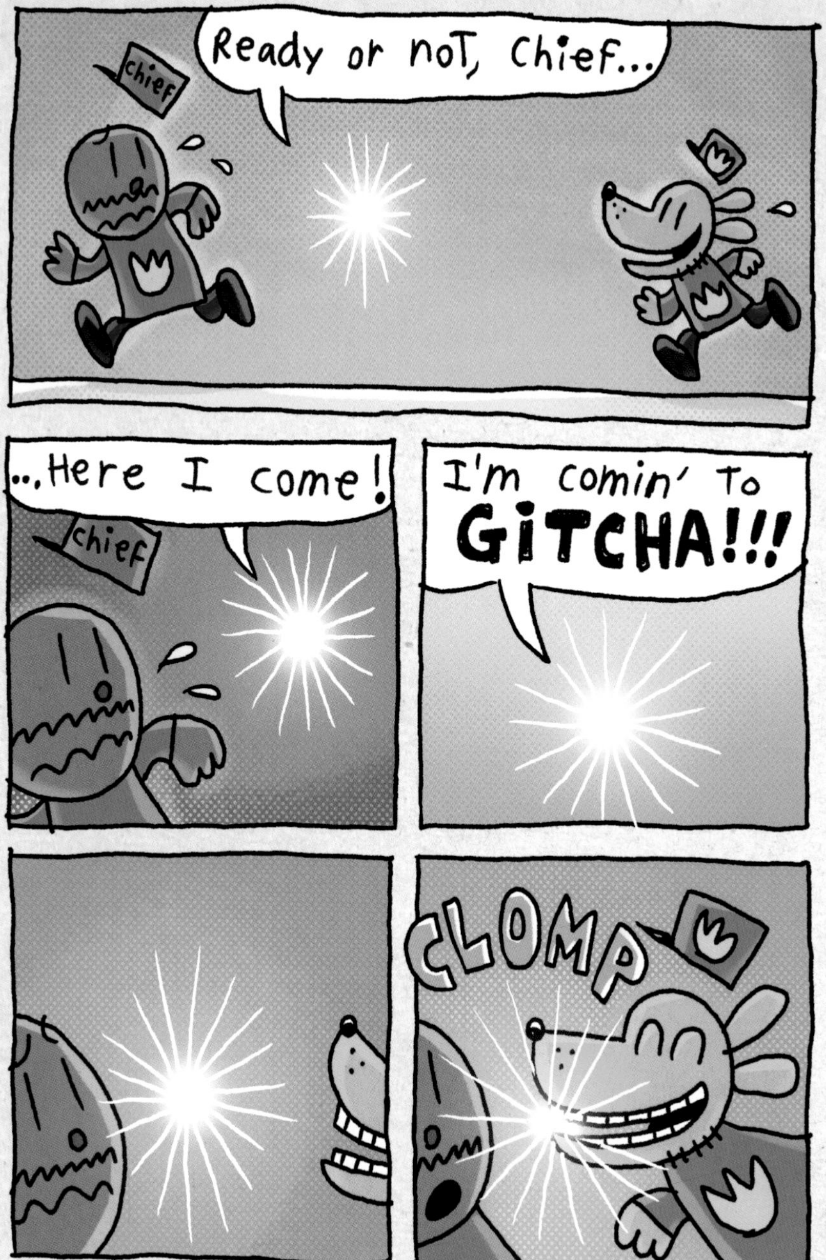

chief
Ready or not, Chief...
...Here I come!
chief
I'm comin' to GiTCHA!!!
CLOMP

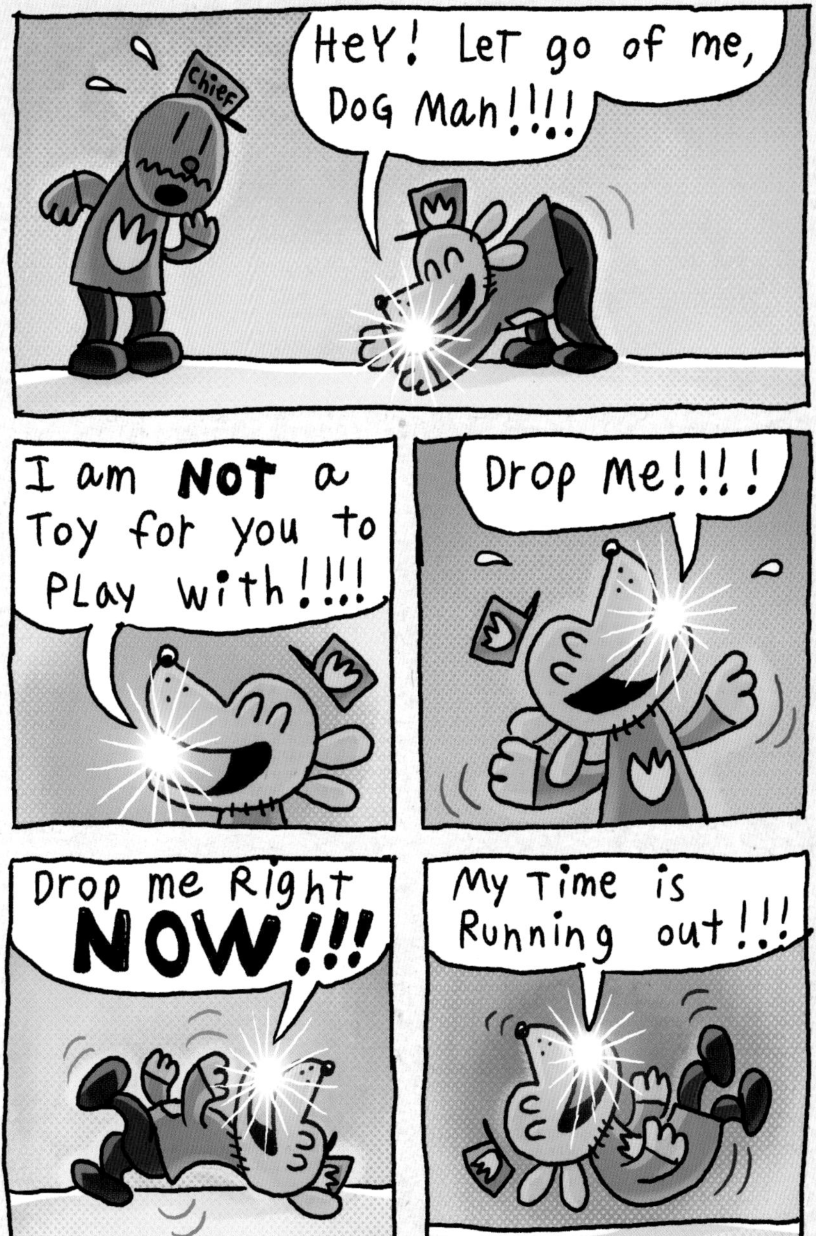
HeY! LeT go of me, DoG Man!!!!
I am NOT a Toy for you to PLay with!!!!
Drop Me!!!!
Drop me Right NOW!!!
My Time is Running out!!!

Chapter 10

An Ice Ending

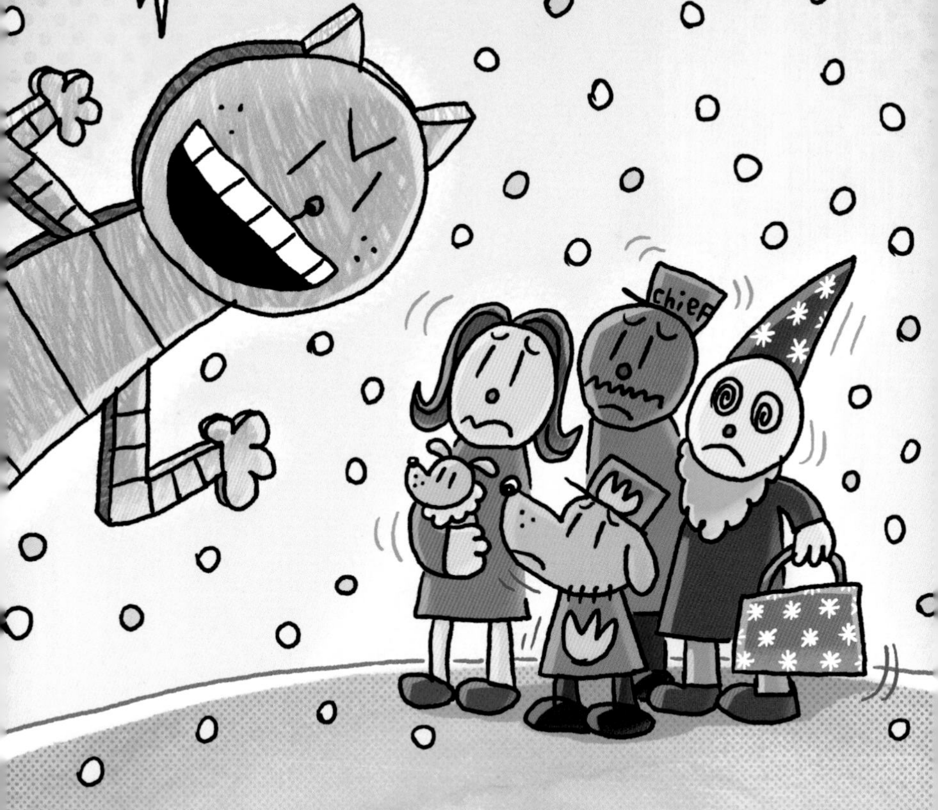
chief

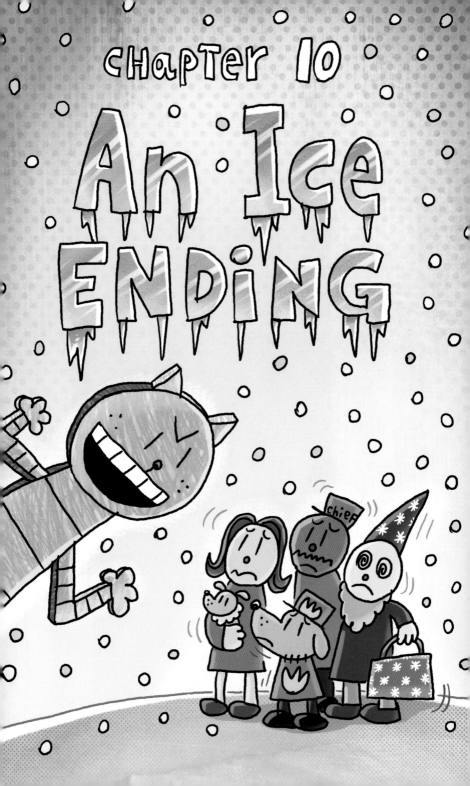

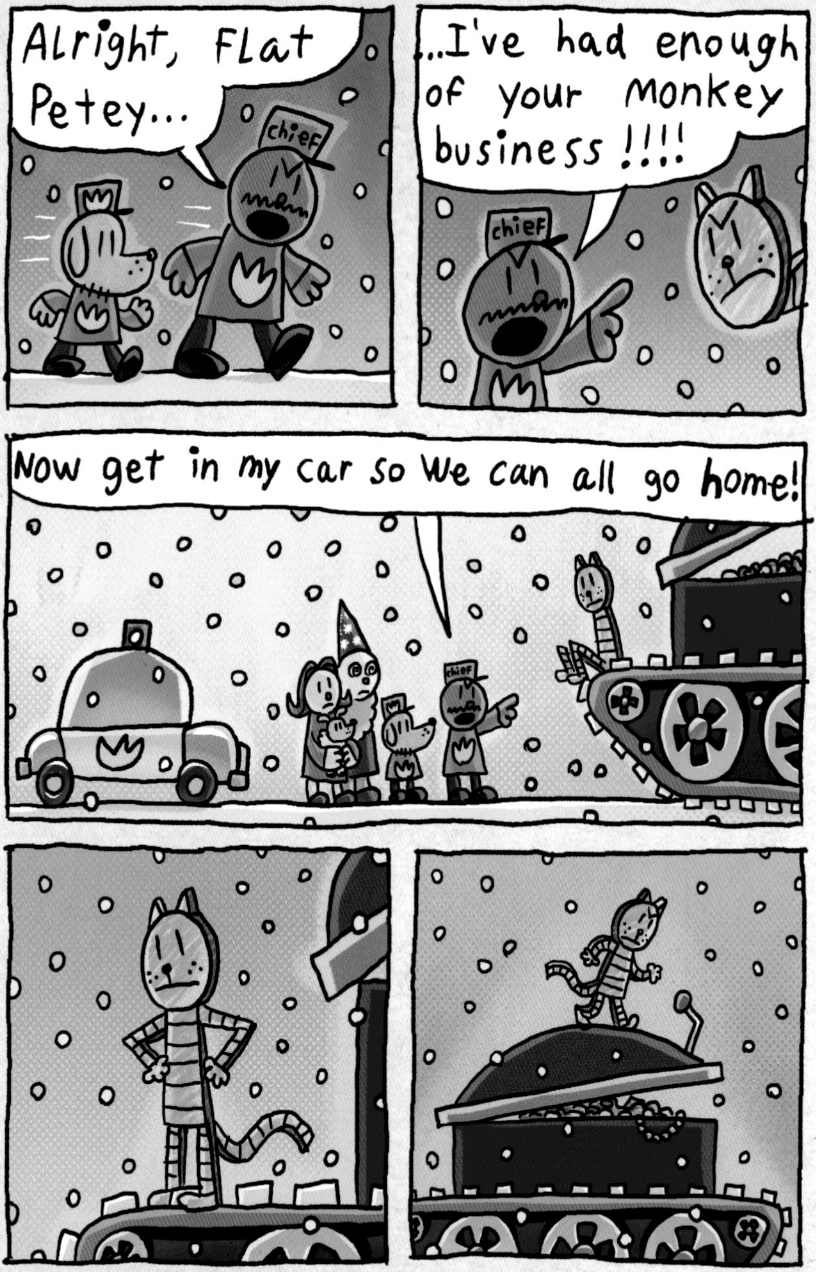
Alright, Flat Petey...
chief
...I've had enough of your monkey business!!!!
chief
Now get in my car so we can all go home!
chief

K·K·KRUNCH!
KUNKAKUNK
Ya mean That car?
chief

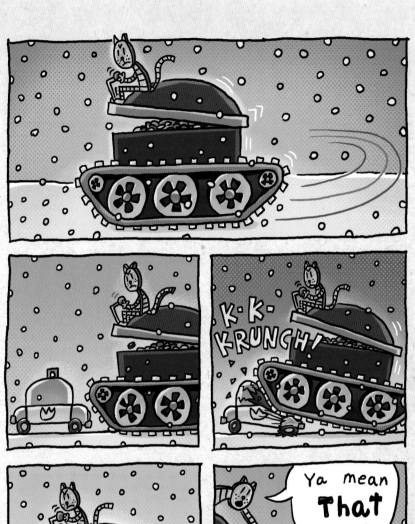

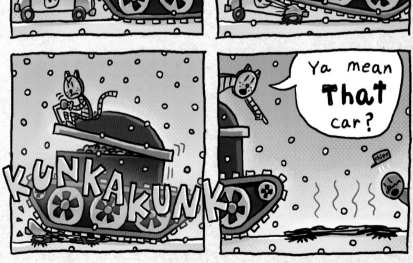

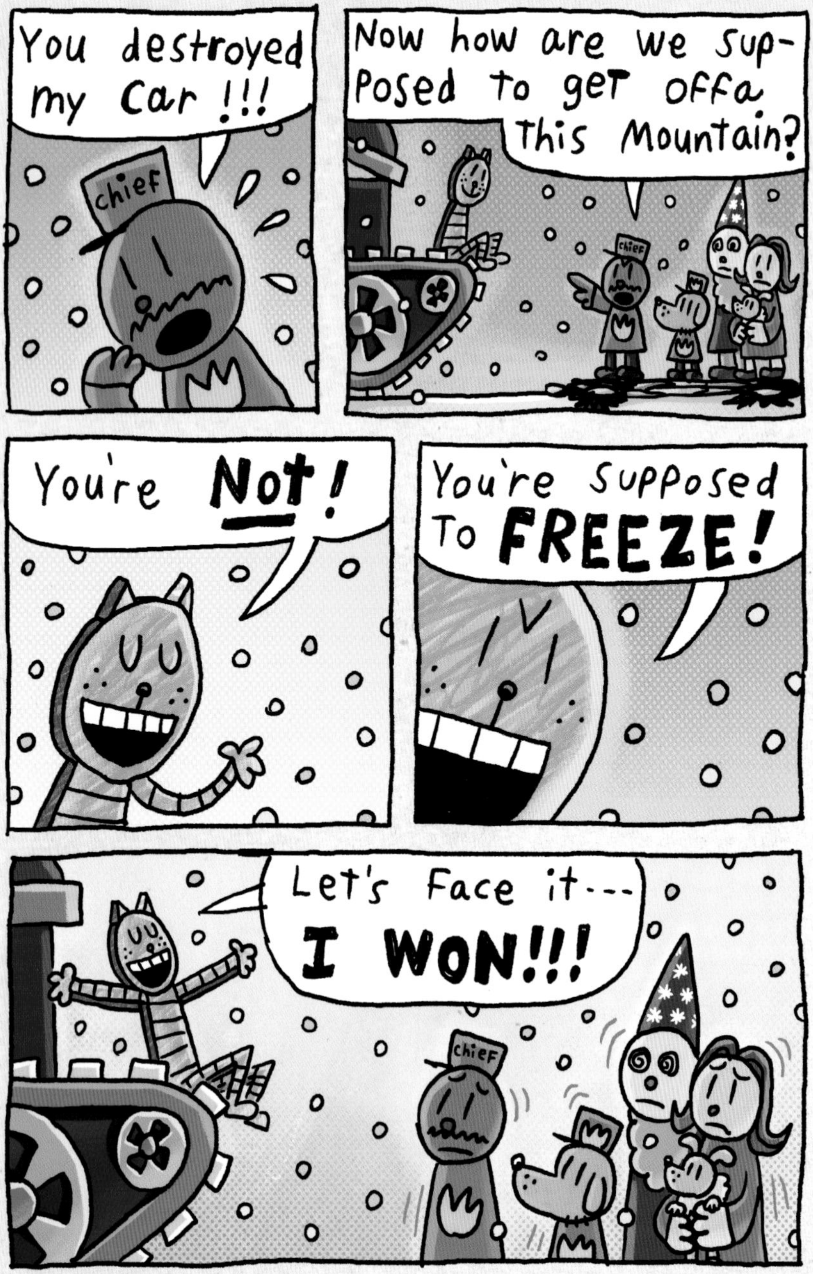
You destroyed my Car !!!
Now how are we sup-posed to get offa This Mountain?
chief
You're Not!
You're supposed To FREEZE!
Let's Face it---
I WON!!!
chief

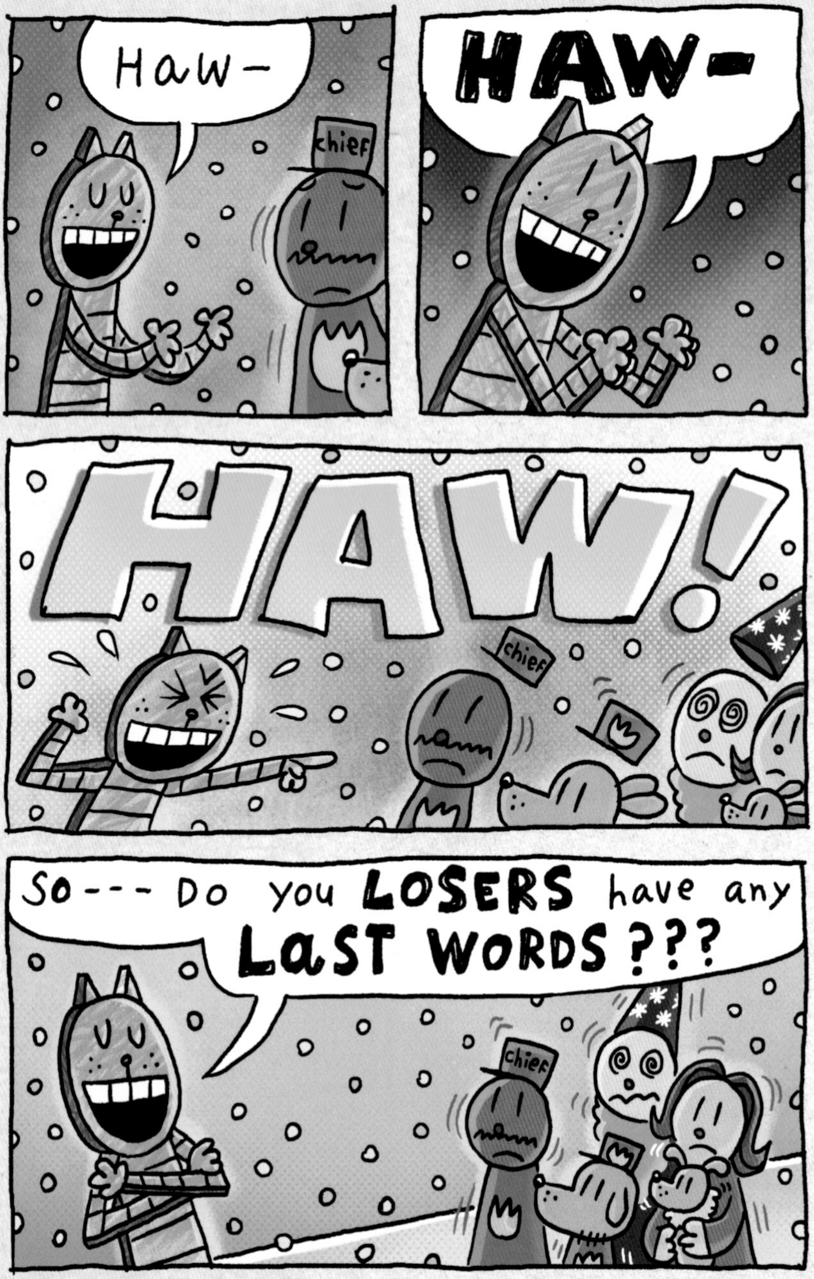
Haw-
chief
HAW-
HAW!
chief
So--- Do you LOSERS have any LAST WORDS???
chief

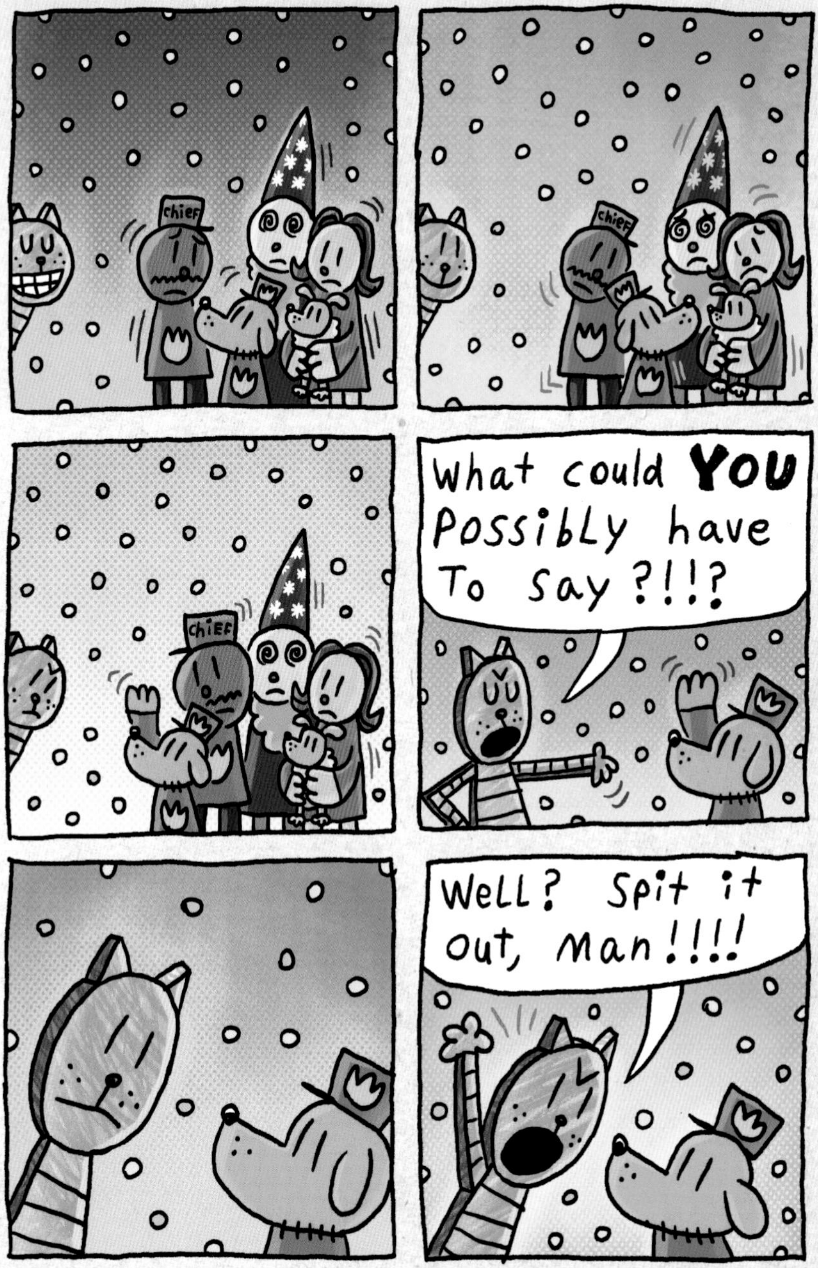
chief
chief
chief
What could YOU possibly have to say?!!?
Well? Spit it out, man!!!!

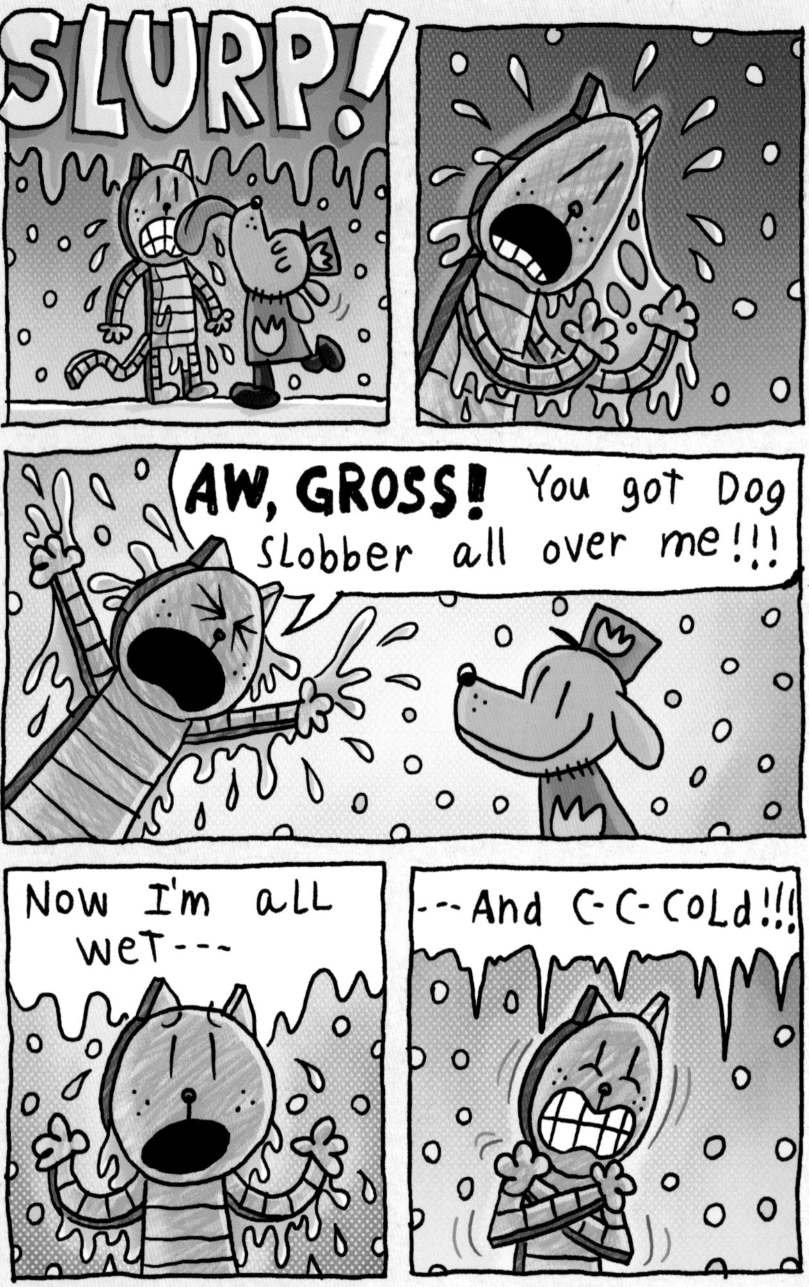
SLURP!
AW, GROSS! You got Dog slobber all over me!!!
Now I'm all wet---
---And C-C-COLd!!!

Flat Petey was RIGHT --- Paper DOESN'T freeze...

...but **WET** Paper freezes very QuickLy!!!

FOOMP

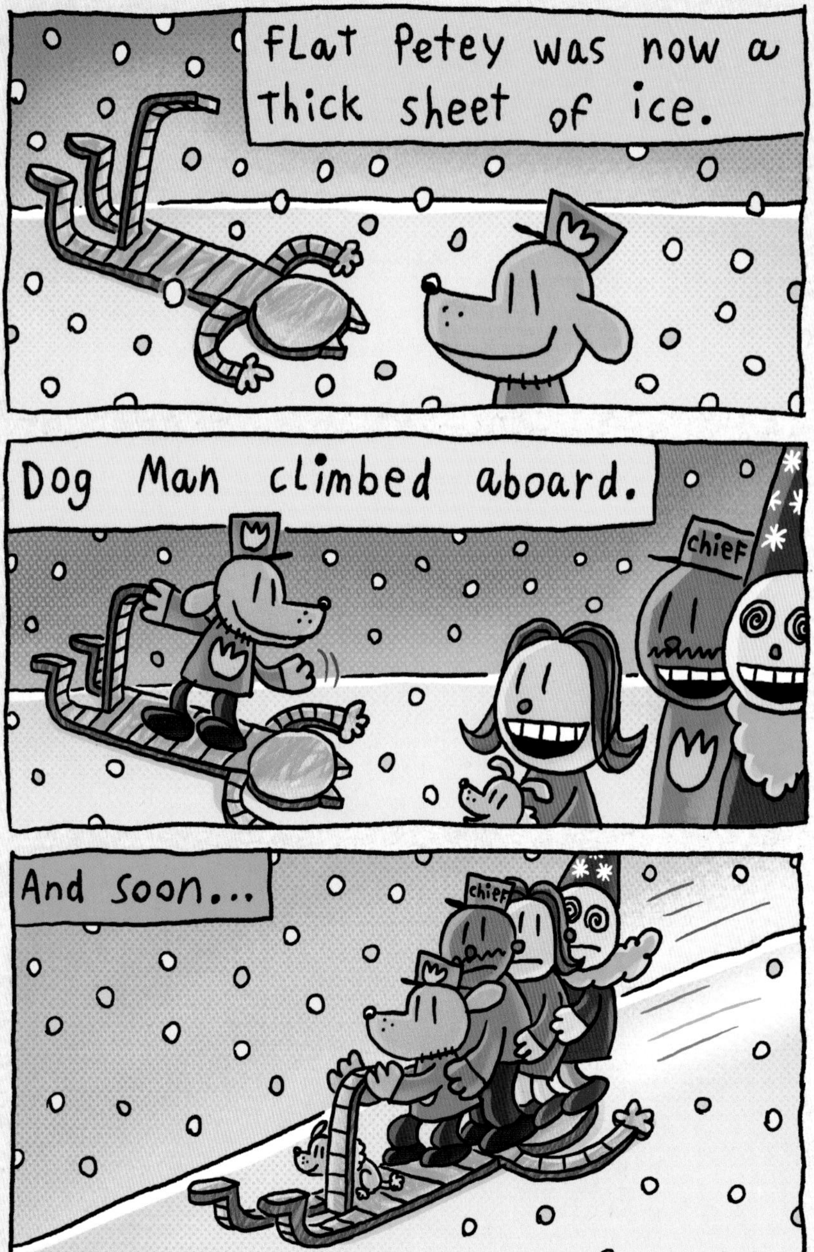
Flat Petey was now a thick sheet of ice.
Dog Man climbed aboard.
chief
And soon...
chief

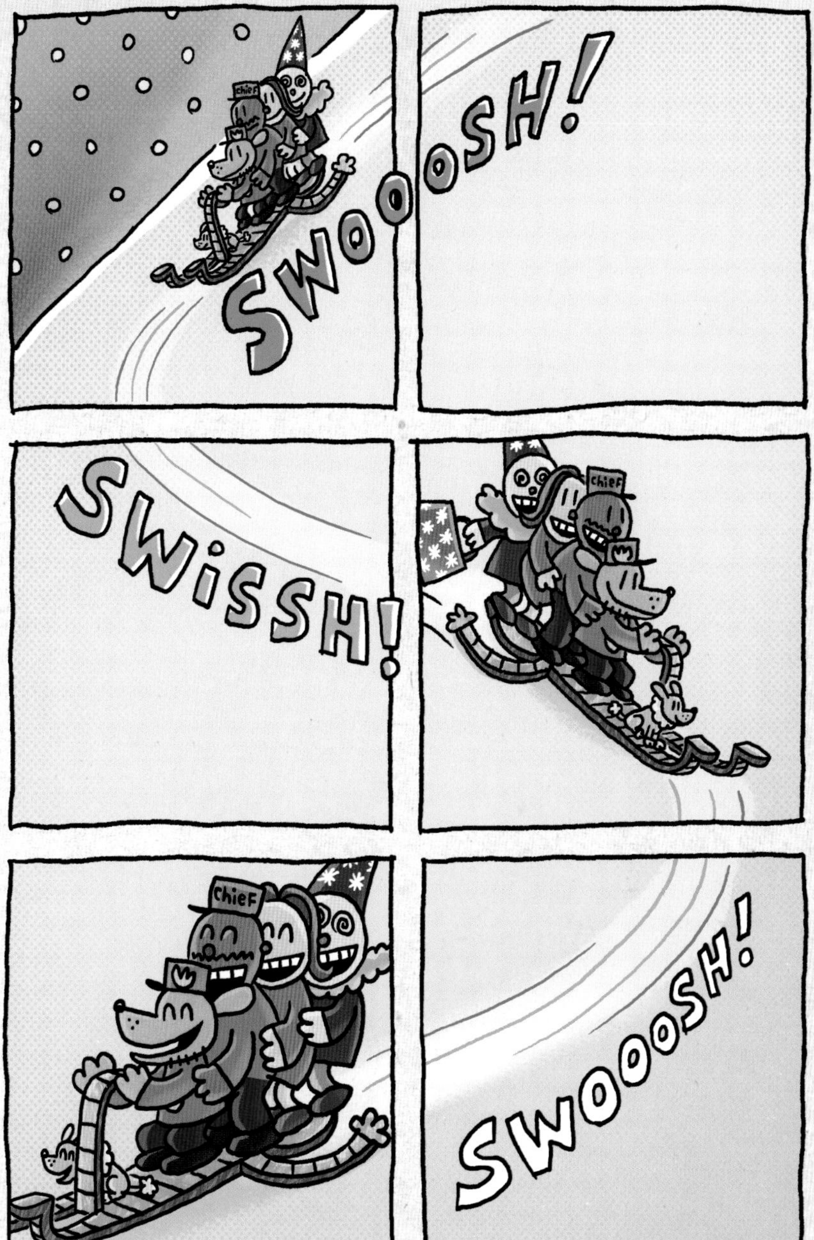
SWOOOSH!
SWiSSH!
SWOOOSH!

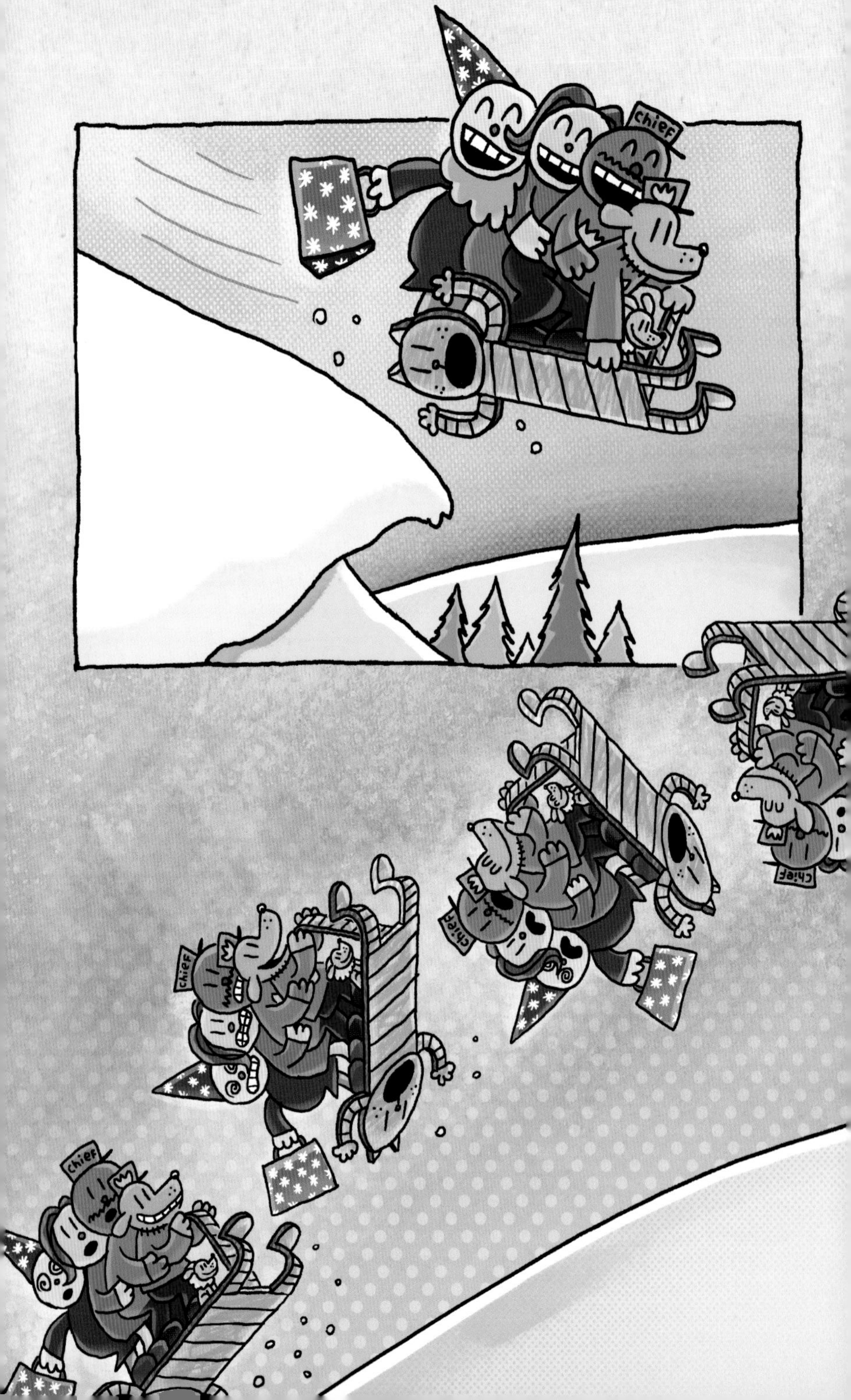
chief
chief
chief
chief
chief

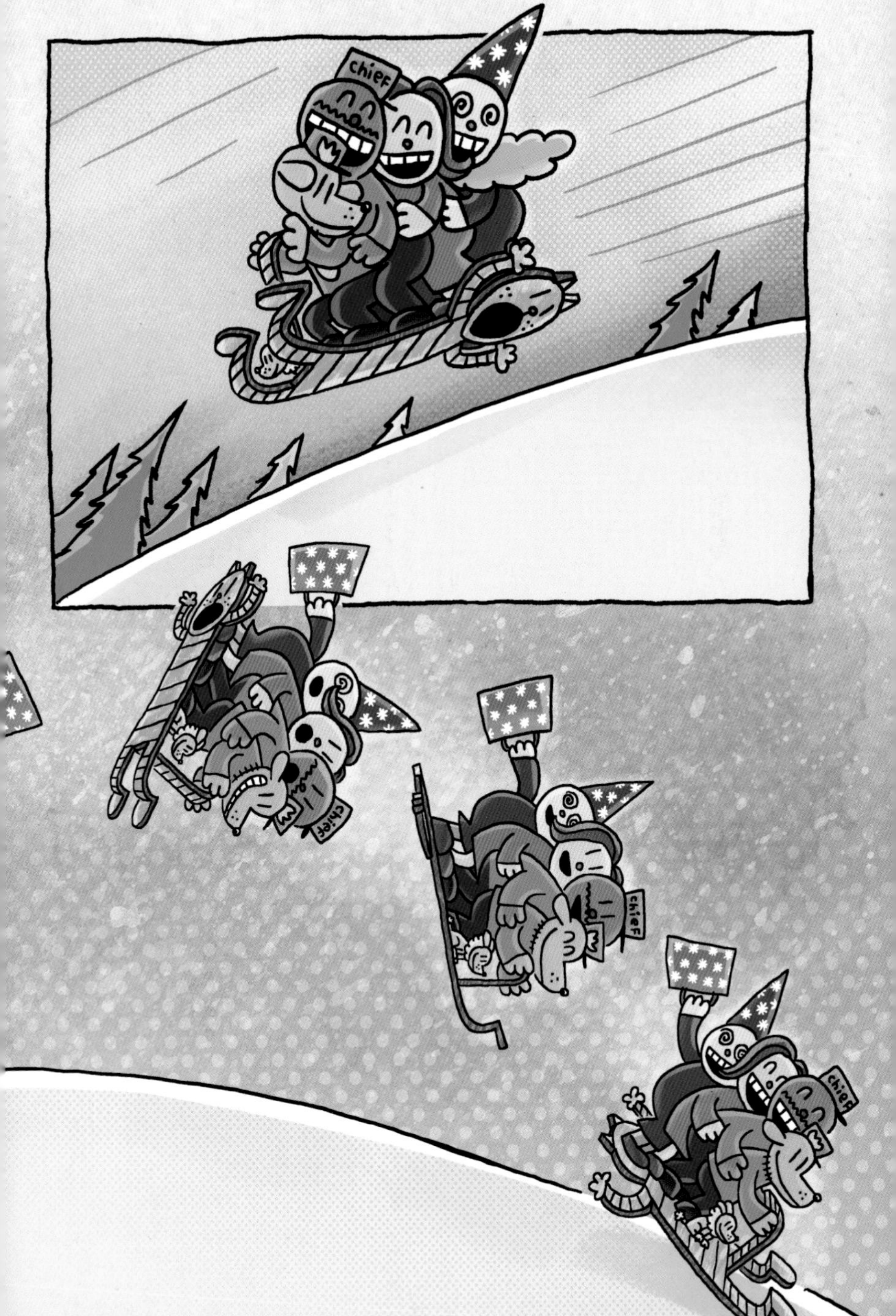
chief
chief
chief
chief

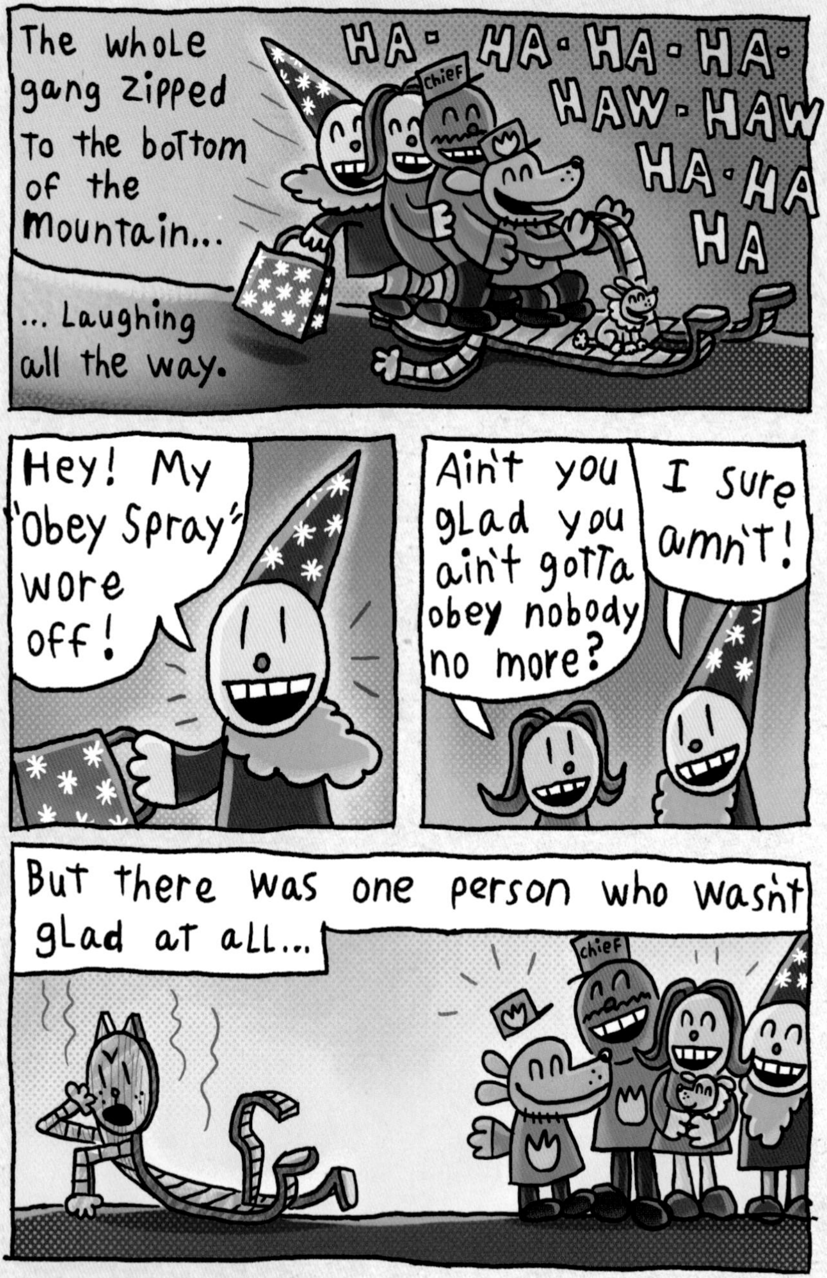

The whole gang zipped to the bottom of the mountain...
HA-HA-HA-HA-HAW-HAW HA-HA HA
Chief
... Laughing all the way.
Hey! My "Obey Spray" wore off!
Ain't you glad you ain't gotta obey nobody no more?
I sure amn't!
But there was one person who wasn't glad at all...
Chief

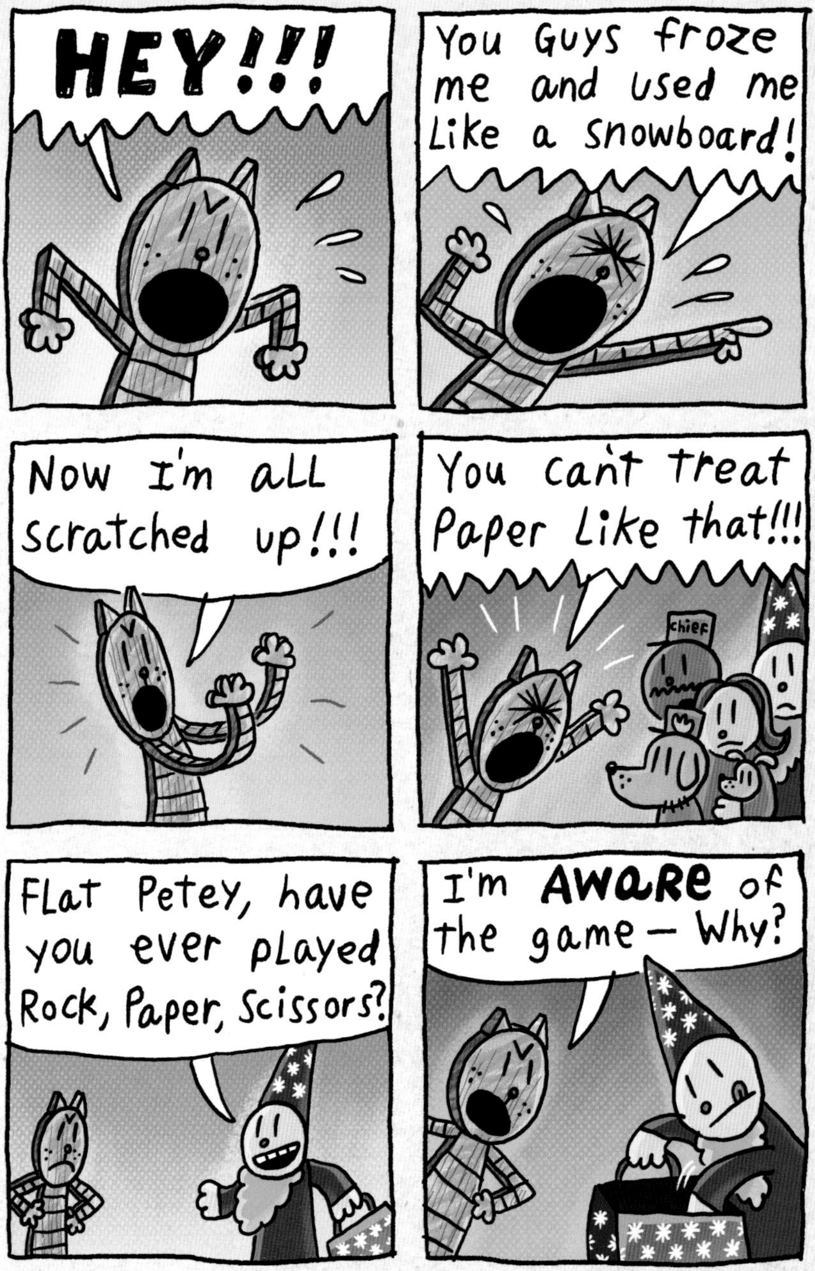
HEY!!!
You Guys froze me and used me Like a snowboard!
Now I'm all scratched up!!!
You can't treat Paper Like that!!!
chief
Flat Petey, have you ever played Rock, Paper, Scissors?
I'm AWARE of the game— Why?

Living Spray
SSSS
Living Spray
'cuz scissors ALWAYS beats Paper !!!!

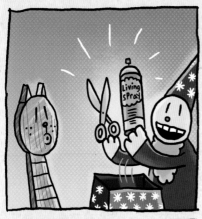

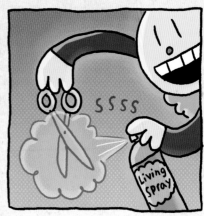

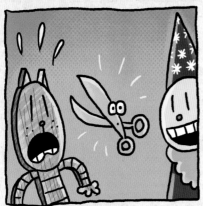

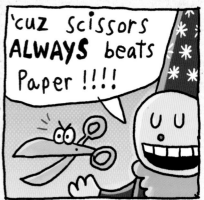

TRIPLE SNIP-O-RAMA

Left hand here.

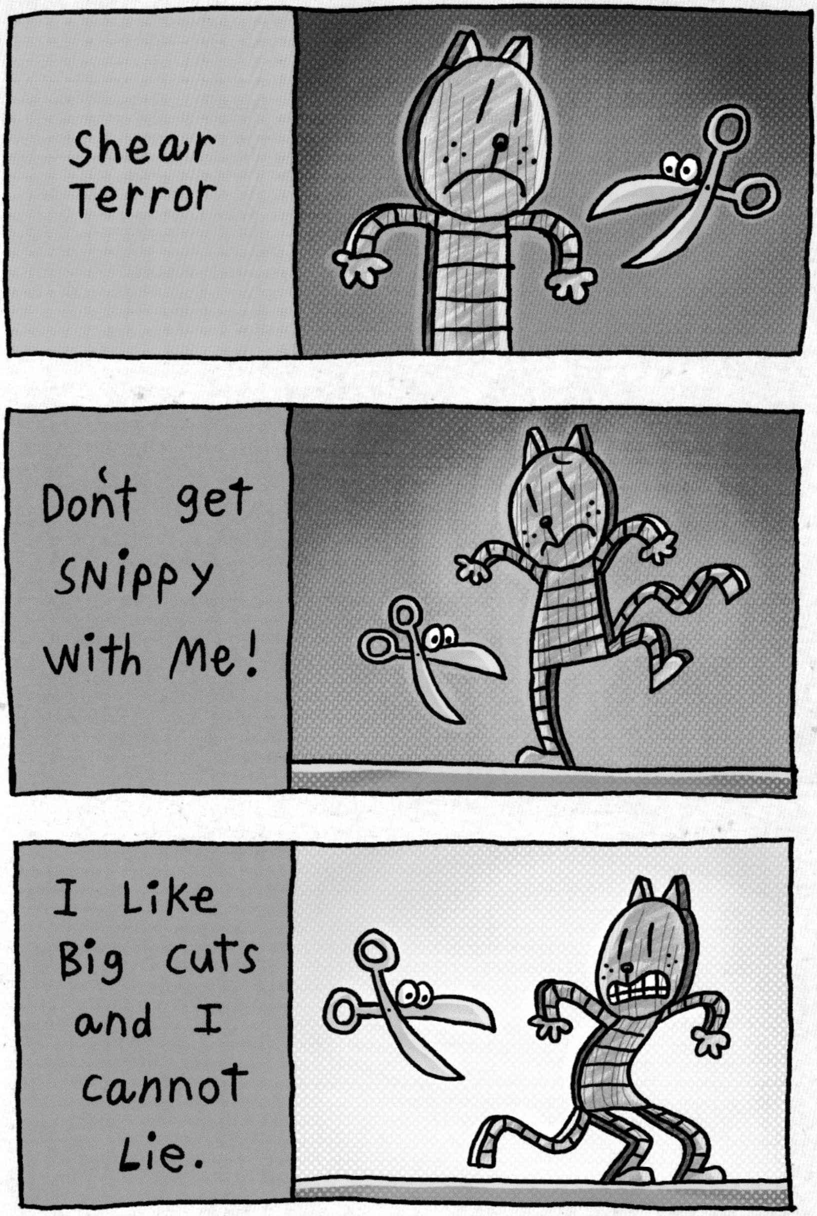
Shear Terror
Don't get SNIPPY with Me!
I Like Big cuts and I cannot Lie.

Right Thumb here.

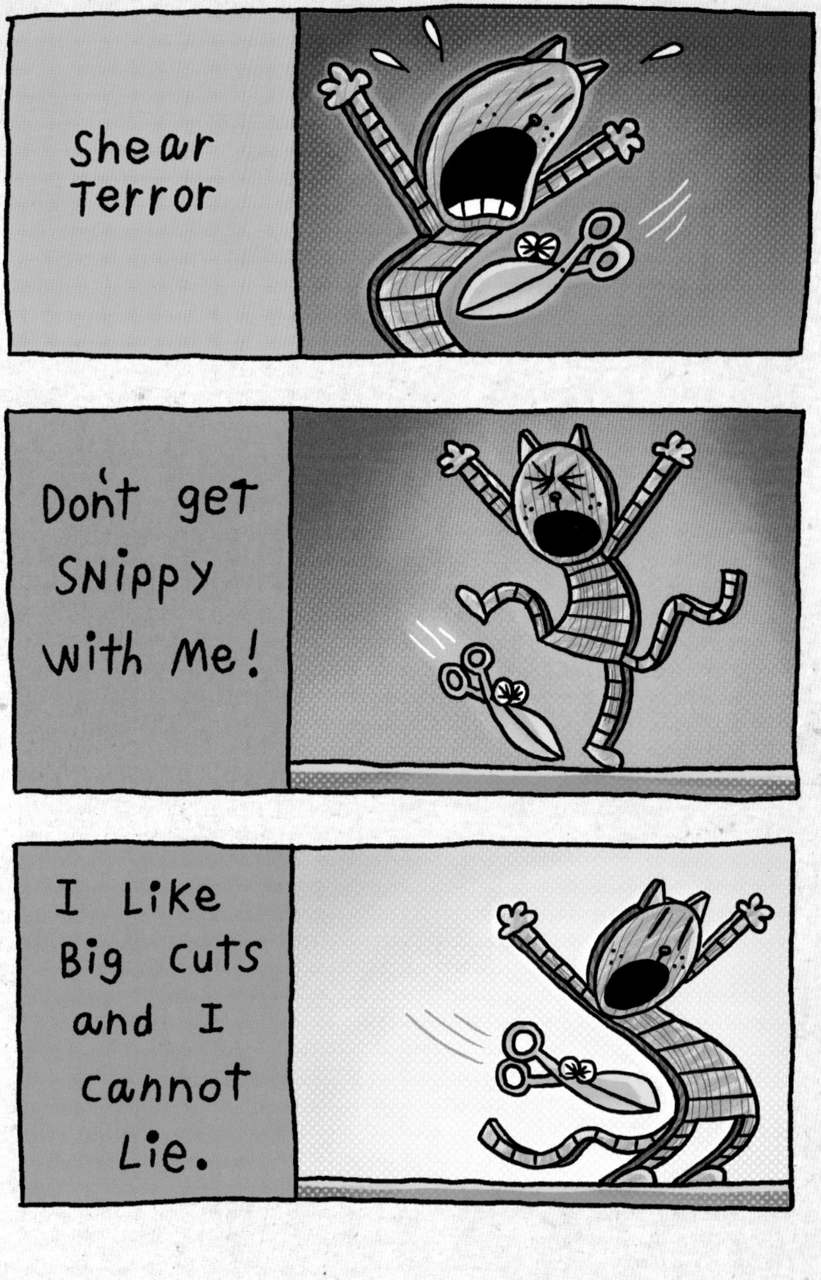

Shear Terror
Don't get SNIPPY with Me!
I Like Big cuts and I cannot Lie.

Good boy, DOG man!

You're our hero!

HOORAY FOR DOG MAN!

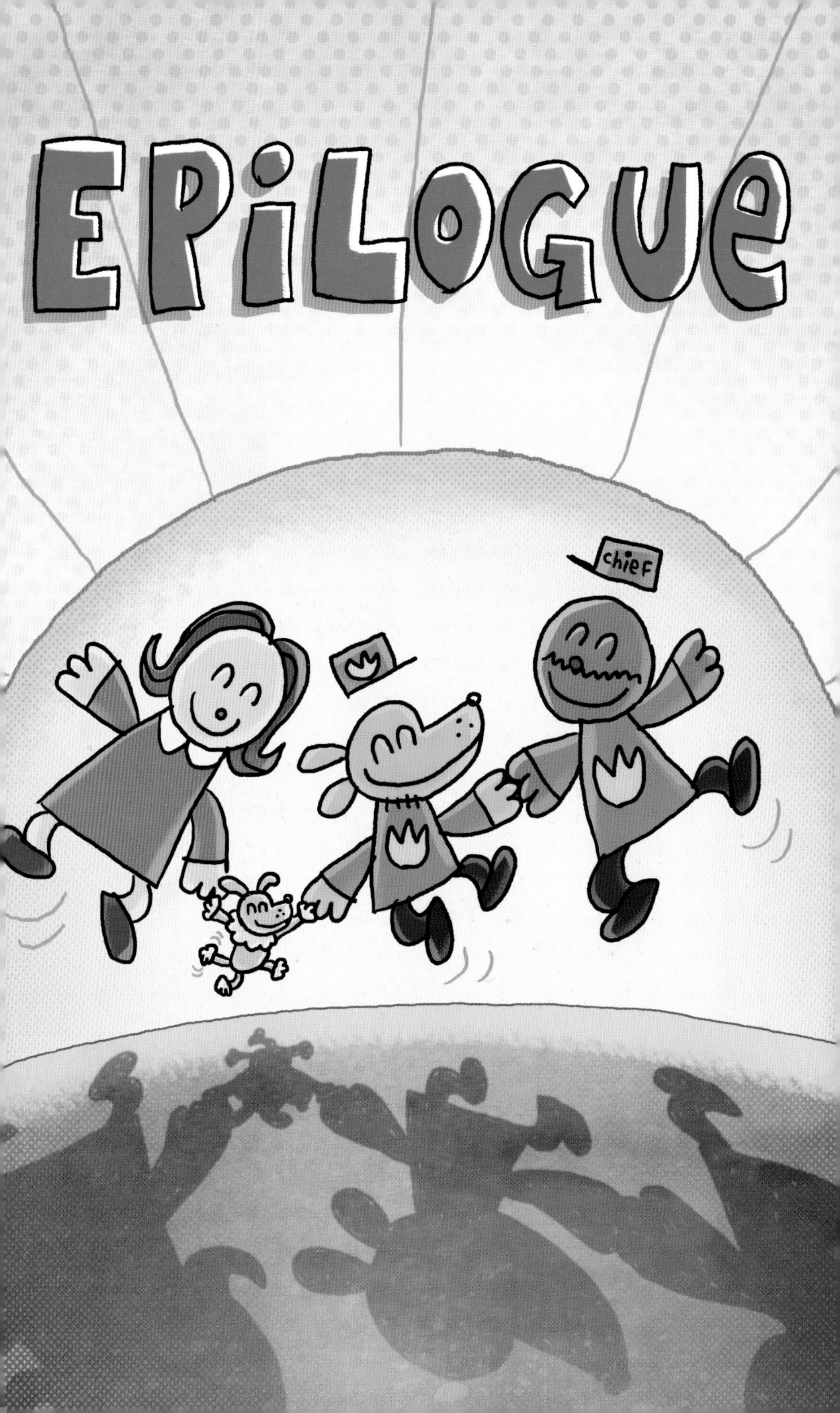
EPiLOGUE
chief

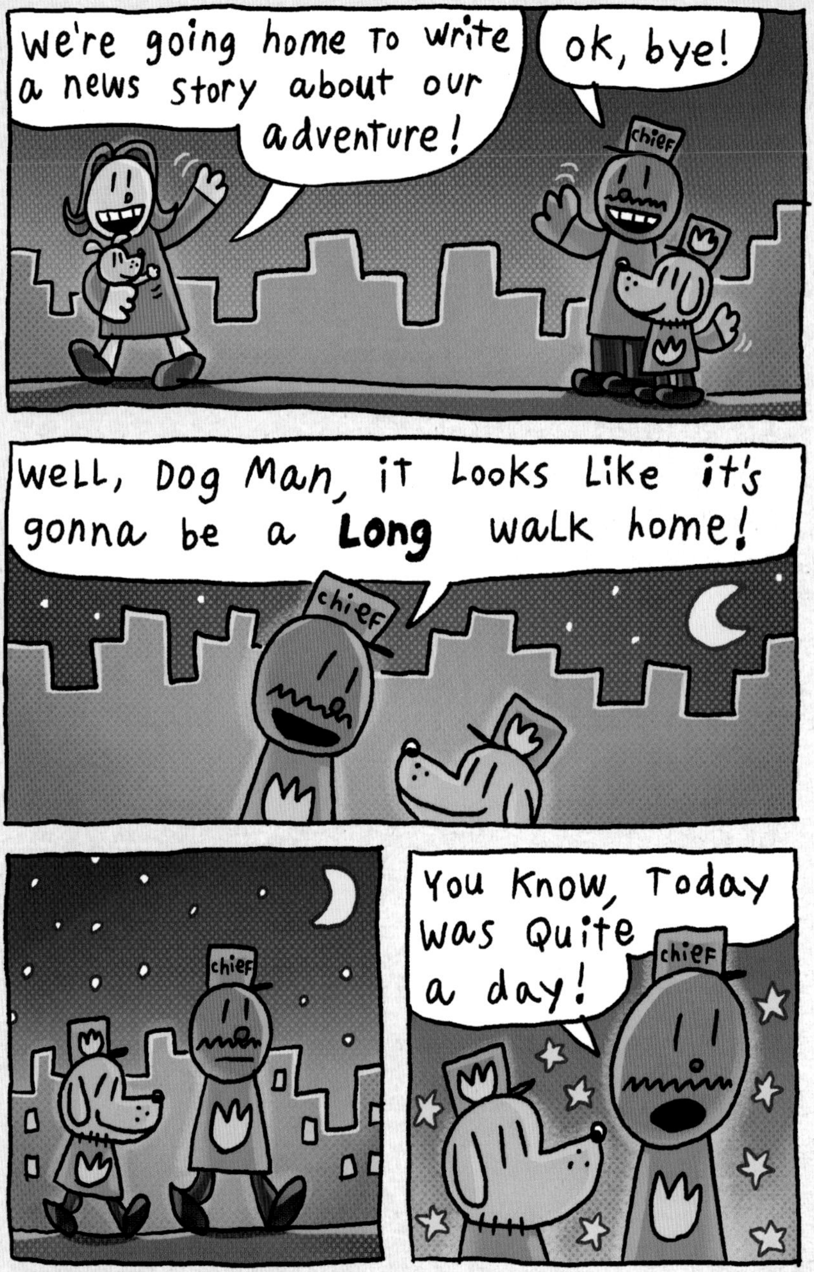
We're going home to write a news story about our adventure!
ok, bye!
WeLL, Dog Man, it Looks Like it's gonna be a Long walk home!
chief
chief
You Know, Today was Quite a day!
chief

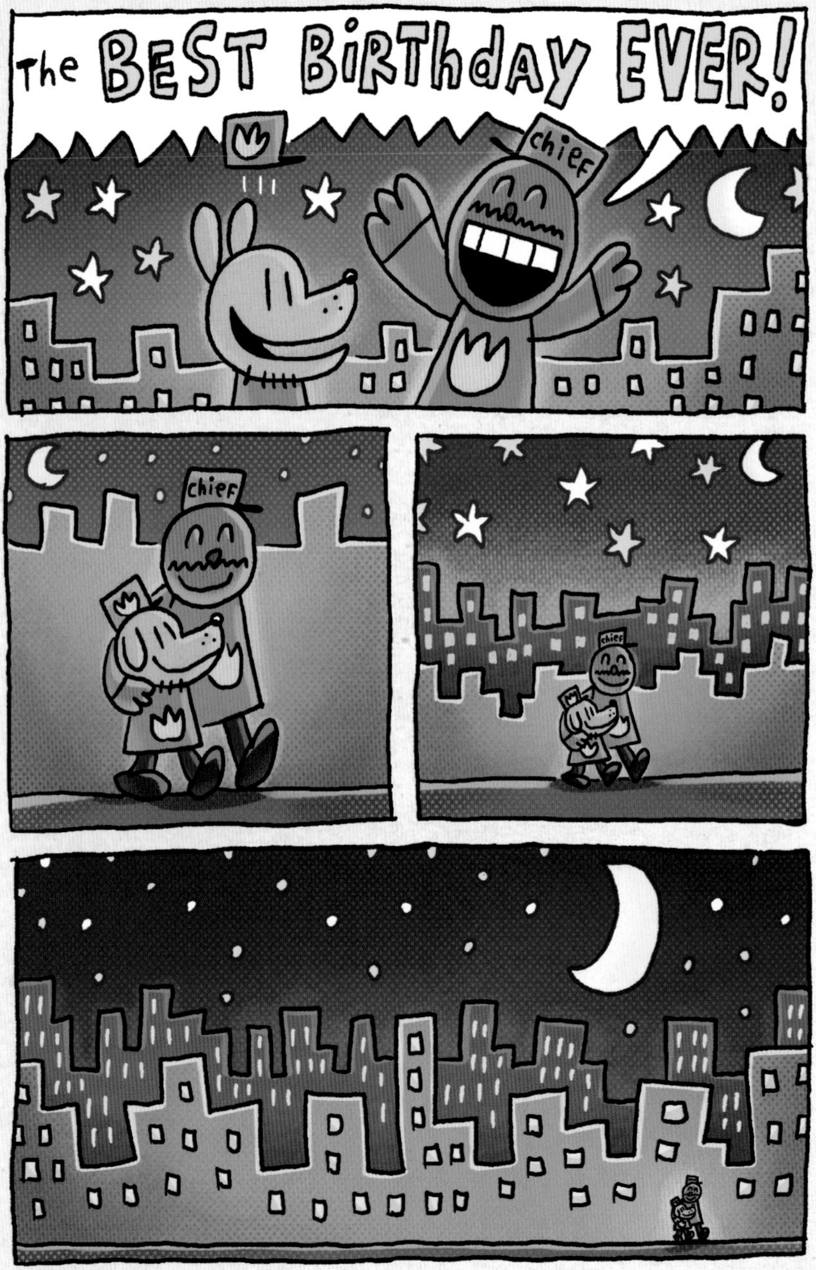
The BEST BiRThday EVER!
chief
chief
chief

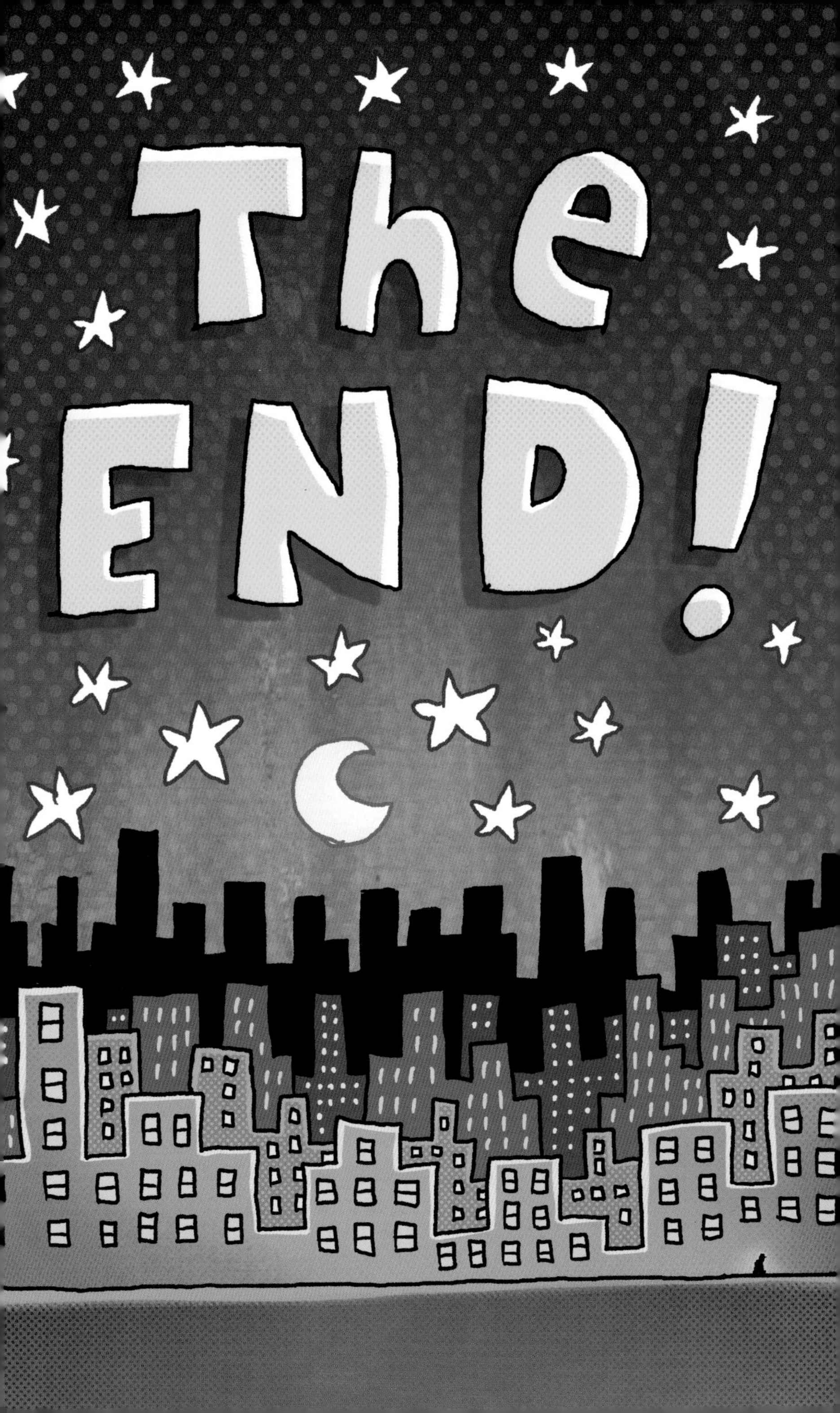
The END!

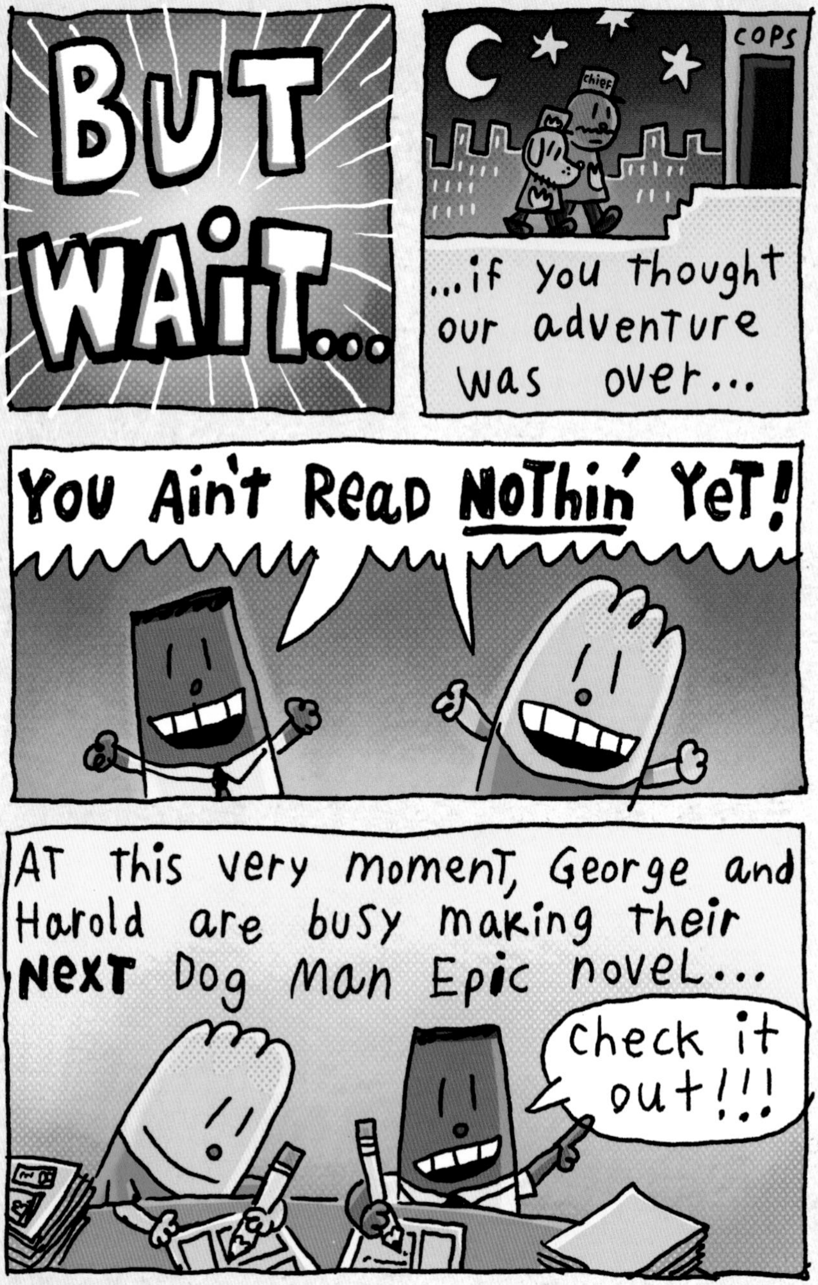
BUT WAIT...
COPS
chief
...if you thought our adventure was over...
YOU AIN'T READ NOTHIN' YET!
AT this very moment, George and Harold are busy making their NEXT Dog Man Epic novel...
Check it out!!!

DOG MAN
A Tale of Two Kitties

He was the best of Dogs...

...he was the worst of Dogs.

IT was the age of invention...

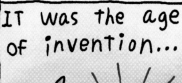

CLoNe 'em
NEW

...it was the season of surprise.

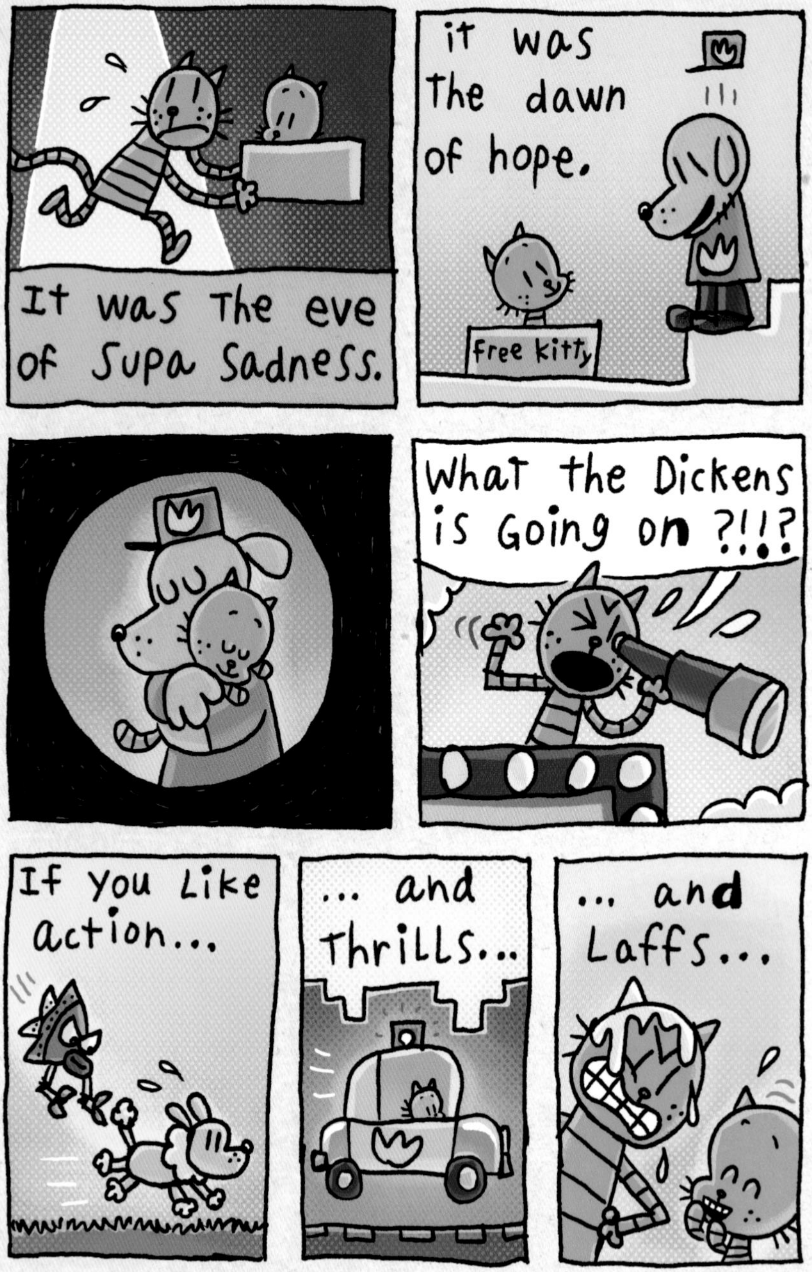
It was The eve of Supa Sadness.
it was The dawn of hope.
Free kitty
What the Dickens is Going on ?!!?
If you Like action...
... and ThriLLs...
... and Laffs...

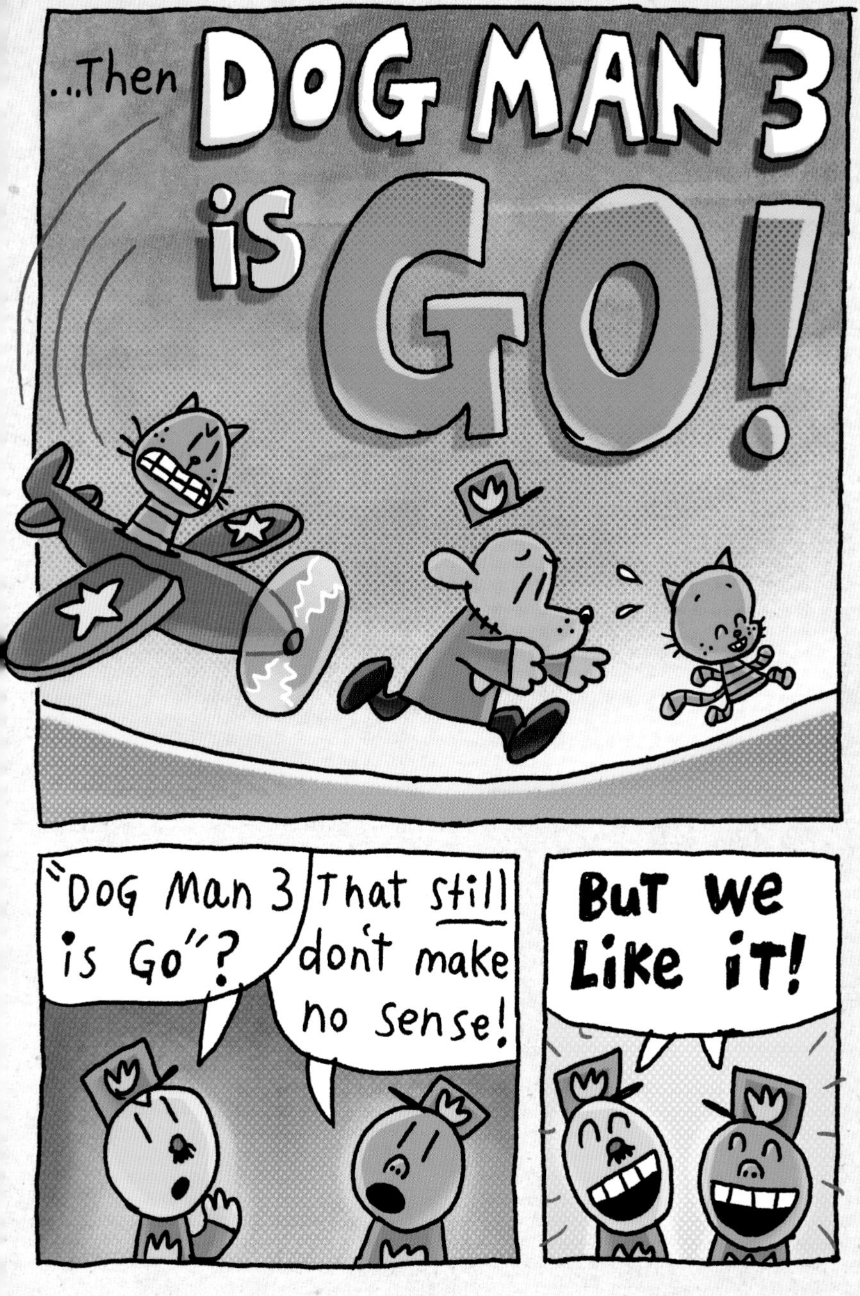
...Then DOG MAN 3 is GO!
"DOG Man 3 is Go"?
That still don't make no sense!
BUT WE LIKE IT!

BONUS COMIX

This next comic was something we made bAck when we were in Kindergarten!

... back in the carefree days of our youths.

Ahhh, I remember them well.

Juice boxes... nap time...

... safety scissors... scented markers...

sniff

MEMORIES!!!

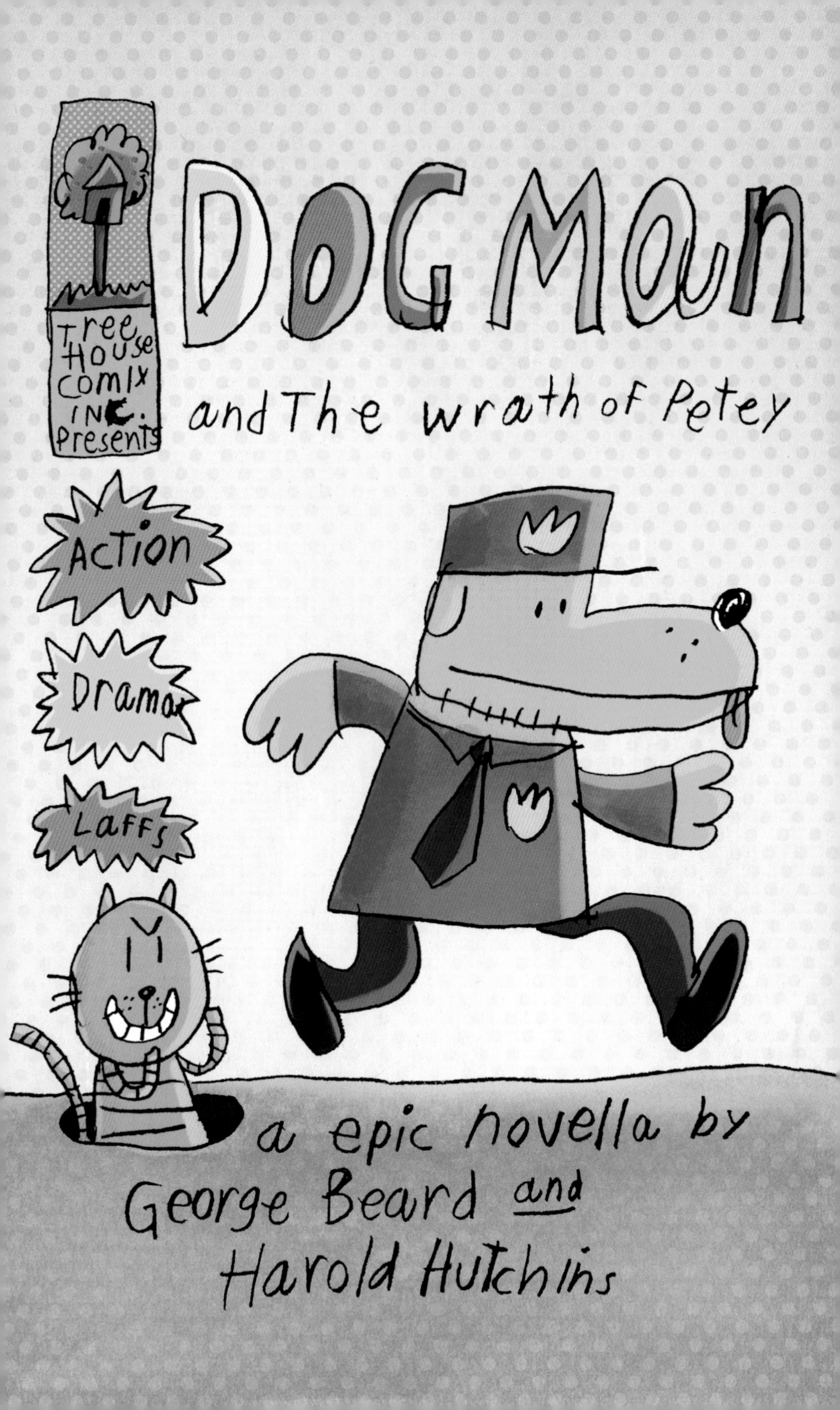
Tree House Comix Inc. Presents
DOGMAN
and The wrath of Petey
Action
Drama
Laffs
a epic novella by
George Beard and
Harold Hutchins

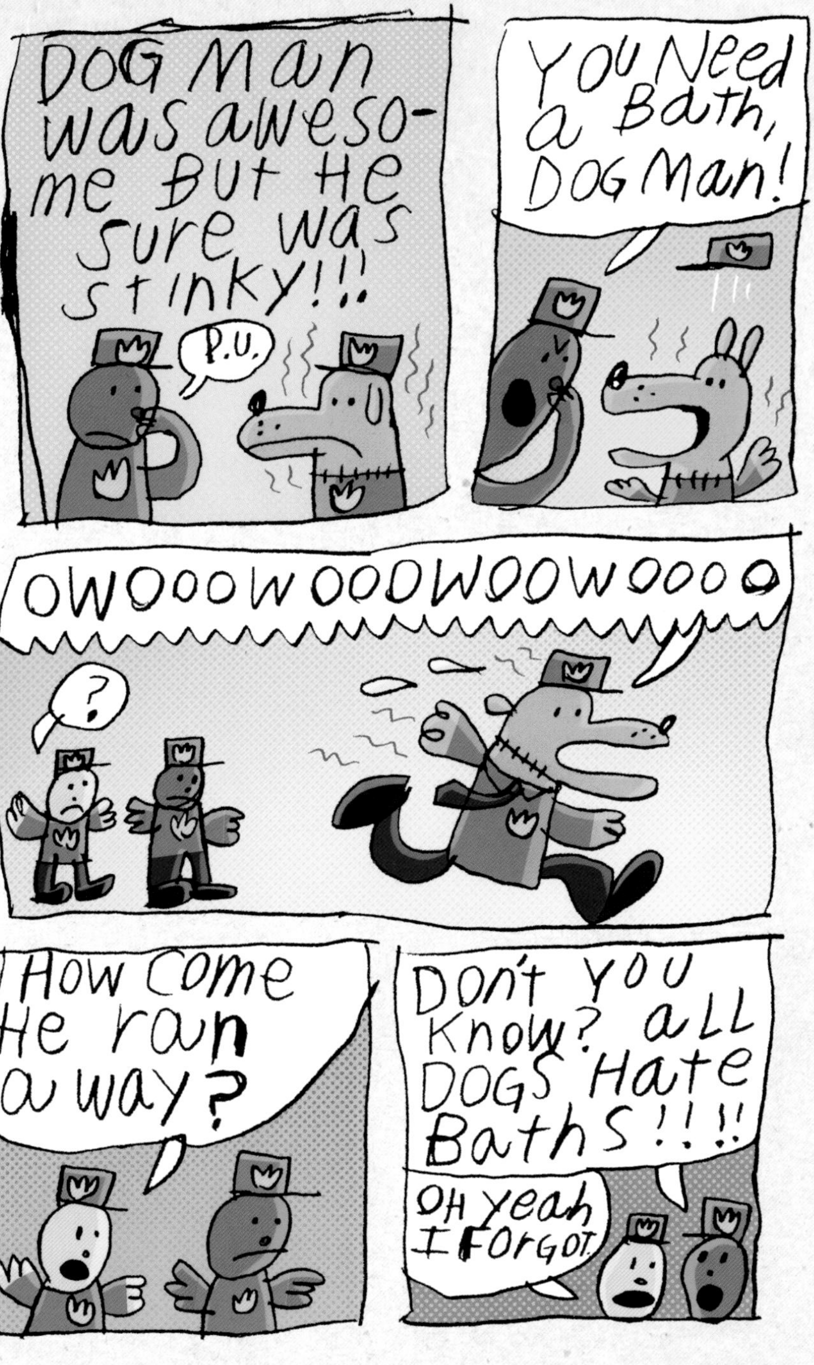
DOG Man was aweso-me But He sure was stinky!!!..
P.U.
You Need a Bath, DOG Man!
OWOOOWOOOWOOWOOOO
?
How Come He ran a way?
Don't you Know? all DOGS Hate Baths!!!!
OH yeah I Forgot.

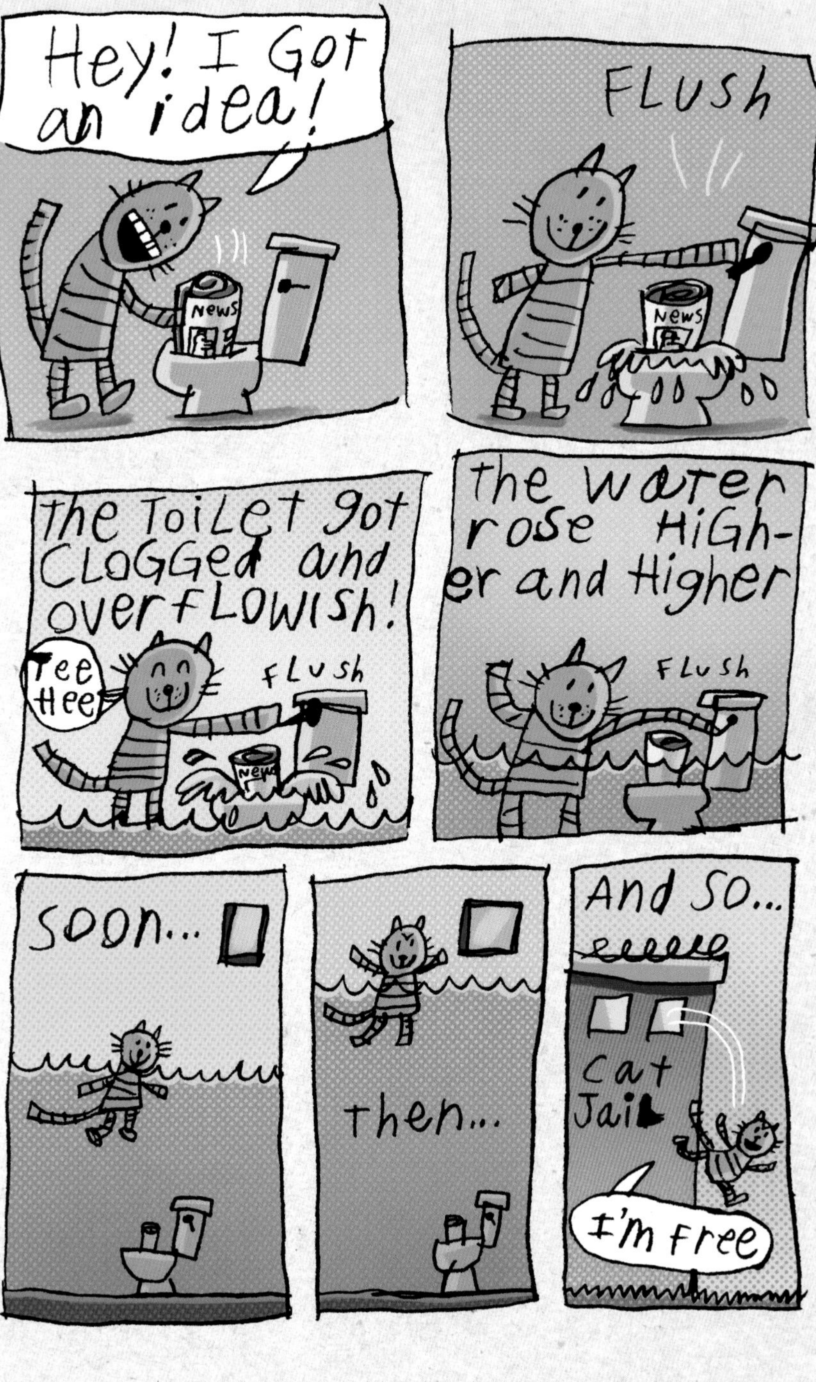
Hey! I Got an idea!
FLUSH
NEWS
The ToiLet got CLoGGed and overFLOWISh!
Tee Hee
FLush
The water rose HiGh-er and Higher
FLush
soon...
then...
And So...
Cat Jail
I'm Free

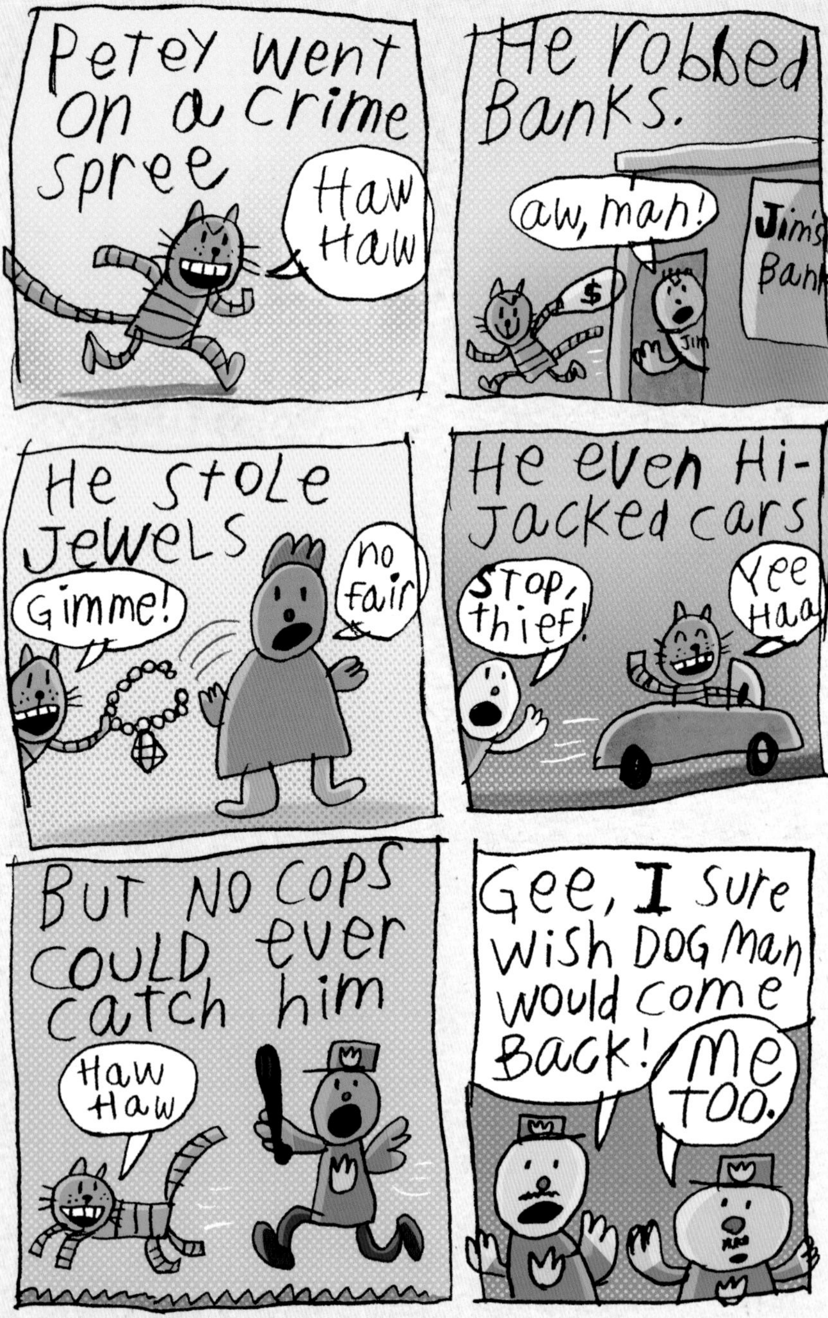
Petey went on a crime spree
Haw Haw
He robbed Banks.
aw, man!
Jim's Bank
Jim
He stole Jewels
Gimme!
no fair
He even Hi-Jacked cars
Stop, thief!
Yee Haa
But no cops could ever catch him
Haw Haw
Gee, I sure wish Dog Man would come Back!
me too.

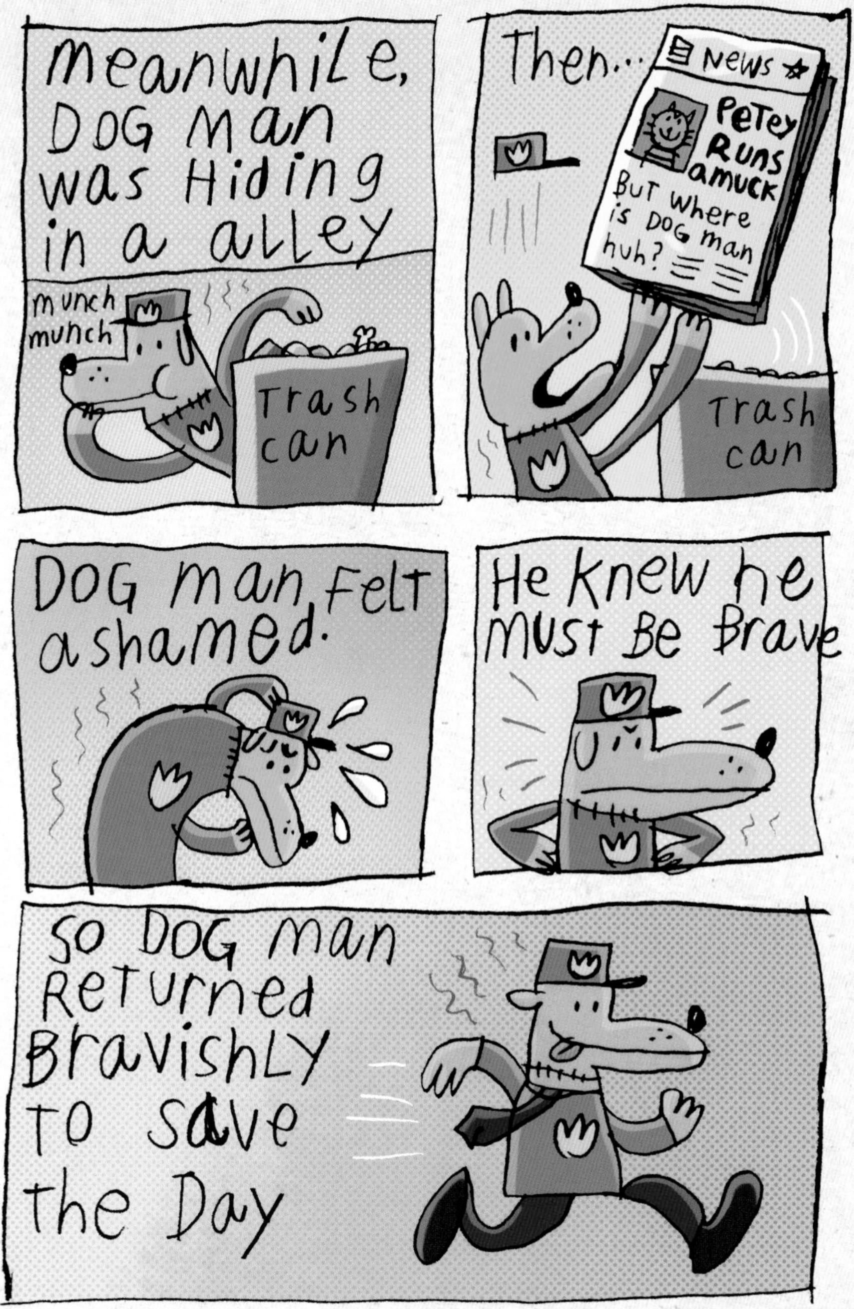
Meanwhile, DOG Man was Hiding in a alley
munch munch
Trash can
Then...
NEWS
PeTey Runs amuck
BuT where is DOG man huh?
Trash can
DOG man Felt ashamed.
He knew he must Be Brave
So DOG man Returned BravishLY TO save the Day

Dog Man Got Scared!

Come and Get It!

SOAP

He digged a hole to get away

Dog man Digged and digged...

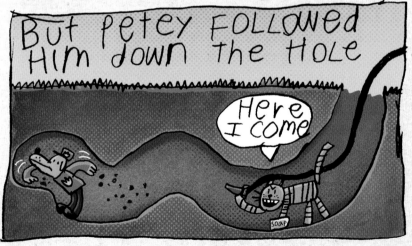

But petey Followed Him down the Hole

Here I come

SOAP

PETEY RAN OUT OF THE HOLE

FLIP-O-rama

Here's How 2 do it.

PUT Your Left Hand There on dotted Line

HOLD the other Page with Your thumb

Flip the page Back and Forth

It makes it look Like a moving Cartoon

Left Hand Here

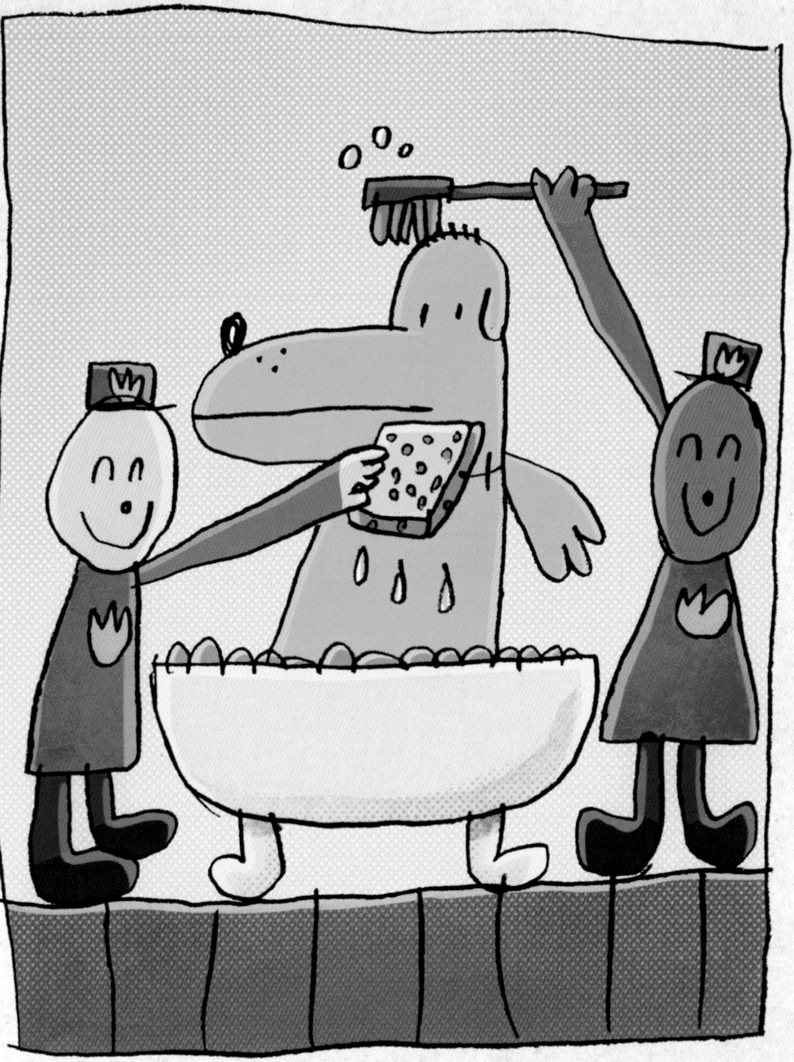

Bathtime for Dog Man

RIGHT THUMB Here

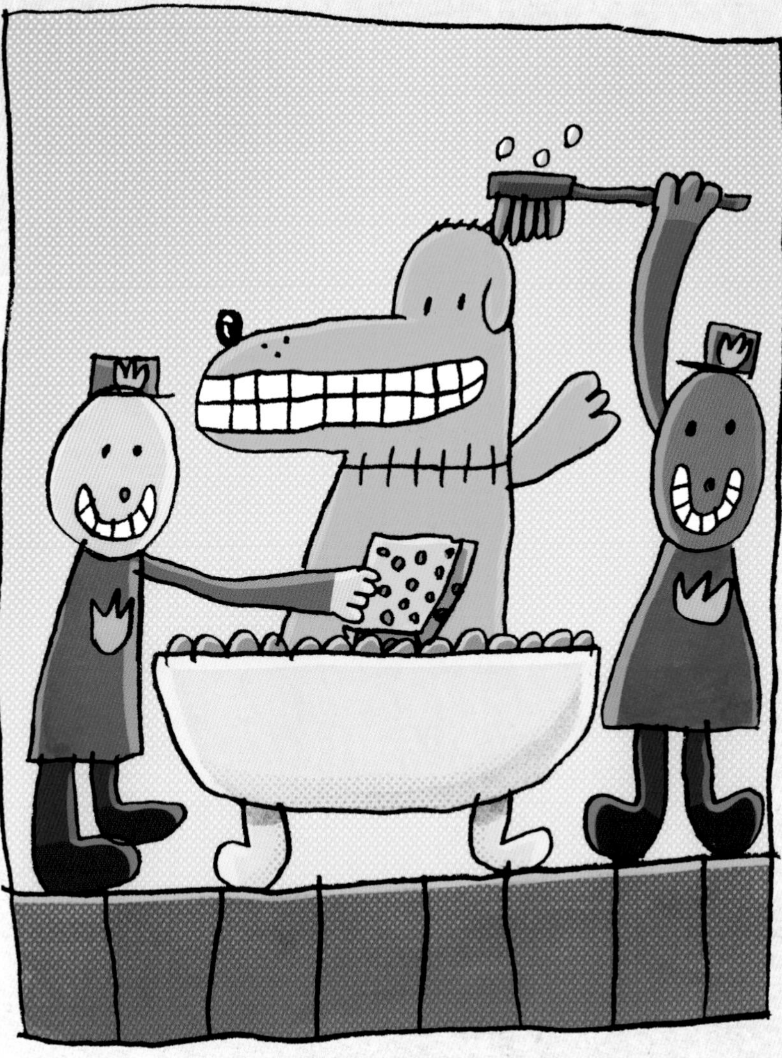

Bathtime
for
Dog Man

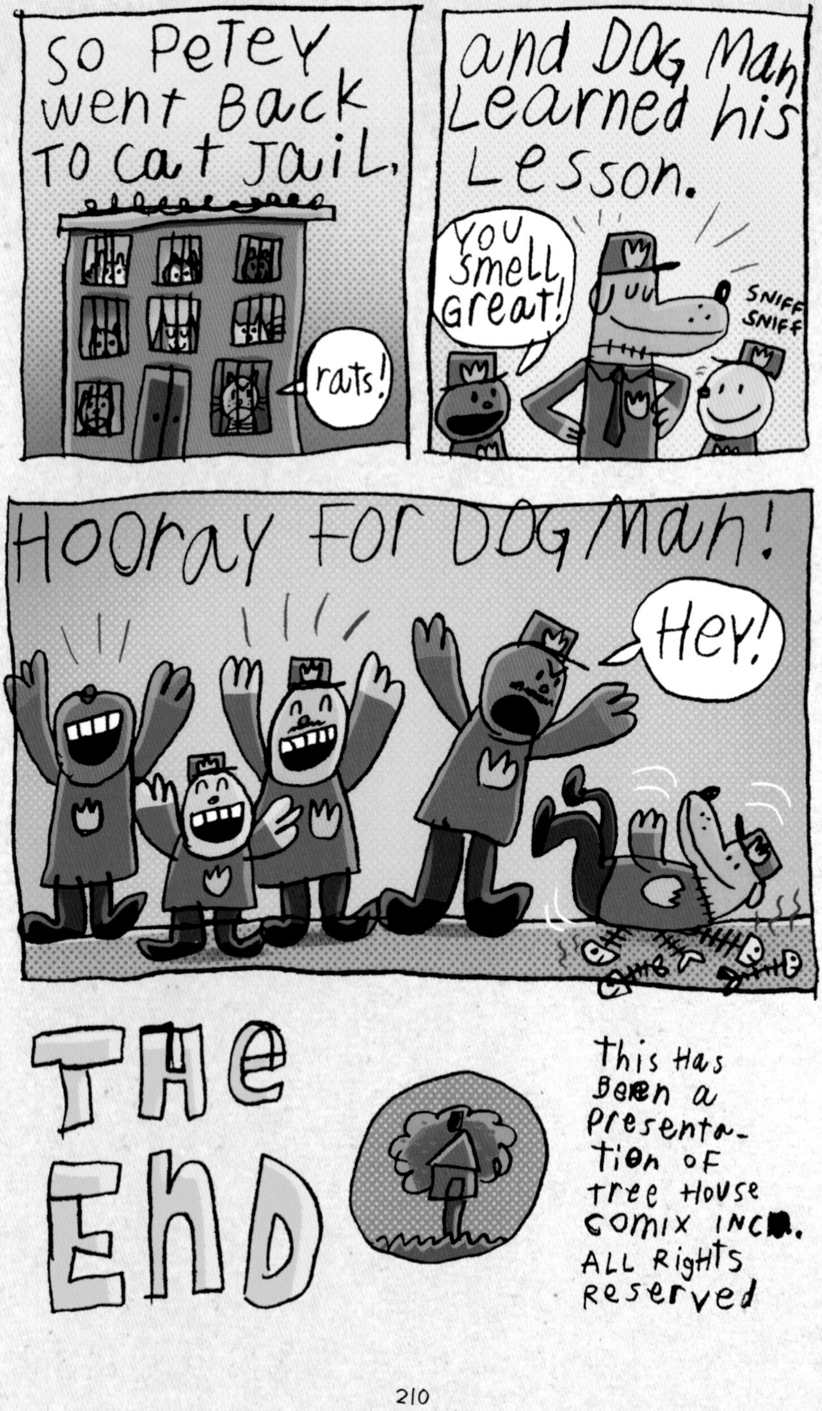
So Petey went Back To cat Jail,
rats!
and DOG Man Learned his Lesson.
You smell great!
SNIFF SNIFF
Hooray For DOG Man!
Hey!
THE END
This Has Been a presenta-tion of tree House comix INC. ALL Rights Reserved

HOW 2 DRAW DOG MAN

in 41 Ridiculously easy Steps!

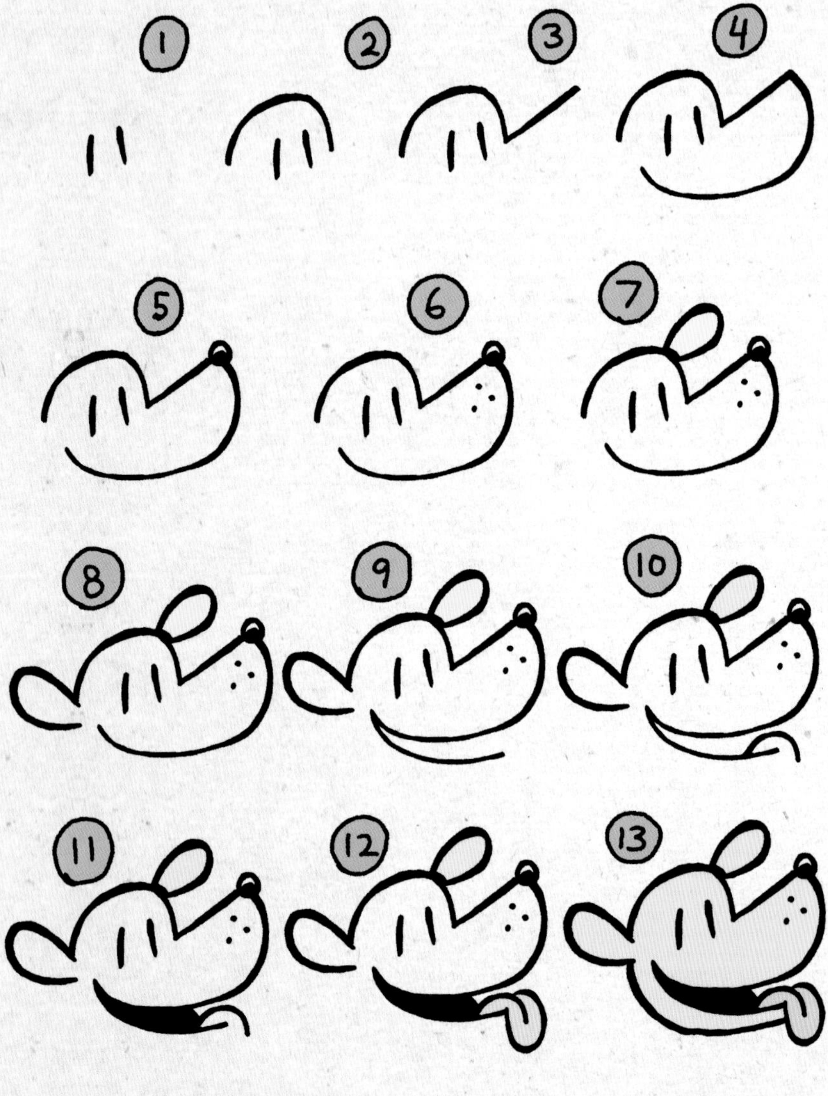

1
2
3
4
5
6
7
8
9
10
11
12
13

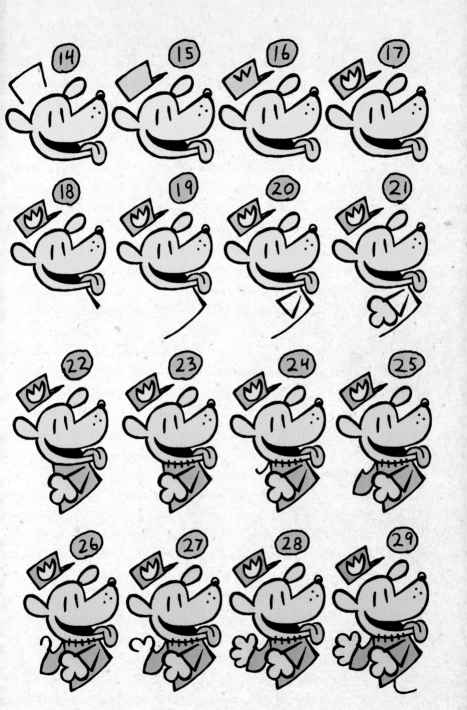

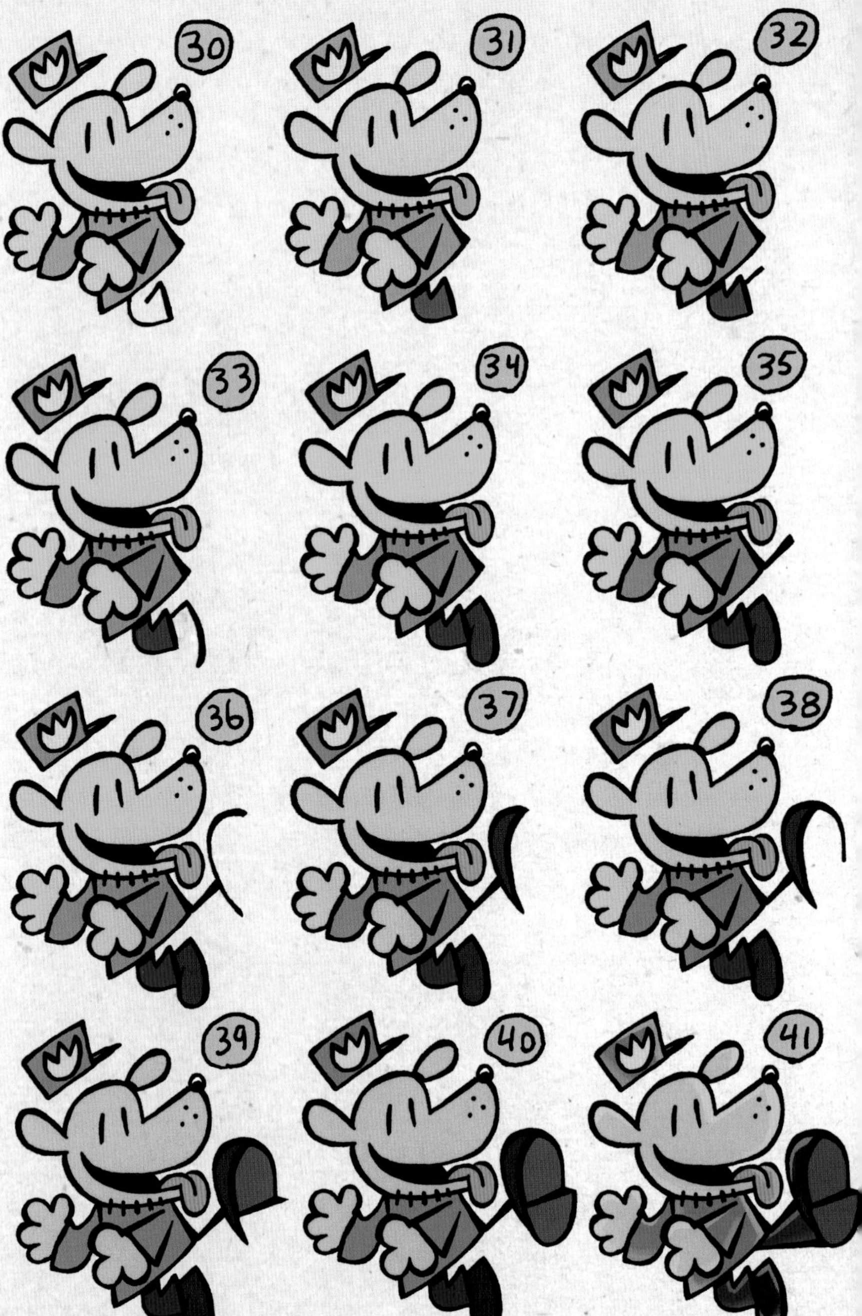
30
31
32
33
34
35
36
37
38
39
40
41

HOW 2 DRAW PETEY

in **28** RIDICULOUSLY EASY STEPS!

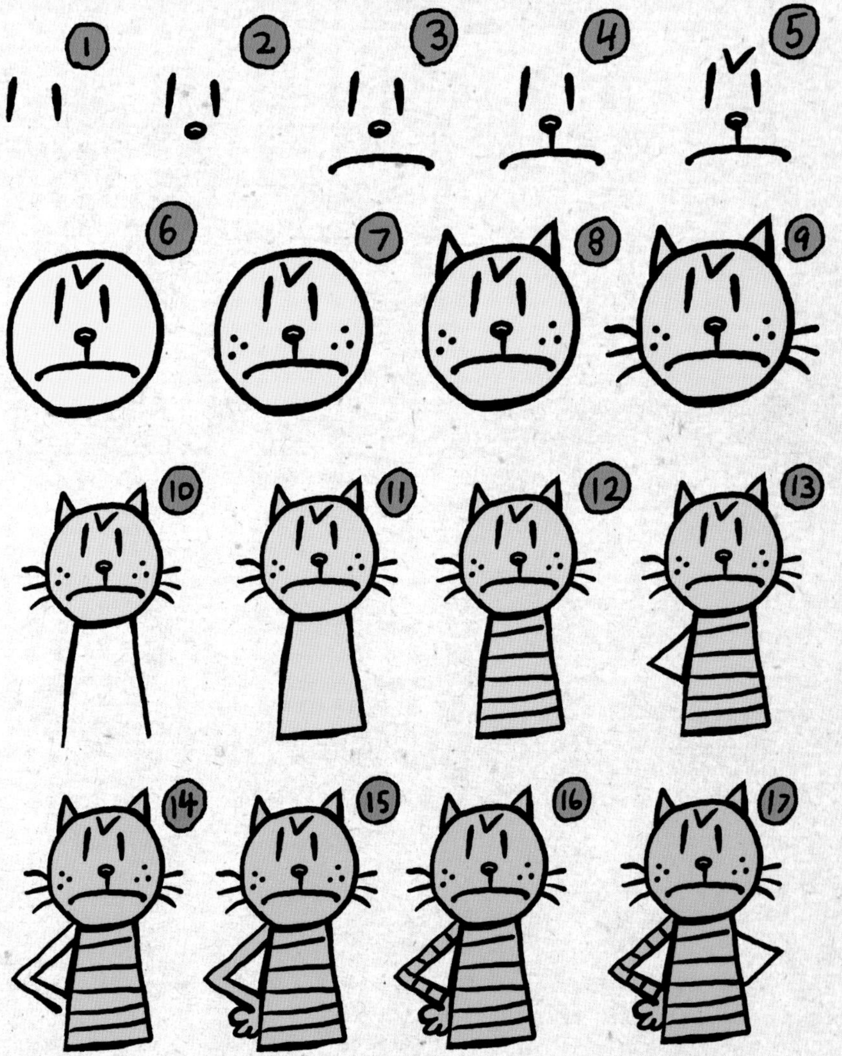
1
2
3
4
5
6
7
8
9
10
11
12
13
14
15
16
17

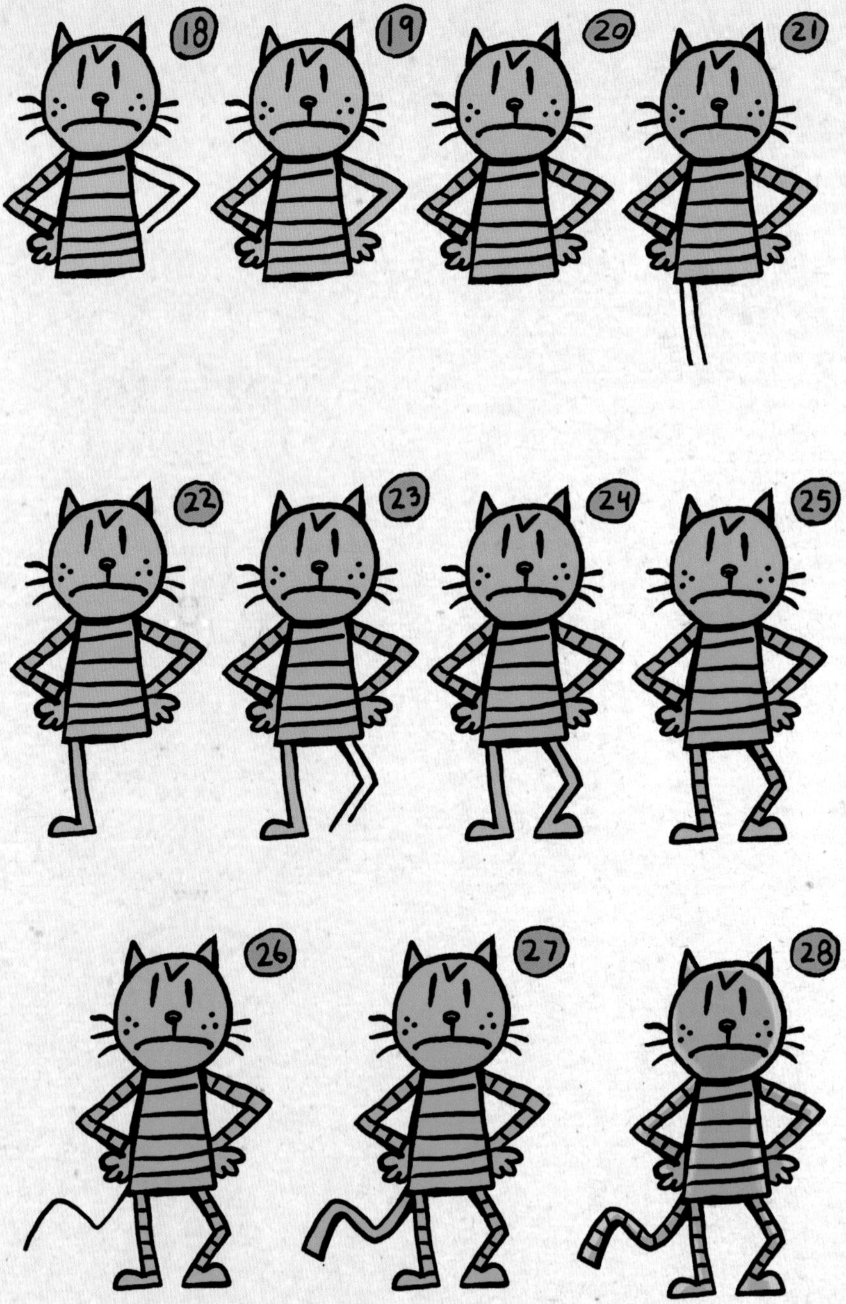
18
19
20
21
22
23
24
25
26
27
28

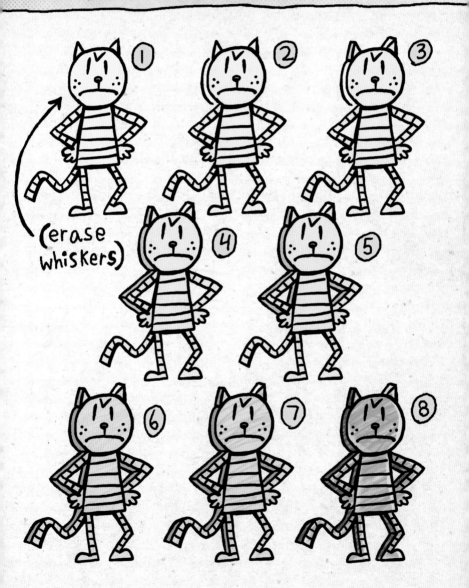

(erase whiskers)

HOW 2 DRAW FLIPPY

in 16 RIDICULOUSLY easy STEPS.

HOW 2 DRAW ZUZU

in 24 Ridiculously easy steps!

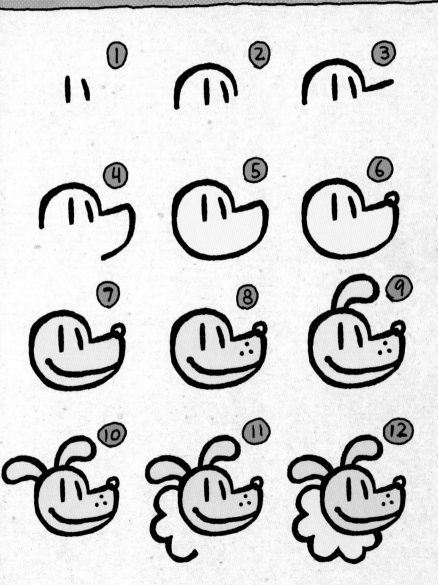

BUT WAIT!

the Fun continues online!!!

GAMES

Make your own FLIP-O-RAMAS!

CRAFTS

Learn to draw SARAH, CHIEF, and MORE!

VIDEOS

at PLANETPILKEY.COM

GET READING W

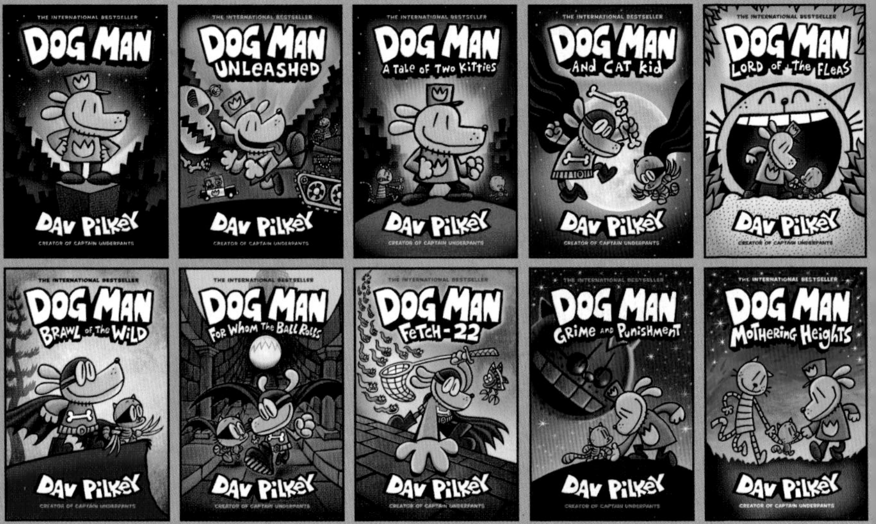
THE INTERNATIONAL BESTSELLER
DOG MAN
DAV PILKEY
CREATOR OF CAPTAIN UNDERPANTS
DOG MAN UNLEASHED
DOG MAN A Tale of Two Kitties
DOG MAN AND CAT Kid
DOG MAN LORD of The FLEAS
DOG MAN BRAWL of the WILD
DOG MAN FOR WHOM The BALL ROLLS
DOG MAN FETCH-22
DOG MAN GRIME AND PUNISHMENT
DOG MAN MOTHERING HEIGHTS

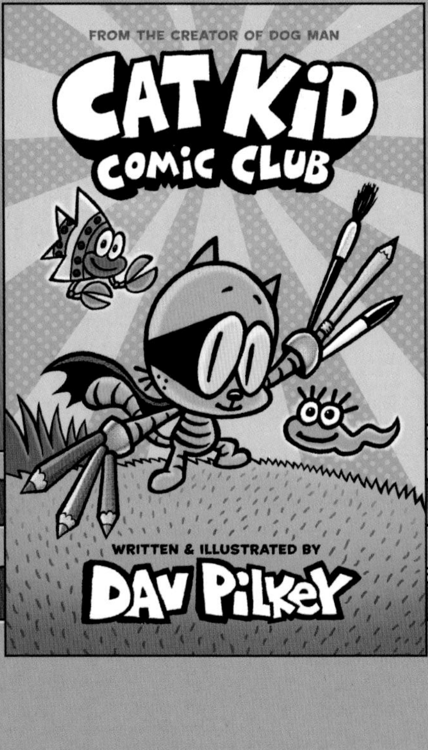
FROM THE CREATOR OF DOG MAN
CAT KID
COMIC CLUB
WRITTEN & ILLUSTRATED BY
DAV PILKEY

★ "Irreverent, laugh-out-loud funny, and . . . downright moving."
— Publishers Weekly, starred review

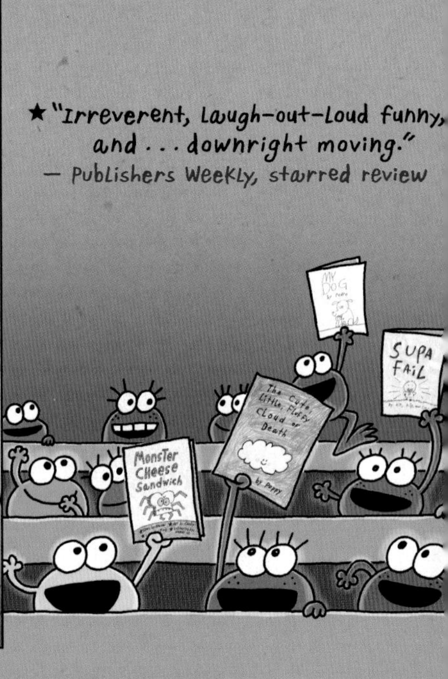
SUPA FAIL
Monster Cheese Sandwich
The Cute, Little, Fluffy Cloud of Death

TH DAV PILKEY!

The Adventures of
CAPTAIN UNDERPANTS
FULL COLOR
THE FIRST EPIC NOVEL BY
DAV PILKEY
CALDECOTT HONOR ARTIST

FULL COLOR
CAPTAIN UNDERPANTS
AND THE ATTACK OF THE TALKING TOILETS
THE SECOND EPIC NOVEL BY
DAV PILKEY
CALDECOTT HONOR ARTIST

FULL COLOR
CAPTAIN UNDERPANTS
THE THIRD EPIC NOVEL BY
DAV PILKEY
CALDECOTT HONOR ARTIST

FULL COLOR
CAPTAIN UNDERPANTS
AND THE PERILOUS PLOT OF PROFESSOR POOPYPANTS
THE FOURTH EPIC NOVEL BY
DAV PILKEY
CALDECOTT HONOR ARTIST

FULL COLOR
CAPTAIN UNDERPANTS
AND THE WRATH OF THE WICKED WEDGIE WOMAN
THE FIFTH EPIC NOVEL BY
DAV PILKEY
CALDECOTT HONOR ARTIST

FULL COLOR
CAPTAIN UNDERPANTS
AND THE BIG, BAD BATTLE OF THE BIONIC BOOGER BOY
THE SIXTH EPIC NOVEL BY
DAV PILKEY
CALDECOTT HONOR ARTIST

FULL COLOR
CAPTAIN UNDERPANTS
AND THE BIG, BAD BATTLE OF THE BIONIC BOOGER BOY
THE SEVENTH EPIC NOVEL BY
DAV PILKEY
CALDECOTT HONOR ARTIST

FULL COLOR
CAPTAIN UNDERPANTS
AND THE PREPOSTEROUS PLIGHT OF THE PURPLE POTTY PEOPLE
THE EIGHTH EPIC NOVEL BY
DAV PILKEY
CALDECOTT HONOR ARTIST

FULL COLOR
CAPTAIN UNDERPANTS
AND THE TERRIFYING RE-TURN OF TIPPY TINKLETROUSERS
THE NINTH EPIC NOVEL BY
DAV PILKEY
CALDECOTT HONOR ARTIST

FULL COLOR
CAPTAIN UNDERPANTS
AND THE REVOLTING REVENGE OF THE RADIOACTIVE ROBO-BOXERS
THE TENTH EPIC NOVEL BY
DAV PILKEY
CALDECOTT HONOR ARTIST

FULL COLOR
CAPTAIN UNDERPANTS
AND THE TYRANNICAL RETALIATION OF THE TURBO TOILET 2000
THE ELEVENTH EPIC NOVEL BY
DAV PILKEY
CALDECOTT HONOR ARTIST

FULL COLOR
CAPTAIN UNDERPANTS
AND THE SENSATIONAL SAGA OF SIR STINKS-A-LOT
THE TWELFTH EPIC NOVEL BY
DAV PILKEY
CALDECOTT HONOR ARTIST

DOG MAN
The Musical
Original Cast Recording

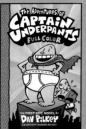

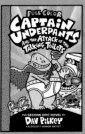

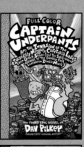

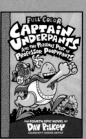

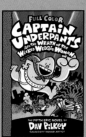

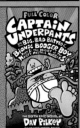

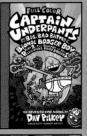

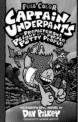

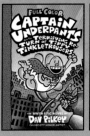

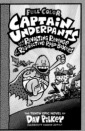

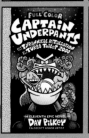

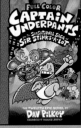

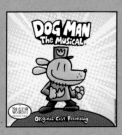

The epic musical adventure is now available from Broadway Records!

PLANET PILKEY

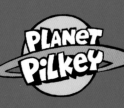

Go to planetpilkey.com to read chapters, make comics, watch videos, play games, and download supa fun stuff!

HOME BASE

SCHOLASTIC

Download on the App Store

GET IT ON Google Play

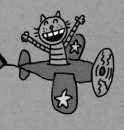

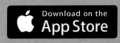

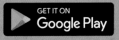

ABOUT THE AUTHOR-ILLUSTRATOR

When Dav Pilkey was a kid, he was diagnosed with ADHD and dyslexia. Dav was so disruptive in class that his teachers made him sit out in the hallway every day. Luckily, Dav loved to draw and make up stories. He spent his time in the hallway creating his own original comic books — the very first adventures of Dog Man and Captain Underpants.

In college, Dav met a teacher who encouraged him to illustrate and write. He won a national competition in 1986 and the prize was the publication of his first book, WORLD WAR WON. He made many other books before being awarded the 1998 California Young Reader Medal for DOG BREATH, which was published in 1994, and in 1997 he won the Caldecott Honor for THE PAPERBOY.

THE ADVENTURES OF SUPER DIAPER BABY, published in 2002, was the first complete graphic novel spin-off from the Captain Underpants series and appeared at #6 on the USA Today bestseller list for all books, both adult and children's, and was also a New York Times bestseller. It was followed by THE ADVENTURES OF OOK AND GLUK: KUNG FU CAVEMEN FROM THE FUTURE and SUPER DIAPER BABY 2: THE INVASION OF THE POTTY SNATCHERS, both USA Today bestsellers. The unconventional style of these graphic novels is intended to encourage uninhibited creativity in kids.

His stories are semi-autobiographical and explore universal themes that celebrate friendship, tolerance, and the triumph of the good-hearted.

Dav loves to kayak in the Pacific Northwest with his wife.

Learn more at Pilkey.com.